I0543817

ABOUT THE AUTHOR

M. A. Anderson has always had a love of things that go *'bump in the night'*, and that's why she enjoys writing dark fantasy.

Having a love of books and reading from an early age, she wrote short stories and song lyrics and progressed to playwriting in her teens.

She is an Australian author who writes Urban fantasy, Supernatural crime thrillers, Contemporary and Paranormal Romance.

You can find out more about M. A. and her books on her website: http://www.m-anderson.com.au or join her on popular social media sites.

DARK LEGACY SERIES
Reece: Prequel
Dark Legacy
Once Bitten
Soul Chaser
Evil Nature
Most Deadly

PARANORMAL ROMANCE
THRILLER SERIES
Written as Maggie Anderson
Wolf Blood
Wolf Curse
Wolf Lover
Wolf Bonds (coming 2022)

ROMANCE
Written as Maggie Anderson
Driving Me Crazy
Love's Twist of Fate
A Night of Passion
A Night of Passion: Clean Romance Edition
Christmas, Mistletoe and You

COLLECTIONS
Dark Musings

NON-FICTION
Write Your First Book: From Page to Publication

MOST DEADLY

ഌﮢ

M. A. ANDERSON

Bella Luna Books
Australia

This is a work of fiction. Names, characters, places and incidences are either the product of the author's imagination or, if real, are used fictitiously and with the utmost respect. Any resemblance to persons, living or dead is entirely coincidental.

Copyright © 2021 M. A. Anderson
Brisbane, Australia

This edition published 2021
Bella Luna Books, Australia

All rights reserved. No part of this book may be reproduced, transmitted or stored in an information retrieval system in any form or by any means without prior written permission from the author

Cover design by Maggie Anderson

ISBN: 9780648483625 (paperback)

MOST DEADLY

୨୦ଓୡ

M. A. ANDERSON

Bella Luna Books
Australia

This is a work of fiction. Names, characters, places and incidences are either the product of the author's imagination or, if real, are used fictitiously and with the utmost respect. Any resemblance to persons, living or dead is entirely coincidental.

Copyright © 2021 M. A. Anderson
Brisbane, Australia

This edition published 2021
Bella Luna Books, Australia

All rights reserved. No part of this book may be reproduced, transmitted or stored in an information retrieval system in any form or by any means without prior written permission from the author

Cover design by Maggie Anderson

ISBN: 9780648483625 (paperback)

"Words have no power to impress the mind without the exquisite horror of their reality." ***Edgar Allen Poe***

CHAPTER ONE

Reece, Andre, Nathaniel, and Tom raced through the hazy legion of tall trees in hot pursuit. They couldn't allow the creature to get away from them again. They were determined to capture it this time. By the time the small group reached the edge of the wooded clearing, the monster had stopped in the center. Haloed by the full moon, its reptilian, multifaceted skin glistened under the milky veil of light. The moon had a lot to answer for. It not only governed humans afflicted by its influence – hence the name lunatic, but also a multitude of supernatural creatures. Reece believed this snakelike monster could be one of them. Sarah, Ed, and Lozano were on the opposite side of the circular, overgrown grassy knoll awaiting the PI's order to move in. Their plan was to lure… or chase the creature here in order to encapsulate it in a hidden trap already in place beneath the layer of leaves, twigs and grass. Thankfully, it worked.

They were one man down, as Todd resigned after Charlotte's death. He couldn't handle the constant reminder she'd never be coming back. Reece figured the ex-detective had been in love with her, his feelings motivating his decision to join their team. He would've been an asset to their cause, although the PI understood why he couldn't stay. Grief did strange things to people and Todd had to deal with it in his own way. Who knew what the future held, although it had already been almost seven years with no word from him. Maybe when he came to terms with the loss, if you ever truly get over losing someone, he might change his mind. The door would always remain open.

Reece tapped the communication device in his ear. "Everyone move in slow 'n steady. We want to catch the motherfucker this time." He glanced over his shoulder, gave his son a nod. Tom shifted into wolf form. The PI wouldn't take any chances with his son's life. "Ok, let's do this."

Ed, Sarah, and Lozano emerged from the towering pines, stopping at the perimeter of the clearing. "Now what?" the chief asked.

"Spread out. Be careful. You know what this thing can do." He'd seen it spit venom at a cop, melting the flesh clean off the guy's skeleton before what remained dissolved into a sticky puddle of red goo. Hence, the reason they were covered from head to foot in dark blue protective gear, the kind that resisted acids and flammable liquids, except for Tom. His sheer size and speed would protect him. His son had adjusted well to his new life, the transition being a difficult one at first. Now that he could turn at will it made his life a whole lot easier, less painful too. When the PI had the father/son talk with him (not the sex talk), Tom remembered being abducted from Charlotte's apartment at the age of ten and driven in the trunk of a car out to a cabin in the woods. Reece and his team had raided the property to rescue him and his mother from the Alpha, who turned out to be Tom's biological father, Dan McCredie.

A shock to everyone, but an even bigger one for Charlotte who ended up shooting Dan in the head because he'd planned to massacre them all. He'd been stunned when she'd pulled the trigger, the look on his face before he hit the ground causing her to throw up at his feet. She never got over the fact their son would, on his sixteenth birthday, become a Lycanthrope. And she had felt betrayed by the man she'd once loved for lying to her all those years ago about what happened to him in the alley while on patrol. He'd attacked his partner and had not been bitten by something huge and fast as he'd claimed.

This reptile demon managed to escape hell somehow, which meant the rift had fractured again. Sarah's incantation held for almost seven years, but they knew it would only be a matter of time before the otherworldly creatures found another way to infiltrate the human world again.

Nathaniel depressed the trigger on the remote device. The cage whipped up around the creature, trapping it in mid-air. It struggled against its restraints, spitting venom through the triangular gaps between the ropes.

The group moved in, Sarah shooting it with the tranquilizer gun several times to make sure she knocked it out.

"Let's get this thing loaded and out to the facility where it won't be able to do anymore damage," Reece ordered.

"You don't wanna kill it?" Ed asked, a deep questioning frown furrowing his already wrinkled brow.

"Not yet. We need to study it. We don't know if this is the only one. If there are more out there we're in serious shit."

"Ok, I guess." Ed shrugged. "If it was me I'd finish it."

"I get where you're coming from, Chief, but we need to know more about these creatures."

"Yeah, yeah, I get your point."

Reece's gaze moved around the bordering trees. "Where's Tom?"

Andre crossed the clearing to the PI. "I gave him the backpack so he can get dressed."

"Thanks."

Ed, Lozano, and Nathaniel secured the creature inside the van. "Will you meet us at the facility?" the black vampire asked.

"Yeah. I want to drop Tom home first, then I'll head out."

Tom joined the group, slinging the gray backpack over his left shoulder. "I wanna come with you."

"You've got homework, don't you?"

"I'll do it when we get home. Come on, Dad, I'm part of the team, aren't I?"

Reece gripped his son's solid bicep. "Of course you are, but…"

"You'd prefer I go home, act like a regular teenager, do my homework. Right?"

"Your mom would've wanted you to have as normal a life as you can…"

"Mom's not here, Dad. And I know what's out there, so don't treat me like a kid. I can help."

"You *have* been helping."

"Then what's the problem?"

"Yeah, Daniels, what's the problem?" Ed asked, walking over to the pair. "What's the problem about what?"

"Dad won't let me come out to the containment facility with you guys. He's taking me home to do my *homework*." Tom folded his arms, letting out a frustrated huff.

Ed cleared his throat. He didn't want to get between father and son. "Yeah, well, maybe you should listen to your dad. He only wants what's best for ya." The older man gave Reece a sheepish glance. As a rule, he'd agree with Tom. He was old enough to be involved in every aspect of their work, being a werewolf, but he knew it wouldn't sit well with the PI if he sided with the boy.

"Argh!" Tom threw his hands up and stalked away.

"Thanks, Chief, I appreciate the support. I know you don't agree with me."

"Yeah, well, I think he's old enough to participate in the other areas of the job, but who am I to tell you what to do. I work for you now, not the other way around." He shrugged.

Sarah came over to the pair. "What's going on?"

"Tommy... Tom wants to come out to the facility with us but Reece told him he has to go home to do his homework."

Sarah's gaze moved to the PI. "When are you going to allow him to grow up?"

"Wait a minute..."

"No, you wait a minute. You allow him to come on raids with us, put his life in danger with us, but you won't let him come out to the containment facility? I don't get it. What could possibly happen to him out there?" She frowned into his eyes.

"Look, I'm trying to do what I think is best for him, what I think Charlotte would want. His father died out there... Charlotte killed him, remember?"

"How could I forget?" Her serious expression softened. "It was a long time ago, Reece. You know Charlotte would want him to be his authentic self not a watered down version of who he is. He's a grown young man, or haven't you noticed? And a werewolf. He's stronger than any of us put together and he has the brains to accompany that strength. Give him a chance to be around the things important to you, to be a part of your world. That's all he wants."

Sarah made a valid point. Reece let out a heavy sigh and raised defensive hands. "Ok. He can come."

"Hey, Tom, you're dad says you can come," Ed called out across the clearing.

Tom bolted through the tall grass and threw himself at his dad in a tight man hug. "Thanks, Dad!" His face beamed. "You won't regret it."

Reece wasn't so sure.

CHAPTER TWO

"Charlotte!" Reece sprang from his pillow, eyes darting around the shadowed bedroom, his raspy breathing the only sound in the silence, his heart thumping against his ribs, beads of cold sweat dotting his brow. He hadn't dreamed about his dead fiancée in a long time. His jumbled, sleepy thoughts wouldn't adhere. He threw back the covers, stumbled out of bed, padded barefoot over to the window, and looked up at the clouded moon. *What prompted the dream?* He frowned into the eyes of his ghostly reflection in the pane of glass, attempting to pull it back into his memory.

A knock echoed into the room, startling him. He jerked his gaze to the back of the door. "Come in, Tom." He knew it was his son because no one else shared their home.

The young man's handsome face, etched with concern, peered around the door. "Are you ok?"

"Yeah. Just a dream."

"You called out mom's name." Tom remained in the doorway, hand on the door knob.

"Oh. You heard, huh?" He crossed the room to his son.

"I couldn't help hear it, Dad. You were pretty loud."

Reece pulled Tom into a tight man hug and held him for a moment before speaking. He felt some of his dreams were omens, they had been in the past, and he didn't have a good feeling about this one. Something unexpected would arrive on their doorstep. He could feel it. "Sorry I woke you."

"It's ok." Tom eased out of his dad's embrace. "Are you gonna be ok? Do you wanna talk about it?"

Reece gave his son a thin smile. "Yeah, I'll be ok. And, no, I don't want to talk about it. But thanks for asking. Go back to bed. Get some sleep. You've got school tomorrow."

Tom eyed his dad with a curious frown before turning on his heel and heading down the hallway to the stairs. He'd chosen the attic for his bedroom because he thought it would be the 'coolest' space in the house. Before climbing the staircase, he glanced back along the hall at his dad standing in the doorway.

"Goodnight, Tom."

"Night, Dad." A ripple of apprehension slithered through Tom's gut. Neither of them had dreamt about his mom in a long time. What could his dad's dream mean?

CHAPTER THREE

A week later, Reece stood at the front door, key in hand, wondering how he would explain what had occurred an hour ago to his son. He filled his lungs with air, breathing deep in through his nostrils and blew it out in a whoosh. A sigh followed. Charlotte had been gone for over six years and he still couldn't get his head around the fact he would never see her again. He missed her every single day. Before he could insert the key into the lock the door swung open and their son, Tom, stood in the entry hall. No longer the little boy Charlotte had loved, he'd be seventeen in a few months, had gone through his transformation, and stood just over six feet tall. A young man she would never get to know.

"How'd you know I was home?" Reece asked, stepping across the threshold and giving his teenage son a man hug before closing the door.

Tom shrugged. "I heard the Mustang before it reached our street."

The PI stared into his eyes. "Your wolf hearing is pretty acute these days."

"Yeah, I guess." He shrugged again. "What's for dinner? I'm starved."

Andre had signed Adrian's house over to Reece so he could raise Tom in a home environment. He told the PI he couldn't imagine himself living there. It nurtured too many memories for him and he liked the apartment he and Reece had lived in, which he shared with Enrique Lozano, once sheriff at the Las Vegas Metropolitan Police Department, now full-time paranormal PI with Double D Investigations. Despite the rift being sealed, there were still flickers of supernatural activity from time to time, smaller creatures that had somehow remained. And the team also took on regular PI work in the interim to keep the business afloat.

"Can I talk to you about something first?" He gripped his sixteen year old son's shoulder, gave it a gentle squeeze.

Tom's frowning gaze roamed his dad's face. *Something's up.* "Sure, what about?"

"Let's head to the living room."

"Ok." He followed Reece up the carpeted stairway, along the hall, and into the large room with a balcony.

Reece motioned to the burgundy, buttoned sofa that had belonged to Adrian. He didn't have the heart to get rid of the author's furnishings so decided to use them instead. "Have a seat."

Tom gave his dad a quizzical stare. "Am I in trouble? Did I do something wrong?"

"Of course not, buddy, I need to tell you something important. And kinda... strange."

"Oh, ok. What is it?" He backed up to the sofa and dropped down onto it, crossing one leg over the other and folding his arms.

Reece sat down in one of the matching armchairs opposite. "I met someone today..."

Tom's face lit up and he leaned forward. "That's great, Dad. You need to start getting out and having a social life. You're always working..."

Reece raised his hand to stop his son from speaking. "Not like that."

"Oh." Tom leaned back against the sofa. "What then?"

"You remember the lawyer who handled your mom's affairs after she... when we found out you could live with me?"

Tom nodded, an expression of worry crossing his young, handsome face. "I can still live with you, can't I?" He scooted forward on the sofa again.

"Yeah, you're stuck with me, warts and all. You're not going anywhere."

Tom smiled then frowned. "Good. So what do you want to tell me?"

"Phillip Pembroke called me today and asked me to come over to his office." He paused, having no idea what he would tell his son about the woman he'd met at the lawyer's firm.

"And? Come on, Dad, just tell me will ya."

Reece stared into Tom's eyes for a long time, not answering. He couldn't believe it, so how would his son take the news. How would he react when he met the woman?

"Dad?" He reached across and whacked Reece on the knee.

"Tommy, it's difficult to explain."

"You haven't called me that in a long time." He stood up, walked around the coffee table and crouched in front of his dad, his concerned frown deepening. "What's going on?"

Reece let out a heavy sigh. "When I got to Mr. Pembroke's office a woman who claims to be your aunt was waiting to see me."

"My what?" Tom shifted up and sat on the corner of the coffee table. "Mom said she didn't have any siblings."

"I know what mom said. Apparently they'd been estranged for years. I don't know all the details yet, but I plan to find out."

Tom's frown deepened even more and his stomach did a nervous flip flop. Something didn't feel right. "So, why did you have such a hard time telling me? If she *is* related to me it's a good thing, isn't it?"

"Of course." He waited a moment. "There's something you need to know about her before you see her."

"She's here?" Tom's eyes widened.

"Yes. She's waiting in her car outside the gate."

The young man's eyebrows knitted together. "You've never been this way with me before, Dad, why are you acting so weird?"

Reece stood up, Tom did too. The PI grabbed his son by the back of the neck and pulled him into another tight hug.

Tom eased his tall frame out of his dad's embrace. "Dad, come on. Tell me."

"Her name is Charlene... she's your mom's identical twin sister."

Tom's knees buckled and his butt hit the coffee table with a loud thud. He looked up at Reece, tears glistening in his eyes. "She looks like mom?"

"Yeah, she does." He remembered his reaction when she'd stood up and turned around. He had thought he'd seen a ghost.

"Man!"

"If you don't want to see her tonight we can arrange another time. She's ok with whatever you want to do."

Tom remained quiet for a while, his thoughts a jumble. *Do I want to meet someone who looks like my mom? Where has she been all this time?*

Why show up now? How did she find out mom died? Didn't the lawyer say mom had no siblings and that's why dad and I were the sole beneficiaries of her Will? He looked up at Reece. "Would it be ok to do it some other time? I don't know how I feel about it yet."

"Absolutely. I'll go let her know so she's not waiting around." Reece headed out the door and along the hallway to the stairs. He'd known it wouldn't be easy for Tom and he'd wanted to make it as simple and pain free as possible for him. The Lawyer had been insistent for Reece to allow Charlene to make contact with her nephew, even though the PI had resisted. He'd wanted to know more about her before introducing her to his son. He felt relieved by Tom's decision because being in the same space with the woman caused his heart to ache for Charlotte. Tears stung the backs of his eyes. She'd died in his arms. Something he would never forget.

Tom jumped to his feet and raced out into the hall. "Wait." He rushed up to his dad. "Should I see her now?"

Reece rested a hand on Tom's shoulder. "It's your decision, buddy. Whatever you decide is fine with me."

"You're sure?"

"Of course I am. You know your well-being is all I care about."

"I'm not sure what to do. What should I do?" Tom looked into his dad's eyes, a serious frown on his face. He needed Reece's reassurance.

"Do what you feel comfortable with. Ok? Don't worry about anyone else."

Tom nodded. "Ok. Maybe we could meet somewhere for dinner or something. I don't feel like having her here right now."

"Tomorrow night too soon?"

Tom gave a heavy sigh and shrugged. "I guess not."

"Ok." He pulled his son toward him and kissed his forehead. "I love you, Tom."

"I love you too, Dad." He frowned as he watched his dad head down the stairs. *Am I doing the right thing?*

Reece opened the gate and stepped out onto the shoulder.

Charlene was leaning against the fender of her dark blue Jeep, smoking a cigarette. When she saw him approach, she dropped it, ground it into the gravel with the toe of her shoe, and pushed herself off the car, an unsure smile on her face – Charlotte's face. "How did it go?"

"He's shocked, as you would expect."

"Oh, of course. I understand." She twisted a strand of hair around her index finger in the same way Charlotte used to when she felt anxious.

"He asked me to organize dinner for tomorrow night. Do you have plans?"

"No. I'm here to see Tommy, sorry, Tom."

"Ok, well, give me your number. I'll call you in the morning with the details after I make a reservation somewhere."

"Oh, sure." She held out her hand for his cell phone, keyed in her number, and passed it back to him. "There you go. I'll look forward to your call."

"Yeah, ok." He watched her walk around the car, climb in, and drive down the steep, narrow, one lane road. Seeing her again messed with his head. He realized now his dream had been forewarning him about her arrival. Until he knew more about her reason for being in LA he would have to keep his emotions in check. He wondered how he'd do that when she looked like the woman he still loved.

CHAPTER FOUR

Andre whipped across the asphalt on his red Ducati Monster heading to Nathaniel's nightclub. The vampire had called and asked him to come by. He needed to talk to him about an urgent matter and didn't want to discuss it over the phone. What had remained of Decadent Desire had been razed a few years ago, after permission had been granted for Nathaniel to rebuild. The new, popular, gothic nightspot had been redesigned and renamed – *Sanguine*.

Once there, Andre pulled into the alleyway and parked his motorcycle in the alcove between the buildings, removed his helmet and sat it on the seat, then walked back to the rear exit. The door opened. "It is good to see you," Nathaniel greeted. "Come through."

Andre eyed him with a curious stare then followed the broad, black vampire along the short passage and into the club. "So what did you want to see me about?"

"Let's go upstairs."

"Sure." Andre stepped up beside Nathaniel and they crossed the dance floor to the staircase in the right hand corner.

When they reached the office, Nathaniel motioned for Andre to step in ahead of him, then followed him in and closed the door. "Please, have a seat."

Andre remained standing, his eyes following Nathaniel across the room to his desk. He walked over to a chair and sat down. "So?"

"There have been more sightings of the reptile creatures. My team has been eliminating them as they find them, but some have managed to escape."

"Reece suspected there'd be more." Andre folded his arms and crossed one leg over the other.

"Yes. My concern is where they have hatched and how many more there are. Snakes can have up to 150 hatchlings. What if these creatures are as prolific?"

Andre's eyes widened. "Hell! That would mean there are dozens of them out there."

"We need to find their birthplace and destroy it."

"What we need to do is go over to Reece's and tell him what you've discovered."

"Tonight?"

"Yes. We'll need to locate what remains of the creatures and get rid of them. We still have the one out at the containment facility that we can study, so the rest can be destroyed."

Nathaniel glanced at the large clock on the wall beside him. "It is late. Do you not think it would be better to leave it until the morning and meet at your office?"

Andre's gaze moved to the clock. "I guess you're right. Tom would be asleep and he needs his rest."

"Very well. I will see you tomorrow at nine." Nathaniel stood up and came around the desk, hand extended.

Andre got to his feet and shook Nathaniel's hand. "See you then."

The disturbing news did not sit well with Andre. Creatures that could melt flesh from bone could do some serious damage while they waited until the morning. He decided to ride around the city to see if he could locate any of the reptiles. As he reached his bike his cell phone vibrated in his jacket pocket. He tugged it free and frowned at the screen. Reece. "Hey, I thought you'd be asleep by now."

"Yeah, well I've got a lot on my mind at the moment."

Andre frowned. "Like what?"

"It's too difficult to explain over the phone. Want to come over?"

"What about Tom?"

"He's sleeping. It'll be fine."

"Ok. I'll see you soon." He straddled his motorcycle, slipped his glossy black helmet on and snapped down the visor. The engine purred to life when Andre turned the key, and he idled down the alley and out onto the road. It would take a little over an hour to get to Reece's, which would make it just after midnight by the time he arrived. He stepped on the gas and the Ducati whisked along the deserted street.

∞

Andre followed Reece upstairs and into the living room. He could sense the tension in his friend and wondered what had happened. The pair entered the dimly lit space and Andre sat in one of the armchairs just as he always had when he lived there. "Sorry, force of habit." He stood up.

The PI raised his hand. "No. Stay there. I'll sit over here." He took a seat on the center cushion of the sofa.

Andre backed into his chair. "So what's up?"

Reece let out a heavy sigh. "I met someone at…"

"Well that's great news. It's about time. What's the problem?"

"Why does everyone think I mean a woman when I say that?"

Andre leaned onto his elbows. "You don't?"

"Well, yes, I do, but not in a romantic sense."

"Oh. Ok. Want to tell me about her?"

"I got a call from Phillip Pembroke, the lawyer that handled Charlotte's affairs. He asked me to come and see him, which I did. To cut a long story short, he had a woman with him… one who claims to be Tom's aunt…"

"But how is that possible? Charlotte didn't have any siblings."

"Yeah, that's what we all thought. But she does. Charlene is her identical twin sister."

Andre's brow furrowed. "What?!"

Reece nodded. "She's her to a T."

"Oh, man, I'm sorry. It must've been so hard for you, meeting her that way."

"Yeah, you could say that. I thought I'd seen a ghost. And it hurt like hell."

A pained expression crossed Andre's pale handsome face. "I get that. So why is she here? Where has she been? And what does she want?"

"One question at a time, ok?"

"Sure, sorry. What about Tom. Has he seen her?"

"First of all, she says she's here for Tom. Where she's been… I have no idea yet. And I don't know what she wants. We haven't gotten that far. No, Tom hasn't seen her, he didn't want to." He waited a beat then said, "You know, I had a dream about Charlotte the other night. I woke up covered in sweat with my heart pounding. My gut told me something was coming and here it is."

"What are you going to do?"

"I've organized dinner for tonight," he said, checking his watch. 12:18 AM. "We'll see what happens."

"You need to ask her where she's been all these years and what she wants. Do you want me to do some digging to see what I can find out before you go to dinner?"

Reece's eyes met his friend's. "I could do it myself, but, yeah, I'd appreciate it. It's a little too close to home."

"Consider it done. I don't need to sleep so I'll get on it as soon as I'm home."

"Thanks. Speaking of home, how's it going with Lozano?"

"Seems to be working out well so far. I can't see any foreseeable issues." Andre stood up. "Oh, by the way, Nathaniel asked me over to the night club tonight. It seems there are more of those reptilian creatures out there. Did you know that snakes can hatch up to 150 baby snakes?"

"Yeah, I saw it on National Geographic once."

"Well, I didn't. Anyhow, that means there could still be dozens of those things stalking the streets of LA."

"What else did Nathaniel tell you?"

"His team has eliminated some of them but he believes we need to find the nest and destroy it."

"Wouldn't they have all left by now?"

"Probably. Who knows?" Andre shrugged. "Ok, I'll head off and see what I can find out about… Charlene?"

"Yeah."

"Charlene Delaney?"

"I think so. I didn't ask."

"She isn't married?"

Reece shook his head. "I don't know. Maybe."

"I should be able to track her details down with her maiden name, if she is married it would be on record, but you'll need to get more information if I'm going to do a thorough search."

"I will tonight."

"I'll let you know what I find out."

"Thanks, Andre. I really do appreciate it."

Andre waved it off. "That's what friends are for."

As he turned to leave, Tom came into the room.

"Hey, Uncle Andre, how are you?" He rushed up to him and gave him a hug.

"I'm good. You?"

"Studying for an exam. Well, not right now, I was sleeping…"

"Sorry if we woke you." Andre released his surrogate nephew.

"Nah, I needed to use the bathroom and I heard voices in here. Did dad tell you about my aunt?"

"Yes, he did. How do you feel about that?"

Tom frowned and gave it some thought. "I'm not sure. I guess I'll find out when I meet her for dinner."

"Well I hope it all goes well." Andre smiled.

Tom's gaze moved to his dad then back to his uncle. "Yeah, I guess." He shrugged. "She looks like mom, you know."

"Yes, so your dad mentioned."

"I hope I don't act like a baby when I see her."

"I'm sure you'll be just fine. You're a strong young man, Tom, don't forget that."

He nodded. "Thanks, Uncle Andre. Well, I'm going back to bed. Goodnight."

"Goodnight." Andre waited for Tom to leave then turned around. "I'll get the information to you as soon as I can." He was concerned for Tom, and for the woman's intentions.

CHAPTER FIVE

The following morning, while Reece worked alone in the office, a knock echoed into the room pulling his gaze from the computer screen to the frosted glass of the pale green wood door. The hazy silhouette of what looked to be a man appeared like an apparition on the other side of the pane. Reece pulled himself out of his chair, crossed the room and opened the door, a look of surprise on his face when his eyes met those of Todd Lassiter. "Well, hello, you're a sight for sore eyes." He opened the door, motioning for the ex-detective to enter the office. "It's been a long time. What brings you here?"

Todd gave the PI a sheepish glance before stepping into Double D Investigations. "Yeah, it has been a while. I'm sorry I left the way I did. I needed some time to make sense of what happened."

"Yeah, we all did." Reece closed the door, motioned to his desk. "Have a seat."

The pair crossed the office. Todd sat down on one of the two chairs facing the window, the PI returning to his swivel chair. "What can I do for you? You don't need our help I hope."

The ex-detective let out a heavy sigh. "I want to work for you again. Is it too late?"

Reece leaned back, folded his arms, and studied his visitor for a moment. "Why?"

"I – I need to be doing something to make a difference."

"Why now after all this time?"

"I feel like I let everyone down, especially Charlotte… I want to make it right."

Reece's suspicions were confirmed. Todd still had feelings for her even though she'd been gone all these years.

Ed Borenko entered the office. "Well look what the cat dragged in." He crossed the room and stood beside Reece's desk. "What took you so long, Lassiter?"

"I needed time to get my head around everything. To try to make sense of what happened to Charlotte. It hasn't been easy, you know?"

Ed folded his arms over his podgy belly. "Yeah, well, we all felt the same but we didn't give up." The chief wasn't sure how he felt about Todd Lassiter turning up out of the blue like this, and it showed on his face.

Todd stood up. "Look… I know… I – I'm sorry. I'm here to make amends, if I can."

Ed's gaze moved from him to Reece. "I'm not the one you should be apologizin' to." He poked the air, pointing at the PI. "He is."

Todd looked across the desk at Reece. "Can you forgive my foolish behavior? Will you give me the opportunity to work with you again?"

Reece ran the idea around his mind. They could use Todd's expertise, his connections, and he'd always maintained he would take him back, if he asked. But what if he decided to skip out on them again? "Let me get back to you. I think we need some time to be sure it's what we both want, don't you?"

"Fair enough, I guess I deserve that."

"It has nothing to do with what you deserve, Todd. It's what's going to work for the business. I need people on my team I can rely on, no matter what."

"Ok, well, let me know when you make a decision. And for the record, you *can* trust me. You know where I am." He turned on his heel, crossed the room, pulled open the door and stopped short. "Charlotte?" Todd turned to look at Reece then back to the woman standing in the hallway.

Reece rushed across the office and caught the ex-detective as his knees buckled. "No, Todd, this is Charlene."

Todd's dazed gaze moved to the PI. His mind couldn't grasp the vision in front of him. "What?"

"This is her sister."

Todd's eyes moved back to the woman who looked like Charlotte. "How?"

"Come in, Charlene. Just give me a minute." Reece led Todd back to his seat.

"Ed's eyes widened. "What the hell's goin' on?"

"Sorry, Chief, I didn't have time to tell everyone yet. I only found out myself yesterday. This is Charlotte's twin sister, Charlene. She came to LA to see Tom."

"What?" Ed's mind felt foggy all of a sudden. Were his eyes playing tricks on him? It felt like something out of that TV show The Twilight Zone.

Reece turned to look at the woman. "Can I ask why you're here?"

"I came to find out about tonight. You said you'd give me a call."

"Oh, yeah. Sorry. My mind has been on other things."

"What's happening tonight, Daniels?" Ed wanted to know.

"The PI's gaze moved to his ex-boss. "Tom and I are having dinner with Charlene so she can meet him."

Both Todd and Ed couldn't take their eyes off the woman with Charlotte's face.

Reece looked at Charlene. "I'll text you the address once I sort these two out. Ok?"

"Of course. I'll wait for your message." Her eyes moved from him to the two men who appeared to be in shock then back to him. "I'll see you tonight." She stepped into the hallway, crossed the landing, and headed down the stairs.

Reece closed the door, walked over to the small corner kitchen, pulled open a cupboard door beneath the sink and snatched up the half empty bottle of whiskey. He grabbed two glasses from off the sink and crossed the room. After pouring the drinks, he handed one to Todd, the other to Ed. "Drink up, it'll help." He glanced across the office at the kitchen wondering if he needed a whiskey himself. Every time he saw Charlene the gaping hole in his heart widened.

"Since when did Charlotte have a sister?" Todd asked, his voice low. "She never mentioned her."

"Maybe not, but she's here and she's very real." Reece folded his arms.

"I thought Charlotte was an only child." Ed said.

"They've been estranged for years."

"How do you know this isn't a demon pretending to be Charlotte's sister?" Todd couldn't get his head around the woman being the exact image of his ex-partner.

"Because we closed the rift. Nothing can get through." Reece didn't want to tell Todd about the new fracture. Not yet.

Still dazed, Todd looked up at the PI. "Have you checked her out?"

"Andre's on it. I'm not leaving anything to chance where Tom's concerned."

"Tom?" Todd frowned.

"Charlotte's son."

"Oh, yeah, Tommy. He must be, what, seventeen by now?" Todd swallowed the last of his whiskey. It helped.

"Almost. He turns seventeen later in the year."

Ed wandered around Reece's desk and plonked himself down in the PI's chair. "What a head spin."

"Yeah, I'm sorry, Chief, like I said I only found out yesterday when Charlotte's lawyer called me. Seeing Charlene in his office nearly blew me away. I thought I'd seen a ghost."

Ed gave him a sorrowful look. "I'm sorry, Daniels. Must've been hard for ya."

"That's an understatement. Every time I see her it hurts like hell."

Todd could relate to those sentiments. "How does Tom feel about it?"

"Confused, upset, as you'd expect." Reece perched himself on the corner of the desk.

The ex-detective huffed out a stunned guffaw. "No kidding. I think we all feel the same way right now."

Reece frowned at Todd. "How are you feeling?"

"Rattled." He held up his glass. "May I?"

"Sure." Reece picked up the bottle, unscrewed the cap, and poured a finger's breadth into Todd's glass. Realizing he did need that drink after all, he crossed the room, snatched a glass from off the kitchen sink, and brought it back to his desk. After pouring himself a much-needed whiskey, he tipped up the glass, swallowed the amber liquid in one mouthful, and coughed as it slid into his uneasy gut.

"Why do you think she's here after all this time? Does she want something?" Todd wasn't convinced the woman's intentions were honorable.

Reece shrugged. "Tonight's dinner should answer those questions." He hoped.

"Todd's right, Daniels. Why would she come here out of nowhere after all these years? It doesn't add up. She must want somethin'.""

"Like I said, Andre's looking into it."

"I knew Charlotte for a lot of years, Reece. Don't you think she would've said something about a sibling?"

"She didn't say anything to me, so I guess not."

Todd pushed his empty glass across the desk. "What if the rift has opened up again? What if Dracula or another creature you've dispatched has sent her here? Who's to say it couldn't happen? I've been doing a lot of reading over the past few years on this stuff. Maybe that's what's happening right now."

"I think Charlotte didn't mention her sister because they were estranged for too many years. It's possible she never expected Charlene to come to LA in search of her… or as it stands, Tom, so why would she involve us in something from her past she wanted to keep private?"

"I don't have an answer." Todd's gaze moved from the whiskey bottle to Reece. "But I've got a bad feeling about this. As Ed said, something doesn't feel right about this whole situation. How did she even know about Tom? You need to be careful, Reece."

"Always. Tom is my first priority."

CHAPTER SIX

Later that afternoon, Reece made the decision to head home and go through Charlotte's things stored in the basement. Would he find something about Charlene amongst them? Surely Charlotte kept some memento of her sister among her belongings... a photo, a letter, something. As he drove his midnight blue Mustang convertible toward the Hollywood Hills an uneasy feeling slid through his gut. *Could Todd be right about her?*

Reece pulled up at the gated alcove, climbed out of the car and headed for the double, carved wooden front doors. He was about to push the key into the lock when a door swung open. "Hey, Dad, you're home early."

Reece glanced at his cell phone screen, checking the time, before his gaze returned to Tom. "What are you doing home?"

"We had a free class last period so I thought I'd come home instead of hanging out at school."

"Oh, ok. Sensible idea." Reece stepped inside, closed the door and gave his son a hug.

"Thanks." Tom frowned at his dad. "Why are you home?"

Reece let out a sigh. "I thought I'd have a look through your mom's things to see if there's anything there..."

"About Charlene, you mean?"

"Yeah."

"Can I help?"

"Don't you have homework?" Reece frowned into Tom's eyes. He didn't want his son upset by going through Charlotte's stuff.

"You always do that." Tom folded his arms, giving his dad a scowl.

"Do what?"

"I'm not a little kid anymore. You don't have to protect me from everything."

Reece let out another heavy sigh. "The reason I do it is because I love you and want to keep you safe."

"I know, but you have to let me grow up. I know what's out there... remember?"

Reece raised defensive hands. "Ok, I get it. If you want to help I'd appreciate it."

The pair headed to the basement.

Opening the door, Reece flipped the wall switch – the dull amber glow providing minimal light – and trudged down the wooden treads, Tom behind him. The boxes with Charlotte's things were stacked against the wall in the right-hand corner. Reece reached up to pull the chain on the second overhead bulb in the center of the basement and the shadowed space lit up.

Tom stood with hands on hips. "Where do you want me to start?"

Reece ran his eyes over the floor to ceiling stack, pointing to the other end of the pile. "Over there. I'll open up some of these."

"Ok, sure." Tom moved to the left, reached up, pulled a box from off the top of the stack and sat it on the floor. He lowered himself onto his butt and used a clawed fingernail to slit the adhesive tape.

Reece glanced over at him. "I don't know if it's a good idea to partially transform like that."

"It's fine, Dad. It doesn't do anything to me."

"Well, just be mindful of not overdoing it. We don't know if there are any permanent side effects to doing what you can do."

"Will you stop worrying so much? If I notice anything I'll tell you. Ok?"

"Sure, ok." Reece's eyes remained on his son for a moment longer before he returned to opening the box he'd set down with a pocket knife.

The pair remained silent for quite some time, lost in their own world of memories, until Tom's voice echoed around the underground space. "Hey,

I remember this." He held up a colorful crayon drawing he'd made in kindergarten of him and Charlotte. "I didn't know mom kept it."

"Mom's tend to keep a lot of stuff their kids make. It means more to them than anything store bought."

Tom's smile widened then his expression turned solemn. "I wish she was still here."

"Me too, buddy, me too."

"There's nothing in here belonging to Charlene, no photos of her with mom... nothing from their past."

"Ok. Seal it up as best you can and start on the next one." Pulling his cell phone from the back pocket of his jeans Reece checked the time. "We're meeting her in a couple of hours so let's hustle."

"Oh, ok." Tom set the box aside and tugged the next one from the stack.

Andre hadn't been in touch either, so they were going into tonight's dinner blind.

The pair continued checking boxes, finding nothing about Charlene in any of them. What could it mean?

CHAPTER SEVEN

Charlene stood outside the restaurant, her gaze roaming the street for Reece's midnight blue Mustang. *They should arrive any minute.* Her stomach did a nervous flip flop. Would she be able to pull this off? The PI's voice startled her and she spun around.

"Hi. Sorry we're late. I lost track of time working on something."

"That's ok. I've only been here a few minutes."

Reece's gaze remained on her for longer than it should have, his mind wandering back to his and Charlotte's first date. Well, it hadn't been a date, as such. They'd arranged to have dinner together to go over the case they'd been working on, which turned out to be werewolf related.

Charlene's eyes moved from Reece to the tall, good-looking young man beside him and she smiled. "So, you must be my nephew." She extended her hand.

Tom knew it would be impolite not to shake hands. He reached out, their palms connecting. "Yeah, I guess."

Reece could tell Tom felt uncomfortable. "Why don't we go inside?"

"Oh, yes, of course." Charlene stepped into the restaurant ahead of them.

Once they were seated at their table, Charlene initiated the conversation. "Tom, I didn't come here to make you feel uncomfortable. I'd love to get to know you, as you're my only living relative now. If you have any questions please feel free to ask." She gave the young man a warm, maternal smile.

Tom didn't answer. His eyes flitted to his dad.

Reece wanted to act as a buffer. "Let's order something to drink, take a moment, and let the evening flow the way it's going to. Sound good?"

Charlene's gaze moved to him. "Yes, you're right. I'm rushing things, aren't I?"

"I understand you're excited to meet Tom, but you have to be mindful of… your appearance and how it's affecting him."

"You're right again. Forgive me." Her eyes moved to the young man. "I'm sorry, Tom. I know this must be difficult for you… me looking like your mom."

Tom frowned into her eyes. "I do have a question. Where have you been all these years?"

The boy's sudden brashness took Charlene by surprise. "Oh, well, I live across the country. I have a job and…"

"You're not answering the question. Why did you come here now, after such a long time?"

"I – I wanted to meet you."

"How did you even know about me?"

"Well, I – I've been keeping track of your mom over the years and…"

"If what you're saying is true why didn't you come see her before she died?" Tom folded his arms.

"She didn't want to see me."

"Why?"

"It's something I'd prefer not to discuss right now. I will tell you when…"

"Ok, so you don't plan on answering any of my questions tonight?"

"I'm happy to answer your questions."

"Just not the important ones." Tom skidded back his chair and stood up. "Dad, can we go?"

"Please, Tom, won't you give me a chance?" Charlene popped up off her chair.

Reece watched the interaction between the pair. "Perhaps we can make this dinner another time. When you're more prepared."

"I am prepared."

"It doesn't seem that way. You don't want to answer Tom's questions… questions he needs answers to."

"There are some things I need to explain at length and a public place isn't appropriate." She returned her gaze to Tom. "Won't you please stay?"

Tom glanced at his dad then back to the woman with his mother's face and sighed. "I don't know." He shrugged.

"Perhaps we can arrange another time. Maybe at the office where you can talk freely," Reece offered.

She nodded. "Yes, all right."

"Ok. I'll be in touch." Reece took his son by the arm and the pair left the restaurant.

Charlene sighed. Dinner hadn't gone at all according to plan.

℘CЯ

When Reece pulled the Mustang into the circular driveway, Tom flung open the door and stepped out. "I'm going up to my room." The silent drive home only solidified the turmoil in his son.

Reece leaned across the console. "Tom, wait. Let's talk about it."

The young man continued across the drive, into the alcove, and disappeared into the house.

Reece opened the door to go follow him when his cell phone vibrated in his jacket pocket. He'd turned in onto silent for the dinner so they'd have no interruptions. Tugging it free, he stepped out of the convertible, frowning at the screen. Andre. "Yeah, what's up?"

"I need to see you. Can you come over to the apartment?"

"I've got a situation right now. Can we make it another time?"

Andre frowned. "What kind of situation?"

Reece gave a heavy sigh. "The dinner did not go well. Tom's upset. He's gone up to his room and I want to go talk to him."

"Maybe you shouldn't. Maybe you should give him some time to process it."

Reece's gaze moved to the open passenger door. He walked around the hood of the Mustang and closed it. "No, he's hurting. I need to…"

"Give him some space."

"Andre, I know you mean well, but you have no idea about kid's emotions."

"I think you should let Tom work it out for himself. He'll come to you when he's ready to talk about it. He always does."

Reece paced in front of his car. *Perhaps Andre is right. Perhaps Tom does need some time.* "Ok. I'm on my way. See you in a bit." He rang off, texted Tom to let him know where he'd be, and pocketed his phone. Gazing up at the small, round, multi-paned attic window he gave another sigh, climbed into his car and headed to Andre's.

ℰᏅ

When Reece reached the apartment, before he could raise his hand to knock, the door opened.

Andre motioned for him to step inside. "I'm glad you decided to come over. I've found some information about Charlotte's sister I knew you'd want to see. Sorry I couldn't get it to you before your dinner meeting."

The PI frowned into his friend's eyes as he crossed the threshold. "What have you got?"

"I'll show you." Andre closed the door and headed down the hallway to his room, his laptop open on the foot of his bed. "Grab the chair."

Reece tugged the office chair out from under the small wood desk, rolled it across the carpet, and sat down. Gazing along the hallway, he asked, "Where's Lozano?"

"He went out for a late dinner with Ed. I encouraged him to go so we could have some time to ourselves."

"Does he know about Charlene?"

"Not yet. Do you want me to tell him?"

"Yeah. He should find out from one of us before he sees her."

"Ok, I'll talk to him when he gets back." His gaze returned to the laptop screen. "What I've got so far isn't a lot. It indicates Charlotte does indeed have a sister whose name is Charlene." Andre perched himself on the edge of the bed, typed something into the computer, then turned it around so Reece could peruse the information on the screen.

Reece's gaze moved from the document he'd been reading to his friend. "All this proves is the twins were born at Valley Presbyterian Hospital, nothing else. I need more information. Is Charlene married? Does she have a family? Where does she live? Does she work? What's her married name? Have there been any run-ins with law enforcement? Even a parking ticket would be helpful."

"My next port of call is public records and the DMV to see what I can find. At least we can safely say she isn't a demon posing as Charlotte's sister. A good thing, right?"

The PI's gaze darkened. "Is it? Just because Charlotte *had* a sister doesn't mean she still does. Maybe check deaths first to see if Charlene is still living." Reece's gut told him something about the woman who claimed to be Tom's aunt didn't add up. He wanted to know why. She always seemed nervous, as though she was hiding something.

CHAPTER EIGHT

Charlene lay on the brown and gold printed cover of the queen-sized bed in her hotel room staring at the ceiling. *How can I convince Reece and Tom I am who I claim to be?* The way it stood right now, the PI was not about to allow her entry into their inner sanctum. She needed to change that. But how? She gave a heavy sigh, swung her legs over the side of the bed, and crossed the room to the window, gazing down at the busy street several stories below. Her plan to reunite with her nephew would be hindered if she couldn't get them to believe her.

Their dinner hadn't gone as she'd expected. Tom appeared to be quite the astute young man, his questions direct. He didn't understand that some answers couldn't be provided in a brief amount of time. Certain things required explanation. She needed to be careful how she handled the situation with the teenager otherwise she would ruin her chance of establishing any kind of relationship with him, which she desperately needed to do.

Reece would pose a problem. Being fiercely protective, it would be difficult for her to get close to the boy, so she needed to figure out a way to relinquish the PI's hold on him in order to gain the teen's trust. After all, they were meant to be family. A smile spread across her lips as she glanced at her hazy reflection in the pane of glass.

A sudden knock echoed into the room causing Charlene to swing around, her eyes moving to the back of the door. *Who could that be at this time of night?* Her gaze drifted to the bedside clock. 11:53PM. She crossed the room with caution, leaned in, peered through the peephole and gasped. Releasing the U-shaped catch on the security lock, she swung the door open. "What are you doing here?"

CHAPTER NINE

Because Andre postponed the arranged meeting with Nathaniel at their office the previous morning, due to the situation with Charlene, he thought it best to call everyone together to discuss their plans to eradicate the reptilian creatures. There hadn't been any new reported cases as yet, but it was only a matter of time before the citizens of Los Angeles became their prime targets. The creature out at the containment facility had died and their research team had begun an intensive investigation into the cause. How many reptiles were still out there? Would they die in the same way that one had?

A knock echoed into the office. Reece and Andre turned toward the sound. "Come in," Reece called.

Nathaniel stepped into the room. "Good morning," he said, closing the door.

"Morning," the pair said together.

Nathaniel ran his gaze around the open space. "Where are the others?"

Reece checked the time on his phone. "They should be here any minute. Have a seat." The PI motioned to the chair beside Andre.

"Thank you. I will remain standing."

Within minutes, the door opened again and Ed, Sarah, and Lozano walked in. "Morning all," Ed greeted.

"Morning," Reece offered. "Grab a chair. Come join us."

Sarah rolled an office chair over to Reece's desk next to Andre. She no longer worked as Deacon for St. Joseph's. She'd resigned after Charlotte's death, vowing to help Reece eradicate as many supernatural monsters that she could. No more innocent people would die – not if she could prevent it.

Ed pulled up a chair from the lunch table next to Sarah. "So, what's this all about, Daniels?"

"I'll let Nathaniel tell you." He motioned for the black vampire to fill everyone in.

"My team discovered the reptilian nest in drains on the outskirts of LA. No creatures were present. They have been eradicating as many as they can but there are still more roaming the city. If we do not contain them they will travel to other parts of the country. We must move on this without hesitation."

"How are we gonna find them?" Ed asked, folding his arms across his pot belly.

"We will divide into pairs. Do a thorough sweep of the city," Nathaniel told him.

"Yeah? What happens if they find us first?" Something slithered in the pit of the ex-Lieutenant's gut. He didn't like the feeling. "Those things spit venom that can dissolve a body –and I, for one, don't want to have to get up close 'n personal with 'em."

"You have safety gear. It will protect you from their venom."

"Don't you think we should be doin' this as a team?"

Reece stepped in. "We can cover more ground this way, Chief." He folded his arms, frowned at his ex-boss. "What's the matter with you? You're usually up for this kind of thing."

"Yeah, well, I ain't gettin' any younger. I'd like to have a few more years on this planet before I die. It isn't a crime, you know?" He shrugged.

Nathaniel crossed the room to Ed and rested a hand on the older man's shoulder. "And you will, if you take precautions. As will we all."

Ed gave the black vampire a surreptitious frown, his cheeks flushing. "You're immortal, I'm not." He knew Nathaniel would die one day. Not for a long time – hundreds more years, perhaps.

Sarah reached across and gave his hand a gentle squeeze. "We're going to be fine. We've been up against worse."

"Yeah, yeah, I know." He gave her a sideward glance. "But aren't you gettin' tired of it all?"

Reece sat on the corner of his desk near Ed. "Do you want to quit?"

Ed's gaze moved to the PI. "Not what I said."

"It kinda sounded like it to me," Lozano told him, a sheepish look appearing on his face when Ed gave him a scowl.

The chief gave a heavy sigh. "I feel like all I've been doing for the past few years is chasing one kind of monster or another. It's wearing me down. This wasn't how I foresaw my retirement, you know?"

A heavy weight sank into Reece's gut. It wouldn't be the same without his ex-boss. "If you want to leave, Chief, you don't need my permission. It's up to you and…" he glanced at the ex-priest, "Sarah to decide." Would she leave too?

Ed stood up, waving off the comment. "I'm not making any rash decisions right now. We need to get rid of those reptile creatures first."

"You are thinking about it though?"

"Well, yeah. Like I said, I ain't gettin' any younger." He shrugged.

Silence circled the office for quite some time before a knock echoed into the room.

Reece walked over to the door and pulled it open. "Todd? What are you doing here?"

"I hadn't heard back from you so I thought I'd stop by to find out if you've made a decision."

"Come in."

The ex-detective entered the office, his eyes roaming the others in the room. "Hi," he said, feeling self-conscious as everyone's gaze moved to him.

Reece returned to his desk.

Todd crossed the room. "What's going on?"

The PI folded his arms, still on his feet. "We encountered reptilian creatures that spit venom so potent it dissolves flesh and bone. We're in the middle of working on a plan to eradicate them. Want in?" His right eyebrow arched.

"Uh, sure." Todd frowned. "How do we protect ourselves against them?"

"We have protective gear that can withstand flammable liquids, including acids," Andre told him.

"Do they work?"

Good question. No one knew for sure because they hadn't been close enough to be attacked by one of the creatures.

"As far as we're aware, yes," Reece offered.

Todd's frown deepened. "You don't know for sure? And you're willing to risk your lives to…"

"You said you wanted to come back to the team. The job involves dangerous situations. So are you in or are you out?" Reece stepped up to Todd, hands on hips. "I need to know."

Todd raised defensive hands. "I'm in. One hundred percent."

With Ed considering leaving the team, and the possibility of Sarah going with him, Reece needed all the manpower he could get. Would Todd prove to be reliable? Only time would tell.

CHAPTER TEN

Andre followed Nathaniel through the dank, pitch black circular drain with caution, aware that some of the reptiles might have returned to the nest. Possible? Yes. Any kind of supernatural organisms were creatures of habit and this particular sewer provided the perfect environment for such creatures. They preferred the dark.

A sound echoed out of the gloom. Both vampires pulled up short, their nocturnal vision widening to survey the tunnel in both directions. Even with their acute hearing, they couldn't ascertain which direction the sound had emanated from. The pair held flame throwers locked and loaded, ready for an imminent attack. Nothing happened.

"Who's there?" Andre's voice bounced off the concrete, vibrating around them.

No answer.

What did he expect? The assailant to jump out of their hiding place at them?

Nathaniel's vampire hearing homed in on breathing further down the tunnel. He motioned with his head – the pair continued forward. The hidden would-be attacker, not too far in front of them, seemed human... or close to it.

"Andre?" Nathaniel said telepathically.

"Yes?" Andre answered in the same way.

"Do you hear breathing?"

"I do. Maybe it's a homeless person sleeping down here."

Nathaniel didn't think so. "I do not believe it is the case."

"What then?" Andre stopped.

Nathaniel turned to him. "I sense a supernatural force. Witch, perhaps."

A figure stepped out of the gloom, flicking on the flashlight of their cell phone. "I wondered how long it would take you to figure it out." The woman dressed in a black leather biker jacket, figure-hugging dark blue jeans, black combat boots stood in front of them. Her flaming red hair and lilac colored eyes were her most attractive features, even though her face was beautiful. "I am here to offer my assistance."

"It is a strange place to introduce yourself," Nathaniel told her.

"This wasn't my intended venue. I planned to pay a visit to Double D Investigations."

"And yet, here you are."

"I came here to eliminate the reptilian creatures. As you have."

"How did you hear our conversation?" Andre wanted to know.

"I have a number of abilities, telepathy being one of them."

Andre frowned into her lilac colored eyes. "Who are you? Where are you from?"

"Maybe we could continue the interrogation outside. There are no reptiles here. I've done a thorough sweep of the drains." She motioned in the direction of the subterranean entrance.

"Why should we believe you?" Nathaniel asked. "You could be a decoy."

The woman gave a sigh. "You would think that, wouldn't you?"

"We have no reason to trust you," Andre added.

"Fair comment, I suppose. If you want answers you're going to have to follow me outside." She stepped around the pair, heading toward the drain's entry point.

Nathaniel's left eyebrow arched as he gave Andre a dubious stare. The pair followed the witch out.

She stood with arms folded across her ample bosom. "To answer your first question, my name is Avalynn Cross. I'm a practitioner of both kinds of magick. I've been in LA for a couple of weeks trying to track down the reptiles. I came here from New Orleans."

"How did you know about the reptilian creatures?" Andre asked.

"News travels fast in supernatural circles. An outbreak occurred back home and I thought I could assist with the eradication of the reptiles here or anywhere else they may show up." She unfolded her arms. "I *am* here to help."

"So far there haven't been any further attacks. As far as we know." Andre's gaze moved to

Nathaniel then back to Avalynn. "We had one contained but it died."

Her lilac eyes widened. "How?"

"Our research team is attempting to determine the reason," Nathaniel offered. "They think it could be environmental."

"Interesting. Can I see it?"

"I think we need to introduce you to the other members of our team first." Nathaniel wasn't sure how Reece would take this new turn of events or the witch's offer of help.

ℰℭ

Reece stood with arms folded scrutinizing the woman standing before him. A witch. Arianne had been a half-breed vampire with witch abilities, but it had served no purpose whatsoever. Dracula had killed her as she attempted to save Andre's life – she had been the daughter of the father of all vampires – his blood. Even though this witch had powers that would certainly assist his team, he wondered what her motives were. Why would she risk everything to come to LA to help them? What did she want in return? There was always a price.

"I understand your lack of trust in me, although I am here offering my help without any strings or payment." Avalynn stepped up to the PI. "That's what you were wondering, wasn't it?"

"There are always strings attached or some kind of payment... not always in cash." Reece stared into her lilac eyes trying to find any deception in them. "Why would you want to help us?"

"Because I have knowledge about the creatures, I can assist with their extermination." She mirrored his movements.

"You were surprised when I told you the one at our facility died. So, it's obvious to me you don't know as much as you think."

"Ok. You're right. But I do know other things you don't."

"Like what?" Reece's gaze remained on her lilac colored, almond shaped eyes.

"They can morph into human form... over time they must shed their reptilian skins, in the same way a snake does, which makes them vulnerable."

"Human form?" This new information caused a lead weight to sink into the pit of Reece's gut.

"Yes. I became friends with one, unaware of what he was. He tricked me. Not long after I learned the truth I killed him." A single tear slipped down Avalynn's right cheek. She brushed it away with her fingertips.

"So you were in a romantic relationship with one and didn't know?"

Her lilac eyes darkened. "Yes. I had no idea when I met him. They are adept at hiding their true nature."

"How did you find out?" Reece perched himself on the corner of his desk.

"Over time, I grew to have my suspicions about him. I'm not entirely sure what prompted them. One night I followed him and witnessed his transformation into reptile form before he disappeared into a sewer. I captured him soon after, extracted information from him about the other creatures. Once we had what we needed we... the witches of New Orleans... traveled into the drains to cast a spell that would destroy the nest and remaining reptilian creatures hiding there. We also fashioned a supernatural force field in case we missed any."

"So they do go back to the nest?" Nathaniel asked.

Her gaze moved to him. "I thought so, only the ones here in LA haven't returned. And they shed their human skins in a different way to the ones we eliminated back home. It seems they are evolving."

CHAPTER ELEVEN

Detective Grant Donovan stood in the parking lot behind the abandoned movie theater, staring at the gooey puddle of red slime as he slipped a stick of doublemint gum into his mouth. The second call out in less than 48 hours. So far, forensics could only determine the collected organic samples were indeed human. *How could someone kill another person this way? What could dissolve a body like that? And why hadn't they cleaned up the crime scene so no one would know about it? Why leave the remains?* He didn't have any answers to these vital questions and it sat heavy in his gut. *Did someone see what happened here?* He'd send out uniforms to door knock. *Someone must've seen or heard something. Anything.*

He heard his name as he scrutinized the crime scene, his gaze moving along the alley. "Reece." He extended his hand. "Long time no see."

"Yeah, it has been a while. How's it going?" Reece's palm connected with his in a firm shake.

Grant stepped out of the way to reveal the macabre evidence. "About as well as could be expected, under the circumstances." The detective knew about the PI's extracurricular activities before leaving the force and wondered if he could shed some light on this new murder investigation.

Reece gave a heavy sigh. "What I tell you needs to be in confidence. For now, at least."

"I get it. You know I won't say anything until you give me the go ahead."

The PI's gaze surveyed the alley, the forensic team doing a sweep of the area. "Can we talk in your car?" He couldn't afford to be overheard.

"Of course." Grant turned around, his eyes roaming the alley for his partner Harrison Killjoy. "Killjoy?" He stuck his fingers in his mouth, gave a loud whistle. "Hey, Harrison."

His partner glanced over his shoulder, got up, turned around and stood with hands on hips. "Yeah, what?"

"I'm heading out front for five. You ok to keep everyone in line?" He gave his partner a cheeky smile.

"Sure thing, *boss*." He returned an equally smart-alecky grin.

"You can stop with the wisecracks now." The joke had worn thin. Grant turned to Reece. "Ok, let's go."

"You get a promotion?"

"Yeah."

"Congratulations."

"Thanks."

The pair headed to the detective's dark blue sedan parked on the street.

"So, what can you tell me?" Grant asked, closing the driver's door. "This can't be a human perp. It has to be something else. Right?"

Reece wasn't sure how much information he should share as they had nothing to go on about the location of the creatures yet. "Definitely something else."

"I knew it." He rolled down the window and spat his gum onto the road. "Do you know what's doing this?"

"I'd prefer not to say until we locate them."

The detective's eyebrows rose. "*Them?* You mean there's more than one roaming our city doing that to people?" He motioned toward the alley with his head.

"As far as we can tell. We've been able to eliminate some of them but there are more. My team is trying to find their location as we speak."

"You know you can trust me. You have before. What are we looking at here?"

Would he trust him this time? What choice did he have? He needed someone with their ear to the ground. Reece sighed. "Reptilian creatures. Their venom is the cause of the puddle of slime you witnessed down there. It's lethal."

"Fuck me!" He unwrapped another stick of gum, shoved it into his mouth. He'd been trying to give up smoking for a few months now and chewing gum helped with the cravings. "So anyone that comes in contact with one of these things will end up a puddle of bloody goo."

"Yes."

"Holy hell!" He glanced at the PI sideways. "And you want to keep this under wraps?"

"It's necessary… for now."

"Why?"

"Because they can take on human form. It's the reason we haven't been able to find them. Who knows where they are… what line of work they're in. They could be in the precinct for all I know."

The detective's complexion paled. "You've gotta be kidding me."

"I wish I was." Reece remembered the cops Ed brought in to help with Charlotte's kidnappings case when they were outnumbered out at the containment facility. Unbeknown to his boss, they had been a werewolf pack, so had their Chief of Police, MacKinnon.

೫ಞ

Reece had just stepped into the Double D Investigations office when the door burst open and Avalynn Cross stormed into the room. "You had no right involving the law in this."

The PI stood with hands on hips. "Don't tell me what I can and can't do. You've been here all of five minutes and think you know this town. You have no idea. The detective I spoke to is reliable." He frowned into her unusual eyes. "How do you know who I've spoken to, anyway? Have you been following me?"

"I cast a spell to keep tabs on you all. For your own safety."

"Don't bullshit me. Like I said before… you want something. What is it?"

"I don't want anything from you. I'm here trying to help rid your city of those creatures." She folded her arms.

"You storm in here telling me I shouldn't involve the police. Why?"

"Because I discovered some of the creatures have been here longer than any of us realize. Some have maintained their human form to avoid detection. They have jobs, homes, and live like regular people."

"Yeah, I figured."

"You did?" Her right eyebrow arched. "How so?"

"We have werewolves in the department so who's to say there aren't other kinds of supernatural creatures working in the system."

"Anything is possible, which is the problem."

No argument there. If the reptilian creatures had infiltrated the precinct the city would be in deep shit.

CHAPTER TWELVE

When Reece arrived home later in the day, he spotted Charlene's Jeep parked on the bend outside the main gate. She wasn't in the vehicle which meant she was inside with Tom. The PI screeched to a halt out front of the portico, turned off the engine, bolted out of the convertible and stormed into the entry hall. He raced up the stairs, along the hallway into the living room. The pair was sitting on the sofa together, laughing.

Reece stood with hands on hips. "What's going on here?"

Tom's gaze moved from Charlene to Reece. "Hi, Dad. Charlene picked me up from school. We've been catching up."

Reece's eyes moved to the woman who looked like Charlotte. "How did you know which school Tom attended? And why didn't you run it by me first?"

Charlene stood up, the smile disappearing from her face. "I didn't think it would be a problem. I drove him straight home. I'm only trying to get to know my nephew. I hope you don't mind?"

She was doing an excellent job of making him look like the bad guy, Reece realized. "It isn't a problem. I'd just prefer you let me know before doing something like this. It's for Tom's safety."

She gave the PI a curious frown. "You don't think he's safe with me?"

"Not what I said." Reece crossed the room. "We've been through a lot over the years – it's my job to take care of my son."

"Of course it is. And I wouldn't do anything to jeopardize that." She glanced at Tom then looked at Reece. "But how am I supposed to get to know him unless I spend time with him?"

"I thought we agreed to take things slow. What happened to the plan of giving Tom a chance to process it all?"

"So much time has gone by already. I don't want to waste anymore. Tom needs me in his life and I want to be there for him."

Again, she made him look like the enemy.

Tom spoke up. "Dad, it's ok. I want to spend time with Aunt Charlene."

Aunt Charlene? "I didn't say it wasn't ok, buddy. I think we should stick to the plan of taking things at a steady pace, not rushing into anything." He could see he was losing ground. What could Charlene have said to get Tom on side all of a sudden?

∞⚬∞

After Charlene left, Reece headed over to Andre's. He needed to find out if he'd learned anything more about the woman. His gut still warned him something wasn't right about her and he needed to listen to that inner instinct. It hadn't failed him before. He pulled into the curb outside the apartment building, turned off the engine, gave a heavy sigh. What had prompted Charlotte's sister to seek Tom out now? What did she really want? To his mind, her only reason for being in LA was to try to place a wedge between them. Could it be her plan? What if she tried to gain custody? He became lost in his thoughts for some time trying to figure out what Charlene wanted.

A knock on the passenger-side window startled him, his body giving an involuntary jerk. His gaze moved to the figure on the sidewalk. He pressed the button for the window and it slid into the door with a quiet whirr. "You didn't have to come downstairs. I would've come up."

"You've been sitting out here for a while now. Something wrong?" Andre climbed into the convertible.

"Yeah, there is. When I got home tonight I found Charlene in the house with Tom. She'd picked him up from school. When I asked her how she knew which high school he attended she avoided the question and turned it around on me." He frowned at his friend. "Have you found out anything else?"

"Yes. There are no death records for her here in California. I've also run checks in some of the other states but haven't found anything yet. I plan to keep looking until I do."

"Thanks." Reece sighed. Remembering what Todd said about demons disguising themselves, when he'd asked Andre to check deaths first he thought something might show up. "Can I see what you've got?"

"Sure. Come on up."

When the pair stepped into the apartment Lozano came out of the kitchen with a mug and a plated sandwich in his hands. "Hey, Reece, want some coffee?"

"Maybe later. Andre wants to show me something first."

"Oh, ok. Knock on my door when you're done." Lozano headed down the hallway to his room.

Reece sat down at the dining table while Andre retrieved his laptop from his bedroom.

When he returned, he sat next to Reece, opened up the computer and clicked a link. "So this is what I've got so far. The problem I'm having is we don't know if she's using a married name."

The PI frowned into his friend's eyes. "So her maiden name hasn't brought up anything about a marriage or the birth of children?"

"Not yet, no."

"Doesn't it seem odd to you?"

"It could mean I haven't found the right state yet."

"Maybe." An anxious tangle of nerves wrapped itself around the pit of Reece's gut and squeezed tight. *Are my suspicions correct about her?* He jerked out of the chair. "I have to go. Let me know when you find something concrete. I've got a nagging feeling about Charlene that won't go away."

"Sure. As soon as I have anything I'll call you." Andre frowned at the back of his friend as he stepped out the door. Reece seemed to be freaking out. Did he have a reason to?

CHAPTER THIRTEEN

A few nights later, Detective Grant Donovan parked his dark blue sedan in the alley beside the abandoned theater, stepped out of his car and closed the door. He couldn't shake the gnawing feeling in his gut. What did he expect to find coming back here tonight? He wasn't sure, but his cop instincts told him he should take another look around the crime scene. The revelation Reece Daniels imparted on him about the creatures causing the deaths made him feel inadequate – and to be honest – scared the shit out of him.

Their door knocking efforts had proved fruitless. No one had seen or heard anything, or if they did they were keeping quiet about it. Apathy caused people to not want to get involved – even if someone had lost their life. It seemed to him that people had become desensitized to the horrors of the world.

Grant had asked the PI to join him because he knew the ex-detective had a nose for this kind of stuff. How would he explain the deaths to his boss? He couldn't go tell him snake creatures did it, could he? Something he'd need to discuss with the PI as well.

Reece's midnight blue Mustang pulled in behind the detective's car. He climbed out. "What do you expect to find here, Grant? Forensics did a thorough sweep of the scene and came up empty." The pair shook hands.

"I don't know. My gut told me to come back here. So here I am."

Reece couldn't argue with a man's gut. Instincts were everything in this business. "Ok, where do you want to start?"

Grant pointed in the direction where the puddle of slime had been found. "Over there, I guess."

The pair crossed the shadowed parking lot to the green metal dumpster behind the building.

"Why don't we split up? We'll cover more ground that way," Grant said.

"Sure."

After fifteen minutes of searching, Grant called out to Reece. "Hey, Daniels, come take a look at this." He pointed the beam of his flashlight at the evidence. "What do you think?"

Reece pulled a small plastic zip lock bag and a pair of tweezers from the right side pocket of his jacket to collect the remnant. Holding the bag up to eye level, with the flashlight shining on its contents, the PI said, "Looks like snake skin."

"Yeah, it does." Grant gave him a frustrated scowl. "It's evidence we can't use, right?"

Reece frowned into his eyes. "How would you explain it?"

The detective gave the question some thought, then shrugged. "Don't know."

"Yeah, it's the dilemma we're up against in this line of work. You might have to let the case go cold. I've had to in the past."

"You're serious?"

"You bet. If you can't explain this," he said, pushing the bag at the detective, "you don't have anything. Who's going to believe you if you tell them what I've told you?"

"There has to be some way to…"

"Believe me, there isn't. No one knows about the things lurking in the dark. Or if they do they choose to ignore it."

℘ℭ℞

Reece drove the unlit lonely road out to the old state prison with the contents of the bag secured in his jacket pocket. Grant agreed not to say anything to anyone about the discovery, at least for the time being. The honest cop wanted to do the right thing for the victims, but knew his hands were tied. If he tried he'd look like a crazy person. The PI had explained he'd felt the same way all those years ago – helpless. So he'd left the force and started his own paranormal private investigative business.

He pulled the Mustang up to the locked gate, left the motor running, got out to unlock it. Once inside, he relocked the double chain gates then drove up to the door. It opened and Ed Borenko stepped outside.

"Did you bring it with you?" the older man asked.

"Yeah." Reece passed the bag to his ex-boss.

"Let's get it inside." Ed turned on his heel.

Reece followed him into the building. "Anyone else here?"

"Sarah."

"The team?"

"Nah, I sent them home an hour ago. They've been workin' round the clock and were ready to keel over."

"Fair enough."

"So we've got two deaths so far, right?"

"Yeah. But it's only a matter of time before there's more."

Ed turned to look at the PI. "Now Donovan knows?"

"He's kind of known for a while."

"Well I hope he keeps his mouth shut." The chief continued along the corridor, Reece in tow.

"I'm sure he will."

"Do you believe the witch? I mean about the fact these things can change into human form?"

"She has no reason to lie."

"She might if she has her own agenda for being in LA."

"I'm sure she does. There isn't much I can do to make her tell me what that is though."

"We need to know for our own safety, you know?" He entered the old Warden's office. Sarah wasn't there.

"Didn't you say Sarah's here?"

"Oh, yeah, she's in the lab looking over what the team has found so far."

The pair made their way to the laboratory.

"Hey, Reece. Did you bring the sample with you?" Sarah asked.

"Got it right here," Ed said, handing her the zip lock bag.

Reece pushed his hands into the pockets of his jacket. "So what has the team found so far?"

"They've discovered a combination of genes."

"Which means what, exactly?"

Sarah motioned for Reece to press his eye against the microscope's ocular lens. "There is human DNA mixed into the reptilian genome," she told him.

Reece jerked his head away from the eyepiece. "So what Avalynn told us is true?"

"It appears to be the case. I've been doing some research." Sarah pulled up an article on the computer about ancient deities called Anunnaki. "They were believed to be reptilian extraterrestrial beings that came to earth from the planet Nibiru, who created the human race out of a need for servitude. Scientists have proved some of the DNA strands in the human genome are not even human in origin, making them something else. Fits the scenario, don't you think?" She pointed to a picture. "See here? These ancient Sumerian carvings show the Gods as snakes with snakes."

"You're thinking these creatures are Gods, not demons?"

"It's possible," she told him.

"It's going to make it difficult for us to locate the remaining ones, with them being able to stay in human form."

"Yes, it is. I'm wondering now if Nathaniel's team actually killed the reptiles they found, or if the creatures, should they be godlike deities, left the bodies."

If this were true where could they be and how could they eradicate them permanently?

CHAPTER FOURTEEN

The iconic, 1893 Bradbury Building in downtown LA was Reece's next stop. He'd been pussyfooting around the fact he needed to speak to Phillip Pembroke, Charlotte's lawyer, to find out what he could about Charlene. The attorney obviously knew more than he'd let on.

Tom had been acting up over the past week, very unlike him, and the PI determined it had something to do with the conversations he'd been having with his aunt.

Pembroke's office, situated on the fifth floor of the bygone era building, sat at one end of the ornate ironwork balcony with a corner view. As Reece approached the frosted glass, honey-colored wood door it swung open and he came face to face with Charlene. "What are you doing here?" he asked, his tone tighter than intended.

"I could ask you the same thing," she replied, without offering an explanation as to the reason for her appointment with the lawyer.

Fair comment, he supposed. "I have business with Mr. Pembroke."

"So did I." Her gaze remained on his green eyes.

He felt heat in his cheeks and diverted his attention to the open doorway behind her. Pointing into the office, he said, "Well, I'd better…"

"Oh, yes, of course." She stepped aside. "We'll have to plan a get together some time soon. I have some things I'd like to discuss with you."

"What kind of things?" Reece's gut shrank into a tight ball. Were his suspicions correct? Did she want custody of Tom?

"Let's talk about it over dinner… or drinks. I'll call you." She headed for the caged elevator midway along the balcony, not giving him a backward glance.

Reece watched her walk away before stepping into the office. *What is Charlene up to? What did she come here to discuss with Charlotte's attorney?* He knew Pembroke couldn't tell him anything because of lawyer-client privilege, so if Charlene did plan to file for custody he'd find out when the court hearing documents were served.

ଋଠଓ

When Reece arrived home, he could hear Tom in the kitchen. He shrugged out of his jacket, hung it on the coat rack beside the double front doors then walked into the galley-style, open work space to greet his son. "Hey, buddy, how's your day been?"

Tom finished putting away the bread and other ingredients he'd used. "Ok, I guess."

Reece stepped up to the center counter. "What do you want for dinner? We could do Chinese or Thai, if you like. Or pizza, if you prefer."

Tom picked up the plated sandwiches he'd made and a can of soda. "I'm good. I'm taking this up to my room." He passed his dad, heading for the entry hall.

Reece turned around. "Hey, Tom?"

The teen gave a sigh, glanced over his shoulder. "Yeah?"

"Can we have more than a two second conversation? We've always spent time in the afternoon catching up, what's changed?"

"Nothing, I have homework. And you know how you feel about me getting it done." He continued into the entry hall.

"Tom?"

He gave a huff. "What?"

Reece walked up to him and frowned into his eyes. "Everything ok?"

"Yeah. I've gotta go study. I've got an exam coming up."

"So all of this is because you're stressed about a test?"

The teen shrugged again. "What else would it be?"

The PI folded his arms. "I don't know. You tell me."

"Geez, Dad, you're reading way too much into it." He averted his gaze. "Can I go now?"

Reece studied his son for a moment. "Sure."

Tom disappeared up the stairs.

Reece walked back into the kitchen. He could feel something was off with him. They'd always maintained an honest, open father-son relationship until recently, with Tom becoming defensive. Why? What had Charlene said to make him react in such a way?

His cell vibrated in the front pocket of his jeans. He tugged it free, staring at the screen. Unknown Caller. He frowned at the vibrating phone in his hand, wondering who it could be. Only one way to find out. "Reece Daniels speaking."

"Hello, Reece, it's Avalynn. Are you available?"

"When?"

"Now."

"Why?"

"I've located one of the creatures. I thought you might want to come down here… help me eliminate it."

"I'm sure you can handle it on your own. I've got other things on my plate right now." He stepped back into the entry hall and glanced up the stairs.

"Are you serious? More important than eradicating these highly dangerous creatures?"

"*Yes*, Avalynn, *I do*."

"No need to bite my head off. Ok, I'll take care of it."

"Wait. Give Nathaniel a call. He'll send one of his team with you."

"No, thanks, I don't work with vampires if I can avoid it. I'll handle it." She rang off.

Reece sighed as he slid his phone back into the pocket of his jeans. Maybe he should've gone with her. Not much he could do about it now, he couldn't call her back as she had a private number, something he'd have to talk to her about. If they were going to work together he'd need to be able to contact her.

He climbed the carpeted staircase, walked along the hall and opened the door leading to the attic. He needed to sort out the current situation with his son. "Tom, can you come down here, please?"

Tom appeared at the top of the wooden stairs. "What is it? I told you I'm studying."

"I know what you told me, but I think we need to have a talk."

Tom huffed out a frustrated breath. "Can't we do this later?"

"No. Now." Reece walked back along the hall to the living room and waited by the door for his son.

Tom clomped down the wooden treads, stepped into the hallway, and banged the door shut. "Dad, I need to study," he said when he reached his father.

"This won't take long."

Tom crossed the room and plonked himself down on the sofa with another huff.

Reece remained standing. "Do you want to tell me what's going on with you? You've been avoiding spending any time with me over this past week. Why?"

"I haven't…"

Reece raised a hand motioning for his son to stop speaking. "*Yes*, you have. I've noticed the change in you since you've been talking to your aunt."

Tom popped up off the sofa. "That's not true."

"From where I'm standing it is. What's going on?"

"Nothing's going on. Geez, why are you so jealous of her?"

Ah, there it is.

"Charlene told you I'm jealous of her?"

Tom gave his dad a sheepish sideward glance.

Reece folded his arms. "Tom?"

The teen let out a long sigh. "She… well… kind of… yeah."

"And you believed her?"

"Well you don't like her, do you?"

"I want to be sure she is who she says she is before…"

"Before what?"

"Before something happens we can't change."

Tom's eyes widened. "Like what?"

"Like her wanting custody of you. If she *is* your biological aunt she can appeal to the court for custody."

Tom swallowed hard, his Adam's apple bobbing above the neckline of his dark gray T-shirt. "I thought no one could take me away from you."

"She may be blood, Tom. And if so, she could. But not without a fight."

"When you say she *may* be blood what do you mean?"

"Your Uncle Andre's looking into her background to make sure she is your mom's sister. Todd Lassiter, you remember him, made a valid point about the possibility of someone sending her here to cause trouble."

"You mean like a – a demon or something?"

"Yeah, it's a possibility."

"Has Uncle Andre found anything?"

"Not yet. He's investigating other states because we don't know where she's from."

"I do."

"What?" Reece's frown deepened.

"Yeah, she told me where she's from."

The PI walked up to his son. "Where?"

"New Orleans."

Something slithered in the pit of Reece's gut. It couldn't be a coincidence… could it?

CHAPTER FIFTEEN

Avalynn coasted her cherry red, Honda Shadow Spirit down the alleyway and parked the motorcycle outside a neighboring apartment block beside the weathered, red brick warehouse under construction. Removing her glossy black helmet, and shaking out her flaming red wavy lengths, she ran her witch gaze over the scaffolded, four-story building, wondering how difficult it would be to get in, get the job done, and get out without being detected by security staff. She could cast a cloaking spell on herself, which would hold for a short period of time, but she preferred not to if she didn't have to, as it took too much out of her and she needed her powers to fight the creature.

A sound close by caused her to swing around, hands raised ready to hurl a jolt of electrical magick into whoever was behind her, and breathed a relieved sigh when she spotted the bulky, dark clad form of Nathaniel strutting along the alley toward her. Even though she wasn't fond of working with vampires she felt relief at seeing him rather than one of the creatures. *How did he know where to find me?* She guessed it had something to do with his vampire radar. Bats used them so why not blood drinkers, seeing as they possessed a supernatural connection to each other. "What are you doing here?"

Nathaniel gave Avalynn a stern stare. "Reece asked me to provide backup for you."

"And you found me... how?"

"I have certain abilities which allow me to track individuals by their vibration."

"Yes, I figured as much." She folded her arms. "The building is semi-finished, some apartments are already leased. There's security inside. Any ideas?"

"And how are you able to provide this information?"

She gave him a perceptive grin. "I also have *certain*... abilities."

Nathaniel surveyed the building. "Do you know if there is a fire escape here? If there is we can get inside from the roof."

"I only arrived a few minutes before you did, so, no. But we can check." She pointed to the back end of the warehouse.

The pair walked the length of the alley, shoulder to shoulder, and turned the corner onto the narrow side street.

"There's another alleyway down there. Perhaps that's where it is." Avalynn headed along the sidewalk, the black vampire behind her.

"Wait," Nathaniel said. "I can transport us onto the roof."

"You mean fly?"

He gave a sharp nod. "Yes." He could sense her aversion for his kind.

"I don't think it's a good idea." He would have to touch her and she didn't want his cold hands or body in such close proximity to hers.

"It would be the most advantageous method. As the construction workers are still here, if you cast a cloaking spell no one will see us ascend to the roof."

He made a good point.

Avalynn gave a heavy sigh. It looked as though the gods wanted her to use her witch powers after all. "Very well." She began to chant an incantation when a voice nearby stopped her. She knew that voice. She turned around, stood with hands on her hips. "Why are you here?"

Reece stalked up to the pair. "Because those reptiles are dangerous and even though you believe there's only one inside there could be more."

"Look, I'm a witch. Do you not think I can handle the situation? I have magick on my side, you don't."

"I've been up against the worst of the worst and it wouldn't be fair to let you go in after those things alone." The PI stepped up beside Nathaniel.

Avalynn's lilac eyes moved to the black vampire. She poked the air with her left index finger. "I have him."

"You'll need more back up if this place houses more than one of those creatures. Remember what I told you Sarah said? They could've ascended from Sumerian gods. They may not be demonic as we first thought. They could possess powers beyond what any of us is capable of fighting. There's always strength in numbers. That's why I brought Andre and Todd with me." He hit speed dial on his cell, pressed the phone to his ear. "You can come around now."

Avalynn glowered at the PI before her frowning gaze moved to the pair turning the corner. "How do you expect us all to get inside unseen?"

❧

The four-story, warehouse apartment building seemed eerily quiet for a semi-leased block at the end of a work day. You could hear a pin drop, and it bothered Reece. Where were the residents? What about security staff doing their rounds? Why hadn't someone stepped out of the caged elevator on the floor below them? Something didn't feel right. His gut churned as he swallowed down the acidic taste of bile. *Could this be an ambush?* His wary gaze flitted to the witch beside him. *Could Avalynn be involved? Is that the reason for her being in Los Angeles?* The group of five continued down the concrete stairwell to the fourth level doorway into the corridor.

When they reached the red metal safety door, Reece raised his hand motioning for everyone to stop. They needed to devise a strategy to get into the apartment, eliminate the creature, and get out without any casualties or deaths… or being seen. He tugged a spray can of black paint from the side pocket of his protective gear pants. "I'll disable the security cameras in the hallway. Once I do, we'll need to get into the apartment before the guys in the lobby realize what's happened. And they will."

"I can open the door," Avalynn said.

"Ok. Good." Reece's gaze moved to Todd. "You've got the stunner?"

Todd raised his gloved hand. "You bet, right here."

"Nathaniel, Andre, I want you to move in from both sides. Keep the creature distracted. Don't get too close."

Both nodded. "We will be fine," Nathaniel told him.

"We're not messing around with the one inside this time. It's a done deal." Reece pulled the navy blue wool ski mask down over his face. "Ok, let's do this." He checked the door for an alarm before tugging it open. Easing his tall frame along the concrete wall so the security camera wouldn't pick up movement, he sidled up to the first one, raised the spray can and squirted two sharp bursts of black paint onto the lens. One down, one to go. Moving across the corridor, he did the same to the camera opposite. "Ok, Avalynn, work your magic on the door lock. We need to get inside *now*."

The witch chanted an incantation as she pointed her right hand toward the lock. The large door popped open. She turned around, giving everyone a satisfied grin. "There. All yours."

Reece stepped up to the door. In a low voice he said, "We need to move in quickly." Pressing his gloved hand against the textured blue metal he pushed the door open and the group moved inside. No one in the living area. They moved through the apartment like a swarm of ants, checking every space. Nothing. The five moved into the center of the large living room. When they reached the woven circular floor rug the lights went out.

CHAPTER SIXTEEN

Detective Grant Donovan sat at his work desk sifting through unsolved cases he now believed could have been perpetrated by supernatural beings. *How is that possible? Why is it possible? And why didn't I know about it sooner?* There were a dozen cold cases spanning twenty years with unexplained circumstances, and the certainty they were part of what had been happening in LA for more than a decade weighed heavy on his shoulders. He wanted to know more. The only way to get to the truth would be to speak to Reece Daniels... at length. He needed answers. He needed to know what he was up against.

Harrison Killjoy wandered across the office to Grant's desk, wheeled a chair over, sat down. "What're you doing?"

"I'm going over some old case files."

His partner folded his arms, leaned back on the chair, crossing one leg over the other. "Why? We already have too much on our plates. What good will it do?"

Donovan sighed. "We know what's out there. Daniels has offered us a free pass on what goes on in this city and I'm going to take every opportunity to get these cases solved. For the families."

"Grant, you know you can't do that. Who'd believe either of us anyway? Reece put his trust in us... in you. Don't let him down."

"What's the point of knowing if we can't do anything about it?"

"Daniels *is* doing something. He's out there fighting creatures people believe are only in their worst nightmares. We have to support his efforts."

The detective sighed again. "Yeah, ok, I know you're right, but…"

"But nothing. We have to have faith it'll all work out for the greater good. He's doing all he can to keep this city safe, and he needs our help to do it. No one wants to know what's out there. Believe me."

"Ok. I still want to do some investigating into these cases on my own time. I need to feel like I'm doing something to help."

Harrison rested a hand on his partner's shoulder. "You are, pal. Otherwise Reece wouldn't have involved you."

Donovan nodded. "Yeah, I guess you're right. Sometimes I wonder why he did."

"Because he needs someone on the inside to provide intel on unusual cases. That's how you're helping him get the job done."

He gave Harrison a thin smile. "I hadn't thought about it like that. You're right."

"I know." His partner gave him a wicked grin. "I'm always right."

"Wise guy." He punched Harrison in the shoulder.

"Ouch. Hey!"

Grant glanced at the time on the computer screen. "It's getting late. We should head home. You don't want to be late for dinner and have Angie mad at you again."

"She understands, at least most of the time."

As the pair headed to the door Grant's desk phone rang. He glanced over his shoulder contemplating whether to leave it or pick it up. Something in his gut told him he should take the call. His gaze returned to Harrison. "You go on home. I'm just gonna grab that."

"It could wait till tomorrow, you know."

"Yeah. I think I should get it."

"Ok. See you in the morning."

"Yeah, see ya." He rushed over to his desk and snatched up the receiver. "Detective Grant Donovan speaking."

∞∞

Reece and his team raced up the concrete stairs and burst through the gray metal door. Once they were on the roof, he said, "Let's get to the ground fast." He should've trusted his gut when he realized the place was too quiet.

The group thrust themselves across the top of the building, but before they could reach the ladder leading to the grated metal stairs, seven figures appeared in front of them blocking their path.

"Spread out!" Reece shouted. "Lock 'n load."

His team pulled their weapons.

Avalynn stepped up beside him. "Let me." She raised her hands, the crackling blue-purple electrical current emanating from her fingertips, and hurled a bolt of magick at the figures.

As it exploded around them, their skins split open and the reptilian creatures sloughed off their human casings. Opening their mouths, their glistening fangs visible, they spat yellow venom across the rooftop towards their assailants.

"Take cover!" Reece yelled.

Everyone dashed behind whatever they could use to protect themselves: air-conditioning units, water tanks, anything to stay clear of the poisonous spray.

೮)෮

The detective pulled his dark blue sedan into the curb outside the warehouse apartments and turned off the engine. Gazing up at the newly semi-renovated, red brick building, he wondered why the PI wanted to meet with him here. His eyes roamed the deserted street around him. *Where is he? It's not like him to be late.* Unclipping his seatbelt, Grant Donovan stepped out onto the road. Once again, he ran his frowning gaze around the street expecting to see Reece coming toward him. He didn't. He checked his watch. 8:48 PM.

Grant walked around the hood of his car to the sidewalk. A sudden chill traveled the length of his spine. He gave an involuntary shudder. Something didn't feel right. He tugged his cell from the pocket of his overcoat, scrolled for Reece's number and hit the call button. No answer. *Where could he be?* He headed along the street to the nearby alley. A dark colored van parked midway looked like the one Reece used for his PI business. *He must be here somewhere. But where? For what purpose?*

Grant decided against contacting Harrison. Angie wouldn't be impressed with him calling her husband out on a job at this time of night. He gave a sigh as he stared at the number on the screen of his phone. "Why aren't you picking up?" An idea popped into his head and he called the precinct. "Hi, Mike, it's Grant Donovan, Homicide. Can you run a trace on a cell number for me? Yeah, it is important. Thanks." He gave the cop the PI's number. After several minutes the uniform came back on the line giving him the address. He was already here. Grant ran his uneasy gaze over the building. Reece had to be inside and could be in some kind of serious trouble.

℘

Reece kept low to the ground as he made his way over to Andre and Nathaniel behind a central air-conditioning unit. "We're outnumbered and definitely unprepared for this fight. We need to find a way out of here." To his mind, it would be their only chance at leaving alive.

Avalynn and Todd whipped across the rooftop to where the other three were secluded. "What are we going to do?" Todd asked, breathless. "I don't think this protective gear is enough to ward off the stuff those things are spitting at us."

A valid point.

"I can continue to contain them with my magick while you make a run for it," Avalynn told them.

Reece frowned. "What about you?" He didn't want to leave her alone.

"I'll be fine. I'll meet you back at your office." Her lilac eyes averted to the creatures moving closer. "You need to leave *now*."

The group of four hurried around the water tanks to the scaffolding. Todd and Reece climbed down the rusted metal labyrinth, while Nathaniel lifted Andre onto his back and leapt off the parapet down to the alley. Once on the ground, they headed for the van. They were about to climb in when Reece heard someone call his name. He turned around. Grant Donovan was marching toward him along the alley.

"What's going on?" the detective asked.

"Sorry. When I called I thought I'd be down here by the time you arrived." Reece tugged the ski mask off over his sandy blond hair.

"So you were here on a job?" Grant shoved his hands into the pockets of his coat.

"Yeah."

"The reptilian creatures?"

The PI nodded.

"Did you eliminate it... or them?"

"Not exactly."

A flash of what looked like lightning emanated from the rooftop of the apartment building.

"What's that?" Grant Donovan jerked his head upward, his eyes moving to the bright shock of light above them.

"You wouldn't believe me if I told you."

The detective folded his arms. "Try me. At this point, I'm ready to believe anything."

CHAPTER SEVENTEEN

Everyone that had been on the roof, along with Detective Donovan, was now back at the Double D Investigations office waiting for Avalynn to arrive. It had been almost two hours since the group left the warehouse apartments – still no word from her.

The door opened and Ed, Sarah, and Lozano walked in.

"So what's up, Daniels? What's the reason for this late night meeting?" Ed asked, following his companions across the room.

"We were ambushed tonight. I don't know if the reptilian creatures or Avalynn orchestrated it," Reece told him, gazing out of the window at the dimly lit street below.

"What makes you think it's the witch?" Ed plonked himself down on a chair from the kitchen table after pulling one out for Sarah.

The PI turned around. "There have been indicators I've chosen to ignore. Now I'm not so sure I can continue to do that."

"What kind of indicators?" Sarah asked, sitting down beside Ed.

"Where she's from for one thing. I found out Charlene is also from New Orleans. Could it be a coincidence or is she involved with Avalynn?"

"It could be a coincidence," Sarah offered.

"Could it? We don't know anything about either of them. They arrived here around the same time." Reece's gut tightened. "Doesn't that seem strange to you?"

"I suppose it could… if you want to get into conspiracy theories." Sarah walked over to the PI. "Do you believe the two situations are related?"

Reece gave a huff. "I'm not sure."

"So wait until you have solid evidence. Keep an eye on Avalynn's movements, see where she goes, who she makes contact with, then you'll have your answer."

Sarah made sense, as usual. The calm voice of reason.

"You're right." Reece nodded, more to himself than her.

"Good. Now we've sorted that out, why are we here?"

"Avalynn said she'd meet us back here once she finished dealing with the creatures. It's been a couple hours."

"Maybe she's injured. Perhaps you should go back just in case," Lozano offered.

"She said she could handle it." Reece moved around his desk. "But you're right. We should go back."

Todd stood up. "Do you want us all to go with you?"

"No, only Nathaniel and Andre this time. Be on standby. If we need help I'll call or text."

"What about me?" Grant Donovan asked.

"Head home. I'll be in touch."

ⅎ℞

The rooftop appeared deserted as the three climbed over the parapet from off the iron scaffolding. Where could Avalynn have gone? Reece moved through the shadows his Glock 9mm raised, Andre close behind, Nathaniel checking the rear, moving past the water tanks and air-conditioning units to where the reptiles attacked them. No sign of Avalynn anywhere. *Why didn't she come back to the office like she said she would? And why hasn't she called?* The PI's gut squirmed. Alarm bells were going off about this whole scenario.

"Avalynn?" he called in a loud whisper. "Avalynn are you here?"

Nathaniel came up beside him. "I do not hear a heartbeat. She is not up here."

"Then where is she?"

Andre walked over to the pair after searching the roof. "Perhaps the creatures have her captive."

"You saw what she could do. Do you think they would have any chance of capturing her?" Reece's eyes roamed the area around them.

"It's possible, if one surprised her."

Reece's squirming gut tightened. "Unless she's working with them. She'd had dealings with them in New Orleans... been in love with one of them before she discovered his true identity. Who's to say she isn't part of it all?"

"Do you believe that?"

"I don't know what I believe at this point. Why would she vanish like this?"

"Maybe she didn't. Maybe she *is* being held captive."

"We need to get inside. They could have her locked in the basement." Reece marched over to the rooftop door, tugged it open. Confronted with a pitch black stairwell, no light anywhere on the floors below, it confirmed what he'd been thinking. He turned to his companions. "They know we're here."

"It would appear so," Nathaniel replied, peering over the railing.

"I wonder if we can get into the building through a window from the scaffolding."

"One way to find out," Andre said. "We'll need to be ready for anything."

Reece's entire nervous system buzzed, the hair all over his body standing erect, his gut squirming even more. Should he get the rest of his team down here or wait to see how the situation played out?

&ORB;

Lozano gazed out of the office window in quiet contemplation. They shouldn't have let Reece, Andre and Nathaniel go back there on their own. He turned, ran his dark brown eyes around the rest of the group sitting in the room. "Hey, I think we should go over there to be nearby in case Reece needs us."

"You heard what he said," Ed told him. "He wanted us on standby."

"Yeah, I know what he said, but it would be better if we were closer. I mean, anything could happen in the time it takes us to get down there."

Ed's relaxed demeanor stiffened. "Good point."

"I agree with him," Todd said, standing. "I think we should go."

"Let's gear up." Sarah stood up. "We're heading out."

When the group reached the street, Avalynn had just climbed off her motorcycle.

Ed marched up to her. "Where have you been? Why didn't you call to let us know you were ok? Reece, Andre and Nathaniel have gone back to the warehouse apartment building looking for you. They thought something happened to you," he told her, gruffness in his tone.

"I didn't say how long I would be before I got back here. Why didn't he wait?"

"Because he thought you were in trouble, that's why. He's one of the good guys."

Todd stepped up beside Ed. "What happened to the creatures?"

"They've been contained in the basement until I can find a more permanent solution. They're not easy to kill."

CHAPTER EIGHTEEN

An unlocked second story window offered access into the building. Reece steadied himself on the narrow plank of wood beneath his feet on the scaffold, flattened his gloved palms on the pane of glass, pushed up the old fashioned wooden sash, and climbed through into the dark space, fanning the room with his phone's flashlight. Ladders, paint cans, stacked bags of plaster, tools, and other work materials were scattered across the empty apartment. No one lived here yet. Good.

Andre climbed inside, Nathaniel followed.

"We need to keep moving," Andre said. "We don't want security finding us before we can get to the basement."

Reece's gaze moved to his friend. "Yeah. Let's go."

Andre crossed the spacious, open plan room to the door. Reece and Nathaniel close behind. Using his vampire senses, he listened for a moment to see if he could hear breathing, a heartbeat, or movement outside. Nothing. He glanced over his shoulder. "Ok, let's go." He swung the large metal door back and stepped into the shadowed hall. The translucent milky light from a street lamp below offered a vague glow to the dark corridor. The stairwell stood a few feet away, but before they could reach it, the door opened and the security guards from the lobby stepped out, flashlights roaming the hallway.

The three dashed back into the apartment, Reece securing the lock as the door clicked shut.

Within seconds, the security guards tried the door.

Reece motioned with his head for his companions to follow him back out the window. Just as he closed the sash, the lock clicked back, the sound echoing around the unfurnished apartment, and the large metal door swung open. All three darted back behind the red bricks.

The two uniformed guards stepped into the room, both of their flashlights fanning the unfinished space. One climbed the spiral staircase to the loft above, checking the bathroom. The pair stepped out into the hallway, the snap of the lock echoing around the empty apartment once again.

Reece blew out a noisy breath. "That was close."

"Yes, too close. We'll need to be more careful." Andre sidled back along the plank to his friend. "Let's try it again."

Nathaniel followed the pair inside, squeezing his large frame through the constricted opening. "Wait. I do not think they have moved off this floor yet."

Before anyone could react, the two guards burst into the apartment. Reece grabbed his Glock firing off two warning shots, hoping the pair would retreat into the hallway. They didn't.

As the group witnessed earlier, the guards skins split open and sloughed off onto the concrete floor as the reptilian creatures emerged from their human casings.

Jerking backwards, Reece shouted, "Get out *now!*"

All three dashed across the room, Nathaniel crashing through a second pane of glass, Reece scrambling to get out of the window, Andre on his heels.

The reptiles spat yellow venom across the apartment, the acidic spray missing Andre by inches.

Reece slammed down the wooden sash then jumped to a plank below him, Andre doing the same. Nathaniel appeared behind the pair, whisked them off the metal structure, and lowered them to the ground.

"It looks like the place is full of those things," Reece said, breathless.

Lozano, Ed, Sarah, Todd and Avalynn raced along the alleyway to the trio, Reece spotting the witch as the group got closer.

"Where were you?" he asked, his voice tight. "Why didn't you call to let us know you were ok?"

"I said I would meet you back at your office. I didn't realize there was a specific timeframe for that." She glowered at him.

Reece's stern gaze wandered the worried faces around him. His frown disappeared.

"Are you all right?" Sarah asked. "What happened up there?"

Reece wiped beads of sweat from his brow with the back of his hand. "The security in this place is reptilian too. Two of them attacked us."

Sarah glanced past Reece, spotting the two reptile security guards racing along the alley toward them. "We need to move... *now*."

Avalynn swung around and hurled a shock of white bolts of magick at the pair from her fingertips. The lightning projectiles exploded at their feet. They kept coming. Everyone took off running, the creatures in hot pursuit.

Whipping around the corner of the building, heading for the van, Reece spun around, running backwards, and fired more shots at the pair. Even with the rift sealed, he still made a habit of loading his weapon with silver cartridges. He hoped the metal might have some kind of impact on the creatures. At least slow them down so they could make their escape. A bullet hit one in the shoulder – it didn't stop. The other reptile gained momentum. Reece fired off continuous rounds until it hit the ground. "Let's get out of here."

The group climbed into the vehicle, the PI ramming the key into the ignition, the wheels spinning on the asphalt as it sped along the two lane road. He'd retrieve the other van later. His eyes darted to the rear view mirror, his anxious gaze roaming the street behind them. Neither creature followed. Did the silver work?

℘

Later that night, Reece rode to the warehouse apartment building on the back of Andre's red Ducati Monster to collect the van Ed had driven there earlier. As Andre pulled in behind the van, Reece pushed himself off the back of the motorcycle, walked over to the vehicle, opened the passenger door and tossed his helmet on the seat.

Andre climbed off the motorcycle, tugged his helmet free, set it down on his bike's seat and joined Reece. "Are you heading back now?"

The PI shook his head. "No, I want to take a look around first. The place is still in darkness."

"Do you think it's a good idea? They could be lying in wait like before."

"I only want to do a perimeter check. I'm not planning on going in alone. You can take off if you like."

Andre folded his arms. "No way. I'm coming with you."

"Ok, let's move." Reece stalked along the alley, turned the corner, Andre right behind him.

When the pair reached the front doors of the building, the PI climbed the three terracotta tiled steps and peered through the glass. Deep shadows fell across the foyer. No sign of security or anyone else. "Looks like they've done a runner."

Andre used his nocturnal vision to scope out the lobby. "Yes, it does."

"Dammit! Now we're back to square one." Reece stood with hands on hips, his frowning gaze roaming the street. "I wonder where they've gone."

"Good question. Now they know that we know about their disguises they'll be vigilant about not being identified."

"I'm sure the ones Avalynn locked in the basement would be gone as well."

"I read that reptiles use pheromones as a form of communication with each other, so it's highly likely the ones in the basement would do the same."

"There's always something to learn about supernatural creatures, isn't there? Right now, Avalynn knows more about those things than we do, so I'll give her a call in the morning. Ask her to do a search. We have to end them before they take any more lives."

✥

Avalynn stepped into the Double D Investigations office the following morning. Reece had left a message on her cell the previous evening rather than wait until today. "You wanted to see me?" She grazed a chair back on the wooden floor, plonked herself down, crossed one leather-clad leg over the other and folded her arms.

Reece's gaze moved from the laptop screen to her. "Thanks for coming in. I need your help. We have a situation."

The witch's left eyebrow arched. "What kind of situation?"

"The reptilian creatures have left the warehouse apartments. I went back last night to pick up the van... the place is deserted. Can you track them somehow?"

Avalynn shifted on her seat. "I can try."

"You know more about their habits than we do. Where would they go?"

"Right now, I don't know." She stood up. "Let me see what I can find out. I'll be in touch." She strutted across the office and out the door before Reece could object.

"That went well," Ed said, sarcasm in his tone.

Reece let out a sigh and glowered at him. "Yeah, I can see that."

"Do you think she'll help?" The ex-lieutenant got off his chair and walked over to the PI's desk.

"I wish I knew."

"You don't trust her, do you?" Sarah asked.

"Not entirely, no. We were ambushed in the apartment building and I'm wondering if she's involved in some way."

Todd crossed the office to the group. "What motive could she have?"

"That's what I intend to find out." Reece came around his desk, perched on the corner, folding his arms. "I think it's time to do what Sarah suggested... keep an eye on Avalynn's movements." His stern gaze moved to his friend. "Andre, can I ask you to track her?"

Andre looked up from his computer. "Not if you want me to continue searching for information on Charlene. I need to focus. Maybe Nathaniel could send one of his team."

Reece's eyes remained on Andre for a moment. His friend made a good point. Finding the information on Charlene was crucial – for Tom's sake. "Ok, sure, I'll call him."

"I can do it," Todd volunteered.

"I appreciate the offer, but we need someone Avalynn can't detect. You'd be easy for her to spot."

"I get it. A vampire can hide in the shadows, yada, yada."

"Yeah, they can. And because I have no idea what kind of powers she possesses we need to be careful not to tip her off, otherwise she won't help us locate those things."

CHAPTER NINETEEN

The next evening, while Reece worked alone at Double D Investigations, his cell vibrated on the desk in front of him. He snatched it up to check the caller ID. Charlene. His gaze moved to the clock on the wall. 9:30 PM. *Why would she call at this time of night?* He jabbed the green button with his thumb and pressed the phone to his ear. "Hello, Charlene, what can I do for you?"

"I thought we could arrange that drink and conversation. Do you have some time now?"

"Now? It's a bit late for a drink, don't you think?"

"It's not that late. We really need to talk."

"About what?" He stood up, walked over to the window, leaned against the frame.

"I think we need to call a truce, for one thing. You seem to think I'm here to cause trouble for you. I'm not, I'm only interested in what's best for Tom."

"You don't even know him. How could you possibly know what's best for him?"

Andre continued to search for information on Charlene but seemed to keep hitting a brick wall, which to Reece's mind sent up a gigantic red flag.

"Look, I understand. You've been in his life for a long time, feel you take precedence, and you do, but I'm his aunt and as such don't I deserve to be a part of his life too?"

"When I know more about you. You've been filling his head with the notion I have something against you. The fact is I'm not putting Tom at risk any further until I have the answers I need."

The line went silent.

"Charlene?"

No answer.

"Are you still there?"

"Yes, I'm here." She didn't respond to his accusation of manipulation. "Do you honestly believe I would put him at risk?"

"I'm wondering why you've shown up now after all these years. You may have been estranged from Charlotte, but after she passed you could've made contact at any time, seeing as you've known where we were. Why didn't you?"

"If you meet me tonight I'll explain everything."

Reece pressed the mute button on his phone, let out a heavy sigh. There were more important matters to take care of right now, although he did want to know more about the woman before allowing her further access to his son. Pressing the mute off, he said, "All right, where?"

ⅎ)(∛

When Reece walked into the elegant bar he ran his gaze around the sophisticated ambient space, spotted Charlene sitting in an orange armchair, cocktail on the small round table in front of her, and a frosty glass of beer sitting on the other table in front of a second orange armchair. The quiet corner she'd chosen felt intimate. As he got closer, she glanced up at him with a smile. "Thanks for coming on such short notice. I appreciate you doing it."

Reece's gut did flip flops under his belt. She had Charlotte's smile, which made it all the more difficult for him to keep his mind on the task of finding out why she'd come to LA. Not being able to dig up anything on her bothered him. *If* she *was* Charlotte's sister there had to be a paper trail of some kind – somewhere. "No problem." He sidled into the space between the table and chair and sat down.

"I took the liberty of ordering you a Budweiser. I hope it's ok."

"Yeah. Thanks." His eyes moved from her to the tall glass of cold beer standing on the round table in front of him then back to her. He frowned. "You were going to tell me about yourself." He wanted to get to the facts and get this meeting over with. Looking at Charlene made his heart ache… he couldn't risk being distracted by her.

"Yes, I will. I thought we could at least have a drink together first." She reached for the jumbo-sized cocktail glass, popping the straw into her mouth and taking a long sip of the rainbow colored concoction.

Reece's heart stuttered in his chest. Being around her threw him off balance. "Ok, sure." He picked up the beer glass and swallowed a large mouthful of the amber liquid.

Charlene ran her gaze around the room. "This is a nice venue, isn't it?"

"It's ok." Reece sat the glass in his hand on the table.

"You don't appreciate having a drink at a nice place like this one?"

"I don't go to bars anymore. I have a drink at home if I want one."

"Of course." Her right eyebrow arched. "Who's minding Tom tonight?"

"Tom's old enough to take care of himself, he doesn't need a babysitter. He'll be seventeen soon."

"I didn't mean…"

"Look, I came here tonight to hear what you have to say. You said you were going to fill me in on who you are and why you're in LA so can we move this along?"

"I hoped we could…"

"What? Become friends? Or something more? What game are you playing?"

"I'm not playing any game. I thought we could get to know each other, that's all." She touched his arm.

The feel of her hand on his skin caused an unsettling reaction in him. He folded his arms. "For what purpose?"

Charlene returned her hand to her lap. "To be good family for Tom."

"So start by telling me the reason you're here."

She let out a heavy sigh. "All I want is for Tom to get to know me. To have some kind of relationship with him. Is that such a terrible thing?"

Reece leaned forward on the chair. "You're stalling."

"I'm not."

"Why won't you tell me about where you come from? Where you've been all this time and why you're here now?"

"I'm going to. It's just… I can't do it in one sitting. There's a lot to explain, as I told you the night we met for dinner."

"How difficult can it be?"

She sighed. "Very."

"Like I said, you're stalling." Reece's patience had worn thin. He stood up. "When you're ready to talk you know how to reach me."

Charlene popped up off her chair. "So that's it? You're not allowing me to see my nephew because I won't tell you what you want to know?"

"You bet. Tom is the most important person in my life. I'll do everything I can to protect him." He headed for the door.

Once again, their meeting hadn't gone according to plan. Reece Daniels appeared to be one tough cookie… and not easy to break.

CHAPTER TWENTY

The following afternoon, Detective Grant Donovan waited at the entrance to the alley behind the Chinese restaurant in Downtown LA for Reece to arrive. He'd contacted the PI the moment the call came in because this body was different to the previous two victims. There seemed to be an epidemic of supernatural murders taking place in his city that he felt powerless to prevent. He spotted the midnight blue Mustang pulling in across the street and stepped onto the sidewalk to greet the PI. "Hey, thanks for coming." He extended his hand, Reece shook it.

"No problem." Reece frowned at him. "You said this body's different?"

"Yeah." The detective pointed to the alley. "You'll see what I mean when you take a look."

The pair pushed through curious onlookers, bent under the yellow crime scene tape, and wandered down to the dead end.

When they reached the body, the uniform tugged back the white sheet.

Reece remained poker-faced. "Ok." He recognized the female casing as one from the apartment building.

Grant Donovan gave the PI a peculiar stare.

Reece picked up on it. "Let's head back to the street." He turned around and walked along the alley, the detective followed.

"What's going on, Reece?"

"Not here."

When they were far enough away from prying ears, Reece said, "It's not a body... as such. It's the human casing of one of the reptile creatures."

Grant folded his arms. "Well, how the hell am I supposed to explain that to my superior? He's going to demand answers."

"I know. I'm sorry. It is what it is."

"From where the department stands right now it looks like a body that's been split down the middle. What am I supposed to do with it?"

Reece shrugged. "Get rid of it, I suppose."

"Are you kidding me? How do you propose I do that?"

The PI gave it some thought for a moment. "Let them take it to the morgue and leave it with me." He turned on his heel, stalked back toward his car. He couldn't have the coroner taking samples of the remains.

"Daniels?" the detective called after him.

"I said I'll handle it." Reece continued along the alley without looking back.

୧୦୯୨

After the successful removal of the human casing from the morgue, and finishing up reports for other Double D cases, Reece closed the lid on the laptop, got up from his desk, stretched, then headed for the door. Tom called to tell him he'd ordered pizza and it would arrive in the next 35 minutes, so he'd have just enough time to get home before the delivery guy knocked on their door.

Grant Donovan didn't ask any questions about how they removed the body from the morgue, he didn't want to know. He told Reece he was grateful it would become a missing corpse not a homicide investigation, at least not until the body showed up, which it wouldn't. Over time it would turn into another unsolved cold case.

Reece headed along the boulevard, turned right, easing the Mustang up the incline and around the bend. He'd be home in five minutes. Once he reached the six foot, cream colored fence of the property, he left the engine running, climbed out, opened the double green metal gates, got back in and drove through, pulling the convertible up out front of the entrance.

The front doors opened and Tom came out into the alcove. "Hey, Dad, the pizza's already here. Come on, before it gets cold."

Reece walked into the entry hall, the aroma of cheese, Italian herbs, and pepperoni wafting into his nostrils caused his empty stomach to growl. They smelled delicious.

Tom chuckled. "Forget to have lunch again, huh?"

The PI gave his son a thin smile. "Yeah, guess so. I tend to lose track of time when I'm focused on work."

After dinner, Tom cleaned up the kitchen counter before heading to the attic to finish a school assignment.

Reece climbed the stairs and walked along the hallway to his room. He needed to take a shower before dropping into bed. He felt wiped out. It had been a long day. As he headed into his bathroom to turn on the faucet, he realized he hadn't heard from Avalynn or Charlene over the past 24 hours. It felt good. Charlene was a complication he didn't need in his life, and the witch?… well, he didn't know what to make of her. Yet.

೮ЭᏟᏒ

The overhead, tubular fluorescent bulb flickered a white shock of light across the sterile room, turning the dark space bright for a nanosecond before giving an electrical buzz and snapping off, leaving the eerie room pitch black. Reece's already tense body gave an involuntary shudder, the hairs on the back of his neck standing static, as he fumbled to tug his cell phone from the pocket of his jeans, flick on the flashlight, and crossed the lab to the metal refrigerators lining the wall ahead of him.

What had prompted him to visit the morgue at this time of night? He glanced at the face of his phone. 11:58 PM. Almost the witching hour, as some believed, as he also believed these days. A rash of goosebumps traveled up the skin of his arms as he stepped up to the refrigerated drawer. Reaching for the handle, he pulled back the spring-loaded lever and the door popped open. Reece swallowed the tangle of nerves lodged in his throat, threatening to cut off his air supply, and swung back the stainless steel rectangle.

The body beneath the white sheet lay still… frozen in time.

He gripped the end of the metal tray, slid its full length out into the space beside him, the body lying on it suspended in mid-air like an audience participant at a magic show being levitated off the floor.

He stared at the obscure, lifeless figure hidden from his view and swallowed hard, his gut churning beneath the belt on his jeans. Who was under that cover and why was he compelled to find out?

A noise in the corridor outside caused him to extinguish his flashlight. Could it be security? Or someone coming into the morgue? The echoing footfalls grew louder. His eyes darted around the dark space, his mind trying to recall if there was anywhere he could hide. There wasn't.

Without a second thought, Reece climbed on top of the corpse, rolled the tray back into place, and pulled the door to, leaving it slightly ajar so he could breathe. A light bobbed about the room, a tiny sliver of its bright beam slicing into the blackness inside the fridge. The body shifted beneath him and Reece jerked up, whacking his head hard against the ceiling of the confined space, his eyes wide.

The sheet slid from the head of the corpse and Charlotte's deathly pale face appeared beneath him. *"Don't* trust her," she warned.

Reece sprang out of bed, his heart thumping against his ribs, his body bathed in beads of cold sweat, his tall frame trembling as he tried to slow his ragged breathing... his anxious mind unable to grasp the horrific vision.

After gathering his shaky composure, he thought about what his dead fiancée had said. 'Don't trust her.' Was it a warning about Charlene?

CHAPTER TWENTY ONE

Tom climbed the stairs, heading to his next class and stopped short when he heard his name echoing along the corridor behind him. He glanced over his shoulder. Jade Maxwell. He let out a long sigh and waited for her to catch up to him. He had always been careful not to encourage the girls around him because of what he was, but for some reason, unbeknown to him, Jade had gotten under his skin. He liked her. A lot. But what could he do about it? Nothing. He couldn't let her into his crazy world. It would be too dangerous.

Jade bounced up the staircase, arms loaded with books, and stopped on the step beneath him. "Hey," she said, a little breathless, "are you heading to Mr. Edwards' biology class?"

Tom gave her a sheepish sideward glance. "Uh, yeah. I didn't think you took the same class."

"Oh, I don't. I'm next door." She stepped up beside him. "Can I walk with you?"

What could he do? Say no? "Sure." He continued up the staircase, Jade in tow.

Once in the corridor, she matched his quick pace. "I thought maybe…"

Tom turned his head sharply. "What?" He hadn't meant for it to sound so acute. "Sorry. What were you thinking?"

"You're an A grade student in all of your subjects, right?"

Tom's cheeks flushed. He wondered how she knew about his grades and where the conversation was heading. "Uh, yeah. Why?"

"Well… I thought maybe you could tutor me. I – I really need help with algebra…"

"Sorry, I don't have the time." He knew he couldn't tutor her, even though he wanted to. It would bring them closer together. Too close.

"I'm happy to pay you whatever you want. I'm not asking you to do it for free."

"It's not about money."

Her pretty face wrinkled into a curious frown. "What then?"

"I'm busy."

"Busy with what?" She gave him an unsure smile. *He's trying to blow me off. I can tell.*

"I – I help my dad after school."

Jade frowned. "Isn't your dad a Private Investigator?"

"Uh, yeah, he is."

"So how do you help him?"

"I do errands for his office. Keeps me pretty busy."

Her face dropped. "Oh. Ok." One of her friends waved her to hurry up. "I'd better go. See you 'round."

"Yeah. See you." He hated having to put her off but he didn't have a choice.

∽೧ೈ

When Tom stepped into the entry hall his dad came out of the kitchen, mug in hand, to greet him. "Hey, buddy, how was school?"

Tom let out a sigh. "Ok."

Reece frowned. "By the sound of that long sigh it doesn't sound ok to me. Want to talk about it?"

"Not really." Tom dropped his backpack onto the carpet and hung up his jacket.

"Might help," Reece coaxed.

Tom headed into the kitchen. His dad followed. The pair sat on a tall stool either side of the center counter.

"What's up?" Reece asked.

Tom remained silent for a moment, contemplating whether to tell his dad or not. "There's this girl…"

Reece grinned and set his mug of coffee on the counter. "Oh."

"I think she likes me."

"So what's the problem?"

He prodded his chest. "I am."

"What do you mean?" Reece frowned into his son's eyes.

"I'm a werewolf, Dad, what else?" Tears stung the backs of his eyes. He blinked them away.

"You're still a teenager. You should have a girlfriend at your age. Enjoy dating and all the fun that goes with it."

A single tear slipped down Tom's right cheek. "I can't."

"Why not?"

"Because… what if I turned and hurt her, or something?"

"You have your wolf under control, Tom. You have for a long time now. I know you can handle it. What brought this on?"

"She… Jade… asked me to tutor her."

"Oh, I see. And you don't want her to get too close to you because you like her."

"Yeah, I do."

"So tell her you'll do it."

"I can't. I already told her I do errands for Double D Investigations after school."

"Ok. Tell her I've given you some time off so you can help her."

"*Dad…*"

"What? You need someone in your life. Isn't that what you're always telling *me*?" He gave his son a humorous grin.

"This is different."

Reece leaned back on the stool. "How so?"

"You're human."

"And you're *half* human. I have total faith in you, Tom. You've got this."

CHAPTER TWENTY TWO

Detective Grant Donovan glanced at the precinct clock as he entered the quiet workspace. 7:24PM. He let out a heavy sigh and headed for his desk, running his gaze around the almost empty room. Harrison, his partner, sat at his workstation two finger typing on his computer keyboard, a report document on the screen.

"Hey, Grant, where have you been?"

"Out."

"Yeah. Where?" Harrison stopped typing and spun around on his chair.

"Need to know."

"Right." Harrison continued typing.

Grant walked over to his partner's desk, leaned in close to speak to him. "If you must know I went home for some dinner. Can't have the Mrs. mad at me all the time for never being there, can I?"

Harrison sighed. "Yeah, I'm hearing you."

On the way across the workroom, his boss, Ken Humphries, stuck his head out of the door of his office. "Donovan, can I have a word?"

Grant gave another heavy sigh. When his boss asked to have a word he knew it meant trouble. He zig-zagged between desks and stepped up to his boss's door. "Yes, Sir?"

Ken waved him in. "Close the door. Have a seat." It wasn't a request.

"Sure." Grant did as he was asked.

"Any news on the missing body?" His boss leaned on the blotter on his desk, giving Grant a serious stare. He wanted answers.

"Uh, no, not yet."

"I wanna know how someone walked outta the morgue with a body. Why would somebody do that?"

"I don't know, Chief. There're a lot of sickos out there."

Ken's brow furrowed into a deep frown. "You think someone did it for kicks?"

"No."

"What did you mean then?" Ken Humphries folded his arms as he leaned back in his chair.

Grant shrugged. "I have no idea at this point."

"Well, find out. I want both cases closed ASAP."

Grant sprang up off his seat. "But Chief…"

"Don't 'But Chief' me. We've got some crazy shit going on in LA right now. Bodies dissolved to puddles of slime, others split down the middle. We need to lock up whoever stole that corpse." He poked the air with his index finger. "Understood? Maybe they're the ones doing the killings. Whoever they are, we need to get them off the streets."

"Yes, boss, but…"

"Again, no buts. Get out there and *do your job*. Get Daniels to assist. He seems to know more than he's letting on these days." He pointed to the door.

Grant knew the interrogation had concluded. He got up, opened the door and stepped outside.

Harrison came over to him. "What did the boss want?"

"The boss wants us to find the missing body, pronto."

Harrison's gaze moved from Grant to their boss's office door. "How are we supposed to do that?" They already knew what happened to it.

ॐ

Reece's cell phone vibrated on the nightstand, waking him from a restless sleep. He reached across, his fingers prodding the wooden surface for his phone, snatched it up and frowned at the glowing screen. Grant Donovan. "Hey, what's up?" he said in a sleepy drawl, glancing at the bedside clock's luminous green numerals. 11:56PM.

"The boss wants me to step up the investigation on the missing body. He wants an arrest soon. He also wants you to assist."

"What?" Reece threw back the covers, swung his legs over the side of the bed and sat up.

"Yeah, I know. Considering we both know what happened to it." He waited a beat. "Please tell me it will never be found."

"It won't." Reece ran his hand over the stubble on his chin.

"I knew this would come back to bite me in the ass."

"Look, the body can't be found so you've got nothing to worry about." Reece stood up and walked over to the window.

"You're one hundred percent sure?"

"It's been incinerated." It hadn't been. His research team at the containment facility would study it. Grant didn't need to know that. No one would find it out there. He could hear the relieved sigh on the other end of the line. "Feel better now?"

"Yeah, I do. Thanks for getting rid of it."

"No problem. It would've been detrimental to our cause if the coroner took samples from it. Better this way."

"Yeah, I know, you're right."

"Anything else, or can I go back to sleep now?"

"Oh, sorry, I didn't realize I woke you."

"It's ok. Don't lose your shit over this, Grant. Play it cool. Don't give your boss a reason to suspect anything."

"I hate to tell you this… but he already does."

Unable to go back to sleep, Reece pulled on his jeans and T-shirt then headed downstairs. If Grant's boss had become suspicious about what he knew it would cause serious problems for him. He knew Ken Humphries. Even though they hadn't crossed paths in quite some time, he doubted the Lieutenant had changed over the years. When Ken wanted something he could be like a dog with a bone. He wouldn't give up until he got the answers he needed.

Dropping a coffee pod into the machine, Reece wondered whether or not he should attempt to diffuse the situation with Ken, before it got out of control, and the Lieutenant stepped into something he'd rather not know about. The man was a stickler for regulations. He wouldn't understand what Reece was doing, which would make him even more determined to do everything he could to shut Double D Investigations down.

Reece turned a clean mug over on the counter, sat it under the nozzle and pressed the button. The coffee sputtered into his cup. He spun around when he heard a noise behind him. "Hey, buddy, what are you doing up?"

Tom rubbed his eyes and yawned. "I heard you come down here. Can't sleep?"

Reece shook his head. "You?"

"Nope."

"Still trying to work out what you're going to do about Jade?"

Tom pulled out a tall stool and climbed onto it. "Why do things have to be so complicated?"

"They don't have to be."

"I know you think I've got my shi – self together. What if I don't?"

Reece came around the counter to him. Gripping his son's shoulders, he said, "Yes, you do. I know you would never do anything to hurt the people you love."

Tom's cheeks flushed. He gave his dad a thin, embarrassed smile. He did love Jade. "Ok. I believe you."

"Good. So go do something about it. Tomorrow."

"Ok." Tom slid off the stool. "I'm going back to bed, unless you want some company."

"I'm fine. You go on."

"Night, Dad." Tom headed out the door.

"Night, buddy."

CHAPTER TWENTY THREE

Avalynn stepped from the empty elevator, strutted along the hotel corridor until she reached room 305. She'd located one of the reptilian creatures, this one she had a personal interest in, this one different from the others. She rested her hand against her leather jacket, the inside pocket concealing something ancient, something precious. Something that would eradicate the reptiles in LA and prevent them from returning. Something that needed to remain her secret.

The reason she'd come to the hotel alone? This particular creature had been in New Orleans, had tricked her into falling in love with it, had let her believe it ascended the night she thought they'd killed it. This time it would… forever.

Leaning into the door, she listened. Movement inside.

Avalynn stepped backwards, glanced along the hallway in both directions. Finding the floor void of people, she raised her right hand and the door flew open. Reaching into her pocket, she whipped out the ancient gold talisman, fashioned in the eye of a snake with an emerald at its center, thrust it toward the figure standing by the bed, repeating the words that would rid the city of this anomaly.

He swung around, defensive hands raised. "Stop."

Avalynn kept chanting as she moved closer.

"Please, Avalynn… stop." He lowered his hands, his smile beguiling.

The witch's conflicted emotions caused her words to stumble. At that moment, the creature rushed forward, knocking the talisman from her hand.

Avalynn thrust out both hands. A white bolt of electricity sent the creature hurtling across the room. "Your kind should not be here. You unbalance the earth." She snatched up the talisman to begin the chant again.

"I stayed for you," he said, staggering to his feet on the other side of the queen-sized bed. "I've never stopped loving you."

"Don't lie to me." She continued chanting.

The creature in human form, the man she'd once loved, crumpled into a heap on the plush blue carpet. "Please, Avalynn, don't do this."

Tears stung the backs of her eyes and she blinked them away as she proceeded with the ritual to dispatch the creature. Her heart still ached for what they'd once shared… before she'd learned his secret. "Your kind kills without restraint. You must be stopped."

"Listen to me."

"No!" She moved closer still, the strength of the talisman wreaking havoc on the reptile's human form. Its body convulsed, the color draining from its skin revealing the snakelike creature beneath the flesh.

When the witch reached the bed, the bathroom door flew open. Two more creatures appeared in the open doorway. One opened its mouth, fangs extended, and spat venom across the room.

Avalynn thrust her left hand toward the pair, freezing the spray mid-air while also suspending the reptiles in the doorway. It wouldn't hold for long. She continued toward the creature on the floor.

At that moment, Nathaniel and Andre burst into the room. "Get back!" Nathaniel shouted.

Avalynn turned to look in the direction of the booming voice. "What are you doing here?"

"We've been tracking you." Nathaniel whipped across the room and took out the two reptiles in the bathroom doorway. They wouldn't stay down for long. The bodies began to split down the middle. Andre threw himself across the room, firing tranquilizer darts into the pair before they could emerge. It would keep them out for quite some time.

Avalynn didn't know whether to be pleased for the backup or angry for Reece having her followed.

Nathaniel stepped up beside her. "Who is this?"

Her gaze moved to the quivering human form. "One reptile that isn't easy to dispatch."

"Allow me." Nathaniel wrenched the male off the carpet and sank his fangs into him. Once he drained the body, he dropped the casing onto the floor. "It is gone."

As Avalynn discreetly pocketed the talisman, a single tear slipped down her left cheek and she brushed it away.

૪૭ભ

Avalynn threw open the door of Double D Investigations and stormed across the office. "Why did you have me followed?" She stopped in front of Reece's desk, folded her arms, and glowered at him.

The PI remained seated, his eyes moving from the laptop screen to her. "I did it for your protection."

"Don't give me the same BS I told you."

Nathaniel and Andre came into the room.

Avalynn glanced over her shoulder before her severe stare returned to Reece.

He stood up. "Look, if you want to go off on your own and get yourself into trouble fine. I'll remove backup."

"I'm a witch. I can take care of myself." Her gaze moved to the pair behind her. "Besides, I don't need the backup of vampires." Her steely lilac eyes returned to the PI. "I think you wanted to find out who I made contact with… not offer protection."

"Think what you like."

"I will. All I've done is come to LA to offer my help and this is how you repay me?"

"I didn't ask for your help." Reece folded his arms.

"Ok. I'm withdrawing my offer."

"Then you don't need to be here." Reece frowned at her.

Avalynn turned on her heel, crossed the room, jerked the door open and left.

Nathaniel stepped up to Reece's desk. "Do you think it is wise to let her go?"

"We'll continue to track her without her knowledge."

"Ah, I understand. She will not be on her guard." Nathaniel gave the PI a perceptive smirk.

"Correct."

Andre sat down. "We need to find the rest of the reptilian creatures. It's strange there haven't been any new reported deaths. Looks like they're laying low."

"And with good reason. They would know about the three you took out."

"But where are the others?"

"An opportunity will present itself. I feel it in my gut." Reece sat down again.

"Let us hope it is sooner rather than later, because there are bound to be more deaths when the creatures cannot contain their urges any longer." Nathaniel sat beside Andre.

Reece's cell vibrated on his desk and all eyes moved to the buzzing sound. He snatched up his phone. "Hello?"

"I have information about the creatures you're looking for. Can we meet?" The voice sounded warped. Reece figured the caller was using a voice distorter. But why?

"What kind of information?" Reece's gaze moved to Andre and Nathaniel. Both moved forward on their chairs, a frown on each of their faces.

"I would prefer to speak with you in person."

Could this be some kind of setup orchestrated by the creatures?

"I'm not coming alone."

"Fine. Bring your vampire friend with you."

How did the caller know about Andre?

"When? Where?"

"Tonight. The old LA zoo."

Why that particular location? It had been part of his life for quite a number of years and, on occasion, haunted his dreams.

"What time?"

"Eleven."

"Where?"

"I'll find you." The line went dead.

"What's going on?" Andre frowned at him.

"Someone with information on the reptilian creatures wants to meet."

His friend stood up. "You want me to come along?"

"Yeah, I do." His gaze moved to Nathaniel. "You too. But you'll need to be discreet."

"I can do discreet."

"What did the caller tell you?" Andre asked.

Reece shrugged. "Nothing more than they could provide information on the reptilian creatures."

"You think it could be a trap?"

"I wouldn't put anything past those things. They know we're on to them, so yeah, I think so."

"What time are we meeting the informant?"

"Eleven tonight."

CHAPTER TWENTY FOUR

Reece screeched his midnight blue Mustang to a halt across the street from the marketplace, threw open the door, climbed out and crossed the road. Grant Donovan had called him, asking him to come to the closed fresh produce store. When the place didn't open one customer queued outside waiting to shop called the local police station. When the Rampart cop arrived, he found the back roller door partially up and, on checking inside, found the horrific scene. This new attack blew Reece's theory about the creatures attacking on nights of the full moon out of the water. It now appeared they attacked any time.

The detective came over to Reece as he stepped onto the sidewalk. Grant, his team, and the forensics guys had been there for hours.

"What have you got?" the PI asked.

"Six puddles of bloody goo."

Reece's right eyebrow arched.

"Yeah, I thought you'd want to be here." Grant motioned for the PI to go in ahead of him. "This is new. I mean more than one body. Do you know what's going on?"

"I wish I could say yes. They must be getting desperate." He continued toward the crime scene.

Grant gripped Reece's arm to stop him. "What do you mean?"

The PI turned around. "I honestly don't know. I would tell you if I did. It's an assumption at this point."

"I need more than guesswork on this. Do you know anything about their habits?"

"Not much, no. We're still working on it."

Grant blew out a noisy, exasperated breath. "They've been quiet for a few days. Why now?"

"Like I said, they must be desperate."

"So you think they kill as a food source?"

"Could be."

Grant's forehead creased into a concerned frown. "Do you have people researching these creatures?"

"Yeah, I do. As soon as I know anything I'll call you." He motioned at the puddles with his head. "Any idea who they were?"

"We think it's the store owner and his family. We won't know for sure until forensics comes back on the remains."

Harrison Killjoy stood up when he saw Grant and Reece standing nearby. He'd been studying the puddle. "Hey, Reece, how's it going?" He smiled, extended his hand. The PI shook it.

"Could be better under the circumstances."

Harrison nodded. "Yeah, I know what you mean."

Grant huddled close to his partner. "Reece has people researching the creatures. He said as soon as he has anything he'll let us know."

"Great. We could use the help. The only problem I can see is how to explain those." He pointed to the puddles.

"I wish I could give you an answer," Reece told him, "but there's nothing you can do to explain it to your boss… or anyone else."

"I understand. Our hands are tied on this." Harrison was contemplative for a moment. "Is there anything more we can do to help you? I'm tired of sitting around waiting for that elusive breakthrough that isn't going to come."

Reece's right eyebrow arched. "You're serious? Because if you are we could sure use the help."

Grant frowned at Harrison. "What are you doing?"

"The one thing I *can* do. Help get rid of those creatures before they kill more innocent people."

Grant folded his arms. "So you're going to moonlight?"

"Yeah, I think I am. What about you?"

The detective blew out another noisy breath. "I – I don't know…"

"Come on, Grant, you said you wanted to do more about this situation."

"I know I did."

"We can't sit on the fence here. People are dying."

A slight pink flush spread across Grant's cheeks. He wanted to help without putting himself in the line of fire. He had a family to consider. So did Harrison. "I'll think about it."

"Fair enough," Reece said. "You know where to find me if you change your mind. Like I said, we could use the help." He turned to look at Harrison. "You know where our office is?" The detective nodded. "Can you come by tonight?"

"You bet."

"Ok. See you there at midnight?"

"I'll be there."

"I have to go. I'll check in with you later." Reece headed out of the building and back to his convertible. Once in his car, he made a conference call to his team. "We've got six more puddles in West LA."

"What do you want us to do?" Ed asked.

"Meet me at the office at midnight tonight. We need to ramp up our search for those reptiles."

"Reece, I haven't found anything more on the creatures yet," Sarah said. "Do you want me to keep looking or come to the office?"

"Come to the office. I need everyone onboard."

"Ed, can you pick me up?" Lozano asked.

"Sure thing."

"Thanks."

"Do we have any leads?" Todd wanted to know.

"Not yet. I've set up a meeting with someone who might be able to shed some light on the creatures, and I want to be ready to move on it." He gave a quiet sigh. "Andre, pick up Nathaniel and meet me at my place. We need to keep that appointment and I'd prefer to travel out to the old LA zoo together. We'll drop Nathaniel off so he can track us." Reece had implemented the suggestion Todd made years ago, when they were in Paris on a job, about having microchips implanted in every member of his team so they could keep track of everyone. It worked well so far.

"Sure. We'll be there by ten."

ഇ⊙ᆼ

Reece's gut tightened and he swallowed the tangle of nerves lodged in his throat as he entered the shadowed, abandoned grounds of the once popular attraction. He'd been here on more than one occasion in the past, on the hunt for supernatural killers he'd known nothing about at the time. They left Nathaniel inside the vehicle, Reece choosing to bring the van tonight, while he and Andre made their way around to the graffitied unfenced cages and expansive treed picnic area.

Reece could feel his breathing go shallow, the hair on the back of his neck standing static. The place gave him the heebie jeebies, if he wanted to be honest about it. Dave, his partner back in the day when he worked on the force, had felt the same way the night they'd come here in search of a werewolf – which to them had been a human murder suspect not a supernatural one. Many years later, Dave had been bitten by one of Jacques' vampires lying in coffins in the underground cavern of St. Gabriel's church and the PI had killed him, something that would haunt him for the rest of his life.

The pair turned the corner, following the concrete path to the cages.

A figure stepped out of the dark, clad in black clothing with a hood hiding their face. It appeared male by the height and build. "You can stop there." He used the same voice distorter making him sound robotic.

"I've done what you asked in good faith. Don't you think I deserve the same courtesy?" Reece asked.

"This is not a game, Detective. The circumstances are dire."

"I'm fully aware of the situation. If we're going to work together…"

"There is no *we*. We are not working together. What I impart to you I will do only once. When you get what you came here for you're on your own." The figure remained obscure in the shadows.

"Why did you want me to come with Reece?" Andre asked. Something inside him told him this figure was someone he knew.

"Because you are his friend… his *best* friend, and as you saved his life here many years ago it seemed the suitable site for this meeting."

Reece stepped forward, his frowning gaze locked on the figure. "How do you know that?"

"I know many things about you and your team." He smirked beneath the hood.

Something slithered in Reece's solar plexus. This figure felt familiar. "Who are you?"

"You don't need to know. What you do need to know is the creatures are leasing a triple-story, beachfront property in Santa Monica. There are eight sharing the home."

"Where?"

"I will send the details once I am away from here."

"Why get us to come out here with no intention of giving us what we need now? I have my team on standby."

"By the time you return to your office you will have the information you require."

"Why are you helping us?"

"I have my reasons."

Reece's gaze shifted to Andre, the pair staring at each other for a moment, both thinking the same thing. It had to be someone they knew. When they returned their gazes to the place the figure had been standing... he was gone.

CHAPTER TWENTY FIVE

Reece threw open the door of Double D Investigations, stalked across the room to his team, Nathaniel and Andre behind him. The scowl on his face told the group the PI wasn't happy about what occurred out at the old LA zoo.

"Did you get the information we need?" Todd asked, standing up from the kitchen table.

"Not yet. He said it would be here by the time we got back." Reece rounded his desk, sat down, opened his laptop to check his email. Nothing. "Dammit!"

Andre came around the desk. "He hasn't sent it?"

"Doesn't look like it." The PI folded his arms, his frowning gaze moving to his friend's serious stare. "Why do we take their word for it? Why didn't we jump him, make him tell us?"

"Because you would have been ambushed," Nathaniel told him, thinking it would be better to convey the information to the PI once they were on safe ground. "He came prepared."

Reece jerked out of his chair, walked up to the black vampire, hands on hips. "You mean he brought backup after telling me to come alone?"

"Yes. I could sense others nearby in the ground level cages."

The PI frowned. "How many?"

"At least eight."

"Human?"

The vampire nodded. "Yes, I believe so."

Reece let out a noisy breath. "I'm tired of playing fucking games with these people… or them playing games with us. Tonight could've gone a completely different way. We were in danger out there and didn't even know it."

"You weren't to know the guy would do a backflip," Todd said.

"Not the point. We…" A musical ding sounded on his laptop. Reece spun around. He dropped into his chair, clicked the link, and ran his eyes over the email. No sender address attached, but it contained what he'd been waiting for… the location of the reptilian creatures' hideout. "Ok. Let's move out. I'll brief you on the way."

Harrison called the PI while they were heading back to the office after their meeting with the disguised figure, apologizing for not being able to make it. Another time, he'd said. Reece understood. The cop's family was his number one priority.

₧₦

They arrived at the triple-story beachfront house around 1:00 AM. The modern concrete and glass structure sat on a corner of a short, dead-end street that backed onto the beach with a row of trees running along the high metal gray fence. The PI did a quick sweep of the property for an entry point they could utilize along the side fence. There were none. The place appeared to be sealed off. He jumped up, gripped the black trim on the top of the fence, and pushed himself up to check the yard. BBQ entertainment area, swimming pool, Jacuzzi with miniature waterfall, steps leading onto another balcony with a row of deck chairs. This wasn't even part of the main building, which was separated by an elegant courtyard. *Some house.*

He made a B-line for the van and climbed into the back with the others. "Looks like we'll have to go over the fence. There isn't another way inside."

"We could try the door from the carport," Nathaniel offered.

Reece's gaze moved to the window and he ran his eyes over the front of the house. "Mm, maybe. The problem is we don't know where they'll be. We don't even know if they sleep."

"Most reptiles sleep," Sarah told him.

The PI's serious stare moved to her. "You're sure?"

"Yes, I've been researching all types of reptiles... a lot of them do sleep."

"These could be different. Seeing as they're not real snakes."

"Maybe. Although they should follow the same sleep patterns as most reptiles."

"Let's hope so. It'll make our job a whole lot easier." He pushed open the van's double back doors. Everyone climbed out. "We need to be discreet. We don't want the neighbors waking up and calling the cops."

Everyone nodded.

Reece checked their ear communication devices. "Hear me ok?"

Again, everyone nodded.

"Good. Let's move in slow 'n steady." He led the way down the drive to the front of the building, stunned to see Avalynn standing behind one of the cars. "What are you doing here?"

"The same thing you're doing." She folded her arms.

"How do you know about this place?" Ed asked, his gruff voice echoing around the under-house space.

Reece swung around. "Chief!"

"Sorry," Ed said in a whisper.

The PI's gaze returned to the witch. He thought they were done with her. "Well?"

"I got a tip." She raised her chin, looked him in the eye. She would not be intimidated by the likes of him.

"When?" Reece folded his arms.

"Last night around nine."

"How?"

"I received an anonymous email with the information."

"You didn't meet them in person?"

Avalynn shook her head. "No. Why, did you?"

"Yeah. He requested a meeting."

"How strange." She frowned at him.

The hunch about it being someone they knew popped into his head. It would have to wait. His intense gaze returned to Avalynn. "Can you get us inside?"

"Of course."

"Ok, let's do this."

The interior of the elegant home appeared quiet. No movement anywhere on the lower floor, the place in darkness. The group surged through the extensive ground level to the stairs.

Reece gave hand signals so everyone knew what to do. They would seize each floor at the same time taking the sleeping reptiles by surprise, so as not to allow them time to react.

Nathaniel, Andre, Todd, and Sarah climbed the stairs to the top level while Reece, Ed, Lozano, and Avalynn took the middle floor.

With everyone in place, Reece gave the order for each group to rush the rooms.

No one.

The teams did a thorough sweep of all levels.

The place was empty.

The group met in the entry hall.

"Someone must've tipped them off," Reece said.

"Who?" Lozano asked.

"Good question." The PI walked up to the witch. "It seems strange to me you're here and they're not."

Avalynn stood with her hands on her hips, a scowl on her face. "You think I did this?"

"Just trying to figure out how they knew we were coming."

"What about the guy who gave us both the information? Maybe he likes having the upper hand. Maybe he's the one controlling them."

Reece gave her theory some serious consideration. *She could be right.*

CHAPTER TWENTY SIX

Reece awoke to his cell vibrating on the nightstand beside his bed. He blinked back the haze of sleep, rubbed the grit from his eyes, snatched up the phone and pressed the button. "Hello?" No answer. He pulled the phone away from his stubbled cheek, checking the screen. Unknown caller. He pressed it to his ear again. "Hello?" He heard the quiet click, then the buzzing dial tone. Reece swung his legs over the side of the bed, sat up, and hit redial. Blocked. Could it have been the person he'd met the previous night? Or maybe a wrong number? With a frustrated huff, he dropped the phone onto the nightstand, and headed to the bathroom for a quick shower.

When Reece entered the kitchen, Tom was finishing up breakfast. "Morning, bud, sleep ok?"

"Yeah, I did. How about you?"

"Yeah, it's the first solid night's sleep I've had in a while."

"That's good. Hey, I gotta go. Is it ok if Jade comes over after school so I can get started on tutoring her?"

"Sure. It'll be nice to meet her." Reece poured himself a mug of coffee.

Tom gave his dad the look. "You won't embarrass me in front of her, will you?"

Reece propped himself on a stool at the center counter. "Now why would I do that?"

"Just don't act like a cop and start asking her heaps of questions. Ok?"

"I wouldn't dream of it." He gave his son a cheeky smile and a wink.

"Dad!"

"Go to school. It'll be fine. I promise. See you tonight."

"Yeah, see ya. Love you, Dad."

"Love you too, buddy." Reece watched his son leave, picked up his mug of coffee and took another cautious sip.

His cell vibrated in his shirt pocket. Tugging it free he checked the screen. Charlene. *Why now?* "Good morning. Why the early call?" He hadn't heard from her for a few days and it had felt good not to have to deal with the drama.

"Morning. Can I see you?"

Did he want to see her? He thought about it before giving her an answer. "When?"

"Today, if possible."

"Is there a problem?"

"Of course there's a problem. You won't let me speak to my nephew."

"I explained the reasons for that."

"Yes, you did. But it's not good enough. I have a right to…"

"No. I have an obligation to look out for Tom's welfare and while you're not prepared to give me the answers I need this is how it will remain."

"I'm not here to hurt either of you. I wish you would believe me."

"If you want to sit down and tell me the real reason you're in LA we'll see how it goes from there."

Silence.

"Charlene, are you still there?"

After a long pause, she said, "Yes, I'm here."

"So, what's it going to be?"

"All right. Will you come to my hotel? We can have coffee in the restaurant downstairs."

"I can be there in an hour."

"I'll see you then." She rang off.

Reece frowned at the phone in his hand. Would she tell him what he wanted to know this time?

⁊ʒג

When Reece entered the hotel lobby, he spotted Charlene outside the restaurant entrance. She gave him an uncertain smile as he crossed the foyer. "Thanks for coming."

"No problem. Shall we?" He motioned into the cafe.

"Yes, of course." Charlene entered ahead of him.

The pair sat at a quiet table in the corner close to a window offering a view of the lush gardens.

A waitress came over to their table and set two menus down. "I'll give you a couple minutes before I take your order."

"No need. Coffee's fine." Reece slid the menu across the table toward her.

"Oh, ok." The young woman turned to look at Charlene. "Coffee for you too?"

"Yes, thanks."

"What would you both like?"

"Black for me," Reece said.

"The same." Charlene shifted in her seat.

The young waitress returned with a pot of brewed coffee, pouring two cups.

They waited for her to leave before beginning their conversation.

Reece clasped his hands on the table and stared into Charlene's anxious eyes. "Are you actually going to tell me this time?"

"Yes. I said I would."

He gave her a skeptical frown. "You've said the same before on two previous occasions."

"I – I know. This time I plan to."

"Whenever you're ready."

"Can we have our coffee first?"

"Sure."

"How's Tom?" She picked up her cup, took a sip.

"He's good."

Her right eyebrow arched. "Is that all you're going to tell me?"

"For the moment."

Charlene gave a heavy sigh. "Ok. Maybe I deserve being treated this way for not being a part of Tom's life sooner."

"This isn't about what you deserve it's about being honest with me."

She swallowed the tangle of nerves lodged in her throat. Could she do this? She didn't have a choice. "I have a son. Tyler. He's a year younger than Tom. He…" Tears welled in her eyes and she blinked them back. "He's sick."

Reece straightened on his chair and frowned. "What's wrong with him?"

Charlene took another sip of her coffee to fortify herself. This was more difficult than she'd anticipated. She set the cup down on its saucer and looked Reece straight in the eye. "He needs a kidney transplant. He's on the list but it's taking too long. His condition is deteriorating by the week."

"I'm sorry to hear that. It must be difficult for you." He frowned at her. "I don't understand. What does that have to do with Tom, and you being in LA?" All of a sudden it dawned on him. "You want Tom to donate a kidney?" Was this what Charlotte warned him about in his nightmarish dream? *Don't trust her.*

She nodded. "He would have to be tested, of course, but if he matched…"

"It's not possible."

A single tear slipped down Charlene's left cheek. She brushed it away. "Why not?"

"Because Tom also has a condition. It's not life-threatening but it makes him ineligible to donate blood or organs."

She frowned into Reece's eyes. "I don't understand."

"I'm sorry. I can't explain it any more than I have."

Charlene's distraught expression turned to a scowl. "You mean you won't, don't you?"

"No. I mean I can't."

"You've been belligerent toward me since I arrived and I can only assume it's because I look like my sister. I can't help who I look like, Reece, and I'm asking for your help. This is serious."

Reece considered his options. He thought about telling her the truth. Should he? What would she do with the information?

She reached across the table and gripped his hand. "I'm asking for you to save my son's life. Wouldn't you do the same for Tom?"

Reece pulled back. "Look, if there was another way…"

"You wouldn't help me."

"That's not true."

"Isn't it?"

"No. And you're wrong about my intentions. I'm only looking out for Tom."

"Tom may be able to help Tyler."

"He can't."

"So you won't even allow me to see if he's a match?"

"Tom's condition is a contagion spread by his blood."

Charlene frowned into his green eyes. "I don't understand. How?"

"If he gave Tyler a kidney Tyler would contract what Tom has."

"Tom looks like a healthy young man to me. If that's the only risk I'm prepared to take it."

"You have no idea what you're saying." Reece leaned back on his chair, folded his arms. He couldn't allow Tyler to become infected with Lycan genes.

Charlene studied his stoic expression. "My son *needs* your help. Why don't you ask Tom and see what he wants to do?"

Reece made the rash decision of telling her the truth. "Tom's a werewolf."

Charlene's eyes widened at the shocking revelation, then she frowned. "That's ridiculous."

"It's not." He leaned forward. "You knew Dan, didn't you?"

"Of course I did." The color drained from her face. "Why are you asking me that?"

"Because he was the alpha of a werewolf pack. He lied to Charlotte... told her he'd been bitten by something huge and fast while on duty. The fact is he'd turned his partner into a werewolf that night."

"You're lying to frighten me."

"I wish I was. When Tom turned sixteen his Lycanthrope genes kicked in. He's great now, but it was a struggle at first."

The pale expression on Charlene's face paled even more.

Reece frowned at her. "What's wrong?"

She shook her head, her voice a whisper. "Nothing."

Reece's stern gaze remained on her, his detective brain ticking over. Why did Charlotte stop speaking to her sister? Her identical twin? Twins were connected in ways no one could understand. Andre and Jacques were inseparable before they were bitten. What happened between Charlotte and her sister to cause such a rift? He straightened on his chair. Charlene had an affair with Dan. Tyler's his son.

"Tyler is Dan's, isn't he?"

Charlene's gaze moved to the table top. "Why would you say that?"

"Because it all makes sense now: the estrangement, Tyler being a year younger than Tom. Do you have a picture of him?"

She nodded, reached into her purse, took out her wallet, opened it and passed it to Reece.

The boy staring back at him was a younger version of Tom. Same hair color, eyes, complexion.

"When does he turn sixteen?" Reece asked.

"In three weeks. Why?"

"Because if he can hold on until his birthday he'll be fine. The werewolf genes will rid him of his kidney ailment."

"You're serious, aren't you? Tom is what you say he is? And Tyler…"

"Will be too."

CHAPTER TWENTY SEVEN

By the time Reece arrived at Double D Investigations, Andre had been at his desk for a couple of hours looking into Charlene's background. He'd matched a New Orleans driver's license by photo comparison. But she had changed her name to Charlene Beaufort, which was their mother's maiden name. He wondered why. The door opened and Reece stepped into the office. "Morning. Been here long?"

"Morning. A couple hours. I've been doing more investigating into Charlene. I discovered she'd changed her surname to their mother's."

"Yeah, I think she must've been hiding from Dan McCredie. I also know why she's here."

Andre crossed the office to his friend. "Why?"

Reece plonked himself into his chair. "She has a son, Tyler. He needs a kidney transplant."

"She told you that's why she came to LA?"

"Yeah, we met this morning for coffee at her hotel and she told me everything."

"She wants Tom to donate one of his?"

"That was the initial plan."

Andre sat on one of the two client chairs in front of Reece's desk. "You told her he couldn't, didn't you?"

"What do you think? Of course I did."

"Ok."

Reece's expression turned sheepish.

"What?" Andre frowned.

"I told her the truth."

His friend popped up off his chair. "What do you mean?"

"I told her about Tom."

"Why would you do that?"

"Because she wanted me to ask him if he'd be willing to get tested. You know I couldn't let that happen. And she would've continued to push the issue because she's desperate to help her son."

"How did she take it?"

"Surprisingly well, considering."

Andre sat down again. "You said she was hiding from Dan. Why?"

"She had an affair with him. The reason for the estrangement."

"Wait. What?"

"I know. Doesn't make sense, considering they were identical twins. Which means…"

"Tyler's a werewolf."

"Not yet. He doesn't turn sixteen for another couple of weeks."

"So she knows once he turns his kidney disease will disappear?"

"Yeah. She said Tyler arrived at her hotel unexpectedly a few days ago after his last dialysis treatment and he's resting there."

"You know she's going to need help with his transformation."

"Of course I know. She'll have to remain in LA until Tyler turns sixteen to make sure the transition is a smooth one. I've been thinking about letting them come stay with us."

"Do you think it's a wise idea?"

"We have few visitors, apart from you, so I don't see a problem."

"Ok, it's up to you. My concern would be Tyler running amok after he turns. You know the first time is beyond difficult."

"The basement is set up with the cage Adrian built so that shouldn't be a problem."

"I hope you know what you're doing."

"I think it'll be good for Tom to get to know his cousin/half-brother. He can help Tyler prepare for what he'll go through."

"What about his treatment?"

"Charlene said the longest he can go without dialysis is about seven days. We'll work something out for him in the meantime. Maybe you could contact Dennis."

"You know what he said. He didn't want to be involved."

"Yeah, I remember. I thought he might consider it because he knows what we do."

"It destroyed our friendship. We haven't spoken in years."

"I know. I'm sorry." He gave Andre a pained look.

"Yeah, I know. It is what it is." He still missed his friend. "Why do you think it took Charlene so long to talk to you about her son?"

Reece shrugged. "I don't know. Maybe she was nervous about asking to have Tom tested, or whether or not he'd be a match."

"At least, you hope that's why."

"What other reason could there be?"

Andre wondered about that.

ℴℂ

Reece stalked along the alley to where Grant Donovan and Harrison Killjoy stood. There had been another attack, the evidence lying on the cracked concrete outside the back entrance to the takeaway café. Another bloody puddle of goo. From what they could ascertain, the owner had been taken by surprise when he came out to put trash in the dumpster. How did the cops come to that conclusion? The back door was found wide open and the metal kitchen bin lay on the ground, its contents of food scraps strewn across the alley.

The detective walked over to the PI. "This has to stop. Have you made any headway on the location of those things?"

Reece folded his arms. "The location was empty when we went in."

Grant frowned. "So, in other words you don't know where they are? Jesus, Reece, you need to get on top of this."

"We're doing the best we can. Someone keeps undermining us. Forewarning them."

"So you have a mole?" Grant folded his arms.

"No, I *don't* have a mole. I think the person who provided the information is the one playing this dangerous game with us."

Grant leaned into him. "Then you need to do something about it fast. I've got my boss on my ass over these deaths. I'm looking at losing my job if we can't catch the perp."

"Maybe I need to have a conversation with your boss. Fill him in on what's happening."

The detective gave the PI an incredulous stare. "You think that'll work? Are you nuts? What makes you think he'll believe anything you say?"

"I'll show him proof."

"What kind of proof?"

"Leave that to me." Reece stalked back along the alley.

Harrison came over to Grant. "What'd he say?"

"He's going to talk to the Chief."

"You mean tell him the truth?"

"Apparently so."

"Frig me!"

"Yeah, agreed."

ℰᘐᘔ

Ken Humphries sat at his desk eating a BLT sandwich one of his guys brought back from the deli down the street. He'd opted to stay in the office for lunch today as he wanted to file away the mound of paperwork on his desk before he left the precinct for the day. A knock echoed into his office and his gaze moved to the window. Reece Daniels. *What does he want?*

He swallowed the gooey wad of food in his mouth, cleared his throat and said, "Come in."

The PI stepped into the office, followed by another man the Lieutenant didn't recognize as police.

"What can I do for you?" Ken asked, setting his sandwich aside.

"I need to talk to you about the current spate of murders." Reece remained standing, so did his companion.

"Oh? What do you know about it?" He motioned for the pair to take a seat.

"You've seen the forensic reports?" the PI asked.

"Of course I have. Doesn't solve the problem though, does it? It's a cop's worst nightmare."

"Yeah, it is. That's why we're here."

Ken frowned at the PI. "What have you got?"

"First, I need to ask you a question."

The Lieutenant tilted his head. "What question?"

"Do you believe in the supernatural?"

Ken Humphries' frown deepened. "You mean like ghosts, demons, that kinda shit?"

"Yeah."

"Do you?" Ken poked the air with his index finger.

"As a matter of fact I do."

"You're nuts. There is no such thing." The Lieutenant folded his arms barring any suggestion the murders had anything to do with spirits or the like.

"What if I could prove it?"

"Then you're a bigger fool than I thought. I heard you left the force to work as a PI. I also heard you were chasing the Boogie Man. Hahaha."

"So you don't have an open mind when it comes to the unexplainable… like these deaths?"

"Not at all. I've never encountered anything that couldn't be explained. These deaths are no different."

"Andre." Reece gave him a sideward glance.

His friend stood up, walked around the desk, perched on the corner close to the Lieutenant. "I want you to look at my face."

Ken's Adam's apple bobbed above his tie, his gut hollowed. Fear washed over him and he swallowed hard, his eyes wide.

CHAPTER TWENTY EIGHT

Later the same evening, after talking to Grant Donovan over the phone to tell him he wouldn't have any further issues with his boss, Reece headed to Nathaniel's nightclub, *Sanguine*, to pick up Andre. His friend's Ducati Monster had died and he needed a lift home. Climbing the stairs to the upper level office, Reece heard the pair in a heated argument with a man whose voice the PI didn't recognize. He eased his tall frame along the wall to the open door.

"You don't have any claim on the night club," Andre said, his voice tight.

"You're wrong," the unknown male replied.

"What do you expect to gain from this?" Nathaniel asked.

Reece peered into the gap between the hinges; the man's back facing him. The shape of the figure seemed familiar. *Who is he?*

"You can come in, Detective," the unknown male told him.

The PI stepped into the office.

When the figure turned around Reece felt his knees weaken.

Jacques.

Only he didn't sound or look quite the same. His hair short, his face shaved, his accent different, he didn't even resemble the Jacques they'd known. Vampires always adapted to their surroundings so which country had he fled to after he'd escaped Dracula?

"What are you doing here?" Reece asked. "Where have you been all these years?"

"I've been abroad. That is all you need to know for the moment." He motioned for the PI to stand with his brother and Nathaniel. "If you please?"

Reece crossed the room. "Why are you here?"

"I'm here to reclaim what is mine."

Andre gave his friend a sideward glance. "He wants to take ownership of the nightclub."

Reece frowned. "You want to come back to live in LA?"

"Why not? It has been far too long."

All of a sudden, it occurred to Reece where he'd seen him. The old LA zoo. "*You* were the one at the zoo." It was more an accusation.

"You are too clever for me, Detective. Yes, it was I."

"Are you controlling the reptilian creatures?"

Jacques gave the question some thought before answering. "Now wouldn't that be an interesting proposition? Alas, I am not."

"Do you know who is?"

"No."

"You always know when something like this happens," Andre told his brother.

"At the moment, little brother, I do not. But I plan to find out."

"To help us?" Reece folded his arms. He didn't think so.

"Perhaps we can come to some arrangement."

"So you're back to wreak havoc on us again?"

"No, I'm not. You are more than capable of dealing with the creatures yourself. If you want my help I will require something from you in return."

"Of course you do. Looks like nothing's changed. Did you warn them?"

"I did not. My dear detective that would be someone you know."

Reece's eyes widened. "What do you mean?"

"As Detective Donovan suggested, you have a mole." He'd been keeping track of Reece.

He shook his head. "Not possible. Everyone on my team is trustworthy."

Jacques' left eyebrow arched. "Are they indeed?" He wanted to rattle the PI, make him doubt those around him.

"How did you know what Grant told me?"

"I have my methods, as you should be aware by now." He gave Reece a smug smirk.

ഇ൭ര

On the way to Andre's apartment, after waiting for Jacques to leave the nightclub, the pair discussed the return of Andre's brother. "What do you think Nathaniel's going to do about the nightclub?" Reece asked.

"I hope he'll stand his ground and not give in to my brother."

"I can't see him giving in. Nathaniel has come a long way since he worked for him."

"When Jacques wants something he doesn't back down, you know that."

"Yeah, I do. I still can't see Nathaniel bending to his will. Did you get a chance to ask your brother where he's been?"

"He wouldn't tell me."

"Remember he wanted to usurp Dracula so he could rule the immortal world? I wonder if he's been in Romania all this time."

Andre shrugged. "Who knows? Maybe. Although, I think he must've gone into hiding to prevent being killed by the ones searching for him, like Eva."

"It's a possibility, I guess. It seems odd he's here now while we're chasing the reptiles." Reece eased the Mustang to a stop at the intersection, waiting for the light to turn green.

"It's too much of a coincidence." Andre folded his arms.

"You think he's lying?"

"I think he knows more than he's telling."

"Yeah, you're right. Dammit! Why did he have to come back?" Reece gave his friend a sideward sheepish glance. "Sorry, I know you've wondered what happened to him all those years ago…"

"No, I agree with you. Him being here makes our job even more difficult, especially if he plans to get involved, which he does."

"I hope he meant what he said about not returning to cause us more pain."

"Yes, me too."

The light changed.

Reece started across the intersection.

A fast-moving black van with a heavy-duty bull bar whipped across the connecting street and plowed into the Mustang on the driver's side, flipping the car onto its roof in the center of the cross roads, before speeding off.

Andre unclipped his seatbelt, crawled from the vehicle, making a dash for the driver's door. Getting down on hands and knees he assessed his friend. Blood poured down Reece's face. *He must've cracked his head on the steering wheel.* "Reece? Reece, can you hear me?"

No response.

He pressed his fingers to Reece's carotid artery.

No pulse.

People were rushing over to the vehicle now.

"Hey, buddy, I called 911," a guy said as he reached the car. "Do you need help getting your friend outta there?"

Andre ripped Reece's seatbelt from the frame and pulled him free of the crumpled convertible. He recognized the pungent smell wafting up from underneath the wreck. "Thanks, I've got him. You need to move away there's gas leaking under the car."

The guy shouted to everyone, "Get back, there's a gas leak."

Those close to the vehicle scurried away, shocked expressions on their faces.

The distant shrill sound of sirens screamed through the air.

Help was on its way.

Onlookers were now on the sidewalk snapping photos and taking videos with their cell phones. The accident would be all over social media in the next few minutes.

The moment the trio cleared the road an explosion rocked the street as the Mustang erupted into a ball of flames.

Andre started mouth to mouth and CPR with a force so fierce it could crack every bone in his friend's ribcage, trying to keep his heart beating. Reece appeared unresponsive.

CHAPTER TWENTY NINE

Reece came to on a bed in a windowed room in the Intensive Care Unit of Cedars Sinai Medical Center, hooked up to a drip and cardiac monitor, his left leg in plaster, a constant dull ache in his ribcage. Andre sat beside him.

"What... happened?" Reece asked, pushing the rubber oxygen mask down under his chin.

Andre stood up. "A black van ran the red light at the intersection."

"On purpose?"

He nodded. "It was too calculated, and they fled the scene."

"Far out." The PI raised his hand to finger the bandage around his head. "Ouch. The Mustang?"

"Totaled, I'm afraid." Andre gave his friend a pained look.

Reece let out a heavy sigh. "I loved that car. How am I going to replace her?"

"We'll figure it out at some point. Right now you need to focus on getting well."

His hazy gaze moved around the compact space. "Where's Tom?"

"He went to get a soda from the vending machine down the corridor."

"Oh, ok." He noticed the glass of water on the metal cabinet. "Can I have a drink?"

"Sure." Andre picked up the plastic glass with a bendable straw and held it for Reece to take a sip.

"Thanks." He eased back on his pillow. "What's the prognosis?"

"You have three fractured ribs and, of course, the broken leg. You also have a medium concussion and stitches to the wound on your forehead."

"So, in other words, I'm out of operation for a few weeks."

"I'm afraid so. I'm going to come stay with you while you're mending."

"You don't have to…"

"Don't even start with me. You stopped breathing. I thought you weren't coming back."

"I'll always come back."

Andre gave him a doubtful frown. "You can't make that kind of promise, Reece."

"Yeah, I *can*."

Tom came back into the room, saw his dad was conscious, rushed over to him, giving him a tight hug. "I'm so glad you're ok." A single tear slid down his right cheek and he swiped it away.

"Yeah, buddy, me too." He ruffled his son's hair.

"I'll go tell the doctor you're awake," Andre said, stepping out of the room.

"I thought…" Tom sniffed back the urge to cry.

"Hey, I'm here. It's ok." The pair hugged again, Tom leaning across his dad for a long time before standing.

"It could've been so much worse. What would I do if…"

"Hey, nothing's going to happen to me. I promise."

"It's a promise you can't keep, Dad. Look what happened tonight."

"I give you my word, as your dad, *nothing* will ever take me away from you."

Andre walked into the room with a familiar face beside him.

Reece's eyes widened. "Dennis."

"Hey, Reece, how're you doing? It's been a while." He picked up the patient chart. "Do you need anything for the pain?"

"Yeah, I do. My ribs are killing me."

"How's the leg feeling?"

"Ok, I guess. It's not hurting."

"Good." Dennis scribbled some notes onto the file. "I'll make sure someone comes in to top you up." He turned on his heel.

"Dennis," Reece called after him.

The doctor turned around. "Yes?"

"Can we talk later?"

Dennis's eyes flitted to Andre, to Tom, then back to the PI. "Sure. I'll stop by before I leave."

"Thanks, I'd appreciate it."

"No problem." Dennis stepped out of the room and crossed the corridor to the nurses' station.

Andre gave his friend a stern stare. "Reece."

"What?"

"What are you doing?"

"Nothing. Why?"

"Why do you want to talk to Dennis?" Andre folded his arms.

"I want to catch up… see how he's doing."

"I know you. Remember?"

"What's that supposed to mean?"

"You're planning to ask him to help Tyler, aren't you?"

"Why would I?"

"Oh, I don't know, maybe because you mentioned it earlier."

Reece raised defensive hands and grimaced when his fractured ribs sent an acute pain up his sternum. "Ok, yeah, I want to talk to him about it. Like I said, he already knows what we do. He's the perfect choice."

"What if he says no?"

"If he says no, I'll do my best to persuade him."

"You mean bulldoze him, don't you?"

Reece gave his friend a faux affronted look. "You think I would?"

"I *know* you would. It's been six years, almost seven, maybe you should think the idea through."

"Let me handle it, will you?"

"That's what I'm afraid of."

⚉

The second dose of morphine caused Reece to doze off and he started awake when he heard someone say his name. Opening his eyes, his groggy gaze moved around the room and landed on Dennis standing at the foot of the bed. "Hey, Dennis, thanks for coming back."

"I said I would." He pulled up a chair, sat down at the side of the bed. "So, what did you want to talk to me about?"

"How have you been? You're in the ICU now?"

"I've been good. Got married three years ago, have a baby on the way. Yes, I feel this is where I can do the most good." He waited a beat. "But you didn't ask me to stop by to chat about what I've been doing, did you?"

Reece gave him a sheepish look. "No, but I'm glad you're doing ok. And congratulations on the marriage and baby."

"Thanks. So what do you want?"

"I could use your medical assistance."

Dennis's right eyebrow arched. "Oh, how do you mean?"

"You saw my son, Tom, earlier?"

"Uh, your son?"

"It's a long story. His mom passed away, we were in a relationship, going to get married… she gave me custody."

"Oh, I'm sorry to hear that, Reece. He looks like a great kid."

"He is a great kid. He's also a werewolf."

Dennis's eyes widened.

"Another long story. His aunt is in LA, she has a son on dialysis…"

"He's a werewolf too?"

"Not yet. He will be when he turns sixteen. In the meantime, he needs help. His kidneys are failing and his mom is worried he won't last the next three weeks."

Dennis gave a heavy sigh. "I'd rather not get involved again."

"Look, he's a fifteen year old kid. You're a doctor who can help prolong his life until he turns. Once it happens he won't need dialysis. You'll be free to walk away."

Dennis gave Reece a dubious frown. "Will I?" He didn't think so. And what would he do about his estranged friendship with Andre? It would be an uncomfortable situation for the both of them. Something he could live without. "Can I think it over?"

"The kid has a couple of days before he'll need treatment again. Don't take too long."

CHAPTER THIRTY

Jade rushed up to Tom at his locker, her face flushed with concern. "Hey, I just heard about your dad. Is he ok?"

The look on her face caused Tom's heart to clench and he wanted to pull her into his arms, hold her close. "Uh, yeah, he's doing ok. He'll be coming home in the next couple days."

"That's good news. I'm so relieved for you." She smiled.

"Thanks. Yeah, me too." He finished stowing his backpack, picked up his books and closed the locker door. "Would it be ok if we postponed the tutoring for a while? I need to…"

She nodded. "Yes, of course. You need to be with your dad once he gets home."

"Thanks, I appreciate it. Yeah, it's going to take several weeks, maybe longer, so…"

Jade waved off the comment. "Oh, take all the time you need. We can catch up later."

"I promise I'll make it up to you with some extra tutoring once my dad's feeling better."

"That'd be great. I'll look forward to it."

The ping, ping, ping of the first bell echoed along the corridor.

"We'd better get going," Tom said.

"Ok, see you later?"

"Sure." He swallowed the nervous lump in his throat, remembering his dad's advice. "Want to sit together for lunch?"

"I'd like that. See you in the cafeteria."

"Yeah, see you there." He smiled.

Jade hurried along the hallway to her classroom.

Tom watched her leave, his heart pumping a little bit faster. She'd said yes.

₭⇒ℂℂ

Jade and her two closest friends, Ashleigh and Chloe, sat at a table near the double doors to the courtyard, Ashleigh studying her friend with a curious frown. *Who is Jade looking for?* It wasn't as though Jade had a crush on a guy, otherwise she would know. They talked about everything.

Ashleigh leaned into Jade. "Um, who are you looking for?"

Jade whipped her head around, the look of embarrassment on her face. "Nobody. Why?"

"Looks to me like you are. Is there a guy you like that you haven't told us about?"

"Don't be ridiculous. We tell each other everything."

"Answer the question." She stared into her friend's eyes. "You *do* like someone."

"Stop it," Chloe chastised. "She doesn't have to tell us, her two besties, everything." She gave Jade a disapproving frown. "Do you?"

"I…"

"Tom Daniels is on his way over here, Ashleigh warned."

Chloe's eyes moved in his direction. "He's kinda cute, but a bit of a creeper."

"He's not a creeper!" Jade defended.

Chloe shrugged. "Well, he's weird. He doesn't have any friends and stays to himself."

"So?"

Ashleigh folded her arms, her frown deepening. "You like *him*?"

"Did I say that?"

"Well you're defending him."

"Because you're both being mean."

"So why is he coming over here?"

"How should I know?"

Tom stepped up to the table. "Hi, Jade." His gaze moved to the other two girls. "Ladies."

"What can we do for you?" Ashleigh's intense stare met his.

Jade eyeballed him.

He frowned at her, not catching on. "I've been tutoring Jade and I wanted to find out when we're studying together again." He knew they weren't studying together right now because of his dad, but he had to say something.

Ashleigh's and Chloe's heads snapped toward her. "Yeah, Jade, when are you studying together again?" Ashleigh wanted to know.

Jade popped up off her chair. "Can we talk outside?"

"Uh, ok." Tom wasn't sure what was happening.

The pair stepped out into the courtyard and Jade found a table away from the windows.

"What's going on?" Tom asked, sitting across from her.

"I – I haven't had a chance to tell my girls we're friends. I've been meaning to…"

"Are you embarrassed to be seen with me?"

"No, not at all, it's just…"

Tom frowned into her eyes. "What happened in there wasn't cool."

"I know. I'm sorry. I *will* explain it to them, I promise." Her eyes darted around the courtyard before she reached across and squeezed his hand. "I – I like you, Tom." She gave him a demure smile, her cheeks flushing.

"I like you too, but I don't wanna be the joke."

"You're not. You won't be. I'll talk to them."

"Ok. So I guess we won't be having lunch together today."

"I'm so sorry. What about tomorrow?" Jade gave his hand another gentle squeeze. She liked the feel of their skin touching.

"Sure, tomorrow." He stood up, stuffed his hands into the pockets of his jacket, and turned to walk away.

"Tom."

"Yeah?" He turned around.

"I really do like you." Jade realized it felt good to say it out loud.

"Yeah, me too." Tom left Jade sitting at the outdoor table wondering how she was going to explain it to her friends.

CHAPTER THIRTY ONE

The following afternoon, Nathaniel and Andre picked Reece up from the hospital and drove him back to Falcon Lair. Because he'd been doing better than expected, the doctor assigned to his case released him a day early on the condition that he take it easy and not try to overdo it. Reece was grateful. It felt good to be home… to be alive. All he wanted now was to get his recovery underway so he could assist his team with locating the reptilian creatures. The accident had put a serious crimp in their plans to rid the city of the venom-spitting monsters, although him being injured was a far better deal than the alternative.

In the meantime, Andre would take the lead while Reece recuperated. Who tried to kill them? Did it have something to do with the creatures or Jacques? Even though the vampire said he had no intention of making their lives difficult, Reece knew he couldn't be trusted, after everything he'd done to them in the past.

Andre helped his friend settle in before heading downstairs to organize some lunch for him.

Nathaniel came into the kitchen. "I will head back to the club. If you need anything call me."

"I appreciate you picking us up from the hospital." Andre walked out with him to his car.

"It is my pleasure." He opened the driver's door. "I'm sending my team out to search for the location of the creatures while you are preoccupied with Reece's recovery."

Andre nodded. "Thank you. Let me know if you find anything."

"Of course." Nathaniel climbed into the black wagon and drove out of the circular driveway, passing Ed's green sedan as he left.

As Andre headed back into the house, Ed pulled up out front. "Hey, Andre, Reece here?"

"He is." Andre walked over to the car and opened the passenger door for Sarah. "He'll be happy to see you."

Lozano opened the back passenger door. "Is it ok for all of us to visit?"

"I don't think it'll hurt."

The trio followed Andre upstairs. "I'm making some lunch for Reece but you can go on in." He headed back along the hallway.

"Thanks," Ed said, knocking on the door.

"Come in."

The door opened.

"Hey, it's good to see you guys." Reece's face lit up. "Grab a seat."

Ed sat on the foot of the bed while Sarah and Lozano pulled up a couple of chairs.

"How're you feeling?" the chief asked.

"Better, now I'm home. There's no way you can recuperate in a hospital."

"Yeah, ain't that the truth."

"Did the doctor say how long before you'll be back to your old self?" Lozano asked.

"About eight to ten weeks." Reece sighed.

"It'll go by fast."

"I hope so because I'm not a good patient."

"You need to focus on getting better," Sarah said. "Take it easy, do what you've been asked."

"Yes ma'am." Reece saluted her.

"I mean it. You could've died. You did die for a short time. This is serious."

"And I appreciate your concern."

She patted his arm.

"Can you get the traffic cam footage from the night of the accident?" Reece asked Ed.

"Already done. We're looking for the van... don't think we'll have much luck, though. Stolen license plates."

"Shit."

"Yeah." Ed rubbed his hand across his stubbled chin. "Think it was Jacques?"

"It's definitely something he'd do." Reece knew he couldn't believe anything Jacques said.

"Yeah, he can't be trusted. You know it, I know it. We all know it." Ed folded his arms across his podgy belly.

"It could've been the reptilian creatures. We've been getting too close."

"Or it could be unrelated," Sarah told him.

Reece's frowning gaze moved to her. "What makes you think so?"

"The rift has fractured and there has been an influx of supernatural creatures coming through."

Ed gave Sarah a stern stare. "You weren't supposed to tell him that now."

"He has a right to know."

"Maybe, but give the guy a chance to heal first." His gaze returned to the PI. "We're on top of it. You don't have to worry."

"When did this happen?" Reece's eyes moved around the three faces.

"About a week ago," Sarah said.

"Frig me."

"Daniels, we've got this. You work on getting better." Ed poked the air with his stubby index finger. "Got it?"

Reece raised defensive hands. "Ok, geez."

"Good. Make sure you do."

∞

Later in the evening, a sharp knock echoed into the entry hall and Andre came downstairs to answer it. He'd made up the spare room next to Reece's so he'd be able to hear him if he needed anything during the night. His instincts told him who was on the other side of the door and he swung it open. "Why are you here?"

Avalynn stepped onto the welcome mat. "I came to offer my help."

"Help? How?"

"Can I see Reece?" She frowned into his suspicious eyes.

"It's late. You could've come earlier in the day."

"I had other things to do."

"Perhaps you can come back tomorrow."

Avalynn's gaze darkened. "Ok. If you don't want a quick recovery for your friend it's up to you." She turned on her heel and crossed the driveway to her motorcycle.

"Wait." Andre followed her out. "What do you mean?"

"As I've mentioned before, I have certain powers. One ability is to remove illness, injury and the like…"

"You're a healer?"

"Among other things."

"I'm sorry for being rude. It's…"

"Yes, I'm aware. Reece doesn't trust me. He's made his feelings perfectly clear."

"Thank you for the offer to help him."

"May I come in now?"

"Of course." Andre motioned for Avalynn to step into the house, followed her in and closed the door. "He's up here."

Avalynn followed Andre up the carpeted staircase and along the hallway to Reece's room. Andre knocked. "Reece, you awake?"

"Yeah, come in."

Andre opened the door and ushered the witch inside.

"What's she doing here?"

"Avalynn came to help you. She's a healer."

Reece's serious gaze met hers. "Why do you want to help me after I said I didn't trust you?"

"Because you need to be on your feet, if you're lying here for weeks those creatures will kill more innocent people."

"Andre's handling things while I'm out of action."

Her gaze moved to Reece's friend then back to him. "No offense, but he isn't tough enough for what needs to be done."

Andre didn't like hearing it. He gave Avalynn a dark stare. "I'll leave you two to talk." He stepped into the hallway and closed the door.

"You didn't have to say Andre couldn't handle the situation," Reece told her. "He's more than capable of heading the team."

"I'm not going to sugar coat things. He doesn't have what it takes to get the job done, despite what you may think."

Reece shook his head. She was some piece of work. "So what happens now?"

CHAPTER THIRTY TWO

The process of removing Reece's injuries had been a painful one for them both. Avalynn's ability to draw out the damage sustained in the accident was physically demanding and left her drained of energy, which would take hours to regenerate. As she sat slumped in the armchair across the room, her concerned gaze on the PI, she hoped he would wake up soon.

Andre paced the floor at the foot of his friend's bed. "Why is it taking so long?"

Avalynn crossed the room. "I'm not sure. Perhaps he wasn't as recovered as the doctor had thought. That would delay the healing process."

"Will all of his injuries be gone?"

"Yes. He should be good as new when he wakes up."

Andre went into the bathroom, opened the top drawer below the hand basin, picked up the pair of scissors and came back into the room. "I'll remove the plaster cast while he's still out so you can check his leg to make sure."

Avalynn gave Andre a stern frown. "I won't need to. It will be healed."

Andre commenced slicing a trail up the thick plaster. When he reached Reece's knee the PI started to stir. "Let's get this off before he comes to."

Andre removed the plaster cast, sliding it underneath the bed until later. "Hey, you're awake."

Reece's blurred gaze roamed the room. "Uh, yeah. What happened?"

"Sometimes the process takes its toll on the recipient's body. You may not have been as recovered as the doctor thought you were. Anyway, it doesn't matter now, you're back."

The PI glanced down at his leg. "So it worked?"

"Of course it did." Avalynn folded her arms.

"Thank you." Reece eased his body into a sitting position. So far so good. He swung his legs over the side of the bed, taking a moment before attempting to stand up.

"Here, let me help you." Andre came around the bed.

Reece raised his hand. "No, it's ok. I can do it." He swallowed the wad of nerves in his throat and pushed himself up off the bed, his heart rate kicking up a couple of anxious notches.

"See. All better." Avalynn crossed the room. "Let me know if you need anything else." She left, leaving the door open.

"Do you want to take a couple of steps?" Andre remained beside him.

"Ok." Reece took a tentative step forward, then another. "I'm better."

"No aches or pains anywhere else? How about the ribs?"

Reece shook his head. "Nope, they're good."

"Great. Just don't overdo it."

"I feel good as new."

Andre nodded. "Ok. Still, don't overdo it."

The pair heard the motorcycle leave, the sound of gravel spraying along the drive behind it.

"Maybe I was wrong about her," Reece said, climbing back into bed.

"Yeah, maybe." Andre headed for the door. "Get some sleep. Goodnight."

"You too. Goodnight."

CR

When Tom came into the kitchen the next morning, Reece and Andre were sitting at the center counter eating breakfast. Tom's stunned gaze moved from his uncle to his dad. "What's going on?"

"Morning, buddy, how'd you sleep?" Reece asked his son.

"Never mind about that. How are you better?" Tom came around the counter, gave his dad a tight man hug, tears glistening in his eyes.

"Avalynn came by last night and healed me."

"She did?" Tom climbed onto a tall stool.

"Yes, she's not only a witch but a healer as well," Andre told him.

"Wow! That's pretty cool."

"Yeah." Reece took a sip of his coffee. "Want some breakfast? There's still some bacon and eggs in the pan."

Tom nodded. "Yeah, I think I do." He walked over to the stove, picked up a plate, scooped scrambled eggs and bacon onto it. "I'm so glad you're better, Dad."

"Yeah, me too. I couldn't imagine lying around for weeks."

"So what's on the agenda for today?" Andre asked.

"You said Nathaniel's team was out searching for the creatures. I think we'll pay him a visit to see if he's found anything new."

"He said he'd get back to me when he did."

"Doesn't matter. We need to get on top of this… fast."

"Sure, ok."

"Do you need me to do anything?" Tom asked.

"Not right now, buddy, just go to school, focus on your studies. When I need your help I'll let you know."

"Ok." Tom knew his dad was shielding him again. He wished he wouldn't because he could take care of himself.

"So how's the Jade situation panning out?"

Tom gave Andre an awkward sideward glance before answering. He didn't want too many people to know in case it jinxed it. "She needs some time to tell her friends."

"Oh, why?" Reece wanted to know.

"Because they think I'm weird."

"Does Jade feel the same way?" Reece set his knife and fork down on his plate, leaned back and folded his arms.

"Of course not, Dad."

"If she cares about you she won't care what her friends think."

"She doesn't. It's peer pressure, you know?"

"Your dad's right, Tom."

"Yeah, I know." He sighed. "I'll talk to her about it today."

"Good idea. If you both like each other nothing should stand in the way." Reece took his plate over to the sink.

"Yeah, you're right." Tom picked up his backpack. "I'm heading out now. See you tonight."

"Have a good day." Reece glanced over his shoulder to watch his son leave.

"Girl troubles. I remember those days. And they weren't too long ago." Andre brought Tom's plate over to the sink, Beth popping into his head.

"Yeah, me too."

ℭℜ

Avalynn's cherry red motorcycle screeched to a stop on the gravel drive as Reece and Andre stepped out into the alcove. Tugging the black helmet off her head and shaking out her long, flaming red waves, she climbed off the bike and walked over to the pair. "Good morning, looks like you're good as new." She appraised his tall frame with her lilac colored eyes, smiling. He was built for a man of his age. "Maybe even better."

"Yeah, I am. Thanks again for what you did."

"You're welcome, but it's not the reason I'm here."

"I figured as much."

"I have a location on the creatures. We need to move now."

"Where are they?" Reece asked.

"Still in Santa Monica in a more remote location on the cliffs."

"Easy to get to?"

"Yes. We'll need to park out of sight to remain obscure from the upstair windows of the building. It has another high security fence around it but we can get in via a staved metal gate near the triple garage."

"You're sure?"

"Yes. It's not going to be a problem."

"Ok. I'll organize my team and we'll head out."

"Good, the sooner the better."

Reece conferenced everyone into the call. "I want you to gear up and meet me here at my place in an hour."

"Are you sure about the location this time?" Todd asked.

Reece gave Avalynn a questioning stare.

She nodded. "Yes, I'm sure. Someone tipped them off at the previous location which, by the way, was also correct."

"Let's hope it doesn't happen again."

"Yeah. Let's."

"Ok, see you at yours in an hour," Ed said, ringing off. Sarah and Lozano were already with him. They'd head to the office to collect their protective gear then drive straight over to Reece's place.

"Andre, ask Nathaniel to come along and bring his team with him. We'll need more assistance on this one. We can't let any of the creatures escape this time."

"I'm on it." Andre tugged his cell from the pocket of his jeans, walking away from the pair.

"How did you get the information about where the creatures are?" Reece asked.

"I received another email, so I thought I'd check it out before coming here. They're there."

Had Jacques sent Avalynn the email? If not, someone was playing a dangerous game with them.

Reece nodded. "Ok. Good."

Andre joined the pair. "Nathaniel's on his way."

The trio stepped back into the house to wait, heading for the kitchen.

"I think I'll keep the location under wraps until we're there," Reece said.

Avalynn's left eyebrow arched. "Oh, why?"

"Jacques told me we have a mole."

"And you believe him? From what I've heard about Jacques Delacroix he can't be trusted."

"That's true, although he has no reason to lie."

"Unless he's behind it." Avalynn folded her arms.

"She's right, Reece," Andre told him. "We don't know what his reason is for being back in LA. He could be involved. You know he likes to play games with us. We can't trust him." Andre frowned at Reece wondering why he felt the need to defend his brother after being so sure Jacques had something to do with the deaths. "You, of all people, should be more than aware. How many times has he attempted to kill us... to kill you?"

"You're right. I know."

"None of us should let our guard down where my brother is concerned. He's a lying manipulator." As much as Andre wanted to believe Jacques, he couldn't. Not yet. Maybe not ever.

CHAPTER THIRTY THREE

A strong ocean breeze whipped up stirring the leaves and debris on the clifftop as the group made their way to the plateau, bands of hazy yellow sunlight filtering through charcoal clouds – signaling a possible approaching storm. The expensive home was well secured, and as Reece ran his gaze over the fenced property he spotted the gate Avalynn had mentioned. He turned to look at her. "Are you sure you can get us into the grounds?"

"The gate will be a piece of cake." She strutted over to the blue-gray fence line. Everyone followed.

No one appeared to be moving about inside. Being the only house on this section of the cliffs, the group could remain ambiguous to other homes set into the distance.

When the teams came upon the boundary of the extensive estate, Reece grabbed Avalynn by the arm to stop her. "Let's get this done quickly."

"That's the plan." She eased her arm out of his grasp and walked over to the black metal gate. Raising her hands, she chanted a short incantation. The gate popped open. Glancing at the PI, she said, "See, what did I tell you?"

Reece turned to the group. "All right. Listen up. We need to get inside, take down the creatures, and get out. You all know what you have to do. Thanks to Avalynn for acquiring a floor plan." His gaze moved to the witch, their eyes met.

The ten moved with caution through the manicured grounds to the locations they would enter the building from and waited for Reece's order.

Inside, they split up, swarming the house like ants.

Reece made his way up the staircase with caution followed by Andre, Todd and Sarah. Nathaniel moved through the living area to other bedrooms on ground level, Ed, Lozano and two of the vampire's team close behind.

Avalynn slipped out of sight.

Once again, as at the previous property, Reece used baseball type hand signals to let his team know what to do. His group followed him down the hallway.

Avalynn stepped outside into the backyard and stood in front of the pool. Looking up, she held the talisman in front of her repeating the incantation she'd used on the reptile creature at the hotel. She hoped it would offer the teams inside some protection. She would not be responsible for more deaths.

Reece motioned for his team to take their positions outside the bedroom doors along the hall. When he gave the signal, they would burst into each room and kill the creatures before they could retaliate. He raised his fisted hand, his fingers rising one by one. One. Two. Three. At the same moment giving the order for Nathaniel and his team downstairs to move in.

The reptiles were prepared. Again, the creatures knew they were coming.

Two spat venom across the room at Reece, the acidic substance hissing on his protective suit. The PI patted at the smoky residue with a gloved hand before it ate through the fabric to his skin.

More venom sprayed across the room.

Andre hurtled himself through the doorway, knocking his friend to the ground. A near miss.

Sarah stormed into the room firing off tranquilizer darts. It would knock the creatures out until they could dispatch them and dispose of the bodies. A dart plunged into one with a dull thunk and it sank to the floor, while the other creature continued to spray venom at them.

She fired again.

The creature's body swerved out of the way of the torpedoing projectile.

Reece jumped to his feet, firing silver bullets at the snakelike creature. Its swift evasive movements left several powdery bullet holes in the wall behind it.

The reptilian creature continued to dart around the room.

Each of Reece's team fired continuous rounds. They couldn't let it escape. Not this time.

Nathaniel, Ed, Lozano, and the two members of the vampire's team secured the lower floor, killing the creatures quickly, before racing up the stairs to assist Reece.

The black vampire thrust himself across the room, reached out to grab the reptile. It sprang at the window, crashing through the pane of glass, and landed on the patio roof.

Avalynn continued to chant the incantation, holding the talisman toward the creature. The magick of the artifact would weaken the reptile, making it easy to apprehend.

Nathaniel hurled his large frame through the shattered glass, gripped the reptile by the throat and squeezed, cutting off its ability to spit more venom. Sliding a large switchblade knife from the pocket of his black pants, he sliced the head clean off the creature and threw the writhing body onto the tiles. The head toppled over the edge of the eaves, landing at Avalynn's feet. "It is done," Nathaniel said.

Avalynn gave the black vampire a severe glare and kicked the reptile head into the swimming pool with the pointed toe of her leather boot before dashing under the patio roof, pocketing the talisman as she took cover from the heavy drops of rain tumbling from the overcast sky.

Reece slid open the glass door and stepped out beside her. "What did you have in your hand?" he asked.

Avalynn had hoped he hadn't seen it. She sighed, pushed her hand into the pocket of her bike jacket and tugged out the talisman. "It's an ancient artifact to immobilize those creatures, among other things. I used it to help you."

"You could've told me about it. Why keep it a secret?"

"It is greatly sought after. If anyone knew it was in my possession my life would be in danger."

Reece searched her lilac eyes for deception but couldn't find any. "Ok. Fair enough."

Everyone headed back to the gate. Once inside the van, the PI would call his cleaning crew who would come out to the property to do a complete clean and repair on the place to conceal any evidence of an altercation.

Heading out of the manicured grounds a heavy rumble grew in intensity behind them. The group stopped outside the fence line and turned around.

The house exploded in a ball of flames.

The force of the blast hurtled everyone through the air along with concrete, glass and other building debris. Reece came to first, the sound of fast approaching sirens in the distance. He staggered to his feet, roaming the members of his team to see who was alive and who might be dead.

Nathaniel and Andre were the next to get up, followed by the two members of Nathaniel's team.

Reece raced across to Ed and Sarah, his ex-boss regaining consciousness along with Todd lying nearby. Sarah remained unconscious. He and Todd helped Ed off the ground. "Are you ok, Chief?"

"Uh, yeah… yeah, I think so." His gaze moved to Sarah lying on the rocky surface. He bent down, pressing two fingers against her throat feeling for a pulse. "Thank God, she's alive."

Nathaniel came across the rocks. "I will carry her back to the vehicle." He cradled Sarah in his arms and headed for the road. She roused as they reached the van.

Reece rushed over to Avalynn. "Are you ok?"

She rolled over, blood trickling down the left side of her face from a deep gash on her forehead. "The bomb was meant for us, wasn't it?"

"Yeah, that would be my guess." Reece gripped her hand and pulled her onto her feet. "Let's get out of here before the emergency services arrive. We don't want to be caught so close to the crime scene dressed like this. It'd be a dead giveaway." He pointed to her head. "We need to clean that up." He knew the police were the least of his concerns. Once again, someone had tried to kill him… *and* his team.

CHAPTER THIRTY FOUR

The musical ding dong of the doorbell echoed into the entry hall and when Reece opened the front door Charlene was standing in the alcove. "Hello. What can I do for you?" he asked, surprised to see her.

She looked at him with concern etched on her face. "I heard you were in the hospital… that you'd been involved in a serious car accident." Her gaze moved up his body from his feet to his head. "How… how are you standing here?"

"It's a long story. Do you want to come in?" As she stepped inside, he leaned out of the doorway and ran his searching gaze around the courtyard. "Where's Tyler?"

"He's resting back at the hotel."

"Oh, ok. Do you mind sitting in the kitchen?" Reece closed the front door.

"No, not at all." She gave him a thin smile.

He ushered her into the large workspace, motioning to a tall stool. "Please, have a seat."

"Thanks." She climbed onto the round wooden circle and set her purse down on the counter.

Reece sat opposite.

"I wanted to thank you for sending Dennis to us. He's been wonderful."

Reece's right eyebrow arched. He'd hoped the doctor's conscience would get the better of him. "Well, I'm happy he could help."

"Oh, he has. Tyler's feeling so much better."

"I'm glad." Reece eyed her for a moment, his heart stuttering in his chest. She reminded him so much of Charlotte. "Want some coffee?"

"Yes, thanks."

Reece popped a coffee pod into the machine and slid a mug under the nozzle. Once the two mugs were filled, he brought them over to the counter, setting one down in front of Charlene before taking his seat again. "I wanted to talk to you about something."

Charlene returned her mug to the counter after taking a cautious sip. "Oh, what?"

"I think you should come stay with us for a while, so Tom can talk Tyler through the transition process."

Charlene's eyes widened. "You want us to stay here with you?"

Reece shrugged. "It seems like the logical solution, given the circumstances. And there's more than enough room."

She didn't answer for a moment, allowing the scenario to permeate her mind. Could it work? They were in desperate need of help. She had no idea what to do with regard to her son turning into a werewolf. And he and Tom would have time to get to know each other. "When did you have in mind?"

"The sooner the better."

"I'd like to discuss it with Tyler first, if that's ok?"

"Of course. Do what you gotta do."

"I'm grateful for the offer…"

Reece waved the comment off. "It's fine. If you decide not to, it's up to you."

"Thank you." She rested a grateful hand on his. "I appreciate you wanting to help us."

"It's necessary." He slid his hand out from under hers. "The first time is pretty rough. I have a cage in the basement…"

A horrified grimace crossed Charlene's face. "Tyler would have to be caged?"

"Yeah. If he isn't he'll kill anyone in his path, including you. He'll be hungry for human flesh and won't have any control over the urge to rip someone to shreds. It takes a while for the creature to gain control of its senses. The first time it's a ravenous wolf needing to feed. But it doesn't take long for a Lycanthrope to gain self-control and live normally. Tom's learned to keep his impulses in check… Tyler will too."

Charlene leaned back on the stool and blew out a noisy breath. "Unbelievable."

"Sorry to be so blunt. There's no easy way to explain it."

"Oh, I – I understand." A tear slipped down her right cheek. She brushed it away. Her baby would become a monster. She shook the thought from her mind. They'd get through it… they didn't have a choice. Damn Dan for hiding the truth. How could he have done this to her? She knew she had to accept some of the blame, knowing she should never have gotten involved with her sister's husband. *Karma always gets you one way or the other.*

Reece felt the sudden urge to move around the counter, take her in his arms, but Charlene wasn't Charlotte. He needed to remember that.

She wanted to change the topic of conversation. Her heart was heavy and she felt like bursting into tears. She swallowed the painful lump in her throat. "You were going to tell me how you're not lying in a hospital bed?" She took another sip of the black brew.

"Oh, yeah, ok. A witch with the ability to heal helped me."

Charlene's eyebrows rose. "What?"

"There's a lot you don't know about the supernatural world we live in."

"I can see that."

"She came here from New Orleans… Avalynn Cross… do you know her?"

Charlene shook her head. "No, I can guarantee I don't know anyone like her." Her face scrunched into a dubious frown. "A witch, you say?"

"Yeah."

"New Orleans is a big city."

"It's a place rife with superstition. Most people who live there know something about the supernatural element."

She shook her head again. "Not me. I keep my nose out of that kind of stuff."

"You do?" Why didn't he believe her?

"Yes." Her gaze met his. "You don't believe me, do you?"

"Not what I said."

"You didn't have to. I can see it on your face."

"See what on my face?"

"The look of disbelief."

"You both come from the same neighborhood."

She frowned. "You've been checking up on me?"

"I investigate anyone who comes into our lives to ensure our safety. I'm a PI, it's what I do."

Charlene didn't know how to feel about that. She climbed off the stool, slid her purse onto her shoulder. "Thanks for the coffee. I'll be in touch about the living arrangements once I've discussed it with Tyler."

"Sure." Reece walked her to the front door. "Look, don't take offense to me investigating you. You're not the only one, like I said."

"I guess you have to be cautious in your line of work."

"I do. It's imperative." He opened the door, waited a beat. "I'll hear from you?"

"You will." She stepped into the alcove and headed for the gate, her car parked on the street.

CHAPTER THIRTY FIVE

Tom stowed his books in his locker, clicked the door shut, and zig-zagged his way through other students along the corridor, heading for the street. The weekend was almost here and he always felt free once he got outside the confines of the school. He hurried down the front steps to the sidewalk. Jade spotted him leaving and followed him out. "Tom, hey, Tom. Tom."

Oblivious to her calls, Tom continued walking. On the third call he turned around. "Oh, hey, I didn't hear you." He smiled.

"Yeah, I thought as much. That eager to get out of here, huh?" Jade's left eyebrow arched.

"I… uh… just want to get home."

"I wanted to ask how your dad's doing. Is he recovering ok?"

Tom's mind recalled the scene in their kitchen this morning. "Uh, yeah, he's doing much better. Thanks for asking."

"I've been thinking about him." She smiled.

"I appreciate your concern. Thanks."

"Are you riding the bus today? Seeing as it's the quickest way home." She pointed across the busy main road.

"Nah, I think I'll walk. At least for a few blocks. I feel like I need the air."

"Mind if I tag along?"

"No, not at all." The pair began their walk.

Once at the boundary of the high school fence, three guys stepped out of the gateway.

"Well, well, well, look what we have here." The tall, dark haired, muscled jock teased.

"Nicholas, what are you doing?" Jade gave her ex a dark stare.

"I'm just saying how cute you two look together." He turned to the two guys standing behind him. "Don't they look cute to you?"

Both nodded and guffawed.

Nicholas turned back to face Jade and Tom. "See, what did I tell you?"

"Why are you doing this?" Jade folded her arms with a huff.

Nicholas shrugged. "Doing what?"

"You're being a bully right now."

"Am I? I thought I was complimenting you. It isn't a crime, you know." His gaze moved to Tom. "Is it, Daniels?"

"All depends."

Nicholas's eyebrows rose in a faux expression of interest. "Oh, on what exactly?"

"Whether you're doing it to be nice or to be a dick."

The jock changed the subject. "I heard you're tutoring Jade."

"Not that it's any of your business, but yeah."

"And are these *tutoring sessions* at her house or yours?" He made quotation marks in the air when he said 'tutoring sessions'. His friends chuckled behind him.

Jade stepped between the two testosterone-hyped teen boys, facing Nicholas. "Can you please stop?"

"Stop what?"

"Just get out of here and leave us alone," Jade told him.

Nicholas's serious gaze moved from her to Tom. "Watch your back, weirdo."

"Or what?" He needed to keep control of his Lycan impulses otherwise Jade would see the real him.

Nicholas dropped his bag on the sidewalk and bounced up to Tom, pushing Jade out of the way as he came almost nose to nose with him. "Or you'll find out."

Tom did his best not to allow his wolf to emerge. He stepped closer to the jock and as he did his wolf eyes glowed honey yellow for a nanosecond.

Nicholas stepped back, the smug, arrogant expression on his face transforming into shock. The guys behind him hadn't seen Tom's eyes change color, but *he* definitely got the message. A wet patch of urine spread across the crotch of Nicholas's gray jeans, traveling down the inner thigh seams.

"Oh, man, what did you do, Daniels?" One of Nicholas's friends said with a chuckle.

Nicholas's head whipped around and he glowered at his friend. "Shut the hell up."

The second friend raised his hand to his mouth to stifle a laugh.

Nicholas snatched up his bag, pushed through his friends, wrapping his jacket around his waist and hurried along the sidewalk, his friends following him.

Jade stepped around Tom, staring up at him. "What did you do?"

"Nothing." He shrugged. "I can't help it if the guy's a pussy."

She remained in place, arms folded. "Why would he embarrass himself if you didn't do something to provoke it?"

Tom raised defensive hands. "You were here. Did you see me do anything?"

Jade frowned. "Well, no…"

"Like I said."

The pair started along the sidewalk again.

After a minute or two, Jade grabbed Tom by the arm to pull him up. She studied his eyes with a frown.

"What are you doing?" Tom asked.

"I'm not sure." Her frown deepened.

"Will you cut it out, kids are gawking at us?"

"I'm checking to make sure you're not…"

"What?"

She shrugged. "I don't know… a vampire or something."

Tom chuckled. He needed to steer her away from where the conversation was heading. "A what?"

"You know, like Edward Cullen in Twilight."

He shook his head. "Who? Sorry, I don't know that show."

"It's a huge book and movie franchise."

"Oh, ok. Still don't know it."

"You've never watched the Twilight Saga?"

"Nope. Why?"

"Because it's awesome."

"Is it a love story?"

"Yes. A beautiful love story."

"Oh, now I know why I haven't seen it."

Her eyes widened. "You don't believe in love?"

"Yeah, of course I do." He sighed. "What's so special about Twilight?"

"It's the story of Bella Swann, who moves to a new state to live with her dad. When she starts school there she sees Edward Cullen and immediately falls for him, even before she knows him." She sighs and a dreamy expression crosses her pretty face. "Love at first sight."

Tom frowned at her and waved his hand in front of her eyes. "Jade?"

Jade came out of her reverie. "Oh, yeah, where was I? Oh, ok. So her new friends warn her off, telling her he's out of any of their league, but she doesn't believe it. Anyhoo, he turns out to be a vampire and she figures it out before he has the chance to tell her himself. And she doesn't care... she loves him anyway.

"Oh, by the way, her best friend, Jacob Black, who's secretly in love with her, turns out to be a werewolf. He belongs to the Quileute tribe of Native Americans and on their sixteenth birthdays they turn into these huge, furry, gorgeous wolves... protectors of the human race." She gave a wistful sigh. "Isn't that awesome?"

"If you say so."

"Come on, Tom, it's romantic."

He shrugged. "Maybe we could watch it together some time?" He realized Jade might be the perfect girl for him. Being into fictional vampires and werewolves maybe she'd be into him too.

A smile spread across her face. "I'd like that."

CHAPTER THIRTY SIX

Grant Donovan pulled open the door and stepped into the Coffee Bean & Tea Leaf cafe, inhaling the pungent, nutty aroma of freshly brewed coffee as his eyes roamed the patrons sitting at tables in search of Reece. When he spotted the PI he crossed the store, slid out a chair and sat down. "You wanted to see me?"

Reece set his mug down on the circular wood-grain table. "Yeah, thanks for coming. Can I get you anything?"

"No, thanks, I don't have a lot of time. You have news about the creatures?"

The PI nodded. "We think we've eliminated them."

The detective's right eyebrow arched. "Are you sure?"

"I'd like to say yes, but right now I can't be sure of anything where they're concerned. We believe the property they were leasing was the only hideout they occupied but we'll keep track. My thoughts are someone has to be controlling them. If it is the case there could be more out there."

"Ok. So where does that leave those of us working on the current investigation?"

"Like I said, we'll monitor the situation to make sure there are no more deaths and I'll keep you informed. We're still searching for the owner of the apartment building downtown. Andre's looking into recent real estate purchases to get a name and location."

Grant folded his arms. "If there is someone controlling those things, there's bound to be more, right?"

"I'm hoping there isn't. All we can do is follow up on anything suspicious."

The detective sighed. "Doesn't instill a lot of confidence in me right now."

"It's the best I can do. You need to keep on top of this too, also any other unusual deaths in the city. There are more creatures out there than any one of us knows about."

"Didn't your priest friend close the rift years ago?"

"She did but it's fracturing again and otherworldly inhabitants are making their way back into our world."

"Frig me!" Grant ran his hand over his face. "So where does that leave us?"

"I've got two teams working on it as we speak. I'm hoping we can get the situation under control soon."

The detective gave him a dubious frown. "I sure hope so. As if these deaths aren't enough, now we have to worry about new supernatural killers in our city."

"Yeah, LA appears to be the epicenter for this kind of activity."

The pair stood up.

"Well thanks for keeping me in the loop," Grant said.

"No problem. If I find out anything new I'll be in touch."

Grant extended his hand. "I appreciate it."

Reece shook it. "We need to work together on this."

"Yeah, we do." He walked over to the door.

"Grant." Reece followed him out onto the sidewalk.

"What?"

"Keep your eyes open and be careful."

The detective swallowed hard. "You think I'm a target?"

"Once they know you, you are."

He gave a heavy sigh. "Good to know."

"It goes with the territory, I'm afraid."

"Thanks for the heads up."

Reece stood for a moment, watching the detective disappear down a nearby alley, then crossed the street and climbed into the Double D Investigations van. He missed his Mustang. Once inside, he started the engine then called Andre on Bluetooth. "How's the search going? Find anything?"

"Not yet. I'm of the belief we got them all."

"I wish it were that easy."

"Maybe it is. There hasn't been any recent activity."

"It doesn't mean there won't be. We need to keep alert." Reece pulled the van out into the traffic. "I'm heading back to the office. Are you there?"

"No, I'm on my way to see Nathaniel."

"Ok. I'll see you later." He rang off.

Traveling along Sunset Boulevard, Reece spotted Tom and a girl he suspected was Jade walking on the sidewalk. He hadn't met her yet because the night she was meant to come to the house she couldn't make it. He pulled into the curb a couple car spaces along and wound down the passenger window. "Hey, Tom, want a lift?"

Tom balked. How would he explain to Jade that his dad recovered virtually overnight? He leaned in the window so she wouldn't hear him. "Dad, what are you doing here?" he whispered.

"I'm on my way back to the office."

Tom glanced over his shoulder, making sure Jade couldn't hear their conversation. "That's Jade. She's been asking about you."

"Oh, ok. Tell her I'm someone that works with your dad."

"I can't lie to her."

Reece gave his son a serious stare. "It's better than the alternative, don't you think?"

Tom nodded. "I guess so."

"See you at home later. Unless you want the lift?"

"No, thanks. We're good."

"Ok. Be safe." He lowered his voice. "Love you."

"Dad!" Tom whispered, glancing over his shoulder then back to his dad. "Ditto."

Reece winked at him, wound the window up, and pulled back into the traffic.

"Who's that?" Jade asked, watching the van driving away.

"A guy that works for my dad. He asked if we wanted a ride."

"I'm glad you said no because I'm enjoying the walk. With you, I mean." She smiled.

"Yeah, me too."

CHAPTER THIRTY SEVEN

Charlene and Tyler had settled into the mansion without any issues, Tyler and Tom were getting on like a house on fire, and Reece felt confident it had been the right decision for all concerned. With Tyler's sixteenth birthday only days away, his health in a much better place than a couple of weeks ago, the PI knew the transition would be better than he'd first anticipated. Tyler acknowledged everything Tom and Reece discussed with him, and looked forward to the change. He'd been sick for so long, he was ready to embrace what would become his new found freedom from illness.

Charlene came into the kitchen to find Reece sitting at the counter working on his laptop. "Hey, is it ok if I sit with you for a while? The boys are up in the attic hanging out and I don't have anything to do right now."

"Sure." Reece motioned to the stool opposite him. "Want some coffee?"

"Thanks." She climbed onto the stool.

"There you go." Reece slid the mug across to her and took his seat again.

Charlene gave him a sheepish glance and picked up the steaming brew, taking a cautious sip. "I want to talk to you about something."

Reece's gaze moved from the computer screen to her. "Oh, what?"

She cleared her throat, set her mug down. "I – I have something to tell you and I don't want it to cause problems between us… seeing as we're all living under the same roof now."

Reece frowned. "Go on."

"I haven't been as forthcoming as I could've been."

"How so?" Reece snapped the lid of his laptop shut and continued to frown into her eyes.

"Well... I – I lied to you..."

"About what?" Reece's heartrate kicked up a couple of notches. He'd allowed this woman and her son to move into his home and now she wanted to make a confession?

"When you asked me if I knew Avalynn Cross and I said no it wasn't entirely true."

"Do you want to explain?"

"We're not friends or anything. I found her by accident one day and we got to talking. I told her about Tyler... she said she was a healer and could help. When she tried it wouldn't take effect."

"That's because witches like Avalynn can't heal supernatural creatures, only humans. They can't even heal themselves because they're not one hundred percent human."

"Yes, I that understand now. We haven't been in contact with each other since, and it's strange we both ended up here at the same time."

"I'm glad you told me, Charlene. You wanted to help your son and there's no harm in trying. You and Avalynn being in LA at the same time has to be a coincidence." He didn't believe in coincidences.

She gave a relieved sigh. "Thank you. I didn't tell you because you were suspicious of me and I didn't want you to have another reason to be. I'm not here to cause you or Tom any harm."

"I know." He waited a beat, then said, "I have a question." His mind wandered back to them running into each other at the lawyer's office.

"Oh, what?"

"Why were you at Mr. Pembroke's office the day I saw you there?"

Charlene gave him a thin smile. "I was wondering when you'd ask me that."

Reece gave her a curious frown. "Oh, why?"

"We never did get around to discussing it."

"Yeah, well..."

"I set up a college fund for Tom. I hope you don't mind. I came into a little money and I wanted to do something beneficial for him – for his future."

"You didn't have to. But I understand your reasons."

"So you're not upset about me doing it?"

"Of course not."

Tom and Tyler came into the kitchen. "Hey, Dad, what's for dinner? We're starved," Tom said. The pair came over to the center counter.

"What do you boys feel like?" Reece picked up his cell phone from off the counter. "We can order in."

"Chinese?" Tom suggested, glancing at his cousin sideways.

Tyler nodded. "Yeah. Can we order Chinese?"

"Sure, if it's what your mom wants." Reece's gaze moved to her.

"Sounds good."

"Great. I'll put in an order for seven." Reece stepped off his stool and headed into the entry hall. He'd place the order then run upstairs for some paperwork he'd forgotten to bring down.

Tyler came around the counter to his mom. "Mom, would it be ok if I share Tom's room with him? There's plenty of space up there."

"Perhaps ask your uncle about it later."

"Oh, ok."

The boys headed back upstairs.

Grateful for all of the PI's help, Charlene would do everything she could not to let him down.

𝓢𝓞𝓒𝓡

A knock echoed into the office of Double D Investigations and Andre got up from his desk, crossed the room and opened the door, surprised to see Dennis standing in the corridor. "Hey, come in." He sensed why the doctor had made the late-night trip to speak to him.
"What can I do for you?"

He didn't answer at first. To Andre it looked as though Dennis couldn't find the right words. "I – I've decided I don't want to be involved in any of what you guys do from now on. My wife knows nothing of what I did to help you before – I'd like to keep it that way. We have a baby due soon and I want to be there for him, not getting mixed up in life-threatening situations that could potentially get me killed – like that time with Ed when he went through the process of becoming a werewolf and kidnapped me.

"And we can't resume our friendship, either. It's in the past. I'm sorry; it's how it has to be. I want you to tell Reece I'm out. This is the last time he can call on me for help. It's the right decision for me and he needs to respect my wishes."

"You know him well enough to know how he operates."

"Make him understand. Please."

"You know, Dennis, you can bury your head in the sand for only so long. You know what's out there. Who's to say something otherworldly won't come knocking on your door one day."

"When it happens, if it ever does, I'll deal with it then. I've made up my mind." He turned and headed for the door.

Andre followed him across the office. "Ok, well, I wish you all the best. Take care of your family… and yourself."

Dennis gave him an uncomfortable glance. Andre had been a great friend before he'd discovered the truth about him. "Thanks, I appreciate it. You too." He crossed the hallway to the staircase, glanced over his shoulder one last time, then walked down the stairs and out of Andre's life for good.

Andre crossed the office to his desk and sat down, his gaze returning to the back of the closed door. He'd missed his friend these past nine years and would continue to do so. Seeing him again brought back the painful memories of when their friendship ended. Vampires seldom allowed humans to get too close, but he'd needed the companionship of someone other than Reece in his life. He and Reece were like brothers which formed a different kind of bond between them. One that could never be broken.

CHAPTER THIRTY EIGHT

The next morning, Reece swung the van into the curb opposite Nathaniel's nightclub, *Sanguine*, turned off the engine, and gazed along the cordoned off alley. Why here? Why now? Could this be the work of Jacques because Nathaniel wouldn't relinquish ownership of the venue back to him? He pushed open the door, gave a heavy sigh, and stepped onto the road. This was going to become a shitshow, he could feel it.

As he walked up to the cop standing in front of the yellow crime scene tape, Grant Donovan came out of the front entrance of the double-story building. "Hey, Reece, thanks for coming."

The PI walked along the sidewalk to the detective. "No problem. What have you got this time?"

Donovan shook his head. "This is not reptile related. Come take a look?"

"Sure." Reece's Adam's apple bobbed above the neckline of his sweater. He waited a moment then followed the detective through the club and out the side entrance into the alleyway.

"Over here." Grant headed between the two buildings.

Reece caught up to him.

The coroner's van parked in the center of the lane, blocked access to any other vehicles, the pair of attendants waiting to bag and tag the body.

Grant nodded to the uniform as he approached and the cop pulled back the sheet.

"Ok." Reece folded his arms, his expression unreadable.

A young woman of no more than 18 to 20 years, drained of blood, lay in the alcove. Jacques' handiwork?

Grant gripped Reece's arm and walked along the alley to a spot where no one could hear them. "Ok? What does that mean?"

"I've seen this before, a long time ago. Let me look into it. I'll contact you when I've got something."

"Come on, Reece, I know better than that, what's going on? This isn't those creatures, so what is it?" Grant frowned into the PI's eyes.

Reece's gaze moved around the alley, making sure he couldn't be heard. "It's a vampire."

Donovan's complexion paled and he ran his hand over his face. "A what?"

"I told you there were things out here you wouldn't want to know about. Now you have no choice. You *know*."

Grant took a quick glance over his shoulder. No one nearby. "An honest to God vampire?"

"Yes."

"Fuck me!"

"Yeah."

The cop folded his arms, his frown deepening. "You think you know who it is?"

"I have my suspicions, but I'd prefer not to lay blame until I'm sure."

"Ok. Fair enough. What happens when you are sure? How do we stop them?"

"*We* don't. *I* do."

"Look, we're in this together. I need to…"

"To what? Get yourself killed? Or worse, turned?"

Grant's pale face drained even more. "I want to help rid our city of these *monsters*."

"Although I appreciate the gesture, I can't be responsible for you right now. This is a whole new ballgame. A far more dangerous one. A vampire won't hesitate to drain you and turn you. Is that what you want?"

"Of course not, but I know what's roaming our streets… like you said, I can't unknow it."

Reece gave a heavy sigh. "It would take up too much time training you. Time I don't have. I need to get on top of this."

"What about someone else on your team? Could they teach me?"

"Let me follow this up first and I'll see what I can do, ok?"

The detective nodded. "Sure, ok."

"Do you know if Harrison still wants to be on the team?"

"We haven't spoken today. He's on a rare RDO. We don't get 'em too often."

"I remember. Can you find out and let me know? If I can organize something I'll be in touch."

"Yeah, sure. I'll give him a call later."

"Ok." Reece headed back along the alley. He needed to speak to Nathaniel.

"Hey, Reece?" Grant called.

The PI turned around. "Yeah?"

"Thanks."

"No problem."

ℰↃℂℛ

Reece climbed the stairs to Nathaniel's office, wandered along the hallway, and knocked. The door swung open and the black vampire motioned for the PI to enter. "Did your detective friend call you? Nathaniel asked.

"Uh, yeah." Reece took a seat.

"Did you offer him any insight into the death?" Nathaniel returned to the chair behind his desk.

"I told him a vampire did it. I didn't say I thought it could be Jacques."

Nathaniel's left eyebrow arched. "Do you think it is him?"

Reece shifted in the chair, resting his right ankle on his left knee, and folding his arms. "Don't you? He wants the club."

"I am not sure it is him. He would not want to bring suspicion upon the nightclub for that very reason."

"So who?"

"A logical question I am unable to answer at this time. There are many master vampires in the world. It could be any one of them."

"I'm not convinced it's not Jacques. This is something he would do. If he can get you out of the way what better strategy? If you're arrested for murder, he has free reign."

"You make a valid point." Nathaniel leaned forward and clasped his large hands on the leather blotter on the desk. "You are going to look into it?"

"You bet I am. He's not going to get away with what he did last time. I can promise you that."

Reece's cell phone vibrated in his jacket pocket as he crossed the street to the van. He tugged it free, checked the caller ID and pressed the answer button. "Hey, Chief, what's up?"

"Are you at the nightclub?"

"I'm leaving now."

"So you know."

"About the death? Yeah." He set his phone to Bluetooth and started the engine.

"It has to be Jacques, right?" Ed asked.

"I'm starting to thinks so."

"Come on, Daniels, it has to be him. Same MO. Body drained of blood, no wounds. Sound like anybody else you know? I'm sure it's him. I'm more than sure. He wants Nathaniel out of the way so he can take ownership of the club again. How obvious could it be?"

"Chief, we still have to check it out. If I find out it's him…"

"We can't have him or any other bloodsucker doin' this again."

"We won't. Just let me get a handle on it."

"I knew he'd be trouble, coming back here."

"Yeah. I wanted to give him the benefit of the doubt when he said he wasn't here to cause trouble, because he's Andre's brother."

"Pfft. Andre's brother? Look what he did to him the last time he was here. Turned him into a mindless robot he could control any time he wanted. He's no brother. You're more of a brother to Andre than Jacques will ever be."

"I appreciate the sentiment, Chief, but we can't go off half-cocked on this. We have to be sure before we make any kind of move."

"Ok, it's your call. If it was me I'd put an end to him."

"I know." Reece's instincts were screaming Jacques. Who else could it be?

CHAPTER THIRTY NINE

With Tyler's birthday only two days away, and with everything else going on in Reece's professional life, he knew he had to make time to be at the mansion for the party, no matter what. It wasn't a coincidence it would be a full moon the same evening. When Tom transitioned into his werewolf state, it had also been on a night of a full moon. His nephew's birthday would be low-key, immediate family along with some of Reece's team to celebrate.

When Reece pulled the van to a stop outside the main entrance of the mansion, the door swung open and the two boys came out to greet him.

"Hey, Dad," Tom said.

"Hi, Uncle Reece." Tyler smiled

"Glad you're home early." Tom wanted to talk to him about something important.

Reece stepped from the van. "Yeah, me too."

"Dad?" Tom gave him a sheepish glance.

Reece noticed. "What's up?"

"Would it be ok to invite Jade over for Tyler's birthday?"

A tricky question.

"Can I get back to you?"

The three entered the house, Reece setting his stuff down by the closed door.

"It's only two days away and it's going to be short notice as it is." Tom folded his arms.

Reece gripped his son by his muscled biceps and looked into his eyes. "I know. I'm sorry. We have to be sure everything goes according to plan. Having someone here who knows nothing about you or what we do can be risky."

He knew what his dad said made sense. "I guess so." His expression changed from disappointment to hopeful. "But you *will* think about it, won't you?" He wanted to invite Jade so they could spend more time together.

"Sure."

"Thanks, Dad." He gave Reece a tight hug, then headed up the staircase with his cousin.

Reece let out a heavy sigh as he walked into the kitchen to find Andre at the counter in conversation with Charlene. "Hey."

"Hey, yourself. You look like you could use some coffee." Andre climbed off the stool and walked over to the coffee machine.

"Yeah, thanks, I could." Reece took a seat at the counter. "You heard the conversation?"

Andre nodded, setting a steaming mug of coffee down in front of his friend. "I did."

"What do you think I should do?"

"I can't tell you what to do with your son." Andre took his seat. "As you said, having someone here who knows nothing about us is a risk. What if things don't go according to plan?"

"My thoughts exactly." Reece picked up his mug, took a cautious sip. "It's taken him a long time to open up to anyone. He really likes this girl and I don't want to disappoint him."

Charlene interjected. "What time will the change take place?"

"Around midnight. But the party is bound to run overtime."

"Why don't we move the party forward? Have it in the afternoon instead. The kids can hang out, have some fun, and Jade can be gone before it gets too late."

A simple solution Reece should have come up with himself.

"It might work," he said, giving Charlene a thin smile then turning to his friend. "What do you think?"

Andre shrugged. "Sounds like a logical solution to me."

"I'll go let the boys know." Reece stepped from the stool and headed for the stairs.

ℰᴑ

Once Charlene retired for the evening, Reece discussed the incident behind *Sanguine* with Andre, and the possibility of Jacques being involved. The pair sat opposite each other, a glass of bourbon in front of them, the half-empty bottle between them.

"You heard about the body in the alley?"

Andre nodded. "Ed called this morning. Gave me an ear-full about how it had to be Jacques." He picked up the etched crystal glass and took a swallow of the amber liquid.

"Yeah, he called me too." Reece frowned into his friend's eyes. "You don't think it's Jacques?"

"I'm not discounting anything where my brother is concerned. My gut is telling me it's him, but I'd like to be sure before going on a witch hunt."

"I agree." Reece swallowed the last of his drink and set the glass down on the counter in front of him. "Do you know where your brother's staying?"

"Why? Are you going there to question him?"

"Yeah, I thought I might. At least we'll have an idea of whether or not he is involved."

"I'll call him when I get home."

Reece hadn't wanted Andre with him when he questioned Jacques. He needed time to suss out the vampire without him trying to hide the truth from his brother. He knew how Jacques operated. He also knew Jacques could get into Andre's head to create an ally, even though Andre knew the truth about him. "Sure, ok. Let me know when you find out and I'll pick you up on the way. We need to get this done tonight."

"Tonight? I thought we'd go there in the morning."

"Strike while the iron is hot, my mom always says." He didn't understand the meaning behind the phrase, although it seemed appropriate for their current situation.

"Ok. I'll call him now and we can leave from here." Andre walked into the entry hall and out the front door.

Reece wondered why Andre felt the need to have a private conversation with his brother. It wasn't as though the PI didn't know what was going on.

Within minutes, Andre returned to the kitchen. "He's at the Roosevelt."

Reece nodded. "Ok. Do you want to ride together or take the Ducati?"

"I'll follow you."

"All right. See you there."

Reece texted Tom as he grabbed his jacket from the coat rack in the hall. His son texted back, B safe. The PI smiled, closed the door, and climbed into the van.

CHAPTER FORTY

Jacques opened the door to the Gable and Lombard Penthouse dressed in elegant charcoal gray pajamas with an Asian-designed, knee-length burgundy smoking jacket over them, and motioned for the pair to enter. He led them into the expansive living area, asking them to take a seat, before sitting down opposite them. Crossing one leg over the other, he clasped his hands in his lap. "Why the need for this late-night visit?"

Reece leaned back against the buttoned sofa and folded his arms. "There has been a death outside the nightclub. Do you know anything about it?"

The vampire's left eyebrow arched. "Why don't you cut to the chase, Detective?" he said, his tone sarcastic.

"Look, it's late and I need to get to the facts." Reece pushed himself forward on his seat and frowned into Jacques' eyes.

"The victim's a teenaged girl, exsanguinated, with no wounds on the body," Andre told his brother. "The work of a master vampire."

Jacques frowned. "Interesting."

"Is it?" Reece hated playing these pointless games with him.

"I can assure you it wasn't me."

"How? Where were you last night?"

"Here at the hotel."

"Can anyone corroborate your story?" Reece wanted answers.

"Perhaps. I did call down for room service at around nine o'clock. Have to keep the charade of being human real." He smirked.

Reece ran his investigative gaze around the opulent surroundings, taking everything in. "Is someone staying with you?"

"Why do you ask?" Jacques' gaze roamed the suite. Nothing appeared out of place so how did the detective know?

The PI jumped to his feet. "Answer the damn question."

The vampire stared into the PI's green eyes for a moment before answering. "All right. Yes, I do have a companion."

"Who?" Reece stood with hands on hips.

"I would prefer not to say at this time."

"Why? Are you thinking they might've killed the girl?"

"I would hope not."

"You can't be sure, though, can you?" Andre stood up.

"Leave it with me. I will look into it and if I find anything I will be in touch."

"Why should we trust you?" Reece didn't, with good reason.

"I told you I am not here to make trouble for anyone."

Reece gave Jacques a skeptical frown.

"I give you my word it was not me. I will do my best to find out who it is."

"Then you'd better do it fast because we both know this is only the first of many."

C&

Back at their vehicles, Reece and Andre talked through the conversation in Jacques' hotel suite. *Who* was accompanying the vampire and why the reluctance to give them any information about the mysterious guest? The PI didn't like the bad feeling gnawing at his gut.

"Do you have any idea who your brother would have staying with him?"

Andre shook his head. "None at all. As you know, we move in different circles. And he's been overseas for the past few years."

Reece gave a heavy sigh. "Do you think he knows who killed the girl?"

"No doubt about it. He's hiding something."

"I'd like to know who's staying with him. It has to be another master vampire."

Andre frowned. "Why would they deliberately go out of their way to bring attention to themselves?" A thought crossed his mind. "Unless they want Jacques out of the way."

Reece frowned, not following Andre's train of thought. "I don't understand."

"Think about it. We can assume Jacques went back to Romania to take over where Dracula left off. What if this vampire traveling with Jacques wants the reins now?"

Reece thought about it for a moment, an amused smirk crossing his rugged handsome face. "Would be kinda ironic, don't you think?"

"Yes, it would."

"It would also mean more innocent teens dying."

"Yeah."

"This can't be happening again." Reece paced. "We still don't know if we've eradicated all the reptilian creatures yet." He remembered he'd asked Andre to look into the ownership of the apartment complex. "Did you find out anything about who owns the building downtown?"

"Not yet, there's always some kind of red tape and laws about privacy. I have someone I trust checking for me."

"I hate to say this, Andre, but I've got a prickling feeling in my gut your brother might be the owner. That these two situations are connected somehow."

"I hope you're wrong."

"Me too, or we're in deep shit."

Heading home, Reece turned the scanner to police frequency to listen to the activity in the area. His ears pricked up at the one eight seven. Another body in an alley behind the abandoned theater where Grant Donovan discovered the reptilian skin caught on some wire. *Is this new crime scene the work of the reptile creatures or the master vampire?* Reece spun the van around, wheels screaming on the asphalt, as he headed to the location.

By the time Reece arrived at the scene, the place was surrounded by squad cars with red and blue strobe lights flashing, making the nearby buildings look like side show alley. He pulled the van into the curb opposite the entrance, got out, and scanned the area for the detective. He'd be with the body, Reece deduced. He crossed the street, flashed his PI license at the uniform standing post, climbed under the yellow crime scene tape and headed round to the back of the building.

Pushing his hands into the pockets of his denim jacket, he walked over to where the body lay. "Hey, Grant. Another one?"

The detective came over to him. "Yeah."

"Drained of blood?"

Grant nodded. "Have you got any leads on this? I could sure use your help."

"I have someone looking into it. Once I hear from him I'll be in touch."

"This has got to stop, Reece. How many more lives are going to be lost before...?"

"Trust me, I get it. It isn't something I want either. I give you my word I *will* find out who's doing this and dispatch them back to hell. You can count on it."

CHAPTER FORTY ONE

The following afternoon, Reece stepped out of the elevator, crossed the foyer, and knocked on the door. No answer. He knocked again. Silence. He gave a heavy sigh, leaned closer, and said, "Jacques, are you in there? I need to talk to you." Nothing. He tugged a small notepad and pen from the pocket of his jacket, scribbled a note for the vampire to call him, and pushed it under the door. Where would he be at this time of day? The PI hadn't forgotten Eva Van Helsing's gift to Jacques of a daywalker ring. Huge mistake. It gave him license to go wherever he pleased, do what he liked, which is why Reece thought he was the one killing these latest victims.

He stepped up to the elevator and jabbed the call button, realizing he should have called before arriving unannounced. Jacques could be anywhere in the city doing God knows what. Something slithered in the pit of Reece's gut, alerting him to the fact he might be on the right track. Jacques did whatever he wanted without any consideration for the consequences. And he did need to sustain his existence.

The elevator door sprang open. Jacques' and Reece's eyes met.

"Detective. To what do I owe the pleasure?" Jacques stepped out of the lift, passed the PI and unlocked his suite's door. "I suppose you'll want to come in." He motioned for Reece to go in ahead of him, picked up the piece of paper from off the floor, dropped it into the nearby waste paper basket, then closed the door behind him. He shrugged out of his calf-length black woolen jacket, hung it on the coat rail, and continued past the PI into the living area of the penthouse. Turning around, he said, "Are you coming?"

Reece followed him into the bright room, a different atmosphere to how Jacques once lived, and took a seat on the sofa. The vampire sat opposite.

"There has been another killing."

"Oh? Where?"

"Doesn't matter. Have you found out anything yet?"

"As I said, I will contact you when I have something viable to offer."

"Not good enough, Jacques. Whoever's doing this will continue to do so until we stop them. Have you given any thought to the fact they may be attempting to implicate you? To get you out of the way?" Andre's hypothesis rang true and Reece thought it might prompt the vampire to talk.

Jacques' stare darkened. "Your concern is unnecessary, Detective. I can take care of myself." He stood up. "When I have information I'll impart it to you. I have a business call to make."

Reece's cue to leave. He got to his feet, headed to the door. Before opening it, he turned around. "You need to be careful. You could be the killer's target."

"Don't concern yourself with my well-being, Detective. As I said, I can take care of myself. Now, if you'll excuse me?"

Reece sighed as he stepped out into the foyer, closing the door behind him. Jacques' feigned offer of assistance bothered him. Could it be a ploy to throw him off the track?

⁝

Ed and Sarah were waiting for Reece when he returned to the Double D Investigations office around 2:30 PM. As the PI opened the door and saw the pair sitting in front of his desk his stomach gave a nervous squirm. Would this be the conversation he'd suspected was coming? Could Ed have made his decision about leaving the team?

Reece crossed the office, walked around his desk and sat down. "Hey, what can I do for you, Chief?"

"I wanted to come tell you in person I've made the decision to leave. Effective immediately. I'm gettin' way too old for all this, and I want to live out the rest of my days enjoying what little quality of life I have left."

The squirming feeling in Reece's gut sank into the pit of his stomach. He'd been dreading this day. "I understand. I appreciate you coming in to talk to me. We're going to miss you, but you have to do what's right for you."

"Thanks, Daniels." He gave Sarah a sheepish sideward glance.

Sarah cleared her throat. "I'm going with him."

Reece's eyebrows rose. "What?"

"It's time for me to stop doing this kind of work and spend time with Ed." Her eyes moved to him then back to the PI. "Ed's asked me to marry him and I've accepted."

"Congratulations. I didn't think you'd be leaving together."

"It's how it has to be. Now that I'm no longer taking blood, I'm going to age quicker than I've been doing for all of these years. I want to be able to enjoy the rest of my life with Ed before anything happens to me."

"Fair enough. Can you send me whatever research you have and any files belonging to the office?"

She nodded. "Yes, I will."

Reece came around the desk to the pair and gave each of them a hug. "I hope you know you're going to be missed."

Ed swiped at an errant tear sliding down his left cheek. "Yeah, yeah, we know."

The PI walked them to the door and opened it. "Please don't be strangers. Don't forget you're part of our family. If you need anything you know where I am."

The pair stepped into the hallway, Ed extending his hand. "Thanks for everything, Daniels."

Reece gave a nod and watched them descend the stairs hand in hand. Returning to his desk, he gave a heavy sigh. Sarah, in particular, had been a crucial member of their team. Her knowledge and skills outweighed the others. How would he replace her?

The door opened and Andre came into the office. "I saw Ed and Sarah leaving. Everything ok?"

"No, not at all. They both resigned."

"What?"

"Yeah, I know."

"Did they give a reason?"

"Ed said he's getting too old and Sarah said she wanted to spend more time with him. He asked her to marry him."

"Well, I'm happy for them, of course. It's not going to be the same without them."

"Yeah, that's a given."

"I have news on the ownership of the apartment building." Andre sat down in front of Reece's desk.

"Were my suspicions correct?"

"No. We were both wrong."

Reece frowned. "Oh? So who's the owner?"

CHAPTER FORTY TWO

Walking home after school had become a regular thing for Tom and Jade. They enjoyed each other's company and Tom could tell they were growing closer every day. He liked the idea of Jade being his girl and planned to ask her… when he got up the nerve. The pair turned the corner into the alley – a short cut to Jade's house – when they reached the center, Nicholas and his two friends grabbed the pair, shoved them into an idling van and sped away.

Jade glowered at her ex. "What do you think you're doing?"

Nicholas gave her a shrewd smirk. "I want to show you something."

"Like what?"

"You'll see."

"And this is the way to do it?" Jade folded her arms and scowled at him.

"It's the only way."

Tom growled in his throat. "You need to stop this van and let us out."

Nicholas folded his arms. "Or what, Daniels? You'll do what you did the other day on the street outside school?"

Tom's cheeks flushed. "What are you talking about?"

Nicholas poked him hard in the chest with his index finger. "You *know* what I mean."

"No, I don't. You do realize this is kidnapping, right? It's a criminal offence."

Nicholas shrugged. "You'll get to go home after I show Jade what she needs to see."

Tom's heart rate kicked up several notches as his wolf tried to emerge. He couldn't let that happen, not in a confined space like this van. He inhaled a deep breath and let it out in a slow, quiet exhale. "You're going to regret this, Baine," he told Nicholas.

"Am I? We'll see who's going to regret it when we get to where we're going."

The van hooked onto the Ventura highway heading away from Los Angeles.

Tom glanced out the side window. Where were they going?

The van pulled off the asphalt road from the exit they'd taken onto a dirt path.

Tom's gut tightened as he recognized the place. The Colorado Street Bridge – better known as Pasadena Suicide Bridge. He swallowed hard. *Why did Nicholas bring us here? And what does he plan to do?* Whatever the reason, the traffic noise and seclusion of the location would make it difficult for anyone to hear them.

The van came to a halt underneath the left-hand side of the two bridges.

Nicholas slid open the side door, jumped out onto red dirt, and gazed around the area to make sure they couldn't be seen. He turned back to the open doorway. "Get out."

"Why did you bring us out here?" Jade asked, a nervous tremor in her quiet voice. Her stomach squirmed.

"Like I said, you'll find out." He pulled a pistol from the pocket of his jacket and pointed it at Tom.

Jade gasped, her eyes wide, her heart racing. "Where'd you get the gun?"

"It's my dad's." He waved the weapon at them both. "Now get out."

Nicholas's friends balked. "Hey, man, you didn't say anything about bringing a piece with you," one said.

The pair scurried out of the van ahead of Tom and Jade and propped themselves beside Nicholas, giving each other an anxious glance.

"It's my insurance policy."

"What does that even mean," the other friend asked. "If you shoot Tom…"

Nicholas swung around and gave him a devious grin. "I'm not going to shoot him." He turned back to look at Tom. "Unless he gives me any trouble."

"This is insane," Jade blurted, her breathing ragged. "Nick... this isn't you. What are you doing?"

"What I have to do."

"Which is?" She could feel her body trembling, a nervous rash of goosebumps spreading up her arms. The situation was way out of control.

"To show you the truth about your boyfriend."

"What are you talking about?" She took a tentative step toward Nicholas, hoping she could talk some sense into him.

"Stop! Don't come any closer. I mean it."

Nicholas's friends gaped at each other. "We can't be here, man. This is so fucked up."

He turned the gun on the pair. "You'll do what I tell you to do. You're not going anywhere. *Understood?*"

Both guys nodded, their Adam's apples bobbing above the neckline of their T-shirts, defensive hands raised. "Ok, man, whatever you say."

Nicholas waved the gun at Tom. "Over there." He motioned with his head to a spot under the bridge then turned to look at Jade. "Now you."

Jade caught up to Tom, terrified Nicholas would shoot him... or them both.

Nicholas and his friends followed the pair, the overcast sky lending an eerie feel to the location. Perfect for his plan.

"Ok, stop. There will do."

"What are you planning, Nicholas, to kill us?" Tom asked.

The agitated teen gave a humorless chuckle. "Could be." He shrugged. "Who knows how this'll play out?"

One of Nicholas's friends, the one doing all the talking, eased himself up beside him. "Hey, Nick, what's this all about? Tom hasn't done anything worth dying for."

Nicholas glowered at him. "Remember what happened the other day? He embarrassed me on the street."

"Ok, yeah, he did, but..."

"He needs payback. And Jade needs to see what he is."

"What he is?" Jade asked. "What do you mean?"

"You'll see." Nicholas turned to his first friend, Jasper, pulled a coil of twine from the pocket of his jacket and threw it to him. "Tie him up."

"Come on, man. This is getting way out of control."

Nicholas turned the gun on his friend, motioning with the weapon for him to walk over to Tom. "Do it!"

Jade's heart lodged itself in her throat, the pounding beat almost suffocating her. She didn't want to witness Tom's death out here. What could she do? Nicholas had lost his mind. "Nick?"

He turned toward her. "Shut up. I don't want to hear anything you have to say."

"Please listen to…"

"I said shut the fuck up."

Jasper pulled Tom's arms behind him and tied his wrists together, whispering, "Sorry, man."

"It's ok," Tom told him. "It's not your fault your friend's a lunatic."

Nicholas strutted over to him. "What did you say?"

"You heard me. This is insane. You're going to jail for this."

"Maybe, maybe not. It all depends on you, doesn't it?" He smirked.

"I don't know what you're talking about."

"Sure you don't." Nicholas thrust out his hand and hit Tom in the face. Hard.

Blood spurted from Tom's mouth as he lurched backwards.

Jade rushed forward. "Nicholas, stop!"

"No. You need to see what I saw." He hit Tom in the face again. Blood trickled from his nostrils.

"Nick!" Jade ran at him, arms outstretched, and shoved him away from Tom.

The teen lost his balance and fell sideways, the pistol flying from his hand into nearby bushes.

Jasper and his friend, Charlie, raced over to pull Jade off Nicholas, Charlie holding her arms behind her.

Nicholas climbed to his feet. "Your boyfriend will pay for that." He stalked over to Tom, balled his fist and punched him square in the gut.

Tom keeled over, air whooshing from his lips, his knees buckling beneath him, and landed in the dirt. He wouldn't fight back, not in front of the girl he hoped would become his girlfriend.

Jade struggled free, rushed over to him and helped him to his feet. "You have to stop this now before something happens you can't take back, Nick. You know you do. This – This is crazy!" Her heart beat so fast her words were breathy.

"Not until you see what I need you to see." He foraged through the scrub for the gun and, at first, couldn't find it. Turning to his friends he said, "Help me find the pistol. My dad'll kill me if I lose it."

Jasper and Charlie prodded around the shrubbery for the gun.

Tom and Jade looked at each other, nodded, and made a run for it.

Nicholas spotted them and took off after the pair, followed by Jasper and Charlie. "Nick, wait," Jasper called, pocketing the pistol.

Tom could have broken free from the ropes around his wrists but didn't because it would be something he couldn't explain to Jade. The pair kept running, making their way back to the road, Nicholas in hot pursuit.

Now he didn't have the pistol it would be more difficult to control the situation... but he would *somehow*.

Nicholas caught up to them, lunged forward, grabbed Jade from behind and pulled her onto her knees. He knew Tom wouldn't leave without her.

Jade struggled against him. "Let me go, Nick. Let me go."

Tom spun around, his eyes glowing in the dull light of dusk, his wolf emerging. He didn't want Jade to find out this way, but he had to do something to stop the escalating situation before someone got killed. He tugged his wrists apart and the rope snapped.

Jasper and Charlie skidded to a halt. "What the fuck's going on?" Jasper shouted, staring wide-eyed at Tom's gleaming eyes.

Tom stalked toward Nicholas. When he spoke his voice sounded deep, throaty. "Let her go. Now!"

Nicholas released Jade, a satisfied smirk on his face. "That's what I wanted you to see."

Jasper tugged the pistol free from his pocket and aimed it at Tom. "Stay back," he yelled, his shaking hands gripping the weapon.

Jade stood riveted to the spot, her heart pounding. "This can't be real."

"I'm sorry, Jade, I would've told you at some point. Yeah, it's real. I'm a werewolf."

Jade's eyes widened. She'd been joking with him about the Twilight movies and all along he knew the truth. Werewolves were real.

"Now you know," Nicholas told her.

Tom stepped forward. "Jade, you have to listen to me."

The exploding crack of the gun echoed in the atmosphere around them. Tom's body jerked backwards, his tall frame hitting the dirt with a thud.

CHAPTER FORTY THREE

When Reece walked through the front door of the mansion, Tyler came flying down the stairs two at a time. The PI frowned as he watched the teen descend the staircase alone. The pair had become almost inseparable and it seemed strange to see the boy on his own. "Hey, Tyler, how'd your...?"

"Uncle Reece, Tom hasn't come home from school. It's been hours. I tried calling him, left voicemail messages, but he hasn't answered or called. I'm getting worried about him."

Reece frowned. "It's not like him at all." He tugged his phone from the pocket of his jeans and speed-dialed Tom's number. No answer. "Did he say where he might be going after school?"

Tyler shook his head. "No, he didn't. I'm worried."

"Maybe he stopped in at Jade's. Is it a tutoring night?"

The teen shrugged. "I don't know. He would've called to let me or mom know, though. He always does if he's going to be late."

"Yeah, I know." Reece's gut tightened. Where could Tom be? "We'll give it another half hour. If he's not here by then I'll go see what I can find out from Jade." He would head over there if Tom didn't come back soon.

His nephew nodded. "Ok. But I've got a bad feeling about this."

"I'm sure he's fine. Probably lost track of time." A squirming sensation in the pit of Reece's gut told him otherwise.
***
Jade let out a sharp, high-pitched squeal. "Oh my God!" She ran over to Tom lying so still she couldn't see him breathing. *Is he... is he dead?*

The three teens took off running, leaving Jade and Tom behind.

She sprang to her feet. "Hey, wait," she called out. "Wait! We need to take him to a hospital."

The trio didn't look back. They jumped into the van, spun the wheels on the red dirt and sped away.

Jade's heartbeat pulsed in her throat as she lowered herself onto the ground beside Tom. She was on her knees helping a – a werewolf. *No, it's still Tom.* She felt around his jeans for his cell. *Yes.* Several missed call messages sat on the phone's screen. She opened one. It redialed Tom's dad.

Reece picked up on the first ring. "Tom, why didn't you call to let someone know you'd be late?"

"Um, Mr. Daniels, it's not Tom it's Jade."

Reece could hear the nervous tremor in her breathy voice. "What's wrong, Jade? Where's Tom?"

"He – he's unconscious. Can I explain later? We need an ambulance *now.*"

The PI's gut shrank into a tight knot of nerves. "Where are you?"

"The Colorado Street Bridge, left-hand side. You know, where all the trees are?"

"Yes, I know where. What are you doing there? How did you get out there?"

"Please, Mr. Daniels, can you send the ambulance right away. Tom's been shot."

∞∞∞

Reece drove the van like a bat out of hell to get to the bridge. He pulled off the road, sped along the dirt track and stopped when he saw Jade in the headlights waving her arms in the air. Throwing open the driver's door, Reece leaped from the van and raced over to where his son lay, unmoving on the ground. He dropped to his knees and pressed his fingers against Tom's carotid artery feeling for a pulse. Weak but steady. Tom would be ok. He turned to Jade. "He's alive."

Jade let out a huge rush of air from her lungs. She felt as though she'd been unable to breathe the whole time she'd been waiting for the ambulance to arrive. "Thank God, I'm so relieved. Is the ambulance on its way?" She gave him a quizzical stare for a moment. "How are you better already?"

Reece looked up at her, disregarding her questions. "What happened here?"

Her mind returned to the scene of the crime, tears tumbling down her cheeks. "We were grabbed and brought out here by Nicholas Baine. He's my ex-boyfriend. He said he wanted to show me something about Tom."

"How did Tom get shot?"

"Nick had his father's pistol with him. He didn't shoot Tom. One of his friends did. Jasper."

"What did he want you to see?"

"I saw it, Mr. Daniels. Tom's a… a werewolf."

Reece needed Andre's help more than ever. "Stay right here, ok? Don't move." He walked away from the van and dialed his friend's number. "I need you to meet me at home. Tom's been shot. But, more importantly, I need you to make Jade forget what she saw tonight."

Andre jumped to his feet. "Is he all right?

"He'll be fine. His Lycan genes will kick in and he'll be ok in a few hours."

"Are you ok?"

"I am now I've seen him. I didn't know if he'd been shot with silver or…"

"The most important thing is he's going to recover. I'll check him out when I get to your place. So what did Jade see?"

"She knows he's a werewolf. I don't know the details yet because she's pretty shaken up. What I need is for her not to know."

"I'll replace the memory she has of tonight with something else."

"Thanks, Andre. I'll get Tom and Jade into the van and head straight home."

"Ok. I'll see you there."

℘⷏℃

Andre arrived at the mansion only minutes after Reece and pulled his red Ducati Monster in behind the van. He removed his glossy black helmet, climbed off his motorcycle and walked over to the back of the vehicle. Reece opened the double doors to lift his son out and take him into the house. "Need any help?" Andre asked.

"No, thanks, I got it." Reece scooped Tom into his arms and carried him over to the double front doors. "Hey, Andre, can you help Jade out of the van and bring her inside?"

"Sure." Andre walked around to the front passenger door. "Hi, Jade, I'm Andre, Tom's uncle. Want to come inside?"

She gave him a vacant nod, her eyes glistening with tears. When he opened the door she climbed down out of the vehicle.

"Let's go in." He directed her to the entrance of the mansion.

Jade stepped into the entry hall and stood to one side, folding her arms around herself in a tight hug, her body still trembling.

Reece had already taken Tom upstairs, with Tyler and Charlene in tow, so she and Andre were alone.

"Want a glass of water or something?" Andre asked.

Jade shook her head. "No, thanks. Can I see Tom? He should've gone to the hospital."

"He'll be ok. I'm a doctor (had been a doctor). Once he's settled in I'll go up and check him out. Please, come have a seat in the kitchen."

Jade glanced up the staircase, her eyes still glistening with unspilled tears. "Are you sure he'll be ok?"

"Yes, he's going to be fine. I give you my word. You've had a pretty nasty shock tonight so come and sit down for a bit." He ushered her into the kitchen and onto a stool. "Are you sure I can't get you anything?"

Jade clasped her hands on the countertop. "Maybe some water. Thank you."

"Sure." Andre filled a glass from the faucet and set it down in front of her. "How are you feeling?"

"I – I'm not sure." She waited a moment, then said, "Do you know about Tom? About what he is, I mean?"

Andre sat on a stool opposite her. "Yes, I do."

"How is that possible? Werewolves are only supposed to be in books and movies."

"There are a lot of unexplained things in the world."

Jade picked up the glass and took a sip of water. "Yes, I know, but…"

"Best not to think about it now. Give yourself some time."

"I can't believe Tom's a werewolf. How didn't I know?"

Andre came around the counter to her. "Jade, I want you to look into my eyes."

She turned toward him, her eyes downward. "Why?"

"I suspect you're in shock and I need to check. It's important."

Jade lifted her gaze up to meet his.

"Tonight you were here with Tom studying. He didn't feel well so he went upstairs to rest. Reece is going to take you home. Everything's fine. You'll see Tom tomorrow when you come by to check on him."

When Reece walked into the room he overheard the scenario Andre planted in Jade's mind. "Hey." He glanced between the two of them. "Tom's resting in bed. He should be feeling much better by tomorrow. Probably a twenty-four hour bug or something." He turned to Jade. "Why don't I drive you home?"

She slid off the stool and smiled. "Thanks, Mr. Daniels."

"Not a problem. Come by and visit tomorrow. I'm sure Tom will be happy to see you. He can spend the day at home recuperating."

"It's a good idea, I think. Wouldn't want to spread it around. I'll come by after school." She turned to Andre. "Thanks for the water. Nice to meet you."

"You too."

Jade headed for the front door.

Reece gave Andre a thankful look then followed her out.

ℴ)∣ℴ

When Reece arrived back home, Andre was preparing to leave. "Tom's sleeping. How'd it go?"

"She doesn't seem to remember anything about tonight. The one problem I can foresee is the boys who abducted them."

"So, what happened?" Andre folded his arms.

"Tom and Jade were on their way to Jade's house when her ex-boyfriend, Nicholas Baine, and a couple of his friends grabbed them and drove out to the Colorado Street Bridge. Nicholas wanted Jade to see Tom in wolf form. I'm not sure how he knew, we didn't get into the specifics, but somehow he did."

"Man."

"Yeah. He'd taken his father's pistol out there with him and one of his friends got hold of it and shot Tom by accident when he started to turn."

"Ok. Do you know where these kids live?"

"No, I didn't have time to ask Jade. She did mention a name though. Jasper."

"We need to find out where they are so I can remove tonight from their memories as well."

"Not sure how we're going to do that yet."

A noise behind the pair caused them both to swing around.

Tom was on the stairs. "I know their names, and we can get their addresses from school."

Reece rushed up to him, surprised he was recovering so quickly. "How are you feeling?"

Tom frowned into his dad's eyes. "Like I got shot." He lifted his T-shirt and gazed at the healing hole in his left side. Lucky for him, the bullet had missed vital organs.

"I'm just relieved you're ok." Reece pulled his son into his arms in a tight hug. "I love you."

"You too, Dad."

"So we're breaking into the high school?" Andre asked.

"It's the only way to prevent those punks from outing Tom and causing problems we can do without right now. We also need to retrieve Jade's and Tom's backpacks. They must still be in the van they were driven out to the bridge in." Reece headed for the door.

Tom and Andre followed.

It looked like it would be a long night.

CHAPTER FORTY FOUR

After breaking into the high school, locating the addresses for the boys, and Andre wiping any memory of the previous several hours from their minds, Reece and his son said goodnight and headed back to the mansion. Jade would come by tomorrow after school to see Tom… all would be right with their world for a while. What would he do without Andre and his ability to replace memories? He'd be in serious shit.

Charlene was still up and sitting at the kitchen counter sipping warm milk when the pair walked in. Tyler was up in the attic. "Where have you two been?" she asked.

Reece hadn't told her when they left.

"Had an errand to run." Reece walked over to the sink, picked up a glass and ran the faucet. Turning around he sipped the water then asked, "How's Tyler taking what happened?"

"He's all right now he knows Tom's ok."

"Good."

Tom gave his dad a conspiratorial glance. "I'm heading to bed. Goodnight."

"Night, son."

"Goodnight, Tom. Pleasant dreams."

Reece sat opposite Charlene and his thoughts wandered back to nights when he and Charlotte would sit together talking about their future. His heart clenched and he took another sip of water.

"What kind of errand can you run at this late hour?" Charlene asked.

"An important one." He didn't elaborate.

Charlene's right eyebrow arched. "I guess you're not going to tell me, are you?"

"Better you don't know."

"Fair enough."

"How are the birthday party plans coming along?"

Charlene smiled. "All ready for tomorrow night."

"Great. I'm looking forward to a little fun for a change."

"Me too. It's been a lot to take in." She climbed off the stool, walked around the counter and sat her mug in the sink. "Goodnight."

"Yeah. See you in the morning." Reece remained seated at the counter watching Charlene leave the kitchen. She was a definite distraction he couldn't let get under his skin.

His phone vibrated on the counter in front of him and he snatched it up. "Hello, Reece Daniels speaking."

"Hey, Reece, it's me," Grant Donovan said on the other end of the line.

"Hi, Grant, why are you calling on a different phone?"

"I accidently dropped mine in the can. What can I say? Stupid, I know. I'm always on a call no matter where I am."

"It's late, what's up?"

"You know how I mentioned Harrison had an RDO?"

"Yeah?"

"Well, he hasn't come back to work and I'm worried."

Reece remembered what Andre discovered about the apartment building. Should he share the information with the detective? Maybe best to wait until they were face to face. "Ok, so what do you want to do about it?"

"Would you meet me at his home? I've got a bad feeling I can't shake."

"Sure. When?"

"Now."

"Now?"

⚡⚡⚡

Reece pulled the van in behind Grant's dark blue sedan parked on the street and climbed out. The detective opened the driver's door and got out of the vehicle when the PI approached.

Grant extended his hand. Reece shook it. "Thanks for coming on such short notice and at such a late hour. Sorry I had to disturb you at home."

The PI shrugged. "No big deal." His eyes moved to the unlit home. "You want to wake them up at this time of night?" He checked his phone. 1:01AM.

"I've been working with Harrison for a couple of years. We get along pretty good, you know? I'd hate for something to have happened to him and his family and we didn't find out for days or weeks."

"Ok. So let's go." Reece walked off ahead of the detective and made his way up the concrete path toward the front porch.

Grant caught up with him. "Wait."

Reece glanced over his shoulder. "For what?"

"Maybe you're right. Perhaps we should do this in the morning... I mean when it's daylight."

The PI turned around. "I need to tell you something."

As they got closer to the front steps a light came on inside the house.

"Shit," Reece whispered. "Let's get back to your car."

The pair made a B-line for the detective's sedan parked a couple of houses down.

"That was close," the PI said, checking the side rear view mirror to see if anyone was leaving the house.

"Yeah." Grant turned in his seat and peered through the back windshield. "Doesn't appear to be anyone coming out though."

"No, there doesn't. I think we should monitor the house for now. What do you think?"

"Yeah, I'm with you."

CR

Once the sun came up, Reece and Grant left the detective's car and wandered along the sidewalk to the front of the home. Killjoy's car stood in the drive, along with a second SUV parked beside it – his wife's. Could Harrison be a reptile creature like the ones residing in the apartment building downtown? *His* apartment building as it turned out. *How could he own a building like that on a cop's salary?* The PI's gut squirmed at the thought. He and Grant were in close proximity to him on many occasions and there had been no way to distinguish any difference.

The pair did a scan of the quiet, tree-lined street, continued along to the driveway and disappeared into the back yard of the property.

Reece motioned for the detective to wait while he stepped up onto the back patio to survey the inside of the house. All seemed quiet. No movement anywhere as far as he could tell. He signaled for Grant to join him, then tried the back sliding glass door. It glided along the track with ease. "I'll go in. Give me a minute and follow me inside. Ok?" Reece told him.

Grant nodded.

The PI pulled his Glock 9mm and eased his tall frame through the kitchen to the breakfast nook. No one. He checked the laundry before stepping into the hallway. Not a sound could be heard throughout the single-level home. He walked along to the first bedroom. The door stood ajar. Pushing it open, he moved into the doorway and scanned the room. Empty. As he headed to the second closed door, Grant called out to him.

"Hey, Reece, in here," the detective said from the living room.

When the PI reached the double width doorway he stopped short. "What the hell?"

The split open bodies of Harrison, his wife, and two kids were lying on the rug in the center of the room.

Grant's face paled. "I can't believe it."

"Yeah, there's no way to tell. Don't go blaming yourself." Reece entered the room and stood beside him.

"But…"

Reece raised his hand. "You couldn't have known, just like I didn't know."

Grant frowned into the PI's eyes. "He wanted to join your team, remember?"

"Yeah. Now we know why. To keep track of what we were doing with the case, so he'd be one step ahead. I guess he didn't do it because we were getting too close."

"He was the mole. Dammit. I told him everything you told me."

"Like I said, you couldn't have known."

"I feel bad for sharing information with him that he used against you."

"No point in stressing over it now. It won't solve anything."

"Where do you think they've gone?"

The PI shrugged. "Don't know. They could be anywhere by now."

Grant swallowed the anxious lump lodged in his throat. "This can't be happening. What am I supposed to tell my boss?"

"Don't say anything. I'm sure when Harrison doesn't turn up your boss will send someone to look for him and it'll be you, being his partner. The place will be cleaned up by then and you can tell him no one was here."

Grant's eyes widened. "You're going to tamper with a crime scene?"

"This isn't a crime scene because no crime has been committed." He motioned to the remains. "Those are shells, nothing more."

The detective's eyes moved to the bodies lying together on the rug. He couldn't get his mind around the fact his partner had been a reptilian creature. He exhaled a long breath. "You're right."

"Let's get out of here," Reece said, heading to the back sliding door.

Grant followed. "So you'll get someone in here to get rid of the bodies?"

"It'll be done tonight. Can't have the neighbors watching."

"Of course not."

"I'll let you know once it's done. If your boss asks you where Harrison is say you don't know, which isn't a lie."

The detective nodded. "Yeah, ok. I'll do my best."

Reece gripped Grant's arm and stopped him. "Make sure you do. We can't have your boss getting suspicious again. It could trigger what Andre already suppressed in his mind."

"Ok."

"You're part of all this now, Donovan, so whatever the department finds out…"

"I get it." He understood his life would never be the same again and his job was on the line and he didn't like it.

CHAPTER FORTY FIVE

The following afternoon, as Reece got ready to leave the office to head home for Tyler's party, Avalynn thrust open the door and marched across the room. "I came to tell you I'm going back home."

The PI stood up, came around his desk, and perched on the corner, folding his arms. He couldn't say he'd be sorry to see her go because he wouldn't. She'd healed him and he appreciated her help, so he'd be civil. "Why? Don't you want to find out if all of the reptilian creatures have been eliminated first?"

"I believe if Harrison was the orchestrator of the attacks here in LA he had to be their leader. With him gone, I can guarantee none of the creatures will remain here alone. Besides, there haven't been any more bloody puddles found, so you have your answer."

Reece frowned into her lilac colored eyes. "How can you be so sure?"

"It's how they operate. We saw it in New Orleans."

"Do you think he's gone there?"

"Quite possibly."

"So you're leaving to track him?"

"I've already been in contact with the city's witch council. They want me back there pronto. They're monitoring everyone entering New Orleans. If he and his cohorts cross the border they'll be captured and killed without question."

Reece stood up. "Well, safe travels."

She stared into his green eyes. "You need to acknowledge your feelings, Reece."

"What do you mean?"

"I think you know." She headed for the open door, then turned around. "Oh, by the way, the vampire attacks... it's someone you already know."

"Who?"

"You'll figure it out soon enough." Avalynn disappeared down the stairs.

Reece raced across the office and stopped in the open doorway, letting out a huff. "Frustrating... wi... woman." He stalked back across the room and dropped into his chair.

Moments later, Todd, Lozano, and Andre came into the office. "What did Avalynn want?" his friend asked.

"She came to tell me she's heading home."

"Doesn't she want to stick around to make sure the reptilian creatures have been eliminated?" Todd folded his arms.

"She believes they've fled the city. Could be on their way to New Orleans. It wasn't her call. The city's witch council summoned her."

"She could've been an asset to our team." Todd took a seat.

"In what way?" Reece folded his arms.

"Isn't it obvious? She's a witch with powers. It would've given us an advantage in fighting other supernatural creatures."

"It's better she's gone." The PI didn't want to discuss it further. "She's needed elsewhere. Besides, we have all the supernatural help we need."

"Any news on the vampire?" Lozano asked, sitting on the chair next to Todd in front of Reece's desk.

"Not yet. Jacques said when he has something viable to offer he'll share it."

"And you believe him?" Todd gave Reece a dubious frown.

"What do you think? Right now we need his help so I'll go along with his eccentric requests. In the meantime, we have to be vigilant. We need to be out at night checking the night spots around town. Anywhere a vampire is likely to frequent."

"Are we pairing up?" Lozano asked. He wasn't sure he wanted to go out on his own.

"Yeah. Safety in numbers. You can go with Andre. Todd and I will work together. We'll start tomorrow night. For now, Nathaniel will send out his team." He checked the time on the wall clock above the kitchen. "We need to get ready for Tyler's party." Reece stood up and came around his desk. "See you there at three." He crossed the office and headed out the door.

₭ℕℛ

When Reece walked through the door of the mansion he couldn't believe the transformation. Tyler's party would be a lot of fun for everyone, including the adults. He closed the door and headed through the living room to the backyard. It looked even better than inside. The creepy environment fitted well with the circumstances of Tyler being in LA. His initiation into Lycanthropy would happen at midnight.

"Hey," Reece greeted, startling Charlene.

She spun around. "Oh! I didn't hear you."

"Sorry." His eyes surveyed the decorated space. "It looks fantastic."

"All Tyler and Tom's idea." She followed his gaze. "It is pretty spectacular, isn't it?"

"Sure is."

The two boys came outside.

"Hi, Dad. What do ya think?"

"Very cool. It's a shame we couldn't have invited more of your friends."

"Yeah, it is, but we get it." Tom glanced at his cousin.

"Yeah, Uncle Reece, it's too dangerous. I'm totally cool with it."

"I'm glad."

Andre stepped out into the yard. "Wow! This is awesome."

"Thanks," Tom and Tyler said together, looking at each other and chuckling.

"When is Jade getting here?" Reece asked. He'd made the decision to let her come to the birthday party because he wanted his son to have someone in his life.

"She just texted. She's on her way."

"Ok. I'll go take a quick shower and change before anyone else arrives." Reece headed into the house.

Tyler turned to Tom. "Your dad is way cool."

"Yeah, he is pretty cool." The pair walked over to the portable refrigerator to grab a soda.

Andre came up to Charlene. "It looks like it'll be a fun night."

She smiled. "I think so." Her expression changed to one of concern. "Tyler's going to be in a lot of pain, isn't he? I mean, when it happens."

Andre rested a comforting hand on her arm. "He'll be fine. It gets easier every time they turn."

She gave a sigh. "I can't help worry."

"I know."

Ed, Sarah, Todd and Lozano came out into the yard. "Hey, this looks great!" Ed said.

Charlene crossed the yard. "All the boys' work."

"Well they did a terrific job." Ed gazed around at the decorations. Black and red balloons, black streamers, fairy lighting for when the sun went down. It looked more like a Halloween party than a birthday celebration. Ed and the others understood the reason behind it. Tyler would be initiated into the supernatural realm tonight and it was his way of dealing with his new life.

The teens came across the yard to welcome their guests. "Hi, thanks for coming," Tyler said.

"It's our pleasure," Sarah offered. "Happy birthday."

"Oh, yeah, happy birthday," Ed told Tyler. "Sorry, wasn't thinkin' when I got here."

"All good." Tyler smiled. "Want something to drink? There's a selection of sodas and some beer too… for the adults."

"Sure, why not." Ed walked over to the drinks sitting in ice.

Jade stepped out into the yard. "Hey, Tom, Tyler." She walked over to the pair and handed the birthday boy a gift. "Happy birthday."

Tyler sat the present with the others on a table close by. He would open them later.

Reece joined his team. "Hey, good you're here."

Ed came back to the group and passed some beers around.

"Thanks," the PI said. "Should be a fun night, as long as everything goes according to plan."

Sarah frowned. "What are you concerned about?"

Reece sighed. "Lycanthropy is unpredictable. We don't know if Tyler will turn at the full moon or if he'll be able to turn at will."

Todd folded his arms. "We need to keep a close eye on him then."

"Yeah, we do." Reece took a swig of beer, his gaze on his nephew.

"Do you think it's safe for the girl to be here?" Ed asked.

"I'll watch out for her," Sarah said.

Reece's gaze moved to her. "Thanks. Wouldn't want Tyler to lose his shit and attack her."

"Don't even put it out there." Andre stepped up beside him.

"We need to be careful. Like I said, we don't know what could happen once night sets in. I'm glad the party's finishing before it gets too late." Reece walked over to the boys. "Hey, how're you feeling, Tyler?"

"Good. Why?" His smile turned into a frown. "Are you worried?"

"Not at all," Reece lied. "We've got this. Just have fun tonight." He gave the teen a smile, as something shifted in his gut. Could it be a premonition? He hoped not.

CHAPTER FORTY SIX

Reece stood watching the kids dancing together, laughing and jumping around to the thumping music oozing out of the amps set up near the fence. So far, the party had gone off without a hitch. The PI breathed a relieved sigh. In a few hours they would face the difficult task of watching Tyler turn into a werewolf in the basement of the mansion. Adrian had set up a solid cage down there many years ago when a rampant werewolf, who didn't know he was one, murdered a nurse. It would now serve a better purpose – keeping Tyler safe during his transition from human to creature... and everyone else around him too.

The music stopped.

Tyler stood in the center of the yard. "I'd like to thank you all for the awesome presents and for coming tonight. It's been a blast."

Everyone clapped.

Jade and Tom stepped up beside Tyler and the three hugged.

"It's been awesome." Jade smiled, her eyes moving to Tom.

"Yeah, it has been a lot of fun." He smiled back at her, his heart beating a little bit faster. He could no longer deny how he felt about her.

"Well, I'd better get going. Dad texted me, he's waiting out front." Jade hugged Tyler then Tom once more before heading to the open double glass doors into the house.

"Wait," Tom said. "I'll walk you out."

As the pair crossed the lawn a sound behind them caused Tom's hackles to rise and he swung around.

Tyler shifted before their eyes and leaped across the yard toward them, bearing his canines, his eyes wild.

Tom shoved Jade behind him.

Reece and Andre rushed forward. "Tyler, STOP!" Reece shouted.

The wolf kept coming.

Charlene backed up beside Sarah. "Oh, my God!"

Tom's eyes glowed and he growled deep in his throat. "Stop!"

Jade screamed. Her eyes wide with fear.

Sarah raced across the lawn, grabbed the girl and pulled her out of the way. "Stay here." She tugged the tranquilizer gun from the holster beneath her jacket, aimed and fired.

The dart torpedoed across the yard into Tyler's torso. It didn't stop him. She fired again.

The wolf kept moving toward the girl.

"Don't, Tyler. I'm warning you." Tom shifted and blocked his cousin's path.

As the wolf neared the group the sedative solution in the darts took effect. He staggered, huffed out a heavy breath, and his large body sagged to the ground.

"What the hell?" Ed said, moving alongside Sarah. "How did you know?"

"I didn't. I always come prepared where supernatural creatures are concerned. I wasn't taking any chances tonight."

Reece stalked over to the pair. "Thank you, Sarah."

"No problem."

Tom changed back into human form and Andre threw him his jacket. "Dad, what happened?"

"We couldn't know if Tyler would turn by the full moon or not. And it appears he can transition at will, like you, which we should've expected. It must be in your particular Lycan genes."

Charlene came up to them. "I – I'm sorry."

Reece frowned into her eyes. "For what?"

"I forgot to tell you the moon would rise earlier tonight. It's one of the shortest days of the year. I saw an article about it online. I'm so sorry." Tears welled in her eyes.

Reece let out a long sigh. "It's all right, Charlene. But the information would've been helpful." On thinking back, the PI remembered Tom had turned on the night of a full moon the first time. It may have been an initial Lycan transition before becoming proficient at turning at will. Who knew? Adrian, Andre's vampire mentor, had been researching the subject when he'd been killed by a werewolf. His knowledge and years of experience with supernatural creatures was indeed missed.

"Why didn't we know about this?" Ed asked.

"We should have, Chief," Reece told him. Under normal circumstances they would have been on top of the moon's cycles. With years of no supernatural activity it hadn't been necessary. The same thought he'd had the night they had captured the reptilian creature crossed his mind: *The full moon has a lot to answer for.*

Charlene rushed across the lawn, knelt down and placed her hand on her wolf son's furry body, the welled tears spilling down her cheeks. She looked up at Reece. "What do we do now?"

"I think we need to take him down to the basement. The cage is set up for him to be comfortable and safe. I'll stay with him to make sure he's ok." Reece and Andre hoisted the heavy beast off the ground and carried it through the open doorway. Tyler wouldn't change back to human form until the drugs wore off. Charlene followed them.

Jade stood fixed to the spot, tears sliding down her face, shock setting in.

Tom threw on Andre's jacket, buttoned it, and rushed over to her. "Jade?" he said, his voice gentle, soothing. "Can you hear me?"

She didn't answer.

Tom turned to look at Sarah. "What's wrong with her?"

"She's in shock. Let's get her into the house. Andre will help once he and Reece have secured Tyler." Sarah took Jade by the arm and walked her into the sitting room. Tom close behind them.

Todd and Lozano followed Ed inside. "That was a close call," Todd said.

"No kiddin'," Ed answered. "If the kid had bitten her we'd be in all kinds of crap."

"Yeah, lucky Sarah came prepared," Lozano told them.

"Damn right about that." Ed's gaze moved to his wife. They'd decided to have a no frills wedding at the registry office with Reece and Andre as their witnesses. "I'm glad you were on top of it, my love." He gave Sarah a relieved glance.

"As I said, can't be too careful where any supernatural creature is concerned."

Andre came back upstairs into the sitting room. He walked over to Sarah, Jade and Tom. "How is she?"

"In shock, as you would expect." Sarah made the girl comfortable in one of the plush, wing-backed armchairs.

Andre moved his gaze to Tom. "I'll take the memory away and replace it with something more appropriate like I did before. She'll be fine."

Tom nodded, his eyes returning to the girl he loved. "Thanks, Uncle Andre." He knelt down in front of Jade.

She cringed away from him. "Don't!"

"Jade it's me." He reached out to touch her hand.

She pulled back. "I said don't!" Tears welled in her eyes. "You're a monster."

Tom got to his feet, his heart heavy in his chest. He frowned down at her, realizing she hadn't meant what she'd said about it being cool to be a werewolf.

"Let's get her onto her feet." Andre gripped her arm, so did Sarah, and they helped her out of the chair.

"Jade?"

She didn't look at him.

"Jade, I want you to look at me."

The girl lifted her face up to meet his immortal gaze.

"You've had an awesome time at Tyler's party. You've danced, laughed, and eaten way too much junk food. It's been heaps of fun."

A knock echoed into the entry hall as Reece reached the front door. He opened it.

"Uh, hi, I'm Scott, Jade's dad."

The PI extended his hand. "Hi, I'm Reece, Tom's dad."

"Good to meet you." Scott smiled.

"Yeah, you too."

"Is Jade ready to go?"

Reece glanced into the sitting room. "Yeah, I think so."

Jade came bouncing out into the entry hall, all smiles. "Hi, Dad."

"Did you have a good time?"

"Yeah. I had a super awesome time." She turned her gaze to Tom. "I'll text you later, K?"

"Sure." Tom's gut twisted into an uncomfortable knot. Jade had lied to him.

CHAPTER FORTY SEVEN

Reece, Andre, and Charlene sat at the kitchen counter, no one speaking. Tyler transitioning into wolf form earlier than expected had been disturbing in itself. At the time, the PI's gut warned him something was wrong, but he hadn't been able to put his finger on what. Now he knew. He needed to follow his gut instinct *every single time* from now on. It could mean the difference between life and death. If Jade had been bitten there would be no coming back from that.

"Maybe I should sit with him," Charlene offered.

Reece's gaze moved from his coffee mug to her. "No, it's best I do it. I know what to expect."

She sighed. "Why did he change?"

"Some wolves can turn at will, like Tom. Others are governed by the moon."

"He wanted to kill Jade, didn't he?"

"Yes, he needed to feed and she was obviously on his mind before he turned." Reece got the impression Tyler liked Jade as well, which could become a problem.

"And there's no cure?"

Reece shook his head. "If someone is bitten and the alpha is killed it breaks the Lycan curse. We don't know how or why. For those born with the gene there is no cure."

"I see." Charlene knew without the Lycan gene her son would have died, so despite the horrific implications, she would do all she could to keep him safe… and everyone else around him.

Reece's cell vibrated on the counter. *Who could be calling at this late hour?* He snatched up his phone and frowned at the screen. Jacques. Of course, who else. "What?"

"I need to see you."

"When?"

"Now."

Why was he not surprised. "Ok. I'll be there in a bit." He rang off, his gaze moving to Andre. "Can you stay? Keep an eye on Tyler?"

Andre nodded. "Sure. What does my brother want?"

"Good question. You know how he operates. Never gives anything away until he hits you with a bombshell." The PI slid off the tall stool. "I'll see you when I get back."

As Reece walked past Andre, his friend gripped his arm. "Be careful."

"Always."

ℝ)(℞

Jacques was in the open doorway to his suite when Reece stepped off the elevator. "Good of you to come." He motioned for the PI to enter the hotel room.

Reece gave him a sideward glance as he passed him in the open space and crossed the living room. "What's with the pleasantries?"

"Can't I be welcoming?"

"It depends."

"Oh, on what?"

"The reason you brought me here at this late hour."

"Ah." Jacques gestured to the sofa. "Have a seat."

"I think I'll stand."

"Suit yourself." The vampire sat down in one of the plush armchairs and wrapped his continental robe around himself, crossing one leg over the other. "I believe the vampire roaming the city is a rogue."

"From where?"

"I don't know as yet. I'm working on it."

"Come on, Jacques. You wouldn't have brought me here if you didn't know more, so spill."

"He traveled here from abroad. I have people looking into it as we speak."

Reece frowned into Jacques' eyes. "You know something you're not telling me. What is it?"

"Believe me, I do not."

"This is a game to you, isn't it? You enjoy toying with people." Reece folded his arms.

"I am doing my best to help you find the vampire. I want you to find him."

"Why?"

"So you can stop him from killing more innocent people. What else?"

"You don't give a damn about us. What's in it for you?"

"Why do you always ask me that?"

"Because I know how your mind works."

"You think you do." A smirk crossed the vampire's handsome face.

Reece headed for the door. "Ok, well, when you have something more substantial to offer let me know."

Jacques stood. "The vampire is someone you know."

The PI swung around, Avalynn's words echoing inside his head. "Do you know who?" He walked back to the vampire. "Because if you do you need to tell me *now*."

"I would if I could. For the moment I cannot."

Reece raised his hand, his index finger close to Jacques' face. "I'm warning you…"

Jacques took a step backwards. "Do not threaten me, Detective. I am your only option right now."

Reece gave a heavy sigh. He couldn't disagree. Jacques was right.

CHAPTER FORTY EIGHT

As Reece pulled the van up outside the front entrance of his home his cell vibrated in his jacket pocket. He tugged the phone free. What was with people calling him in the middle of the night? Grant Donovan's name appeared on the screen. "Hello, Grant, what's up?"

"We have another drained body."

"Where?"

"Behind the Roosevelt. Can you come down?"

Reece started the engine. "I'm on my way."

Why now? He'd spoken to Jacques only a short time ago about the rogue vampire. Now another attack had taken place near the hotel. Coincidence? He didn't think so.

When he arrived at the scene the place appeared deserted. Reece turned off the engine, pulled the key from the ignition, stepped out of the van, and ran his frowning gaze around the area. This was the right location. Something in his gut squirmed. He'd been brought here on a wild goose chase. A noise in the dark caused him to swing around. No one. He swallowed hard, his Adam's apple bobbing above the neck of his T-shirt. "Grant? Are you here?" No answer.

The hair on the back of his neck stood static. Something about this whole scenario felt wrong. As he headed for the hedged driveway he heard a car behind him. He turned around as Grant pulled in behind his van and got out of his dark blue sedan.

"Hey, what's happening?" the detective asked, walking over to him.

Reece frowned. "You tell me. You're the one who got me to come down here."

Grant gave the PI a curious stare. "No, I didn't. You texted me." He pulled his phone from the pocket of his jacket, scrolled through his messages and showed the text to Reece.

Both men glanced around themselves, an icy chill crawling up their spines.

"I knew something wasn't right." Reece peered into the parking lot behind the hotel. The semi-lit space filled with cars seemed ominous.

"Someone brought us here for a reason," Grant told him. "But what?"

"It has to have something to do with the rogue vampire."

"Ok, why here? Why now?"

A shrill scream echoed into the atmosphere not far ahead of them. The pair frowned at each other and took off running toward the sound, which seemed to be coming from the nearby alley. They skidded around the corner and wandered past the apartment building to the dimly lit back end.

Two shadowed shapes appeared beside a blue metal dumpster. The street light above broken, offering no definition to the figures in the dark.

Another scream.

"Hey," Reece called out, raising his phone's flashlight in their direction.

The woman in the man's grasp slumped to the ground.

Reece rushed forward. "Stay where you are."

As he got closer, Grant right behind him, the bright beam of light lit up the male figure's face.

The PI's eyes widened. *No, it can't be.*

Grant skidded to a stop beside him. "Isn't that…?"

The figure before them vanished.

Reece stood fixed to the spot.

"Come on, Reece, let's go after him." Grant took off running, following the perpetrator.

It took a moment for Reece to get a hold of his senses. He rushed over to the young woman lying on the ground, got down on one knee, and pressed his fingers into her carotid artery feeling for a pulse. None.

Grant ran back along the alley, puffing, his face red from exertion. "He got away." The detective noticed the young woman. "Is she dead?"

"Yeah."

"Reece. You saw his face. It was…"

"No." The PI shook his head and stood up.

"Reece…"

The PI's serious gaze moved to the cop. "I said no."

Grant raised defensive hands. "Ok, whatever you say, but…"

"There are no buts."

Grant figured the PI was in shock. He'd let it go for now and attempt to reason with him later.

"I'll call it in." Grant reached for his cell.

"Don't." Reece tugged the phone from the cop's hand.

"Reece, I have to. This is a murder."

"Give me some time to find out what's going on. Can you do that for me?"

The detective swallowed hard, thought it over for a moment. His ass would be on the line if anyone found out. "Ok. But I can't hold off for too long. What am I supposed to do about the body?"

"I'll have someone take care of it."

"Jesus, Reece, we're tampering with evidence. You know what this means."

"Yeah, I know." He gripped the detective's shoulder in a gesture of comradery. "Thanks."

Grant gave a heavy sigh. "Offer your thanks after we *don't* get thrown in jail for breaking the law."

"Can you wait here until my guy shows up?"

"Well, yeah, I'm not going to leave a body lying in an alley."

"I've got a blanket in the van. I'll go get it."

"Sure, ok."

Reece raced along the alley toward Hawthorn Avenue. He'd drive back to the detective. It would be quicker that way.

❧☙

On the ride home, Reece couldn't comprehend what he'd seen in the alley. *How is it possible? Could Jacques be behind it? He has to be.* It seemed strange he'd been summoned to the vampire's hotel suite and only moments later a woman is murdered by… he couldn't bring himself to say it, not even in his head. It couldn't be him. *Something is wrong about this whole situation.* But, then, Jacques did have control of Andre's mind back when they were chasing Dracula. Could he have been like a sleeper cell, lying dormant until his brother awoke the bloodlust inside him?

He screeched the van to a stop on the gravel drive, threw open the door, and marched into the mansion. "Where's Andre?"

Charlene came into the entry hall from the kitchen. "He's with Tyler. Why?"

"Are you sure?"

"Yes, of course I am. What's going on, Reece?"

He headed to the basement. Charlene didn't follow him. He seemed distressed about something and she thought it best to stay out of it.

The PI stormed down the wooden staircase. "Andre? Where are you?"

Andre stepped out of the shadows. "I'm here."

"Have you been here the whole time I've been away?"

His friend stared into his frowning gaze. "You asked me to stay…"

"Answer the damn question."

"Yes, I've been here the whole time." Andre frowned. "Why?"

"Because I just saw someone who looks like you kill a woman near the Roosevelt Hotel."

"Wait. What? Didn't you go to see Jacques?"

"Yeah, I did. As usual, he gave me the runaround so I left. I'd only just arrived back here when I got a call from Grant Donovan. Well, it turned out not to be him. We were both asked to go to the location where a supposed body had been discovered. When we arrived there was no body or crime scene. We heard a scream, raced along the street to a nearby alley, and found someone who looks like you attacking a young woman."

"You know me, Reece. You know I wouldn't lie to you. You *know* I wouldn't do what you're suggesting. I've been here the whole time. Ask Charlene." He motioned to the stairs.

"I did." Reece folded his arms. "Your brother has something to do with it. I can feel it."

"Could it have been him?"

"How? He doesn't look like you anymore." Andre gave him an incredulous frown. "You know what I mean. He's changed his appearance."

"It has to be him. Who else could it be? He called you over there to set up the scene."

Reece gave his friend's hypothesis some thought. "Yeah, you could be right."

"So Grant saw the vampire too?"

"He did."

"Shit."

"I know."

"What about the body?"

"We're hiding it for the time being. I got our guy to pick it up."

"And the detective's ok with that?"

"He doesn't have a choice."

Andre wasn't so sure. "People always have choices, Reece. Remember, his career is on the line."

"Let me worry about Donovan. We need to locate your lookalike vampire. Remember what happened when Jacques turned up the first time. You were arrested for those murders."

"How could I forget?"

CHAPTER FORTY NINE

The PI didn't wait until morning. He and Andre drove to the Hotel Roosevelt to confront Jacques. Reece needed to know the identity of the vampire attacking young women in the city. This time Jacques *would* tell him. No more games.

"Jacques is doing what he does best. Toying with us." Reece swung the van around the corner into Orange Avenue, took a right and pulled the vehicle up opposite the hotel parking lot.

"I had hoped he meant what he'd said about not being here to cause trouble." Andre climbed out of the van onto the sidewalk.

Reece came around the back of the van to him. "He can't be trusted... no matter what he says."

"You're right."

The pair crossed the street, walked back to Hollywood Boulevard and entered the hotel.

Andre pressed the elevator call button.

"We also have to remember if he is involved he can move around at any time of the day because he still has the ring Eva gave him. If the lookalike works for him he'd be using the ring and you'd be arrested for the attacks."

"Something I don't want to go through again. Ever. Why would he do this to me?"

The PI shrugged. "Revenge perhaps. You didn't go along with his plan to kill me when we were at Dracula's compound."

"I was at his command until Adrian talked sense into me. His spirit, I mean."

The elevator door glided open and the pair stepped inside.

"I still don't get it. It doesn't mean I don't believe it. I'd believe pretty much anything these days after everything I've seen." Reece folded his arms, his gaze moving to the lighted numbers above the door.

"You thought I'd gone a little mad at first."

"No I didn't."

Andre gave him a thin smile. "Yes, you did."

When they reached Jacques' floor the elevator door slid open.

"Ok, let's do this." Reece strutted along to the door and knocked.

No answer.

He knocked again. Reece's uneasy gaze moved to his friend. "Where is he?"

"Look, I'm not defending him, but just because he's not here doesn't mean he's out attacking someone."

Reece's frowning gaze moved to him. "You believe that?"

Andre shrugged. "I want to."

"No point in waiting around for him to come back. Let's go." The PI stalked back to the elevator. When he reached it the doors opened and Jacques stepped out, a young woman hugging his side.

"Detective. What are you doing here?"

"I need to talk to you." Reece's eyes moved to the vampire's companion.

Jacques handed the electronic keycard from his pocket to the woman. "Why don't you go in, make yourself comfortable, and I'll be along in a moment."

She smiled up at him, slid the plastic disc from his hand, sauntered over to the door, unlocked it, and stepped inside.

Jacques' dark eyes moved to Reece. "Now, why are you here?"

"A young woman was attacked down the street from this hotel. Coincidence?"

"Of course it is." He gazed at his brother then back to the PI. "Surely you don't think I would do something as ridiculous as attack someone in such close proximity, do you?"

"You have before... or have you forgotten the young woman in the dog park next to Sunset Towers."

"A foolish error on my part. One I will not repeat."

"I saw the vampire." Reece folded his arms.

"Oh?" Jacques' eyes wandered the carpet.

"Yeah. He looks like Andre."

"Is that so?"

Reece grasped Jacques' arm.

The vampire gave him a stern look. "Remove your hand."

"Tell me what you know." He didn't let go.

Jacques stared into the PI's eyes. "I said remove your hand, Detective."

"Or what?"

"Do not provoke me."

"Then tell me the truth about the vampire killing people in my city."

"You will have to find out for yourself. Now take your hand off me."

Reece thought it best not to antagonize Jacques any further – although it felt good. He released his grip on the vampire. "What do you mean?"

"What you think you know you don't."

"This is something you've cooked up, after assuring us you didn't come back to LA to cause trouble, isn't it?" Reece glared at Jacques.

"I'm not the one causing the problem." He crossed the hallway. "Goodnight, Detective." He gave Reece one last smug smile and closed the door.

"That was pointless," Andre said. "He's changed his mind about helping us. Now I'm positive he knows what's going on."

"I don't think he ever intended to help us. This is turning out to be another of his twisted games."

"So who's the vampire? Because it isn't me."

"We need to find out... fast."

The pair stepped into the elevator.

"I agree. How?" Andre pressed the ground floor button.

"We'll stake out the hotel. Find out who he interacts with. Maybe this rogue vampire is staying with Jacques."

"Or not. What about the girl? She could be staying with him."

"I think she's a distraction. Someone he can drink from without any consequences, someone he wants us to think is staying with him." Reece's gaze moved to the numbers above the elevator door. The damn thing wasn't moving fast enough.

"Do you think she's in danger?" Andre frowned at him.

"No. I think Jacques will be more cautious now. He doesn't want to draw attention to himself."

"I don't understand why he's doing this… if he's the one doing it." Andre leaned against the back wall of the elevator and folded his arms. "He set me free. At least in my dream he did."

"Andre, you can't trust him. No matter what he says. None of us can."

"I know."

Reece turned to him. "Look, I know you want to believe he's changed but he's here to wreak havoc on our lives again and we have to be prepared."

"I wish he'd never been resurrected by that sorcerer in the first place."

"Look at it this way, he brought you back and I'm grateful for that." He gave his friend a man hug.

The elevator door opened.

"Let's head back to the mansion."

The pair walked through the hotel lobby. Two could play Jacques' game.

CHAPTER FIFTY

The killings stopped. Two weeks went by and no sign of Andre's lookalike rogue vampire or any more bodies turning up in alleys or dumpsters around town. It only solidified Reece's suspicions about Jacques. The team worked allocated nights staking out the Roosevelt Hotel without success. Of course Jacques would put a halt to his plan with Reece getting too close. While there were no further killings there wasn't a lot they could do. They would continue to monitor the hotel in the hope they would get the break they needed. If Jacques initiated the attacks, which Reece's gut told him he did, he was one step ahead of them once again.

Reece was at the center counter drinking coffee and reading the digital edition of The Los Angeles Times on his tablet when Tom came into the kitchen.

"Morning, Dad."

"Hey, you're up early."

Tom poured himself a glass of orange juice from the jug on the counter and slid onto a tall stool opposite his dad. "Yeah, I've got a class project I need to finish today so I'm going to school early."

"Oh, ok. Do you need a ride?"

"Nah, I'll catch the bus."

Reece got off his stool, walked over to the sink and rinsed his mug, setting it down on the stainless steel drip tray. "You're sure?" he said as he rounded the counter.

Tom nodded. "Yeah."

"You ok?" Reece frowned at his son.

The teen let out a heavy sigh. "Yeah… well, no, not really."

Reece tugged out the stool at the end of the counter and sat down again. "What's up?"

"The night of Tyler's party when everything went to hell, Jade called me a monster."

"Ah." Reece rested a comforting hand on his son's arm. "You know she was in shock and didn't know what she was saying, right?"

Tom shook his head. "I think she meant it, even though she told me it would be cool to be a werewolf when we were talking about the Twilight movies on the way home one afternoon."

"Look at me."

Tom raised his gaze to his dad.

"Those movies romanticize the supernatural. Make it seem wonderful, something to transform the ordinary into the extraordinary. Look, I'm sure she did mean what she said at the time. Seeing something with your own eyes is a whole different story. Cut her some slack. Don't let something she said ruin what you're trying to establish with her." He leaned in, his eyes meeting Tom's. "You still like her, don't you?"

His son shrugged. "I – I'm not sure anymore."

"Have you spoken to her?"

"No. I've been avoiding her."

"For two weeks?"

"Well, yeah. What she said hurt."

"You need to keep things normal. We can't have her wondering what's going on and remembering something about the night of the party."

Tom's eyes widened. "Could she?"

"Yeah. It's happened before."

"Man."

"Go to school. Find the girl, talk to her. Keep it real. Don't give her any reason to suspect something's wrong."

"So what am I supposed to tell her about why I haven't been talking to her or answering her texts?"

"You've been busy with your project because you were on a deadline."

Tom nodded. "Yeah, I think that could work." He slid off the stool. "See you tonight."

"Have a good day, buddy."

ℰℭ

Tom was at his locker when someone tapped him on the shoulder. He spun around. Jade. "Hey." He grabbed an armful of books, closed the locker door and gave her a thin smile.

"Why haven't you returned any of my texts or calls?"

"I'm sorry. I've been kinda busy with a school project that's due today."

"I thought I did something to upset you. Then I wondered why when Tyler's party was so much fun and we'd had such an awesome time together."

"Yeah, no, like I said, I've been busy with school stuff."

"Can I walk with you?"

"Sure."

The pair headed along the corridor to their respective class rooms.

Jade couldn't shake the nagging feeling Tom wasn't being honest with her. "You're sure we're ok?"

"Of course." He stopped outside a classroom. "This is me."

"Oh, ok. Can we have lunch together?"

"I… don't know. It all depends on how the project goes. If I get it finished… sure."

"I'll text you later to see how you're going with it."

"Sure, ok."

"See you later."

"Yeah, see you." *That wasn't awkward at all.* Tom sighed, opened the door and stepped into the classroom.

CHAPTER FIFTY ONE

Reece was about to head out the front door when his cell phone went off. He snatched it from the inner pocket of his black leather jacket to check the display. Grant Donovan. "Hey, everything ok?"

"No. We've got another bloody puddle."

"What?!"

"I'm at the old LA zoo. Can you meet me here ASAP?"

Reece groaned inwardly. *Why there?* "Yeah, sure, I'm on my way." He closed the front door climbed into the van, revved the engine and hurtled around the circular gravel drive, loose stones pinging against the metal body of the vehicle as it sped out of the yard.

Hadn't Harrison's posse high-tailed it back to New Orleans along with him? So why now right after the vampire attacks stopped? Were the two connected as Reece first thought? Did Jacques have something to do with the reptilian creatures as well? The PI wouldn't put anything past the vampire. He'd come back to LA to cause them pain, nothing more. Reece knew it.

On the drive out to the abandoned zoo, he attempted to put the pieces together. The reptiles arrived around the same time as Jacques, at least the deaths started then. When they stopped the vampire attacks began. Too much of a coincidence? He didn't think so.

∞

The PI pulled the van onto the shoulder outside the dilapidated, graffitied main entrance to the old zoo, climbed out of the vehicle, flashed his PI license at the uniform standing in front of the barrier and headed into the grounds.

As he approached the crime scene, Grant came over to him. He peeled off one latex glove, extended his hand to Reece. "Thanks for coming out here. I know this place gives you the heebie jeebies so I appreciate it."

Reece shook the detective's hand. "Yeah, well, a lot of creepy shit's gone down here that I've been directly involved in and it's not a place I want to be, if I can avoid it." He ran his gaze around the extensive picnic grounds. "Where's the... evidence?" No point in saying body because there wasn't one.

Grant pointed into one of the unfenced enclosures. "This way."

The pair climbed over the rocky low-level base that once held a chain-link fence and headed inside.

"So I gather an urban explorer or some kid called it in." Reece followed Grant into the gloomy space.

"Yeah. One of our guys is questioning the group down at the precinct."

Reece stopped. "Why now?"

Grant turned around. "Good question. I thought Killjoy would've been long gone."

"What if it's not him?"

The detective's eyebrows rose. "You think there're others?"

"Could be. We can't be complacent where supernatural creatures are concerned."

"Then we need help."

Reece's right eyebrow arched. "You want me to get in contact with Avalynn?"

"She knows more about these things than we do."

The PI let out a sigh. "Ok. I'll give her a call when I get back to the office."

"Thanks."

"Do you need me for anything else?"

Grant took Reece by the arm, walked him away from the scene and prying ears. "Yeah, as a matter of fact I do. What are we going to do about you know what?"

"Let's leave things as they are for the moment. My guy's reliable. He won't say anything about the cleanup."

"Yeah, ok. Look, we can't keep it on hold indefinitely. I'm gonna have to call it in at some point."

"Do you? Have there been any missing person reports?"

"Well, no, not yet…"

"So let it go until there is. We'll deal with it then. Your ass will be fine. If all else fails I'll take the fall for the decision."

Grant frowned at him. "That's not my concern."

"Isn't it?" Reece's right eyebrow arched.

"Of course not. I like to do things by the book. It's who I am."

"Yeah? Well, in this line of work sometimes you can't."

Grant glanced around them, making sure no one could hear their conversation. "Ok, but…"

"There are no buts, Donovan. If no one calls in a missing person report we dispose of the body. Simple." He shrugged. "We can't have the city in a state of panic, which it already is because of this situation. Have you noticed how quiet the streets are at night nowadays?"

The detective gave a sharp nod. "Yeah, I have. It's kinda creepy."

"It's even creepier with a vampire on the loose."

"He hasn't attacked anyone in the past couple weeks."

"It's only a matter of time before he does. A vampire's bloodlust controls them. They're driven by it."

The pair walked back outside to the picnic grounds.

Reece stopped beside Grant. "Don't lose your shit over the body. Ok? There's nothing anyone can do for the girl now anyway. She's dead."

Grant frowned into the PI's stern stare. "Callas, Reece."

"Look, it is what it is. What we need to do now, to help her and any potential victims, is find the bastard and dispatch him to hell."

"I did think it was Andre for a moment. Only for a moment, though, because I don't believe he could do something like that. He's a good guy." The detective's eyes roamed the grassed expanse before his gaze returned to the PI. "And, yeah, you're right. We do have to find him before he kills again."

"Ok. So forget about the body from the alley. Keep alert. If this vampire's in cahoots with Jacques he could start killing during the day."

Grant frowned at Reece. "I thought vampires could only venture out at night… well, except for Andre and Nathaniel."

"Jacques also has a ring which allows him to move around during the day. If he's controlling the attacks he could send his vampire mercenary out at any time of the day or night. We need to be on our guard at all times."

Grant blew out a noisy breath. "Frig me, Reece, this is so fucked up."

"Yeah, it is."

"What am I supposed to tell the guys I'm working with?"

"Don't tell them anything. If another body shows up treat it as routine."

"Routine? How can a body drained of blood with no visible wounds anywhere be routine?"

"We need to keep the supernatural element of these killings, both the reptilian and vampire, out of the investigative equation. Understand?"

Grant's face paled. "Yeah, understood."

"Good. I'll be in touch." Reece turned on his heel and headed out of the zoo. He had a visit to make.

CHAPTER FIFTY TWO

A knock echoed into the office startling Reece, his attention focused on the report he'd been working on. His frowning gaze darted from the laptop to the frosted glass door. Perhaps it was a prospective client. The business could sure use an injection of dollars right about now. "Come in, door's unlocked." He rounded the desk.

Avalynn walked in.

"Thanks for coming on such short notice," Reece said. He'd wished Grant hadn't asked for her assistance. He'd been relieved when she had gone back home.

The witch closed the door and crossed the room. "No problem. This can't be the work of Harrison Killjoy, as you first suspected, because our hunters captured his group lying low just outside the border of New Orleans. They're dead."

"Yeah, I figured. It could be one of his nest though. Who's to say at least one didn't survive the attacks we orchestrated."

"Possible." Although she didn't think so. "What if it's a new group?"

"Let's hope not, because if it is all hell will break loose in the city before we can get on top of it." Reece perched himself on the corner of the desk, folded his arms. "We have another situation as well."

Avalynn's left eyebrow arched. "What kind of situation?"

"A rogue vampire is roaming LA. He's already killed a couple of women, but it seems he's gone underground."

"What? As if we don't have enough to deal with."

"I know. When it rains it pours."

"Do you think Andre's brother is involved?"

"You bet I do. Andre doesn't want to believe it even though he knows what Jacques is like."

"Have you confronted him?"

"Yeah, on more than one occasion. He denied it, of course. But I'm not buying it."

"Have you been keeping him under surveillance?"

"What do you think? Him. The hotel. Anyone he interacts with."

"Ok. So we need to get him to talk."

Reece's serious gaze remained on her lilac eyes. "How? He's not about to provide us with any information that will jeopardize whatever plan he's set in motion." The PI stood up, walked around his desk and sat down. "I think he wants to implicate Andre because he couldn't control him back when we were fighting Dracula."

Avalynn sat down opposite him. "Dracula, huh?"

Reece gave her a thin smile. "It's a long story."

"One you'll have to tell me about sometime."

Reece leaned back in his office chair and folded his arms. "Maybe."

Her gaze roamed the empty office. "So where's your crew?"

"Andre is chasing up a lead on the lookalike vampire. Todd's on a personal day. Lozano's staking out the hotel."

"You need a bigger team."

"Tell me about it. When Ed and Sarah made the decision to quit I wasn't surprised. They want to spend whatever remaining years they have together enjoying their life. I don't blame them. Wish I could too, but I know what's here as well as what's on its way with the rift fracturing again. Someone has to stop the things coming through."

"Exactly. So I'm offering to stick around to help you."

Reece wasn't sure how he felt about her offer.

ᏸᏣ

With Avalynn back on the scene, it brought to mind what she had said to him the day she left Los Angeles, 'You need to acknowledge your feelings.' As he sat across the kitchen counter from Charlene, he wondered if he should say something. Like what? He liked her? He hadn't at first because he thought she came to LA to cause problems for him, and, perhaps, wanted custody of his son… of Charlotte's son. Now he knew otherwise.

Charlene moved her gaze from the magazine she'd been reading to him. "Something wrong?"

Reece shook his head. "No, nothing."

"O…K. It's… you have an uncertain expression on your face. I've never seen that look on you before. You're always so sure of yourself."

Reece's right eyebrow arched. "Am I?"

"Well, to me you are." She picked up her mug of cooling coffee, took a sip. "So what's on your mind?"

He waited a beat. "This might sound teenage-ish…" He swallowed hard. "I like you."

Charlene smiled. "Good, because I like you too. Makes for amicable living arrangements, don't you think?"

Reece shook his head again. "No. I *really* like you."

Charlene's cheeks flushed pink. "Oh." She closed the magazine on the counter and looked into the PI's green eyes. "Reece… I…"

He waved off her awkward response. "All good. Forget I mentioned it."

She reached across and rested her hand on his. "No, wait. Uh, I appreciate you telling me, I do. There's only one problem, how do I know if you like me for me or because I look like my sister?"

Reece frowned into her eyes. Good question.

"I – I've been thinking about moving back to New Orleans, to be honest. We've been here for longer than expected and…"

The PI's frown deepened. "You want to leave?"

"We should. We have a home there. A life. Tyler has friends. I have…"

"Someone to go back to?"

Charlene withdrew her hand. "No. I've been consumed with Tyler's illness."

"You know he's not ready to be on his own, right?"

"Yes, and I've been in touch with Avalynn. She told me the witch council can assist with Tyler's adjustment. They have werewolves working with them."

Reece couldn't believe it. He'd opened himself up to the woman and she'd planned to leave.

"I – I'm sorry, Reece, I think it's the best thing for all of us. You and Tom are more than welcome to come visit when you have the time. We'd love to see you."

He should've known better than to listen to the witch. She always seemed to be working against him. "Ok. You have to do what you have to do." He climbed off the stool. "I hope it all works out the way you hope it will. When do you plan to leave?"

"By the end of the week."

"So soon, huh?" Could there be another reason for her spontaneous decision to head back? Could she have feelings for him too? "Well I'm going to bed. Goodnight."

Charlene gave a quiet sigh. She knew she'd hurt his ego. "Goodnight. Sleep well."

Reece climbed the stairs, walked along the hallway, opened the door and stepped into his room. He walked over to his bed and plonked himself down on the duvet. He'd made a fool of himself tonight. Not something he did often and it didn't feel good. He kicked off his boots, tugged off his socks – about to undress and take a shower when his cell went off.

CHAPTER FIFTY THREE

Reece screeched the tires of the van into the curb, pulled the keys from the ignition, climbed out and dashed across the deserted wet road. Another body drained of blood in a dumpster in an alley, of all places. This killing reminded him of the series of supernatural murders he'd been investigating back in 2010, and his first encounter with Jacques. He'd been chasing what he believed to be a human perpetrator, unaware creatures like vampires existed. Then he found out about Andre… that had been a difficult pill to swallow. He'd felt betrayed by his friend. They'd known each other for more than ten years at the time. Ten years. Andre's confession to being a vampire came about because he couldn't hide the truth any longer. His brother had been killing innocent teens and he had to make Reece aware. He hadn't believed Andre at first, but it didn't take long for him to realize he actually knew nothing about his city, the supernatural aspect, at least.

The cop standing point gave him a nod and raised the yellow crime scene tape as Reece approached. "How's it goin', Daniels? Long time no see."

The PI gave the uniform a perplexed frown as he ducked under the barrier, glancing back over his shoulder as he wandered down the alley to Grant. *Who is he? Do I know him?* He'd known a lot of cops during his time on the force, although he didn't recognize the one at the mouth of the alley. He shrugged off the disconcerting feeling and walked up to the detective. "What have we got?"

Grant turned around. "Hey, Reece. Young woman in her 20s drained of blood. She struggled with her attacker because her body's covered in heavy bruises and scratches. A couple of her fingernails have ripped off too."

"Jesus."

"She fought hard to stay alive. Under the circumstances she didn't stand a chance."

The pair moved off to the side away from the forensic team and other cops scouring the area.

"No luck on finding this… guy?" Grant looked over his shoulder to make sure they were far enough away from everyone working the scene. He'd almost said *vampire* out loud.

"Not yet." Reece frowned at the covered body. "Maybe he isn't associated with Jacques." He hated to admit it. "We've had the hotel under surveillance. There hasn't been any movement from Jacques or the lookalike."

Grant folded his arms. "You said Jacques is a manipulator. Maybe he gets out of the hotel by bribing staff."

"Like I said, we've got the place covered. I've also spoken to the Concierge and gave him a story he'd believe. He promised to keep an eye on Jacques. As far as he's aware no one's staying with him."

"Then where the hell is this monster hiding out? We have to find him." Grant's forceful frustrated tone rang in his ears.

Reece's frown deepened. "You think I don't know that?"

The detective let out a heavy sigh. "Yeah, yeah, sorry. Sometimes I wish I didn't know what's out here."

"Me too, but someone has to protect the people of this city."

Grant sighed again. "I know. You're right." He stared into Reece's eyes. "So what's our next move?"

"I don't have one at this stage."

"Did you get in touch with Avalynn?"

"Yeah, she's back in town."

"Is she going to assist with this?" He motioned to the scene behind him with his head.

Reece nodded. "She is."

"Good. We need all the help we can get," Grant lowered his voice, "especially with the new reptilian attack."

Reece's gaze roamed the alley. "Can we talk about this later? Somewhere private?"

"Oh. Yeah. Sure."

"Ok. I'll give you a call in the morning. We can grab a coffee."

Grant walked over to the crime scene and Reece headed back to the van. As he got to the entrance of the alley he noticed the cop who'd spoken to him wasn't there, another uniform stood in his place. He'd wanted to quiz him about where they'd known each other. Would it have been the precinct or Rampart? Something slithered in the PI's gut. He didn't like the feeling. It would nag at him until he could find out.

℘ↄ☙

Tom let out a blood-curdling scream and sprang up in bed, beads of sweat trickling down the neck of his T-shirt, his breathing ragged, his body trembling.

Tyler launched himself across the attic. "Hey, are you ok?" He lowered himself onto the foot of his cousin's bed.

Tom's heart beat so fast it felt like it would claw its way out of his chest. "I – I think so." His sharp breaths caused him to feel light-headed. "I hope so."

The door at the bottom of the stairs flew open and Reece rushed up the wooden treads. "Are you ok?"

Tom threw back the covers and swung his legs over the side of the mattress. "I…"

"Bad dream?" Reece stood at the end of his son's bed.

"Yeah, I – I think so." Tom frowned. "I can't seem to remember now I'm awake."

Reece could empathize. On numerous unsettling occasions he'd been pulled from sleep sweating and short of breath. "Do you want me to make you some warm milk with honey?" He remembered Charlotte always made the soothing drink for Tommy when he'd had a bad dream. Tom wasn't that little boy anymore. He was a teenaged werewolf.

Tom's troubled gaze moved to his dad. "Mom used to make that for me whenever I had a bad dream."

Reece gave him a thin smile. "Yeah, I remember. So do you want some?"

"Uh, no, I think I'll be ok."

"You're sure?" Reece's concerned stare remained on his son. Tom seemed shaken by the dream he couldn't remember. Or had he said he couldn't remember so he didn't have to explain it?

Tom nodded. "Yeah, thanks, Dad. I'm going to see if I can go back to sleep."

"Ok. If you need anything you know where I am." Reece turned on his heel, glancing over his shoulder at his son and Tyler before heading down the stairs. "Try to get some sleep, guys. School tomorrow."

Tyler waited until Reece closed the door. "You remember the dream, don't you?"

"Yeah. I just didn't want to tell dad."

"Why?"

"Because it was about him."

CHAPTER FIFTY FOUR

Reece and Grant met the following morning at The Coffee Bean & Tea Leaf café on West 8th Street around 9:30 AM. The crime scene hadn't been the optimal location for a conversation about supernatural creatures running amok in their city. They needed to keep it under wraps for as long as they could. The PI knew a body drained of blood with no visible wounds would draw suspicion, something he couldn't do a lot about right now. Jim Peters had retired a few years ago, leaving Reece without an ally in the Coroner's Office. He wondered what the examining forensic pathologist would conclude. What would he note in his findings? He took a sip of his strong black, his gaze moving to the detective sitting opposite him giving him a curious frown. "What?"

Grant sat his mug on the table. "Just wondering what's going through your mind. You seemed far away."

Reece set his cup down on its saucer. "Sorry." He gave a sigh. "I was wondering what the forensic pathologist will decide about the body from the dumpster."

"Yeah, me too." He leaned back on the wooden chair, folded his arms. "There won't be any kind of marks on the body, will there?"

"Nope." Reece sipped his coffee. "A master vampire has properties in their saliva to heal the wounds. I've been there before. It almost drove me nuts not knowing the truth when Jacques went on a killing spree all those years ago. I thought I was in search of a human serial killer."

"So is Andre a master vampire?"

Reece straightened on his seat and gave the detective a dark stare. "Don't go there."

Grant waved the PI's comment off. "I'm not. I'm wondering if the vampire out there is exactly like Andre. It would tell us a lot."

Reece jerked forward on his chair, frowning at Grant. "What did you say?"

The detective frowned back. "What do you mean?"

"Repeat what you just said."

Grant took a moment to remember his exact words. "I – uh – I said I'm wondering if the vampire is exactly like Andre. It would…"

Reece jumped from his seat. "That's it!"

Grant stood up. "What's it?"

"I have to go. Let's catch up later to discuss the latest developments, ok?"

"Uh, sure, ok." Grant watched the PI rush out of the café and wondered what he'd said to get him so riled up.

ഗോര

Reece pounded on the door of Jacques' hotel suite. No answer. He thumped the wooden door harder. "Come on, Jacques, I know you're in there." Still no movement. The PI gave a heavy sigh, turned on his heel and headed back to the elevator. He'd speak to the Concierge to find out what he knew.

When the elevator reached the ground floor, Reece thrust himself through the opening and marched over to reception. The young woman behind the desk looked up, giving him a pleasant smile. "Good morning, Sir, is there something I can help you with?"

Reece strummed his fingers on the countertop. "Yeah, I'd like to speak to Mr. Sherwood please."

"Oh? Can I give him your name?" She lifted the digital handset to the phone on the counter.

"Reece Daniels. He knows me. We've had recent conversations about one of your patrons."

"Ok. Just give me a minute." The receptionist turned her back to him while she made the call. Within seconds, she hung up and turned around. "Mr. Sherwood is…"

She was about to give Reece the information, when the door opened.

"How can I assist you, Mr. Daniels?" The concierge motioned for the PI to enter his office.

"Like I said before, call me Reece."

"All right. What do you need?" Mr. Sherwood took his seat behind his desk, motioning for Reece to sit down.

"Thanks, I'll stand." Reece folded his arms. "As you're aware, I'm keeping Jacques Delacroix under surveillance. Do you know where he might be?"

The man looked perplexed. "I assumed he'd be in his suite. He took an early breakfast but didn't mention anything about needing a car or leaving the hotel."

"Well he's not answering."

"I'm sorry. I don't know where he could be." Mr. Sherwood stood up, opened a drawer behind him and removed a master keycard. "Let's go take a look, shall we?"

"Appreciate it. Thanks." Reece followed the concierge out of his office to the elevators.

When they reached the top floor, the pair stepped out into the hallway, walked along to the Gable, Lombard suite and before entering, Mr. Sherwood knocked. "Mr. Delacroix, it's the hotel manager. Are you there?"

No response.

He knocked again. "I'm coming in."

Mr. Sherwood swung the door back then motioned for the PI to go in ahead of him, leaving the door open as they stepped inside.

Reece did a quick search. No sign of Jacques.

"He's not here." Reece came back to Mr. Sherwood waiting in the open doorway.

"I'm sorry, Mr... Reece, I wasn't aware he'd be leaving the hotel."

Reece ran his gaze around the spacious, elegant suite once more before following the man out into the hallway. "Not to worry. He has to come back sometime."

"Yes, indeed."

ℴℛ

Tom felt a tap on his right shoulder as he waited at the bus stop. Turning his head, he saw Jade standing behind him. "Hey," he said, feeling awkward as he'd blown her off when she'd texted him about catching up for lunch.

She frowned up at him. "Are you mad at me for some reason?"

Tom groaned inwardly. He didn't want to have this conversation right now. "No. Why?"

Jade shrugged. "Oh, I don't know, maybe because you've been avoiding me since Tyler's birthday party. What's going on?"

"I explained already."

"I don't believe you. You seem different toward me… *when* I see you. I thought we were…"

"Look, Jade, I've got a lot of stuff going on and…"

"…you can't fit me into your hectic schedule." Jade folded her arms. "Lamest excuse I've ever heard. The least you can do is tell me the truth."

Tom frowned into her eyes. "There's nothing going on other than I'm busy right now."

She blew out a noisy, frustrated breath. "Ok, well, if you don't want me hanging around I won't. See you later." She turned on her heel and walked away.

Guilt rose in his throat. Heat flushed in his cheeks. He felt bad. "Jade, wait."

She didn't look back.

CHAPTER FIFTY FIVE

Reece and Todd Lassiter sat in the van across the street from the Roosevelt Hotel, having a late afternoon snack Todd had picked up at the cafe around the corner. Andre and Lozano were in the other van out front keeping an eye on the main entrance, while Avalynn made her way back through the rear parking lot after doing a sweep of the ground floor lobby. As she headed for the van, a black limousine with tinted windows pulled out of the drive. If Andre's lookalike was in possession of the daylight ring, Jacques would need to travel in a car with heavy tint like the one disappearing down the street.

Avalynn climbed into the van through the sliding side door. "Did you catch the limo?"

Reece glanced over his shoulder. "Yeah, I think we should follow it." He wiped his mouth on a napkin, dropped the crumpled paper cloth into the center console, turned the key. They follow the limousine at a safe distance. "Hey, Todd, let Andre know we're heading out."

"Sure." The ex-detective got on his cell phone.

Avalynn leaned between the front seats. "What if it's not him? Or what if it's a decoy?"

Reece's gaze moved to the rear view mirror, his eyes meeting hers in the reflection. "Better to be safe than sorry, don't you think? Besides, Andre and Lozano are out front keeping surveillance on the hotel. If it's not Jacques, Andre will let us know if he makes a move."

"Andre's asking if you want them to follow us," Todd interrupted.

The PI shook his head. "Not yet. Let's see if we're on the right track first. We could be following anyone."

Todd told Andre to stay put, they'd be in touch.

The limousine entered the freeway.

Reece missed the light. "Dammit! It'll get away from us."

Avalynn flicked her finger at the traffic light and it turned green, vehicles on the adjoining road screeching to a sudden stop, trying to avoid a collision with cars in front.

Reece pressed the accelerator down and sped up the on ramp wanting to make up time. "Where'd it go?"

Todd's eyes roamed the vehicles on the multi-lane carriageway. "I don't see it."

Avalynn's arm poked between the pair, her index finger locating the black vehicle not far ahead of them. "There."

The PI gave a relieved sigh.

After a while, the limo merged onto an off ramp connecting to the Long Beach Freeway.

"Where's it going?" Reece frowned through the windshield.

"What's out here?" Avalynn asked, not knowing anything about Los Angeles and the surrounding areas.

Todd straightened in his seat. "The abandoned asylum. They shut it down years ago after some unexplainable occurrences scared the shit out of staff and patients. At one point, it got so bad people stopped being sent there. Anyone who's ever been inside it swears it's haunted."

Reece gave him a dubious frown. Not because he didn't believe the asylum wasn't haunted, but because Todd never seemed like the type of cop who believed in ghosts.

Todd noticed. "Hey, I'll believe just about anything nowadays. I've seen too much not to."

Reece wasn't about to argue.

ᏍᎧᏇ

The black limousine cruised through the open gate of the old asylum, stopped on the other side, the driver emerging to relock it before climbing back inside and continuing through the grounds.

Todd gave a heavy sigh. "How are we supposed to get in there now?"

Avalynn slid open the side door and stepped out of the van. She strutted up to the locked chain-link gate, chanted an incantation, and the padlock popped open. She pushed back one gate allowing enough space for the van to squeeze through, closed it and climbed back into the vehicle.

Todd glanced over his shoulder. "I'm glad you're here, Avalynn. What would we do without you in situations like these?"

"I'm glad I can offer my help." Her lilac gaze moved to the rear view mirror meeting Reece's stern stare. She gave him a smug smirk. "I *am* useful for *some things*."

"You're not kidding," Todd told her.

Reece spotted the limo about half way through the grounds parked outside a double story building. He pulled the van off the drive under a group of low-lying trees and turned off the engine. Swiveling in his seat he said, "We need to find out who was in the limo. My money's still on Jacques."

"Ok. Let's do this." Avalynn slid the door open and jumped out.

Reece gave an exasperated sigh. The witch's reckless behavior could end up getting them killed.

"Wait," he called after her.

Avalynn poked her head around the open doorway. "For what?"

"We need a plan."

She folded her arms and gave him an incredulous stare, her right eyebrow arching. "What good would it do? Do you know the layout of the building we're about to enter?"

Todd looked at him sideways. "She has a point."

Reece sighed. "Ok. Let's stick together and watch each other's backs in there."

"Always." Avalynn marched across the dried grass to the cream colored building, keeping out of sight of the limousine.

Reece and Todd came up behind her, the PI stepping in front to peer around the corner wall. "The driver has to be inside."

"I can take care of him," Avalynn said, moving around the edge of the building and heading over to the driver's window.

"Wait," Reece whispered loudly.

Avalynn ignored him. Within seconds, she waved the pair over.

Reece leaned into the open limousine window. The driver was out cold. "What did you do?"

"I thought he could use a little nap. He'll be fine." Avalynn smiled up at the PI. "Now, let's get inside. We don't know who's here or why." She rounded the vehicle and strutted over to the open double wood doors.

Todd looked at Reece again and shrugged. "Another good point."

Reece gave his companion a disgruntled scowl before following Avalynn into the shadowed graffiti-filled corridor. As the disappearing sun slid into the distant crimson horizon, the PI's gut shrank. Soon they would be in the dark and he didn't like the idea of being in a building he didn't know without an escape route. What if Jacques had another nest of vampires like the ones at St. Gabriel's all those years ago? If he did, they were in deep shit.

CHAPTER FIFTY SIX

Nathaniel rapped on the passenger window of the van giving Lozano a start. The ex-cop rolled the pane of glass down, his heart thumping against his ribs. "Jeez, N, you scared the crap outta me."

"I am sorry. I wanted to find out how the stakeout is going. Has there been any movement?"

Andre peered around his passenger. "A limo left here about an hour ago and traveled out to the old asylum in Long Beach. Reece, Todd, and Avalynn are checking it out. Todd sent a text with the address, emphasizing Reece wanted us to remain here on surveillance."

The black vampire's left eyebrow arched. "And you think it is wise for only three of you to be inside an abandoned complex without backup? Do you believe a limousine would drive out to a disused asylum that did not have Jacques inside? It is a trap."

Andre straightened in the driver's seat. "My instincts told me the same thing."

"Someone has already made an attempt on Reece's life. I believe that someone is Jacques. We need to get out there *now*."

Andre didn't give it a second thought and started the engine. "Ok. Get in."

Nathaniel climbed into the van through the sliding side door, his huge frame taking up most of the padded gray vinyl seat.

Andre sped along the highway, zipping across lanes to take the exit to the Long Beach Freeway. When they reached the unlit compound,

Nathaniel climbed out of the van and pushed back both gates, leaving them open.

As they cruised along the drive, Lozano spotted the other van parked under a clump of low-lying trees. "Over there," he said, pointing in the direction of the vehicle.

Andre's eyes roamed the area around them. "There's the limo."

The trio climbed out of the van, crossed the grass, and shielded themselves behind the side wall of the pitch black building.

"Someone has to be inside," Lozano deduced.

"Yeah." Andre whipped across the road in a blur. He waved the pair over to the vehicle. "Looks like Avalynn's handiwork."

"Shouldn't we tie him up in case he comes to and blasts the horn to alert whoever's inside?" Lozano surveyed their surroundings. He swallowed hard. *Creepy atmosphere.* He tugged his cell phone from his pants pocket to check it was on silent, and flicked on the flashlight.

"I don't think it'll be necessary." Andre's frowning gaze moved to Nathaniel. "They've been out here for over an hour, anything could've happened to them by now."

Nathaniel closed his eyes, focusing his hearing on any sounds. "I hear three human heartbeats."

"Thank God." Andre headed for the open entry, Lozano and Nathaniel behind him. "Which direction?"

Nathaniel pointed down a long dark corridor to their left. "This way."

"Ok, let's go." Andre took the lead.

ℰᏫℭ

Tom opened the front door and stepped into the entry hall to be greeted by suitcases sitting at the bottom of the stairs. He'd decided to walk home, as he sometimes did, to clear his head. He had to stop thinking about Jade. Better to leave things the way they were. His eyes roamed the ground floor level of the mansion. *Where is everyone? And what's with the luggage?*

At that moment, Charlene and Tyler hurried down the staircase. "Oh, Tom," his aunt said, her cheeks flushing pink. "I didn't expect you home so soon. I thought you were with your dad."

"No, I figured he'd be here by now. I already tried calling and he didn't pick up." Tom pointed to the suitcases. "Going on vacation?"

"Uh, not exactly." Charlene glanced sideways at her son then returned her gaze to her nephew. "We're heading home."

"What?" Tom frowned at her. "Why?"

"I think it's time. I have people there who will help with Tyler's situation. We need to get back to our normal lives."

Tyler gave Tom a grimaced look and shrugged. What could he do? Tell his mother he wasn't going?

Tom stepped backwards up to the double front doors. "Can you at least wait until dad gets home?"

"I – I think it's better this way, Tom." A horn beeped out in the courtyard. "I'm sorry." She picked up her suitcase, Tyler doing the same, and headed over to the door. "Please step out of the way."

Tom sidestepped to his right, swung one door back, and watched as the pair loaded their luggage into the trunk, and got into the taxi. His aunt hadn't even given him a goodbye hug. What was that all about? He walked back into the house, tugged his cell phone from the pocket of his jeans and tried calling his dad again. Still no answer.

₲⁙

Reece's mind wandered back to the underground cavern beneath the old church Jacques had laid low in all those years ago, his gut clenching tight. If the vampire did have a nest somewhere the three of them couldn't hold them off. He turned around. Todd was alone. "Where's Avalynn?"

Todd did a 360 degree turn, his eyes roaming the gloom. "I don't know."

"*Just great.*" Reece stood with hands on hips. "If Jacques has other vampires with him we're in deep shit." He tugged his phone from his shirt pocket, held it up and scanned the long pitch black corridor, the white beam of the flashlight fanning only a few feet ahead of him. He gave a frustrated throaty growl. *Damn woman.* "You're sure you didn't see her leave?" Reece frowned at his companion.

"I swear. I didn't."

"Shit." Now what could they do? Without the witch's capabilities they were in serious danger. "Why would she wander off like this?"

"Maybe she…"

A loud bang echoed along the dark corridor, coming from the direction they were traveling towards.

"What the hell *was* that?" Todd whispered, his stomach flipping over beneath the belt on his pants.

Reece thumbed the flashlight off, leaving the pair in total darkness. "I don't know. But it can't be good."

❧ ❧

Nathaniel walked a couple of paces ahead of Andre and Lozano, his super sensitive immortal hearing listening for any footfalls. Wherever Reece, Todd, and Avalynn were, they had moved swiftly.

Andre came up alongside him. "Anything?"

The large black vampire shook his head. "No, nothing."

"I'm worried. They could be anywhere… and in danger."

"We are bound to catch up to them sooner or later." Nathaniel moved ahead.

Lozano stepped up to Andre. "This complex is massive. They could be in another building for all we know."

"Nathaniel thinks they're here."

"Ok. I hope he's right. I don't like being in here in the dark. Makes us easy targets. Makes them easy targets too."

"I know."

The trio continued along the corridor.

❧ ❧

Tom climbed the stairs to his room in the attic wondering why his dad hadn't returned his missed calls. *Where is he?* He frowned at the phone in his hand. Maybe he should call his uncle to find out if he knew. He hit speed dial for Andre and waited, anticipating him picking up. He didn't. *What's going on?*

Flopping onto the edge of his bed, Tom continued to frown at the screen of his cell. *Where could they be?* They had to be working a case otherwise someone would've answered. Tom jumped up and paced his room. How could he find out where they'd gone? He stopped short, remembering the vans were fitted with tracking devices. He raced into his dad's room, snatched the laptop off the nightstand, sat down on the bed, and opened the computer.

What would his dad's pin number be?

He tried his birthday, his dad's birthday, his mom's birthday. The computer wouldn't unlock. *What can it be?* The foot of his crossed leg bobbed up and down as it always did when he concentrated. His gaze moved to the offending foot and it stopped. *Come on brain, think.* An idea popped into his head. He typed in his dad's cell phone number. *Bingo!*

His eyes skimmed the files. There it is.

He opened it up and clicked on the tracking program. Two flashing red dots appeared on a map of the city.

"Where is that?" Tom said as he copied the coordinates and pasted it into the search bar for an address. "It's an abandoned asylum?" His frown deepened. "Why would they be out there?" Tom's gut twisted and a bad feeling pulsed its way through his already tense frame. Were his dad and the others in danger? Of course they were. He needed to get out there. Now.

℠)л

Andre checked his phone. Tom. He'd felt it vibrate in his pocket a few minutes before but ignored it. He realized no one had let the boy know they were on a job and he'd be worried because Reece hadn't gone home. He told Nathaniel and Lozano he would be right back and disappeared in a blur along the corridor.

When Andre reached the outside of the building, he whipped across the grass to the waiting van and climbed in, speed dialing Tom as he did. "Hey, Tom, what's up?"

"What are you guys doing at the old asylum?"

Andre knew his adopted nephew was a resourceful young man. He'd discovered their whereabouts. "We're on a job."

"Is Dad with you?"

"He's inside."

"Why do I get the feeling something's wrong?"

"I don't know."

"Uncle Andre, tell me what's going on."

Andre didn't have an answer. He hated lying to Tom. Under the circumstances, what else could he do? All of a sudden, the passenger door swung open and Tom climbed in, Sarah and Ed standing behind him on the grass.

"What are you doing here?" Andre asked, his eyes moving to the pair behind the boy.

Ed spoke up. "Tom was worried about his dad and when he told us about this place we brought him straight out here. What are ya up to, Andre?"

"We came here looking for Reece and the others. Nathaniel thinks it's a trap set up by Jacques."

"Why the hell didn't you call?" Ed gave Andre a stern frown.

"You retired. Remember?"

"Yeah, yeah I know, but if Reece is in danger we'll always be here." Ed gave Sarah a sideward glance.

"Yes, we have weapons in the trunk," Sarah told Andre. "Have you located them?"

Andre shook his head. "Not yet. Nathaniel has heard three heartbeats so..."

Sarah frowned. "Three?"

"Uh, yes, Avalynn came back to LA because of the new reptile murder."

"There's a new reptile murder?" Ed balked.

"Look, can I fill you guys in later. We need to get back inside." Andre climbed out of the van. Tom did too.

"Let's see what you've got in the trunk."

Sarah led the way around the back of the building where Ed's sedan was parked and opened the trunk. "I thought these could be useful." Ultraviolet weapons. The ones they had used when they were attacked by Dracula years ago. Ones bequeathed to her by the Knights Templar.

"Yes, they'll come in very handy," Andre picked up one and stuck it in the waistband of his jeans under his shirt.

Tom reached into the trunk.

Andre grabbed his arm. "You're staying here."

"The hell I am, my dad's in there in danger somewhere so I'm coming with you." Tom's eyes glowed in the dark, his wolf trying to emerge.

Andre stared into the teen's wolf eyes for a moment. "Ok. Stay close. Your dad wouldn't want anything happening to you on his account."

"Thanks, Uncle Andre." Tom glanced over his shoulder and smiled at Ed and Sarah, turned around and chose his weapon. He wouldn't allow anything to happen to his dad. He'd almost lost him once already.

CHAPTER FIFTY SEVEN

Grant Donovan had been trying to get in touch with the PI since late afternoon to discuss the new case, but hadn't been able to reach him on his cell. Pulling into the curb outside Double D Investigations, the detective snatched his phone from the center console and tried again. Still no answer. He gave a heavy sigh as he pocketed the device, tugged the key from the ignition, opened the door and stepped out onto the road.

He entered the triple-story red brick building, gazed up the wooden staircase and began the climb. He thought he'd give it a shot before heading home, although by the unlit windows he'd glimpsed getting out of the car, figured no one would be there. When he reached the second floor landing he could see the office was locked up tight. He reached into the inner pocket of his coat, pulled out the police issue notebook and ballpoint pen, scribbled a note for Reece to call him when he got it, then shoved the torn off piece of paper under the door. Glancing up, his eyes met his distorted reflection, a phantom in the frosted pane of glass, and an icy chill crawled up his spine. Something wasn't right. His gut could feel it. Where were the PI and his crew?

Grant stepped out of the lobby and down the front steps. As he crossed the sidewalk he heard his name and turned around, thinking it was Reece. It wasn't.

A uniformed cop approached him. "Detective Donovan, what are you doing here?"

The detective eyeballed the cop's name tag, Evan Osborne, his gaze moving to the guy's face and he didn't answer right away. He frowned into the cop's dark eyes. "I could ask you the same question." His frown deepened. "Weren't you at the last crime scene? Didn't I see you talking to Reece Daniels?"

The cop's smile vanished. "Uh, yeah, you did."

"So what are you doing here?"

The cop removed his hat and spun it around between his hands. "Me and some guys I know helped him out with a problem a few years ago."

Grant folded his arms. "What kind of problem?"

"I'd rather not say, if you don't mind."

"Actually, I do." He glanced up at Double D's windows. "No one's here and I'm worried about them." His gaze returned to the cop. "You wouldn't know anything about where they've gone… would you?"

The cop's bushy eyebrows rose and he shook his head. "Who me? No sir."

"I'll ask you again. Why are you here?"

"He didn't seem to recognize me the other day so I came by to talk to him."

Sounded plausible.

"Ok. Do you know what Reece does?"

"Sure. He's a private dick."

Grant scowled at the cop. "I think you know more than you're saying."

The penny dropped. "So you know about…?"

"Yeah, I do. We're working together on the reptile killings."

"Ok. Good."

"I haven't been able to reach him all afternoon so, like I said, I'm worried about him and his team. Any suggestions?"

"Not at the moment, no. Leave it with me. I'll see what I can find out." He passed his cell to Grant. "Give me your number… I'll be in touch."

The detective keyed in his number and handed the phone back, his scrutinizing gaze studying the cop. Something seemed off about him. Could he be a reptile or some other creature? He thought about asking. Did he want to know? "Are you…?"

It was as though the cop could read his mind. Did he? "Do you really want me to give you an answer?"

"Maybe some other time."

"Good call, Detective." The cop headed back along the sidewalk.

An icy sensation washed over Grant as the suspicion that he'd been speaking to another supernatural creature prodded his mind. But what kind?

CHAPTER FIFTY EIGHT

Andre almost collided with Avalynn as she flew around the corner of the corridor he, Tom, Ed and Sarah were about to enter. She pulled up short with a gasp when she spotted him and the others, her face ashen, her eyes wide. "Why aren't you with Reece and Todd?" Andre asked, gripping her by the arms to prevent her from falling backwards. She seemed disoriented, her breathing ragged, her body unsteady. Fear in her eyes.

"I – I…"

Andre gave her a moment to compose herself. "Where are they?"

"I wanted to do a sweep of the building, to see if I could find whoever got out of the limousine, then go back to Reece and Todd to let them know I'd found their location."

Andre frowned into her lilac eyes. "So what happened?"

"I don't know. One minute I'm on the staircase leading down to the basement, in the next I'm here."

"How's that possible?"

"There's another witch here. I can feel the dark energy."

"You're a witch."

Avalynn shook her head. "Not with the capabilities of this one."

Andre frowned. "You're sure they're a witch?"

"More like a sorcerer. An ancient with incredible powers.

Andre knew the sorcerer. The one Jacques commanded to resurrect him. He swallowed hard. They were in serious danger. "Where are Reece and Todd? We have to find them *now*."

"They – they should be almost at the end of this corridor or in the connecting one."

"Take us there." Andre kept a firm hold of Avalynn, marching ahead of the others.

When they reached the end of the dark hallway the pair was nowhere to be found. The group continued around the corner into the adjoining corridor. Still no sign of them.

Something slithered in Tom's gut. He moved up alongside Andre. "Where's my dad?"

Andre rested a hand of reassurance on the teen's arm. "We'll find him, I promise." He tugged his cell phone from the pocket of his jeans, opened the tracking app to check it. Something he should have thought of when they first arrived. No dots moving or stationary. Reece and Todd were microchipped, like the rest of them, so where were they?

Nathaniel appeared out of the shadows, Lozano behind him.

"We have been to the end of this hallway. There is no one on this floor," Nathaniel told them.

"Can you hear any heartbeats?" Sarah asked, the grim look of concern etched on her face.

Nathaniel paused, closed his eyes, and used his immortal hearing once again. After a few seconds, he opened his eyes, shook his head. "No, I do not."

Tom's eyes glowed as his wolf attempted to emerge, adrenalin pumping through his tense frame.

Andre released Avalynn, stepped up to the teen and gripped his arms. "Tom, try to control it. We have to stay focused."

The young man let out a throaty growl, his inner Lycanthrope gaining ground.

"Tom, look at me."

His glowing eyes stared into Andre's.

"You've got this. You have to stay human for now."

"I have a tranquilizer gun if..." Sarah offered.

Andre raised his hand. "It's ok, Sarah, Tom's got this."

Tom's tall frame folded as he let out a guttural roar that echoed around them.

"Come on, Tom, do it for your dad. He needs us."

The teen's head whipped up, his frowning stare directed at Andre. "All right."

Within moments, Tom's wolf subsided.

Ed moved past Sarah. "Andre, the sorcerer... is he the one that brought you back?"

"I'm thinking so, yes."

"Shit."

"Let's hope he hasn't found Reece and Todd. Maybe they've wandered into another building." The fact he couldn't track the pair concerned him.

"I'm with you," Ed said, stepping back beside Sarah again.

The group continued through the gloom to the end of the adjoining corridor.

When they reached the double doors leading out into the compound Andre's cell buzzed in his pocket. He whipped it out. *Is it Reece?* It wasn't. "Hello?"

"Hi, Andre, Grant Donovan here. Do you know where Reece is? I need to speak to him. It's urgent."

"Uh, Grant, yes, we're on a case right now. Can I get him to call you back when we're done?"

The detective hesitated before answering. "Look, I don't know if this means anything but my gut is telling me something's wrong. Is it?"

A long pause ensued.

"Andre?"

"Yes, I'm still here."

"What's going on? Are you guys ok?"

"We're in the middle of something... dangerous. Can we postpone this until later?"

"No, tell me where you are. I'll come to you."

"Grant, listen, you don't want to get involved in this." Andre walked along the corridor, then turned and walked back to the group.

"I'm already involved. Now where are you?"

Andre waited a beat before saying, "We're at the old asylum off the Long Beach Highway. Do you know where it is?"

"Frig me. Yeah, I know. What the hell are you doing out there? That place is haunted... among other things."

"I'll fill you in when you get here. Once you come through the gates continue down the drive. You'll spot the vans under a group of low-lying trees. I'll meet you there."

"Ok. See you soon."

Sarah frowned into Andre's eyes. "You're going to let the detective come out here and get himself killed?"

Andre raised defensive hands. "Hey, I did try to prevent him from coming here. You heard me."

"Yeah, he did, hon, and you should know better than to tell a cop not to get involved. We *always* get involved." Ed slid an arm around Sarah's shoulders. "Hence the reason we're out here now."

"We've all been trained for these kinds of situations. Grant Donovan hasn't." Sarah's gaze moved from Ed to Andre. "Are you planning on giving him a crash course on how to fight vampires?" She folded her arms.

"I'll keep him close."

"How will you protect him when all hell breaks loose?" Sarah wasn't convinced.

"We'll *all* keep an eye on him."

Sarah gave a disgruntled humph. "I guess it's all we *can* do." She believed Andre shouldn't have allowed the detective to come out to the abandoned asylum, although she knew the truth of what Ed said – law enforcement always got involved in any unrest or danger in the city. Grant Donovan was no exception.

☙❧

Reece woke up to pitch black. *Where am I? Where's Todd?* He waited a few minutes to give his eyes a chance to adjust. He still couldn't see anything around him, not even his hand up to his face. He felt around his clothing for his cell phone. Gone. He let out a heavy sigh. "Todd? Todd, are you here?"

A low groan echoed around him.

"Todd?"

Reece heard movement, the sound of something dragging through debris. He swallowed hard, wondering if someone or something else shared the dark space with him. His gut shriveled into a tight knot, a queasy sensation rolling through his abdomen.

"Yeah, I'm here. What happened?"

"Good question. Do you have your phone?"

He heard the rustle of clothing.

"No. What about you?"

"No, it's gone."

"Any idea where we are?"

"Your guess is as good as mine." Reece climbed to his feet. Strange they hadn't been restrained. "I'd say in a basement somewhere." He felt a sharp sting in his left shoulder blade. "Ouch!" His searching fingers reached over his shoulder, prodding the painful spot. "I think whoever has us removed our microchips."

Todd reached over his shoulder. "You're right."

"It's going to make it impossible for Andre to find us. If he's looking. Right now he wouldn't realize we're in danger."

"Knowing Andre, I'm sure he's looking for us." Todd climbed to his feet. At least he hoped so.

Reece reached out until his hand touched Todd's arm. "I guess we should feel around for a door. See if there's a way to get out."

"Yeah, we should, but who knows how big this space is."

"No point in standing here guessing. Let's get moving. We need to find a way out of here."

CHAPTER FIFTY NINE

"Perhaps we should check below the building," Nathaniel suggested. "We know how Jacques' mind works. We also know he loves to play games in his quest to unnerve his victims. And, right now, we are his intended prey."

Nathaniel's words rang true.

Andre knew this was the work of his brother. It could be no one else. He should have known Jacques couldn't be trusted. Ever.

"You mean go down into the basement or morgue?" Lozano asked, swallowing the lump of nerves lodged in his throat. He wasn't a coward by any means. He'd been in many compromising, life-threatening situations as part of Reece's team and during his time in law enforcement, but there had always been a method to eliminating the monsters, both otherworldly and human, not a supernatural creature like Jacques whose methods of self-preservation came at a deadly cost.

"Yes." Nathaniel's serious gaze rested on the ex-cop. "Do not tell me you are afraid."

"I – I'm not afraid." He waited a beat. "Ok, yeah, I *am* afraid. We," he said, pointing to Ed, Sarah, and himself, are human. We don't have nocturnal vision or super powers. We're at the mercy of the dark down there, which could get us killed."

"You have been working with Reece for almost seven years. Why have you not mentioned this to anyone before now?"

"Because I haven't come up against a vampire like Andre's brother before. I know what he's capable of. Yeah, it scares the crap outta me. I've heard the stories."

"Very well, you stay here while we go downstairs." Nathaniel gazed at Andre on his left then Avalynn on his right. They both nodded.

Ed stepped up next to Lozano. "It's ok, Enrique. I've got your back. So does Sarah. We need to stay together. Splitting up is never a good idea where Jacques is concerned."

The ex-cop's Adam's apple bobbed above the collar of his pale blue button through shirt. "You're sure about that?"

"Yeah, I am. Have I ever let you down before?"

"No, you haven't."

"So let's get going. We have to find Reece and Todd." Ed marched ahead of the group.

"Wait," Nathaniel called. "We will go down first. You follow."

"Ok, sure." Ed stepped aside so Nathaniel, Andre, and Avalynn could descend the concrete stairs ahead of them.

Once at the bottom of the staircase, Nathaniel did a sweep of the long corridor with closed doors branching off into rooms on either side. "You can come down now."

Ed, Sarah, and Lozano moved down the staircase into the bowels of the building.

Lozano waited for his vision to adjust. When it did he still couldn't see much. "Can I turn on my flashlight?"

"Yes, of course. Try to keep it obscure by placing your hand over the light to minimize its brightness," Nathaniel told him.

"Ok, thanks, will do." Lozano tugged his cell from his pants pocket and flicked it on, breathing a relieved sigh. "So what now?"

"We go this way first." Nathaniel moved along the pitch black corridor, everyone following him. About twenty feet along, he stopped short. The group stopped as well. He turned around. "There are other vampires here."

Andre walked up to him. "Yes, I can feel them too."

"How many?" Sarah asked.

"Several," Nathaniel answered.

"We have the ultraviolet weapons which should take care of 'em," Ed said.

"Let us move with caution." Nathaniel continued through the gloom.

Avalynn stepped up beside Andre. "Can Nathaniel pinpoint where these vampires are? Are they awake?"

Nathaniel turned around. "I am certain they are awake. It is night, after all."

"Maybe, if you can locate where they are, I can contain them," Avalynn offered.

"They are nearby," Nathaniel told her. "Inside the Morgue."

"Ok, move aside. I'll cast a containment spell." Avalynn pushed past Nathaniel. As she approached the morgue, the double doors flew open and a swarm of vampires poured out into the corridor, crawling overhead along the walls.

Sarah dashed up beside Avalynn, raised her ultraviolet weapon and pulled the trigger.

The pitch black corridor exploded into a bright shock of light.

One vampire disintegrated in front of them, the veil of ash covering the pair. "Run," Sarah yelled, firing again.

An ear-piercing screech could be heard in the background as another vampire burst into flames, dissolving in a cloud of black ash.

Five vampires flew along the dark corridor, gaining ground.

Tom turned around and fired off his weapon missing one by inches.

Ed fired his weapon, hitting the third vampire. "Take that bloodsucker."

The group continued to fire as they moved back toward the stairs.

The vampires kept coming.

$\mathcal{SO CR}$

Grant Donovan pulled his dark blue sedan in underneath the trees alongside the vans. He checked the clock on his dash. Almost midnight. His gaze moved from the digital numerals to outside. The place had a chilling vibe to it at the best of times, even more so at night. He swallowed hard. Did he make the right decision by coming out here? Hell, yes. Reece helped him when he needed it, and he wanted to return the favor. His eyes roamed the area outside his car. *Where's Andre? He said he'd meet me here.*

A knock on the passenger side window startled him and he jolted in the seat. Andre was standing on the other side of the glass.

Grant unlocked the central locking.

Andre opened the door.

"Hey, you scared the bejeepers outta me," the detective told him.

"Sorry. You need to leave. Now."

"Why? What's going on?"

"There's a coven of vampires here. We've managed to eliminate some of them, but there will be more. I'm not prepared to risk your life."

Grant tried to swallow the lump of tingling nerves traveling from his throat to his gut. Even though he was scared shitless at the prospect of coming face to face with a real life dangerous vampire he knew he had to stay. "You're not risking my life and it's my decision. I'm not leaving."

Sarah leaned into the vehicle. "Please, Detective, go while you can."

Grant scanned the faces outside. "Where's Reece?" The detective stepped out of his car and came around to the group.

"Uh, he's not here." Andre closed the passenger door.

"Where is he?"

"We're not sure. We've been trying to locate him and Todd Lassiter for the past couple hours without any luck."

Sarah walked over to the detective. "You should leave. It's not safe for you here."

He shook his head. "I'm not leaving here until I know Reece is ok. Ok?"

Ed came up alongside Sarah, a deep frown creasing his already wrinkled brow. "Hey, Donovan, don't say we didn't warn ya."

"I won't." His gaze moved to Andre. "Don't you all have microchips implanted? Can't you track them with those?"

"We've tried. I'm unable to get a signal," Andre told him. "My guess is they've been removed to prevent us from finding them."

Grant blew out a noisy breath. "Frig me."

"Yes, they could be anywhere in this compound... time is running out."

"So this is Jacques' doing?"

"I believe so." Andre folded his arms. "I think you should leave for your own safety."

"Like I said, I'm not going anywhere."

CHAPTER SIXTY

Reece stumbled in the pitch black basement, his foot catching on something beneath his boot, his body lurching forward. He thrust out his arms in an attempt to steady himself but his tall frame toppled like a falling tree, and he landed hard on his knees on the concrete floor. He heard Todd's voice close by in the dark.

"Are you ok?" his companion asked, concern in his strained voice.

The PI climbed to his feet, brushing the dirt off his jeans, his knees smarting. "Yeah, I'm fine. Tripped on something. Maybe an old beer bottle or something kids have left behind."

"That fall sounded painful," Todd told him. "Are you sure you're all right?"

"I'll have some bruises, maybe a scrape or two, otherwise, yeah, I think so." He stood with hands on hips, pivoting in the gloom. "We have to find a way out of here. There has to be a door somewhere."

"I know you're right, but where?" Todd said, exasperation evident in his tone.

"Let's keep looking. We need to speed this up. Who knows when Jacques or some of his vampires will show up?"

"So you're convinced it's him?"

"I am now. This is the kind of thing he'd do. He always has an entourage of bloodsuckers with him, which puts us in a dangerous position."

Todd coughed as dry saliva slid down his throat, the sound echoing off the surrounding walls. "Do we stand a chance of getting out of here alive?"

"There is always a chance. We're not done for yet." Reece kept moving. "Come on."

"We've been walking around here for ages. What if we're going in circles and don't realize it?" Todd stopped.

"This must be a long basement. I don't recall making any detours so we'll have to come to another wall sooner or later."

"You hope." Todd continued to follow Reece.

"I *know*. They put us in here so there's a way out."

A door not far ahead of the pair creaked open, a shadow standing in the opening, a minute glow of muted light pushing through the darkness. "Reece, Todd, come on."

The pair quickened their pace. When they reached the doorway Reece hugged his friend. "How did you find us?" His gaze moved past Andre. "Where are the others?"

"Nathaniel heard your heartbeats. They're waiting upstairs."

Both men breathed a relieved sigh and followed Andre out of the basement.

ℰᗝᏕ

The detective moved up alongside Ed Borenko. Although he'd never worked with the ex-Lieutenant, the man's reputation preceded him. They'd crossed paths from time to time, and Grant Donovan had a lot of respect for the veteran cop. "Hey, Ed, what if we split up? We can cover more ground that way?"

Ed glanced sideways at the detective. "Donovan, I know you mean well, but we need to stick together. Trust me."

"Ok, so what if we do two groups of four? If you're worried about Reece's safety wouldn't it be more efficient, under the circumstances?"

Sarah stepped between them. "He could be right, Ed. It does make sense."

Nathaniel came up to the trio. "We are well-equipped to deal with the vampires. We have Sarah's weapons."

Ed gave the black vampire a stern glare. "Yeah, I know. Safety in numbers, remember? We've been through this before with Jacques. You, of all pe... vampires should know that. And it didn't end well. We lost good people."

"I know. I am sorry. If we want to locate Reece and Todd expediently we need to make a strategic move. This would be it." Nathaniel stared into the older man's frowning gaze. "Do you want to lead the second group?"

Ed let out a noisy breath. He knew Donovan and Nathaniel were right. They were never going to find the pair at this pace. "Yeah. Ok."

"Good. We will await Andre's return before searching the compound."

"Where'd he go, anyway?" Grant asked.

"He wanted to check out the rest of the basement now there are no vampires down there." Nathaniel studied the detective. "Are you sure you want to remain here? You can always choose to leave."

Grant shook his head. "Nah, I'm good."

"Very well." Nathaniel turned to Ed. "Do you want to pick your team?"

"Yeah, ok." Ed gazed around the group. "Avalynn, Tom, and Lozano."

"All right." Nathaniel passed his ultraviolet weapon to Grant Donovan. "Remain close."

The detective nodded, then frowned at the unusual device in his hand. "What do I do with this?"

"Once we are ready to search I will show you." Nathaniel strutted over to Avalynn. "Stay close to the humans."

She gave a sharp nod. "I will. I won't let anything happen to them."

❧❦

The trio came upon an open doorway leading into a large empty space. "This way," Andre told the pair.

The PI stopped in the opening, Todd pulling up short behind him. "Andre, I thought the others were upstairs."

His friend turned around. "They are. There's a set of stairs through here."

Reece's abdomen clenched. Something seemed off to him. "You're sure?"

"Of course I am. Come on." Andre continued through the gloom.

"What's wrong, Reece?" Todd asked.

"My gut is telling me something's not right."

"Well, you know what I always say? Trust your gut."

Reece called out to Andre. "Hey, I think we should go this way. We'll be outside faster if we do."

Andre came back to the pair. "But it won't take us to where everyone's waiting."

"Why didn't Nathaniel come with you? Why'd you come alone?"

"Because I knew there are no vampires down here." He gripped his friend's arm. "Why are you doubting me, Reece? What's going on with you?"

The tight band of tension in the PI's solar plexus dispersed. He wondered if his feeling of unease was connected to the experience of waking up in the dark not knowing how he and Todd got there. "I – I'm not." He waited a beat then said, "Ok, let's go."

Andre moved ahead of them. Todd grabbed Reece by the arm. "Trust your gut. If you think something's off it probably is."

The PI shook his head. "It's all good. Come on."

Todd wasn't so sure.

CHAPTER SIXTY ONE

Evan Osborne, the uniformed cop who spoke to Grant Donovan outside Double D Investigations, shoved his cell phone into the pocket of his shirt with an exasperated huff. The detective hadn't picked up on any of his calls and no one in Homicide knew his whereabouts. Workplace health and safety required tracking devices to be installed in all work phones and vehicles attached to the precinct, so Evan decided to head to the tech department to get help locating the detective.

He knew a couple of the guys they nicknamed *The Geeks* so it wouldn't be difficult to coerce one of them into helping him. He pushed open the metal and glass door and stalked along the narrow passage to the technical support office. Oliver was alone. Evan smirked to himself as he stepped into the small space. "Hey, Oliver, how's it goin'?"

The young man's body stiffened and he swiveled on his chair. "Oh, hey, Evan," he said, swallowing hard, "Yeah, things are ok." He waited a beat. "Can I help you with something?" He realized his mistake the minute the words left his lips and wished he'd never uttered them.

Evan pulled up a chair and sat beside the nervous young man. "As a matter of fact you can." "I need to locate Detective Grant Donovan. I know he has tracking for his cell and his vehicle so you can find him for me. Right? I don't want to have to make a formal request. It'd take too long."

"Is – is it work related?" Oliver pushed his black-rimmed, Buddy Holly glasses up the bridge of his nose.

Evan stared into the guy's blue eyes, frowning. "Yes… and no. That's why I came to you. Is it going to be a problem?"

Oliver leaned away from the cop. "All depends."

"On what, exactly?" The cop's frown deepened.

"On whether or not it can get me into trouble."

Evan reached across and slapped a firm hand on Oliver's back, a thin charming smile spreading across his rugged handsome face. "Of course it's not going to get you into trouble. You know you can trust me."

Oliver's Adam's apple bobbed above his white collar and navy blue tie. "That's what you said the last time."

"Yeah, I'm real sorry about that."

"I'm lucky I still work here, you know?"

"I'll make it up to you. Ok? Promise."

The technician let out a heavy sigh. He knew he'd regret the decision. He could already feel it. "Give me his cell number and license plate? I'll check both."

"Thanks, pal. I knew I could count on you."

ༀ

The old asylum stood cloaked in deep shadow against the night, the vastness of the complex of dilapidated buildings hidden by the heavy charcoal clouds smothering the hazy, soft yellow glow of the moon. Evan pulled his sports car up at the open gate, his Lycan olfactory senses attuned to the vampires within. Most werewolves couldn't pick up a vampire's scent. It took years of practice, which he'd undertaken for the sake of everyone's protection. And the skill served him well. Why would the detective come out here by himself? The cop homed in on the sounds around him, picking up human heartbeats… so Grant wasn't alone.

Evan switched off the headlights, eased his foot down on the accelerator, and cruised through the gates, traveling along the cracked asphalt drive toward the once main reception building, his werewolf vision guiding his way in the darkness. As he drove, he spotted a group of vehicles under a low-lying cluster of trees. Pulling off the road, he parked behind a dark colored sedan, turned off the ignition and remained in his car. He hadn't come alone. A few of his buddies would arrive any minute.

The bobbing white glow of headlights in the rear view mirror caught his attention. He tugged the key from the ignition, threw open the door, and stepped out of the coupe. His friends had arrived.

Once the SUV pulled in under the trees, five bulky figures emerged from the four wheel drive.

"Hey, Bro, how's it goin'?" one guy greeted.

"Hey, Ryan, thanks for coming." Evan and his Alpha gripped each other's hand and shoulder bumped.

"So what's the situation?" Ryan asked.

"Not sure yet. There are vamps here. I caught a whiff of their scent."

Ryan's left eyebrow arched. "Oh, there is, is there? Well we can deal with those bloodsuckers."

"Fuck yeah," another guy said, stepping up alongside Ryan.

"Wade, glad you could make it." Evan extended his hand.

"No problem, Dude."

The group made their way across the grass to the first building.

"I think we should check this one out. I caught a whiff of Reece Daniels' scent so he must've gone in here." Evan stepped up to the threshold of the reception center.

"Wait," Ryan said. "Wouldn't it be more expedient if we split up? We're all more than capable of dealing with a few vamps, besides it'll get the job done a lot quicker."

Evan turned around. "We need to be careful. A vampire bite will kill us, don't forget."

"I haven't forgotten. I know the risks." Ryan ran his gaze around the shadowed complex. Being their Alpha, he was responsible for his pack's safety. "Ok, we'll do it your way for now. If we don't make any headway we'll split into pairs and do a wider perimeter. Ok?"

"Sure."

The six stepped through the doorway, passed the graffitied, windowed reception desk, and turned into the left-hand corridor.

℘)℘

Nathaniel's patience had worn thin. "We cannot remain here any longer. Let us do a brief search for Andre before we split into teams." He stalked along the corridor to the basement stairs.

Sarah caught up to him. "Don't you think we should wait? He may have moved on to a different building and won't be able to find us."

"We need to stick with the initial plan to locate Reece and Todd before more vampires arrive to attack us." Nathaniel gave her a stern stare.

"Nothing ever goes according to plan, as we all know. We need to make sure Andre is safe as well."

The group stopped at the top of the staircase.

"So what now?" Ed asked, rubbing a hand across the stubble on his double chin while his gaze roamed the darkness around him. His gut wasn't happy. And when his gut wasn't happy something always went wrong.

"Sarah has made a valid point, so we will return to our initial location until Andre gets back."

"Do you think he found them?" Lozano asked. "He should've called by now."

"Maybe he's in a dead zone without any reception," Avalynn offered.

Lozano turned around. "I sure hope you're right."

"Hey, Nathaniel, can you still do that telepathy thing with Andre?" Ed asked.

Nathaniel's stern gaze met the older man's. "It is not a thing. It is an immortal connection."

"Yeah, yeah, whatever. Can you do it?"

"Of course."

"Ok. See if you can contact him." Ed folded his arms across his pot belly.

Nathaniel gave the ex-Lieutenant a severe stare. "Very well." *Andre? Can you hear me?* Nothing. *Andre?* "He is not responding."

"So what does that mean?" Ed pressed.

"Andre is either out of range or he has been rendered unconscious."

Ed stepped up to the black vampire. "Then we need to find out where the hell he is, right now."

ℰℭ

There didn't appear to be another set of stairs as Reece and Todd followed Andre through the basement room. *Where's he taking us?* The PI ran his suspicious gaze around the dark space, wondering why he had chosen not to listen to his gut. "Hey, Andre, wait up."

His friend kept moving.

Todd stopped beside Reece. "This doesn't seem like the way out of here, does it?"

Reece gave his companion a sideward glance. "No, it doesn't." He sighed. "Let's keep moving. We need to find another way out."

As the pair stepped through the doorway Andre had disappeared into, a loud bang ricocheted off the dank, dark concrete walls around them as the door behind them slammed shut.

Reece swung around and groped for the handle, his sweaty palms connecting with the rusted metal. He tugged with all his might. The door wouldn't budge. "It's locked."

Todd's anxious gaze roamed the dark. "Well there has to be another exit because Andre's not in here with us. What's he up to, anyway?"

The PI stood with hands on hips, his gut tight as a guitar string. "I have no idea. It doesn't make sense."

"I wonder where he went."

"Good question. One I want an answer to when we catch up to him. Let's go."

The pair kept moving through the gloom. Another open doorway.

Reece felt they were being led somewhere... where? Why? And what had gotten into Andre?

CHAPTER SIXTY TWO

"Wait." Nathaniel stopped short, everyone pulling up behind him. He raised his head and inhaled a long draft of musty air, his immortal hearing homing in on the approaching footsteps. "There are dogs heading this way." His nostrils flared. He hated the earthy wet dog smell of lupine scent. It played havoc with his olfactory senses.

Ed Borenko stepped up alongside him. "You mean werewolves, right?"

Nathaniel turned his head, gave the older man a severe stare, his left eyebrow arching. "Of course. What else would I mean?"

Ed shrugged. "How the hell should I know? Could be guards with dogs doin' their rounds."

"It is not. There is a wolf pack in the building."

Grant Donovan came up beside Ed. "You mean those things are real too?"

Ed turned his head and squinted at the detective. "Yeah, among many other things out there that no one knows about. I thought Daniels explained it to ya."

"He said it was on a need to know basis."

The ex-Lieutenant let out an exasperated huff, shaking his head. "Dammit Daniels." His gaze moved back to Grant. "When we have time I'll talk you through it, ok? Right now we have other things to worry about."

Grant nodded. "Thanks, I'd appreciate it."

A group of six figures cloaked in shadow turned the corner and stopped in their tracks when they spotted Nathaniel's group. "Who are you? What are you doing here?" one asked.

Grant stepped between Ed and Nathaniel. "Evan?" He recognized the voice.

The figure moved into a dusty beam of moonlight filtering through a high window above a door, one of many leading off the corridor. "Donovan, I've been looking for you."

Grant turned around. "It's ok, he's a cop."

Nathaniel's upper lip twitched with distaste. "It is not ok. He is a wolf."

Grant's eyes widened. He swung his head around, frowning at the cop. "Are you?"

Evan took a couple of steps forward. "Yeah, I'm part of this pack. We're here to help you. "

The other figures behind him emerged from the shadows into the muted light.

₧₨

Reece and Todd felt their way around the large room, stumbling over broken chairs and other debris lying around the floor. The PI wondered why his friend had disappeared, leaving them alone. It didn't make sense. His probing fingers slid across a narrow gap and onto a splintered wood door. "I think I've found a way out."

Todd came up beside him. "Where?"

Reece felt across the chipped paint until he found the handle. "Here," he said, tugging the door open, its rusty hinges groaning with resistance.

"We're in the basement, there can't be many more rooms down here," Todd told him.

"Yeah, I know. My guess is we're being led somewhere specific. Like the morgue or some other containment location."

"Why?"

"I wish I knew. I've got a feeling Andre…"

A bright floodlight flashed on and both men spun around, shielding their eyes from the glare.

₧₨

Evan and his friends joined Nathaniel's group. "What's going on?" He folded his arms and ran his gaze along the corridor. "Are you aware there are other vampires here?"

Nathaniel eyed him with suspicion. "Yes, we are."

"Why are you out here?" Evan's honey colored eyes moved back to the black vampire. His aversion to bloodsuckers was strong. Nine times out of ten they couldn't be trusted. At least the ones he'd known. He would give this one the benefit of the doubt. For now.

"Reece Donovan and Todd Lassiter are missing. We've been searching for hours but have not located them. And it also appears we've lost another member of our group. Reece's friend, Andre Delacroix," Grant offered.

"Ok, well, I guess we split up to cover more ground." Evan glanced at his Alpha who nodded in agreement.

"We have already chosen our teams and plan to do a sweep of the complex," Nathaniel told him.

"Good. Let's get out there and see what we can find."

"You will need to move around the compound with caution. If a vampire bites you, you will die," Nathaniel warned.

"We've handled vamps before," Ryan said. "We'll be fine." He glanced at his digital watch. "Let's meet back here at the entrance in an hour."

Everyone headed out. All except Nathaniel's team who would continue downstairs into the pitch black bowels of the building.

∞⋐⋙

"I knew you were behind all of this, Jacques. Who else would go to these elaborate lengths to get us out here to a deserted location? Why lie about it?" Reece folded his arms. He wasn't about to show fear, even though fear pushed adrenalin around his trembling body. He knew they were in deep shit. "Why didn't you kill me at your hotel? Would've been a whole lot easier? And while I think of it where's Andre?" His stern gaze moved to the imposter standing beside Jacques. "Because he's not him."

A smug smirk spread across the vampire's handsome face. "How perceptive of you, Detective." He gave the lookalike a sideward glance. "He is a duplicate… as am I."

Reece's eyes widened. "What are you talking about?"

"I am not the Jacques you encountered six years ago. The resurrected Jacques died at the hands of Dracula when he was held prisoner at Decadent Desire."

Reece frowned. "So you're telling me you're *a clone*?"

"No, I am a new improved version. The sorcerer had in his possession more of Andre's and his brother's blood and had strict instructions from the resurrected Jacques if anything were to happen to him to resurrect us both for the purpose of finishing what he'd started."

"To get rid of me, you mean?" Reece's eyes roamed the area behind the vampire, spotted the sorcerer standing in a nearby shadowed corner, and knew they were in danger.

"Not only you, Detective. Your entire team." His dark stare moved to Todd then back to the PI. "You have meddled in our affairs for far too long, something that needs to be remedied."

"I thought we came to an understanding."

The vampire's left eyebrow arched as he gave a humorless chuckle. "Did you? He allowed you to believe an agreement had been made. You stood in the way of him becoming the world's vampire principal Master, and he despised you for it. He would have controlled the earth's entire vampire populace." Jacques' duplicate stepped forward. "Now you will pay the price you owe."

Strong hands grabbed the pair from behind and held them in place. Todd struggled against the firm grasp. Reece told him it was pointless.

"You didn't answer my question," the PI reminded.

"Didn't I?"

"Where's Andre?"

"He is safe. For the moment."

"So what now?" Reece's eyes remained on Jacques' double.

"Now we wait for the cavalry to arrive."

₭⇛

Nathaniel stopped at the bottom of the dark stairwell. "I believe we are heading in the right direction." His immortal hearing picked up the faint sound of heartbeats. "This way." He stalked along the length of the underground corridor. Sarah and Grant Donovan close behind.

"This has to be Jacques' doing," Sarah said.

"Yes, I am beginning to think so," Nathaniel told her.

"Why go to these lengths, though. He's had ample opportunity to implement some kind of assault on us... pick us off one at a time."

"He is one for dramatics as you should be well aware."

"This is extreme, though, don't you think?"

"I think he wants to eliminate us and here is the perfect place to do it."

Grant Donovan ran his nervous gaze around him, unable to see anything. He bumped into something and it skittered across the passageway ahead of him with a rusty squeal. "What was that?" His nervous breathy whisper echoed around him.

"A wheelchair." Nathaniel waited for the detective to catch up. "Do you have your cell phone?"

"Uh, yeah. Why?"

"Use the screen for illumination."

"Won't it give us away?" Grant asked.

"They are already aware we are here."

The detective's queasy gut churned, the burning gush of bile rising in his throat. He attempted to swallow the acidic lump welling beneath his Adam's apple, threatening to choke him. "They do?" His words were strangled by fear.

"Yes. Now let us keep moving."

CHAPTER SIXTY THREE

Nathaniel, Sarah, and Grant reached an unlocked door and the vampire stopped, picking up Reece's and Todd's anxious vibrations lingering in the atmosphere around him. "This way." He stepped into the open doorway, his large black clad form evaporating into the veil of darkness.

Sarah was about to follow him when Grant gripped her arm. "Do you think we should be going in there on our own? Shouldn't we get the others down here? As Reece always says, 'safety in numbers'."

"I understand your concern, Detective, but we know what we're doing. Trust us." She shrugged out of his grasp, stepped through the doorway and disappeared.

Grant swallowed the nervous lump in his throat, shone his phone's flashlight into the dark space and followed, his anxious eyes roaming the shadows, his gut swirling. *Where'd they go?* "Sarah?" he whispered, the hush of his voice resonating around the walls. "Nathaniel?"

No reply.

He glanced over his shoulder at the doorway he'd stepped through. Should he turn around and go back upstairs? No. *I'm a cop for God's sake. I need to get a grip.* He called again in a louder whisper, "Sarah? Nathaniel?"

A hand reached out of the dark and grabbed his arm.

Grant let out an echoed yelp, his body jolting backwards.

"It's me," Sarah said. "Come on, stay close."

"You scared the shit outta me," Grant told her, stepping up beside her.

"Sorry. You need to keep focused, Detective Donovan. Your nerves could get you killed."

Grant gave the priest a frowning sideward glance. "We need backup down here."

"I've called the others. They're on their way back."

The detective gave a relieved sigh. "Good."

"It may not make a difference only put more people in harm's way."

The pair caught up to Nathaniel.

"Anything?" Sarah asked him.

"Yes. They are down there. I can hear heartbeats."

Grant shone his flashlight in the direction Nathaniel had pointed to. It revealed a closed wooden door. "So we're waiting for the others, right?"

"We're here," Ed's voice echoed around them. His group moved closer. "Are the wolves coming down as well?"

"Yes, I contacted Evan. He and his friends are on their way," Grant told him.

"So what do we do while we're waiting?" Ed stepped up alongside Sarah.

"We wait for the others to get here then we look for another entry point apart from that one," Nathaniel told him, pointing to the door along the expansive space. "We need to take them by surprise, *if* it is possible."

Avalynn joined them. "There has to be another way in. Maybe a couple of us should go out and take a look around."

"Very well. Sarah, will you accompany Avalynn?"

"Of course."

"Hey, shouldn't one of us go with them?" Ed offered, concerned for his wife's safety.

"Why?" Avalynn asked, her left eyebrow arched. "I'm a witch and Sarah has ultraviolet weapons. We'll be fine."

Tom stepped up. "I'll go."

"No. You are to remain here." Nathaniel gave him a stern stare. "If anything happened to you your father would never forgive me."

"You all need to understand I can take care of myself."

"He's right," Sarah said.

Avalynn stood with hands on hips. "We won't be long. We're just checking out the corridor."

Nathaniel ran his serious gaze over the three. "All right. Do it quickly."

ℝ℞

Evan, Ryan and the other members of their pack headed back along the pavement toward the reception building. When they turned the corner, they were confronted by a group of vampires standing several feet ahead of them. The pack stopped in its tracks. One bite from a vampire would mean a slow, painful death. And there were more vamps than there were wolves.

"We're bigger in wolf form than they are. Let's finish them off," one of the guys said.

Ryan glowered over his shoulder at him. "If you want to get yourself killed go right ahead."

The guy gave him a sheepish look.

"What do you want us to do?" Evan asked.

He weighed up the situation. Not all vampires could pick up their scent which could work to their advantage. "Make a run for it."

The pack took off.

Some vampires took to the air, following individual pack members, while others whipped through the grounds pursuing the rest.

ℝ℞

"Where are those damn wolves?" Ed asked, pacing the room.

"I do not know," Nathaniel said. "They should have arrived by now."

"Let me call Evan," Grant offered. No answer. "He isn't picking up."

"It could mean one of two things. Either they are almost here or something has happened to them." Nathaniel ran his stern gaze around the dark. "We need to come up with another plan. Perhaps they have left us."

"Look, I don't know Evan all that well, but he doesn't seem like the type to bail on anybody," Grant told him. "He came out here to help... and brought back up. He didn't have to."

"Then we can conclude something untoward has happened to them."

"So it's just us?" Ed said, swallowing the nervous lump in his throat.

"Yes, it would appear so," Nathaniel replied.

Avalynn, Sarah, and Tom returned.

"There's another door at the end of the corridor. It could lead into the room or into a closet. I can't be sure," Avalynn told Nathaniel. "Why don't I cast a spell to blow a hole in the wall? The door over there is bound to be locked."

"Think about it," Sarah said. "It would give whoever's inside time to prepare an attack on us. We'd be going in blind. If we can storm the room from two entry points we have a better chance of picking the vampires off before they have time to react."

Sarah made a logical point. Avalynn didn't argue. She knew her magick would be weak against vampires so there wasn't a lot she could do. "Ok, you're right."

"We will split into two teams and use the ultraviolet weapons Sarah has provided," Nathaniel told them. His eyes moved to the detective. "Here, let me show you how the weapon works."

⁎ᏬᏣ⁎

Evan ducked into an open doorway on his left, darted around the corner into the shadows and pressed his large frame against the wall as a vampire whipped past. A close call. He'd dropped his phone in the tall grass as he'd made his escape and had no way of contacting Ryan or anyone else. His heart thumped against his ribs as he wandered through the pitch black building. He wanted to get back to the others. Maybe some of his pack would head back too. He hoped so because they'd need all the help they could get against the legion of bloodsuckers.

A sound echoed along the corridor ahead of him, causing him to stop dead in his tracks, his Lycan hearing pricking up. A vampire? He sidled along the passageway wall in the direction of the sound. If he could catch the vamp off guard it would be one down. A bite from a werewolf would also kill a vampire.

He inched closer to where he'd heard the sound emanate from. *There it is again.*

Swallowing hard, he yanked open the door and thrust his large body into the room. "Ryan!"

"Evan."

The pair gave each other a man hug.

"I'm glad you're ok," Ryan said.

"Yeah, me too. I mean I'm glad you're ok."

"Do you know where the others are?"

Evan shook his head. "No. I'm hoping they made their way back to the reception block. With all these vamps running around, Grant and the others are going to need our help."

"Yeah, you're right. C'mon, let's go." Ryan tugged open the door and stepped into the corridor, Evan hot on his heels.

⁊ʕ

When Evan and Ryan reached the exit a blur came hurtling toward them. Ryan pushed his companion behind him. He expected a vampire to materialize out of the haze, Zac appeared instead.

"Hey, dudes, we need to get the hell outta here. There's a group of vamps heading this way," he told them.

"Where are the others?" Ryan asked.

Zac shrugged. "Don't know. They could be anywhere. We have to go. *Now.*"

Ryan and Evan followed Zac through the knee-high grass back to the reception building.

"We need to find out where the others are before they're ambushed," Ryan said.

"Yeah, the last thing we need right now is more bloodsuckers." Evan picked up his pace, so did Ryan and Zac.

As the trio reached the back end of the building they heard a blood-curdling scream.

"What the hell was that?" Evan said, his werewolf eyes roaming the surrounding pitch black compound.

Zac thrust out his arm, pointing across the grass into the trees where the cars were parked. "It came from over there. Should we check it out?" He swallowed hard.

"Yeah, we should." Ryan whipped across the road, Evan and Zac close behind. The three moved with caution, eyes scanning the area around the vehicles.

Evan's ears pricked up. "Over there." He raced around the detective's car.

Sam lay on his back beside the sedan, a single stream of blood gurgling from his lips, bite marks on his neck, hands and face.

"No! No, no, no," Ryan said, dropping to his knees beside his friend.

Sam coughed. A spray of blood spattered Ryan's shirt.

Ryan lifted Sam's head up off the grass. "Man, I'm so sorry."

"Kill me." A tear spilled from the corner of Sam's left eye.

"What? No." Ryan shook his head.

"You know you have to. If you don't I'll suffer a horrible death. Please do this for me."

"There has to be something we can do," Zac said, his eyes brimming with tears. "We can't…"

Ryan stood up, frowning at him. "If there was don't you think I'd do it?"

"Then you have to do what he asks. We can't let him suffer."

"I'll do it." Evan stepped up beside Ryan.

"No, I'm your Alpha," he said, swallowing the painful lump lodged in his throat. "I'll do it."

The three stood over Sam reciting the sacred Lycan prayer, then Ryan asked Evan and Zac to step away. He tugged the inscribed silver dagger from its sheath at his hip, the ebony handle a protection from the life-taking blade, knelt beside Sam, rested a hand on his friend's shoulder, and plunged the metal into his heart. A flash of golden rays emanated from the wound, a plume of white leaving Sam's lips and dispersing into the atmosphere above him. He was gone. Ryan remained beside him, tears sliding down his cheeks. The bloodsuckers would pay for this. He'd make sure of it.

CHAPTER SIXTY FOUR

Reece couldn't believe they were trapped in another life-threatening situation like this at the hands of Jacques – or as it turned out Jacques' *new improved* model. The master vampire had ensured someone would come back to Los Angeles to finish the job he'd started all those years ago. Why? Because he envied Reece's and Andre's friendship. They were like brothers, and Jacques couldn't grasp the true meaning of brotherhood. His vendetta had always been about the bond they shared. Nothing more.

"So you orchestrated the collision. The explosion at the house in Santa Monica too."

The vampire gave him a severe stare. "I hoped for a more satisfying outcome on either front." He'd expected the PI to die in the collision. That hadn't happened so more drastic measures were taken. Even the vampire's resuscitated memory reminded him of the fact that Reece Daniels was a difficult human to dispatch.

"What do you plan to do with the first Andre? Are you going to kill him like you plan to kill us? He isn't going to bend to your will, you know?" Reece wanted to stall for time. He knew his team was here by what Andre's lookalike told them. At least they stood a fighting chance now.

Jacques paced, hands behind his back, stopped and turned around, his wary gaze moving to the PI. "Yes, it does pose a slight conundrum." He walked across to Reece. "As yet, I haven't decided."

"I guess the thing is, if you plan on keeping him around, allowing him to believe you are his brother, which you are in a way, what's going to happen to *him*?" Reece jerked his chin at Andre's look alike.

The vampire realized the PI's plan. "Enough. You will remain silent until your friends arrive." He raised the left side of his head to listen. "Ah, they are already here." A satisfied smile spread across his face.

Reece's eyes roamed the shadowed corners of the room, his breathing quickening. He had to alert his friends. "He has a vampire team in here with him and the sorcerer," he called out, his anxious voice ricocheting off the dank concrete walls.

Jacques double thrust out his black leather-gloved hand, connecting with the center of Reece's face, knocking him unconscious. The PI sagged on his feet, blood trickling from the corner of his mouth, his body still being held by the vampire behind him.

Todd darted sideways, eyes wide, breathing ragged. *We're all going to die here.*

A loud explosion rocked the building as Avalynn's team stormed into the underground room through the jagged hole in the wall, Nathaniel's team entered through the now fractured door on the other side of the expansive space. Both teams fired off ultraviolet weapons across the bright center and Jacques' vampires scattered, some being taken out by the futuristic devices, agonized screams echoing around the room, their bodies disintegrating into clouds of ash.

Nathaniel thrust his powerful body across the room, landing on top of the vampire holding Reece, knocking the pair to the ground. He twisted the vampire's neck, scooped the PI up and moved him to a safe corner by the shattered door. Todd darted out of the way and fired off shots to cover Nathaniel as he laid Reece on the dirty, debris strewn concrete floor.

Tom shifted into wolf form and attacked a vampire attempting to escape before pursuing Andre's brother.

"Tom. Stop," Nathaniel's deep voice boomed across the concrete room. Tom stopped in his tracks. "Leave him to me." The black vampire strutted across the room. He had a score to settle.

Avalynn stood center using her electrical current to knock out as many vampires as she could. She knew it wouldn't hold them for long.

Sarah fired off her twin ultraviolet arrows. They rocketed across the room into a vampire attempting to escape. The body hit the floor, exploding into a cloud of black ash.

As the residue cleared, Ryan's remaining wolf pack shifted as they surged into the room, spread out and attacked the vampires, their huge muzzles latching onto limbs and throats before the vamps had a chance to bite back.

Ed raced over to Reece, lowering himself onto his knees to shake the PI awake. "Hey, Daniels?" He shook harder. "Come on, come on, wake up."

The PI remained unconscious.

The ex-lieutenant climbed to his feet, pointed his weapon at an approaching vampire and fired. "Take that bloodsucker!" Another one followed. "And that!"

Sarah called out to him. He glanced over his shoulder at Reece before hurtling back into the fray. He really was getting too old for this shit.

Tom's large wolf form bounded across the room when he spotted his dad lying on the floor.

"Tom, we need you." Sarah's voice echoed across to him. His conflicted wolf gaze moved from his dad to her then back to his dad. He wanted to stay to protect him.

Grant Donovan's eyes roamed the chaos and he saw Tom with Reece. Darting around the room, he made his way over to where the PI lay. "It's ok. I'll stay with him," the detective told the wolf, raising his ultraviolet weapon to confirm he wielded protection for them both.

Tom flew back into the fight, blood spraying in all directions as the supernatural conflict continued.

CR

Nathaniel whipped along the corridor in hot pursuit of Jacques. *Where has he gone?* Jacques had managed to elude him. How? He had only been seconds behind him. His immortal hearing pricked up as he heard the engine of a car idling nearby. The black vampire burst through an already broken window out into the cool night air and followed the sound. He could not allow Jacques to get away this time.

The master vampire climbed into the back of a black SUV.

Nathaniel flew through the air to get to the vehicle before it left the compound. As he reached it a burst of pale blue ultraviolet light shot out from the back of the wagon. Nathaniel dived into a nearby clump of bushes to avoid being disintegrated by the deadly beam.

Jacques had thought of everything to maximize his escape.

§Ɔ

The bright flood light smashed when it was knocked over during the fight and the humans in the group remained still, unable to see in the dark. Everything was silent. Had they beaten the vampires? Were they safe?

Nathaniel stepped into the pitch black space, his nocturnal vision roaming the expansive room. The vampires were dust, or if any survived, had made a run for it. They would live to fight another day alongside Jacques.

"Is everyone all right?" the vampire asked.

Multiple responses echoed around the room.

"Very well, let us collect Reece and leave."

Ed flicked on the flashlight of his phone, moving it around everyone in the group to make sure they were ok, especially Sarah. "There you are." He walked over and wrapped his arms around her in a brief hug before moving the light across the room to where Reece lay. "Hey, where's Daniels and Donovan?"

Everyone's eyes moved in the direction of the corner.

"Could the detective have taken him outside?" Sarah suggested.

"Let us get upstairs and find out." Nathaniel headed for the door.

The group made their way from the basement to the main entrance. No sign of either man.

An unsettling feeling gripped the vampire's solar plexus. Had Jacques taken the pair? That would be the only explanation for their disappearance.

CHAPTER SIXTY FIVE

The group congregated under the trees beside the vehicles. There were injuries to be taken care of. None of them had come out of the fight unscathed. Thankfully, no one had been bitten or scratched during the fray. A blessing in itself. They would meet back at Double D Investigations to decide how they would find Reece, Grant, and Andre.

Evan's pack had headed back to the city, the cop giving his word he would assist with the search for the PI and the others. Being part of it now he would do everything he could to help locate them.

Everyone climbed into the parked vehicles and left the abandoned asylum. Ed, Sarah, and Tom rode with the vampire in the van Reece had driven out there in, while Todd took Grant Donovan's sedan. Lozano drove the other van with Avalynn as passenger.

Once back at the office, the group climbed the stairs, filed into the room and sat down. They were all exhausted.

Sarah made a B-line for the First Aid kit in the kitchen before joining the rest of the team at Reece's desk.

"The bloodsucker has Daniels, Donovan, and Andre otherwise where'd they go?" Ed asked, worry wrinkling his already creased brow.

"Yes, it is my theory as well," Nathaniel said.

"We have no idea where the vampire is right now. He wouldn't have gone back to the hotel," Lozano deduced.

"No, he would not. He would have a second, even a third location for his own protection."

"So how can we find him?" Todd paced. "We have to get everyone back... alive."

"And we will." Nathaniel knew the real Jacques better than anyone. He had served him for hundreds of years before the master vampire died – the first time. "My team will do a thorough search of the city, check other hotels and realtors. We *will* find Jacques' location. You have my word."

Sarah's gaze moved to Nathaniel as she dabbed iodine onto Ed's wounds. "Do you have any idea where he would go?"

"Perhaps an old church or another abandoned building."

"Ok... narrows it down somewhat," Todd said, grabbing the laptop from off Reece's desk, plonking himself down at the kitchen table and opening the computer. "There's a church undergoing renovations in Long Beach, not far from the asylum. What do you think?"

"A logical possibility." A thought jumped into the vampire's head. "I think I may know where he has taken them."

"Where?" everyone said together.

"The old LA zoo."

"That's where he met with Reece that night. And it's where the real Jacques had Andre resurrected." Ed flinched as Sarah dabbed another wound. "Ouch! Take it easy will ya."

"Yes, I am aware." Nathaniel's gaze moved to the ex-lieutenant. "I will go there to check it out. It would be the perfect location for him to hide Reece, Andre, and the detective. There are a number of underground cages out there Jacques could keep them hidden in until he decides what is to be done with them."

"What about urban explorers?" Lozano asked. "Wouldn't they come across Reece and the others and help them?"

"Jacques' sorcerer would cast a cloaking spell to prevent anyone from finding them."

"I'm coming with you," Ed told Nathaniel.

"There is no need for..."

"I'm coming anyway." The ex-lieutenant folded his arms, giving the vampire a severe scowl. "It's not a negotiation."

"Very well."

"Me too," Sarah said.

"And me," Todd added.

Tom crossed the office from the kitchen. "I'm coming too. He's *my* dad."

Nathaniel's left eyebrow arched. "I understand how you feel. Nonetheless, we cannot all go. I need some of you here."

"I'll stay," Lozano offered. "If you need backup you can call me. I'll contact Evan and get his pack out to you."

The office door flew open.

Grant Donovan staggered into the room and passed out on the floor. He was covered in blood from head to foot and looked like he'd been beaten.

"Let's get him onto the cot," Sarah said.

Todd and Lozano lifted the detective off the floor and laid him on the bed in the corner of the office.

"I wonder how he got away," Ed pondered, standing with hands on hips.

"It is something we will discover once he is awake," Nathaniel told him.

"Don't you think it's strange they let him go?"

"Perhaps he escaped. Maybe his injuries were sustained from jumping out of a moving vehicle," the vampire speculated.

Ed folded his arms. "What if they weren't?"

"We will find out soon enough."

Sarah threaded through the group carrying the First Aid kit. "I'll clean him up." She knelt beside the cot and proceeded to attend to the detective's wounds.

The others moved back to Reece's desk.

Avalynn remained standing, arms folded. "I go along with Ed. How did the detective managed to escape?"

Nathaniel's serious gaze turned to her. "He may have been released to deliver a message. We will not know anything until he comes to. Perhaps it is best not to hypothesize until we have the facts."

℘)Cℛ

Reece came to in a pitch black room, wondering if he was still in the basement at the abandoned asylum. He had to be. "Hello?" he called, his voice echoing around the walls hidden from his view in the dark. The PI eased himself off the dirt strewn floor onto his feet, his head spinning. "Anyone here?" He closed his eyes, pressed the palm of his right hand against his throbbing forehead, his mind a jumble. *What happened? Oh, yeah, now I remember. Jacques, as usual.* He'd been knocked unconscious by a punch in the face. Reece licked his dry lips, tasting the tang of blood in the corner of his mouth. *Bastard.*

The PI prodded the pockets of his jeans for his cell phone before remembering it had been taken at the asylum. What had happened to everyone? Were they dead? A slithering feeling squirmed in his gut. With outstretched hands, he shuffled across the space making his way to a door, he hoped. It was obvious to him now he wasn't in the asylum. *Where the hell am I? And who brought me here?*

℘

Andre's eyes snapped open. *Where am I?* His nocturnal vision widened as he took in his surroundings. The old LA zoo? Why here? He raised himself up off the debris strewn ground in one fluid movement and stood with hands on hips, gazing around the dank animal cage. His ears pricked up and locked onto a heartbeat. Another prisoner. He walked across the rocky space to the padlocked staved door. "Hello?" His voice echoed along the narrow passageway behind the empty cages.

"Andre?" Reece called back.

"Reece? What happened? Why are we here?"

"Jacques happened."

"That answers a lot of questions."

"Where are you?"

"At the end of the passage. I'm going to attempt to unlock the padlock. Give me a minute." His vampire eyes focused on the heavy metal lock and he used all the immortal energy he could to snap it open.

"Did it work?" Reece's anxious voice echoed along the passage.

"Not yet. I'll try again." He focused on the lock once more. "Dammit!" He thrust out his hands in frustration and hit the metal staves. The lock popped open and fell to the floor, the gate squealing backwards on rusty hinges. "Hey, it worked."

"I had total faith in you, buddy. Now get me outta here."

Within seconds, Andre stood in front of Reece's cage. "Ok, step back. I'm going to try it again."

It took a couple more attempts before the lock popped.

"Let's get out of here." Reece raced along the passage, Andre in tow.

When they reached the narrow rocky steps leading up to ground level they found another locked door. Climbing up, Andre used whatever immortal energy he had left to pop the lock. Because he'd been unconscious for so long his abilities were depleted. "We need to go before someone comes back."

"I'm with you." Reece climbed the last few steps out onto an asphalt drive.

Andre came up beside him.

Reece knew where they were. On the road leading to the main entrance. "Ok, let's go."

The pair stayed close to the rocky concrete wall and made their way up to the dilapidated wooden building.

Reece stopped behind the corner of the wall to check for a guard. No one. To his mind their escape was too easy. His gut did a nervous flip flop beneath the leather belt on his jeans. "I don't like this."

Andre frowned. "What?"

"*This*. It's too easy. Something's not right here."

"Jacques has other things to occupy his mind right now. My guess is he thought we'd be unconscious for hours."

The PI shook his head. "No, that's not it."

CHAPTER SIXTY SIX

"What was that?" Reece gasped. A noise behind the pair caused both of them to swing around.

Andre roamed the darkness with his nocturnal vision. Nothing, as far as he could tell. "Maybe it's some birds in a tree or something," he offered.

"Yeah, it's the 'or something' I'm worried about. We should keep moving. We need to get out of here while we can." The PI stalked along the drive, his gut tight. He knew something wasn't right about their easy escape.

Andre followed, glancing over his shoulder to ensure they weren't being pursued.

Another sound came out of the gloom.

"I *know* I didn't imagine that." With no way to defend himself or his friend, Reece felt vulnerable. He'd left his Glock in the glove compartment of the van.

"No, you didn't."

Approaching headlights lit up the driveway in a white haloed glow and the PI raised his hand to shield his eyes from the glare.

Andre headed along the inclined drive when he realized the van was one of theirs. They were safe now.

Nathaniel, Ed, Sarah, and Todd stepped from the van, each one relieved the pair was all right.

A high-pitched squeal came out of nowhere and echoed along the driveway. Reece spun around. Two reptilian creatures stood behind him.

"Reece!" Andre yelled and made a dash for him.

Ed grabbed his arm to stop him. "Don't."

The PI took a slow backward step, another, then another, defensive hands raised in front of him, his heart pounding, his breathing ragged. The reptiles closed the distance between them.

Nathaniel flew into the air. He would scoop Reece up and move him out of harm's way. As he swooped in to pick up the PI both creatures spat a spray of venom at Reece. The shower of yellow acid covered him from head to foot, his saturated clothes disintegrating from his body, flesh and bone dissolving into a bloody puddle where he stood.

"Nooo!" Tom screamed, leaping from the van, shifting into wolf form and hurtling his large body toward the snake-like creatures.

Sarah snatched up the flame thrower from the back of the vehicle. "Tom, get out of the way!" she shouted.

The wolf backed up.

Sarah pulled the trigger as she marched down the drive.

A bright orange burst of fire hit one reptile then the other. Both slumped to the ground screaming in agony, their bodies sizzling, skin peeling as the flames licked their bodies.

She continued to hold the trigger in place until the reptilian creatures were burnt to a crisp. She no longer cared whether they were gods or demons; she would make sure they didn't live, either. They had killed Reece.

Tom gave an agonized howl as he returned to human form, tears tumbling down his face. "Daaad. Nooo."

Andre covered him with a blanket from the vehicle, gripped his shoulders and raised him off the ground. "Come on. Let's go back to the van."

Tom shrugged out of Andre's grasp. "No, I want to stay here."

Ed and Todd stumbled down the driveway unable to believe what had just happened. Reece was gone. *Really* gone.

Tears slipped down Sarah's face as she fired one last burst of flames at the dead reptiles for her own satisfaction.

Nathaniel landed on the drive only inches from the puddle. "I – I thought I could save him."

"Yeah," Ed said. "Me too." He swiped at an errant tear sliding from the corner of his left eye. "Jacques is gonna pay for this."

"He brought the creatures here to get rid of us both." Andre realized.

"He wants to get rid of us all," Nathaniel corrected. "And he won't stop until he does. We must be one step ahead of him."

"How? We have no idea where he is right now." Andre gave Nathaniel a serious frown.

"I *will* find him." A bloody tear slid from the vampire's right eye. "He *will* die this time. You have my word."

Sarah shoved the weapon at Ed, gave him a painful, teary glance, and walked over to Tom. "Hey, hon, we need to go."

Tom's head snapped up, his tear-filled eyes glaring at her. "I'm not going anywhere." He returned his gaze to what remained of his dad. "I'm staying."

She could hear the heartbreak in the young man's shaky voice and wanted to hold him tight. Now wasn't the time. They had to leave – for everyone's safety. "Hon, there's nothing more we can do here. I'll pray over your dad. We can take the remains with us… to have a memorial for him." Tears continued to slip down Sarah's cheeks. She needed to keep her voice steady for the boy, although she wanted to sob.

Tom raised his tear-streaked face again. "Ok," he said, his voice almost a whisper. He realized his dad wouldn't want him to be difficult at a time like this, and he wanted to live up to that. For him. He climbed to his feet, pulling the blanket closer around his naked body. "I'm sorry. Thank you."

Sarah nodded without speaking again because she knew if she did her voice would break, just like her heart had.

Andre and Ed came over to the boy, both wrapping a comforting arm around his shoulders before walking him back to the van.

Nathaniel waited for Sarah to say a prayer and collect Reece's remains, his nocturnal vision scanning the shadowed trees nearby. Were there more creatures they didn't know about? Or had these two been lying in wait for Jacques' command? He suspected they had.

ᔕᓂᑫᔕ

Instead of going back to the office, Nathaniel drove the group to *Sanguine*. The nightclub was a neutral space – not Double D Investigations where they worked and not the home Tom shared with his dad. He wanted to make it as easy as possible for the young man, who had now lost both parents. The vampire pulled the van into the alley. He turned to look at the other grieving faces before opening the driver's door, stepping out and rounding the back of the van to the sliding side door. He opened it. "We are here."

"Why did you bring us here?" Sarah asked.

"I thought it best for the moment. And I believe everyone could use something strong to drink." His gaze moved to the dazed young man huddled against the wall of the van still wrapped in the blanket.

"I sure could use a drink," Ed said, crouching to step out of the vehicle.

"Yeah, me too." Todd followed him.

Sarah's gaze moved from Tom to Andre. "I'm so sorry." She climbed out into the alley.

Andre turned his head to look at them. "We'll be in in a minute."

The group headed for the back door to the nightclub leaving the pair alone.

Andre pulled a duffel bag out from under one of the seats and slid it across the floor. "Here, get dressed."

Tom's welling eyes met his uncle's. "Why did it have to be my dad?"

"Because Jacques wants us all dead, as Nathaniel said."

"He's a monster, Uncle Andre. He's nothing like you."

"Yes, he is a monster." Andre moved across to the bench seat beside Tom. "We're going to finish him once and for all. I promise you he won't do this to anyone again."

"I wish he hadn't done it to my dad." Tom leaned into his uncle and sobbed, the pain in his broken heart unbearable.

"Me too." Andre swallowed the aching lump in his throat. He wanted to cry as well. Instead, he wrapped his arms around the boy, held him tight and allowed him to grieve.

Minutes later, bright headlights pulled in behind the van. A car door clicked shut and Andre heard rushing footsteps before Lozano's ashen face appeared in the open doorway. "Is it true?" He spotted Tom sobbing against Andre's chest and stopped himself from saying 'Reece is dead?'

Andre nodded.

"I can't believe it."

Nathaniel appeared beside the ex-cop. "Come inside."

Lozano looked up at him with tears in his eyes, nodded, and followed the vampire into the nightclub.

Tom eased his tall frame out of his uncle's embrace. "I'll get dressed now."

"Ok. I'll wait for you in the alley." Andre stepped down out of the van.

"Uncle Andre?"

"Yes?"

"Thank you for being here for me."

"Always."

Once dressed, Tom climbed out of the van. Giving a heavy sigh, he said, "Do we have to go inside?"

Andre's right eyebrow arched. "You don't want to?"

Tom shook his head. "Everyone's sad... it's... it's too hard right now."

"Where do you want to go?" He knew the answer before the young man said it.

"Home."

"Ok. I'll text Sarah so she can explain to everyone." He tugged his cell from the pocket of his jeans and sent the message.

"Let's go." Andre climbed into the van, Tom in the passenger seat, and drove along the alley. "I guess you're not hungry."

Tom shook his head. "Not at all."

"We'll stop by my place so I can grab a few things then head over to yours. Ok?"

"Ok."

As they drove toward Andre's apartment, he'd noticed a set of headlights behind the van that seemed to be on their tail. Were they being followed?

CHAPTER SIXTY SEVEN

Andre pulled the van into the curb outside his apartment building, turned off the engine and climbed out. Tom stepped out of the van as he came around the vehicle.

"Is something wrong, Uncle Andre?" Tom's eyes roamed the busy road from one end to the other. "You were driving kinda fast. And you kept checking the rear view mirror."

"I thought we were being followed. Thankfully, the car turned off down a side street before we got to the intersection."

"Oh, ok. That's good."

"Do you want to wait in the van while I race up and grab some things?"

Tom stuffed his hands into the pockets of his hoodie. "Can I come up with you?"

"Of course. Let's go."

The pair took the elevator to Andre's floor and as they stepped out into the corridor they spotted Avalynn waiting outside the front door to the apartment.

"What are you doing here?" Andre asked, tugging the key from the pocket of his jeans to unlock the large white door.

"I came because I heard about..." Her lilac eyes shifted to the teen. "I'm very sorry for your loss, Tom. Your dad was a good man." Her gaze moved back to the vampire. "And you, too, Andre. I know you were friends for a long time."

"Thank you." Andre gave her a serious look before stepping into the living room.

"Yeah, thanks." Tom followed Andre inside.

Avalynn stood at the threshold. "May I come in?"

"Why? There's nothing anyone can do to bring Reece back so what's the point of your visit?"

"I know where Jacques is."

৪৩ ଓ

Nathaniel stood behind the bar and poured everyone another shot of whiskey. He slid the individual glasses across the shiny black surface then poured a drink for himself. He raised the glass in his hand. "To Reece."

Everyone raised their glasses. "To Reece." They each swallowed the amber liquid in one shot and pushed their glasses onto the bar for another.

Ed coughed as the whiskey hit the spot, warming his insides. "I still can't get my head around what I saw tonight. It doesn't make sense. How could it happen?"

Nathaniel felt a pang of guilt for not being able to reach the PI in time to save his life. "I am truly sorry Reece is gone."

Everyone's eyes moved to him.

"It isn't your fault," Sarah told him, placing her hand on his.

The vampire poured another round of whiskey. "I could have done more... moved faster..."

"No, you couldn't. You did everything you could. Reece wouldn't want you to feel this way." Sarah picked up her shot glass and swallowed the entire contents again.

"Yeah, Sarah's right, Nathaniel. You did your best. Those creatures were there to kill Reece and Andre and they would've killed them both if we hadn't shown up. You can't blame yourself." Ed swiped at an errant tear sliding down his left cheek, the painful lump in his throat threatening to choke him. He wanted to sit somewhere, alone, cry until he couldn't cry anymore. He'd known Reece for too many years and now he was gone.

"So how are we going to find Jacques?" Lozano asked, his quiet voice cracked and he sniffed back the urge to cry. "We have to get rid of him for good."

Nathaniel's cell vibrated on the counter.

Andre.

He pressed the phone to his ear. "Yes?"

"Avalynn is here at my apartment. She knows where Jacques is. Get everyone ready. We're going in to dispatch him and anyone else he has with him. I've called Evan. His pack is coming as well. They'll meet us at the location."

Nathaniel's grief-stricken expression changed to one of hostility. "Where is he?"

"We're on our way to the club. I'll bring you all up to speed when we get there."

Nathaniel set his phone down on the counter top. "Andre, Avalynn, and Tom are on their way here. The witch has found Jacques. We're going in."

"Someone needs to go back to be with Detective Donovan," Sarah reminded.

"No they don't," Lozano said. "I wouldn't leave him on his own in his condition. I asked a friend to stay with him. She's a nurse at LA Community."

Sarah's right eyebrow arched.

Lozano recognized the inference. "Nah, we're just friends."

With everything that had happened tonight they'd given little thought to the detective. Who could blame them under the circumstances?

"He's still unconscious?" Sarah wanted to know.

"Uh, yeah. He hadn't come to by the time I left. I hope he's going to be ok."

"Yes. We all do." Sarah slid off the tall metal stool. "Well, I guess we'd better get ready."

They secured a few locations throughout the city where they housed protective gear and weapons, *Sanguine* being one of them.

"Yeah, you're right." Ed came up behind her.

Todd and Lozano followed them, while Nathaniel waited at the bar for Andre's arrival.

❦

Andre, Tom, and Avalynn were sitting at the bar when the others returned, geared up, weapons in hand. He eyed each of them and wondered how they would handle the raid. They were all grieving. That, in itself, could cloud their judgement. He turned to look at Avalynn. "Do you want to explain?"

She shook her head. "You're in charge now."

"Ok." He turned back to his team. "Avalynn accessed Jacques' hotel suite and took a hair sample from his brush. She proceeded to do a locator spell, knowing it would be the best way to find him... and it worked."

"So where is the bloodsucker?" Ed asked.

CHAPTER SIXTY EIGHT

Grant Donovan came to with a loud gasp and sprang up on the cot, his anxious eyes roaming his surroundings. When he realized he was in a safe place, he swung his legs over the side of the bed and eased his painful body into a sitting position. He raised his hand to his throbbing head. *What happened?* It all came rushing back to him. *The vampire's cronies grabbed us and shoved us in the back of that SUV.* He sucked in another gasp as he remembered what Jacques told him.

Gentle hands gripped his arms and a woman's voice said, "Hey, you need to take it easy. You have a concussion, among other things."

The detective looked up into her lovely, soft features. "Where's everybody?"

"I'm not sure. Enrique asked me to keep an eye on you because you're injured."

"Where's Andre?"

She shrugged. "I'm sorry, I have no idea. If you lie down again I'll call Enrique and find out for you."

Grant nodded, swung his legs back onto the cot and eased his body onto the firm mattress. "Thank you. Please, do it now. I need to tell them something... something crucial."

She walked over to a nearby desk, opened her purse and took out her cell phone. The line rang for several seconds before it went to voicemail. She rang off. "He's not answering."

Grant groaned as he pulled himself up off the cot, leaning his arm against his painful ribs. "Call back... leave a message. I'll tell you what to say."

She pressed redial. "Hello, Enrique..." When voicemail kicked in Grant snatched the phone from her hand. "Lozano, it's Grant. I need to talk to Andre about Reece. Get him to call me as soon as you get this. Tell him not to go anywhere until he speaks to me." He passed the phone back to the woman whose name he didn't know – yet. "Sorry about that. I'm anxious to get a message to Andre and I need someone to call back ASAP."

The woman gave him a thin smile. "So I heard. I'm sure Enrique will call back as soon as he gets your message." She held out her hand. "I'm Anita by the way. And you're Grant. A detective I see."

He shook her hand. "Uh, yeah, sorry again for not introducing myself. There's a lot going on and I hope someone calls me back soon." He felt around his ragged clothes for his cell. Not there. *Of course.* He'd been thrown from the moving vehicle into the bordering trees after being beaten by two of Jacques' men. They planned to kill them both, so why dispose of him and not Reece as well? The vampire had imparted vital information about the PI and it would be the only reason he was still alive. To let the others know.

No one called back.

Grant stumbled to his feet, holding his ribs.

"Where do you think you're going?" Anita asked.

"I have to find them. I have to tell Andre..."

"No, you don't. What you have to do is rest."

Grant raised a defensive hand warning her to stay back. "Don't." He crossed the office and began sifting through pieces of paper on Reece's desk. There had to be something to tell him where they were. He wondered if they'd contacted Evan. If so, he could tell him where they went. *What's his number?* He ran a series of cell numbers around his foggy brain. *No. Not it. Think!* He picked up the desk phone and punched the keypad with his thumb hoping it was the correct number.

"Hello?" the voice on the line said.

"Evan?"

"Grant?"

"Yeah, it's me."

"How are you? I heard..."

"No time right now. Do you know where Reece's team is?"

Evan's chest felt heavy. The detective didn't know what had happened. "Grant, there's something you need to know…"

"Evan, there's no time. Where are they?"

"There's no easy way to say this... Reece is dead."

"What?" Grant blinked then frowned as what Evan told him swirled around his hazy brain. "What did you say?"

"Sorry to be so blunt with the information. Reece was killed by reptilian creatures out at the old LA zoo."

Grant shook his head. "No. No. You've made a mistake."

"I'm sorry, Grant, he's gone. We're on our way to help his team kill Jacques and his cronies."

"Jacques did this?" He'd believed what the vampire told him but it had been a lie… a ruse to throw them all off Reece's track. Grant was meant to tell the team the PI was being held captive at Greystone Manor.

"Yeah, he's been controlling the creatures all along."

The information settled into the processing center of the detective's brain and tears slid down his cheeks. "He's dead?"

"Yeah, I know, it's a lot to take in. Who would've thought? Reece was like a superhero – indestructible. Or so we all thought."

Grant still couldn't make sense of it. Everything seemed pointless. "You're sure?"

"Very sure. Some of his team went out there just as Reece and Andre were making their escape. Two reptiles appeared outta nowhere and sprayed Reece with venom. His team watched him die… his son too."

"Oh my God, Tom."

"Yeah. Poor kid."

"So where are you going?"

"Avalynn did some kind of spell to find Jacques' location. We're on our way out there now."

"Are you still in LA?"

"On the outskirts of town. Why?"

"Can you swing back to Double D and pick me up?"

Anita crossed the office to the desk. "Grant, you need to rest."

"I think it would be better if you stayed put," Evan told him. "You were unconscious for a long time. Maybe it's best you take it easy. We've got this."

"I considered Reece a friend not just an associate. I want to be there when Jacques dies. I need to be there. To be sure he gets what's coming to him."

Silence.

"Evan?"

"Grant, you're injured. What do you think you can do out there? Get yourself killed, maybe?"

"If you're not going to pick me up at least tell me where you're going so I can meet you there. Please."

Evan sighed. "Got a pen?"

Grant jotted down the address, hung up and looked at the woman standing in front of him. "Will you drop me off somewhere?"

"You know you shouldn't be going anywhere, Detective," Anita told him, a frown forming on her face, her arms folded.

"I have to. I don't have a choice. I take full responsibility for my actions and any setbacks they may cause, ok? Now will you drive me or do I have to drive myself?"

୫୦୧୫

When Anita pulled her red Honda Civic into the curb, keeping the motor running, Grant swung open the passenger door and climbed out, holding his injured ribs. He tugged the piece of paper he'd scribbled the address on from the pocket of his suit coat and held it up to his face under the street light. The address he'd been given belonged to the vacant block. "Damn you, Evan."

The cop had given him a bogus address, because he'd been injured, to prevent him from being involved in the death of Jacques Delacroix. Grant let out a frustrated huff. He guessed he couldn't be too pissed at the cop. He was only trying to look out for him.

Anita leaned across the car. "Is this the right address?"

"Yeah. I just realized Evan sent me here because I'm in bad shape."

"Then perhaps you should get in the car and let me drive you back to the office where you can rest."

Grant sighed. "Yeah, I guess you're right."

CHAPTER SIXTY NINE

The vehicles pulled up to the curb, one behind the other, beside the treed parkland fifty feet from the parking lot of Watts Towers Art Center. Andre gazed through the windshield at the ominous three metal spires. The sculpture reminded him of Gothic churches back in France during the 16th century. Why would Jacques be here, and where was he? There appeared to be no movement within the complex, or a nearby vehicle he would travel in. He preferred luxury transportation.

Andre glanced over his shoulder at Avalynn. "Are you sure this is the place?"

She nodded. "Yes. This is the location on the map."

"All right. Let's take a cautious look around. Stay close." Andre stepped out of the van.

Tom came around the front of the vehicle. "This seems like a strange place to be hiding out, don't you think?"

Andre's gaze moved from the spired monument to him. "This Jacques is unpredictable, so who knows why he chose this place."

Tom's eyes roamed the gray metal spires and he pointed upward. "Maybe for those. They look dangerous."

Andre's eyes followed Tom's direction. "Yes, deadly in fact."

Nathaniel stalked up to the pair. "Is this the correct location?" His dark gaze moved to the witch.

Avalynn stood with arms folded. "Yes, it is."

"It does not seem like a place he would be." Nathaniel gazed up at the tall spires.

"Remember, he's not the same Jacques. So who knows what he's thinking," she told him.

"I may not know a lot about reincarnation or resurrection, but I do not think it would alter someone's personality too greatly." Nathaniel's eyes returned to her. "Do you?"

"I don't know," Avalynn told him with a shrug. "This is where the locator spell brought us. Maybe he left already."

The others joined the four standing in front of the van.

"How did I get back into this?" Ed asked, the question rhetorical. His retirement had been short-lived.

"Because Tom needed our help," Sarah reminded.

"Oh, yeah." Ed's eyes followed the tallest spire and he pointed upward. "Looks dangerous."

"Yes, exactly what Tom said." Andre glanced over his shoulder. "I think a couple of us should check the perimeter. Jacques may not be here now."

"What if he is?" Lozano was concerned for their safety. His mind wandered back to Dracula in Las Vegas several years ago and the havoc he wreaked. Jacques was too much like him. Devious. Dangerous. Deadly.

"We'll deal with him." Andre made sure everyone had their ear communication buds in. "Nathaniel and I will check out the exterior first. If we run into any trouble we'll let you know. Grab your weapons. Be on standby."

Todd's gaze roamed the quiet, car-lined residential street. "I've got a bad feeling about this. It feels like a setup to me."

Andre's gut tightened. He'd felt the same thing. Knowing how his brother... or his brother's duplicate worked they were sitting ducks in the open. "Acknowledged."

When he and his companion reached the staved and wire mesh fence they found the gate open. The invitation clear.

"I don't think they should've gone alone," Ed said. "Jacques is an expert at separating his victims so he can pick them off one at a time – or in this case two at a time. He has a vendetta against Nathaniel because of the nightclub, and Andre for not being his puppet when we were in Bucharest. To his mind, he has every right to kill them."

Tom glanced in the direction of the trio of metal spires. "We should follow them. It doesn't matter what Uncle Andre said, we need to make sure nothing happens to them."

"You're right, Tom," Sarah said, "but Andre's in charge now and we have to respect his decision."

"My dad's dead. I don't need to lose my uncle too. He's the only family I have left. He's my Godfather so he's going to be my legal guardian. What happens to me if something happens to him? I'm too young to live on my own."

"Ok, let's cut across the park through the trees and stay close to the buildings. Don't let Andre or Nathaniel see you," Sarah told them.

Tom gave her a smile. "Thank you."

"Don't thank me. I agree with you. We can't take any chances where Jacques is concerned."

"So you do think he's here?" Todd asked.

"No doubt about it. This may be an arts center… it's also a dangerous location. Look at the sculpture of spires. Anything could happen up there." Sarah clutched her trusted crossbow, loaded with silver arrows with ultraviolet tips. "Let's keep moving."

"Wait," Avalynn said. "I'll cast a spell to create a force field of silence so the nearby residents are not disturbed by the commotion and someone calls the authorities."

"Good idea," Sarah agreed. "It's the last thing we need right now."

ʘʀ

Andre and Nathaniel stepped through the gate into the compound where the metal structure stood. The place seemed deserted, but they weren't taking any chances. The black vampire made hand signals to Andre and they split up, wandering through mosaic tiled pieces, planted shrubbery, flowers, and other metal sculptures to the spires at the end of the fence, meeting at the base.

A voice echoed down at them from above. "Glad you could join me. I knew it wouldn't be long before someone discovered my whereabouts. The witch I presume?"

Andre's and Nathaniel's eyes roamed the dark structure until they spotted Jacques on the third level, his knee-length black jacket billowing around him like a cape in the wind.

Andre ignored the question. "You said you didn't come back to LA to cause trouble for us. Now we discover you've been manipulating the reptilian creatures all along. And you murdered my friend." His eyes remained on his brother's duplicate.

"It has taken this long to do what your brother set out to do all those years ago. Except for one last thing."

"Which is?" Andre began climbing the metal sculpture. He would not allow anyone else to die. This would be the final countdown for Jacques. Andre would make sure there were no more ingredients to create another copy of his brother or himself.

"To be rid of you all so I can continue what he started."

This new version of his brother was far more maniacal than the original Jacques.

"How do you plan to do that?" As Andre climbed to the first level of the structure he glanced across the park and saw his team heading toward the fenced compound.

"Andre, no!" Nathaniel started climbing after him.

Andre spotted him. "No, Nathaniel, this is between me and him." His eyes moved to Jacques.

The black vampire stopped climbing. If needed, he would fly up and grab Andre from the monster's clutches. No one else would die tonight.

The team continued to weave its way through the park, moving closer to offer backup. As the group reached the corner of the arts building vampires emerged from every location. They were outnumbered.

CHAPTER SEVENTY

Andre continued to climb the steel structure. Glancing down below him, he could see the pointed sculptures close to the base. From the top most height of the spires, a fall would impale and kill. The very reason they were here. Jacques planned to kill him by throwing him off onto the sculptures below. What this Jacques didn't know was Andre's abilities had enhanced with his resurrection. He could hover off the ground. So if Jacques did do as he suspected, Andre wouldn't fall to his death. The thought crossed his mind; *does he have the same ability?*

Nathaniel began to climb again, realizing what Jacques planned to do.

"Why here, Jacques?"

"It reminds me of 16th century France. The gaudy Gothic Cathedrals built to intimidate their parishioners."

"You were never in France in the 1500s," Andre told him, continuing to get closer.

"Doesn't matter. Jacques' memories remain with me. And this place is perfect for what I have planned."

Andre, now only feet below him, remained far enough away so as not to get pushed off the structure before he could get onto the platform. He pulled himself up onto the same level. "Nothing ever goes according to plan."

"I can assure you this will." He motioned to the parkland. "See for yourself."

Andre's gaze moved to the treed reserve. Vampires were attacking his team. "They have nothing to do with this. Your grievance is with me and Nathaniel. Let them go."

The vampire smirked. "Now why would I do that? Once you are out of the way they would continue to pursue me. With all of you gone I can do whatever I please."

"You're insane."

"Perhaps. Nevertheless, I will have what I want. And I want you dead." He already possessed another Andre he could manipulate.

"Not going to happen." Andre pointed toward the park. "I think your plan is already unraveling."

Evan and the remaining pack members were tearing vampires limb from limb, while Sarah and the others fired off ultra violet weapons. All hell had broken loose on the ground.

Andre turned to Nathaniel. "Go help them."

The black vampire shook his head. "No. I will remain here with you. My team has arrived."

Gazing back to the ground, Andre saw Nathaniel's team emerging from out of the shadows. His friends were not outnumbered now.

Nathaniel continued to climb, his severe stare remaining on Jacques. He would not allow the vampire to harm Andre. No matter what the cost.

Jacques made a dash for Andre. Andre darted backwards, realizing there wasn't a lot of room for error, his feet at the end of the platform, teetering on the edge. He knew he'd be ok if he stepped off, at least if Jacques didn't try to attack him mid-air.

The irrational look in Jacques' eyes caused Andre's gut to squirm. *What is he planning to do?*

Nathaniel climbed up behind the vampire.

"Stay back, I'm warning you," Jacques ordered, swinging around, hands raised in front of him.

Nathaniel stepped closer.

"I said STOP!"

"You have murdered our friend. You are not going to get away this time," Nathaniel told him, his face dark with loathing.

Jacques was sandwiched between Andre and Nathaniel. He had nowhere to go except up. He began to climb the tallest spire from the inside.

The black vampire followed Jacques up.

"Nathaniel, don't," Andre called after him. "He can't get away."

He didn't listen.

"You will regret this," Jacques told him as he continued to climb. There wasn't any room left. He reached the pointed summit of the open metalwork spire, Nathaniel close on his heel.

Jacques held on and kicked down, his polished, pointed toe shoe connecting with the vampire's face.

Nathaniel slipped, one hand letting go.

"Nathaniel!" Andre gasped.

The vampire regained a foothold again and continued to climb. He would not allow Jacques to escape.

Jacques turned around, his back to the metal, and kicked down again.

Nathaniel grabbed and twisted Jacques' foot. A loud crack could be heard as the vampire's ankle snapped.

Jacques let out a yelp of pain before hopping up onto another metal rung.

Nathaniel followed. "You will die tonight, monster."

♃

A vampire sprang from the branches of a nearby tree, landing on Todd and knocking him to the ground, his mouth open, fangs bared ready to sink them into Todd's neck.

The ex-detective pushed his weapon between them and fired. Nothing happened. He pulled the trigger again. Still nothing. Tugging his hand free, he smashed the vampire in the head with the futuristic gun and clambered to his feet. The vampire raised himself up in one fluid motion, continuing the chase.

Evan bounded across the grass, leaping at the vampire and latching onto his throat.

Todd stopped in his tracks, panting. "Thank you." He was grateful for the wolf's help. The last thing he would want is to be turned into a bloodsucker. As he turned to race across the park to help Sarah, another vampire sprang from above, shoved Todd to the ground and sank his fangs into his neck. The vampire drained him to the last drop.

"No!" Sarah screamed, raising her weapon at the vampire.

The creature disappeared before she could get a shot off.

Sarah rushed over to Todd and fell to her knees, checking for a pulse. Nothing.

Ed raced across the grass. "Is he…"

She nodded.

"No."

The pair pressed their backs to each other and fired at the other attacking vampires, blasting them into ash one by one.

℘

Andre began to climb up behind Nathaniel. He didn't want his friend to risk his life fighting his brother's double. "Nathaniel, come down. He can't get away. We have him cornered."

Nathaniel's gaze landed on Andre. "He always finds a way to escape." He climbed up beside Jacques. "You will pay for what you have done."

Jacques grabbed Nathaniel by the front of his black sweater and tugged him off the metal sculpture, as he did, Nathaniel gripped the vampire's arms and they fell down the center of the tall spire together. The pair landed with a loud metallic thud on the platform where Andre stood, Jacques on top of Nathaniel, the impact rocking the metal around them, the sculpture groaning with the weight.

Jacques leaped to his feet, making his way across to the ladder, his ankle already mending.

Nathaniel propelled himself at Jacques. Both lurched off the end of the structure into the air before falling, the black vampire unable to levitate with the weight of Jacques on top of him.

"Nooo!" Andre raced to the end of the platform. The sickening sound of tearing flesh and cracking bone echoed up at him as he peered over the edge.

Both Nathaniel and Jacques were skewered on top of the ground-level metal spire.

Andre leaped off the structure, lowering himself onto the path. As he rushed over to the sculpture the pair disintegrated into a cloud of black ash.

Ed and Sarah ran along the path to where Andre now stood, tears sliding down his cheeks.

"Not Nathaniel too?" Sarah gasped.

"We lost Todd as well," Ed told him. "A vampire drained him before anyone could help him."

Andre turned his blood-streaked face to the pair. "Did you dispatch them all?"

Sarah shook her head. "The vampire that killed Todd got away.

"We need to find out where Jacques hid my lookalike. He needs to be eliminated too." Andre stepped around the pair and headed to the park. He wanted to thank Evan for coming to their aide.

Once the wolves were gone, Andre told everyone to head back to the office. He would meet them there in a while for a debrief.

"Where are you going, Uncle Andre?" Tom asked.

"I need some time alone. I'll meet you back at Double D soon." He knew the sorcerer would be in Los Angeles, somewhere. He planned to find out where and pay him a visit.

CHAPTER SEVENTY ONE

Before he died, Reece had several of his informants searching for the sorcerer. Andre followed up, sending out text messages asking they get back to him ASAP. It was imperative to find the spell caster before he initiated another resurrection of his brother, which he would have instruction to do in the event something happened to Jacques' duplicate. Tonight, he found a voicemail message on his cell with a location.

Andre parked the van outside his apartment block, headed upstairs to change into his riding gear, then traveled down in the elevator to the basement where his Red Ducati Monster sat. He pushed the glossy black helmet onto his head, snapped down the visor, straddled his motorcycle and rode out of the building. Good people were lost tonight – his best friend; Nathaniel, Todd. What would he do without his best friend? And Nathaniel? They were family who had been through so much together at the hands of monsters trying to kill them. How could Jacques' double have succeeded where, for so many years, his brother had failed? A single tear slid down Andre's face beneath his helmet as he whipped across the asphalt heading to The Georgian Hotel in Santa Monica.

What would he do once he got there?

He didn't know. One thing he did know for sure was if the sorcerer didn't hand over whatever was left of Jacques' and his genetic material he would pay with his life. Andre wasn't playing games with these creatures any longer. He couldn't afford to have another Jacques or Andre appear in the future to wreak havoc on him and his team… nor their city. This ended tonight.

Andre turned right off Broadway along Ocean Avenue to the hotel, did a U-turn and pulled his motorcycle into the beachside curb opposite. Removing his helmet, he gazed up at the spotlighted, Art Deco turquoise façade, twin palm trees swaying in the breeze outside. This hotel once hosted celebrities like Carole Lombard and Clark Gable as well as infamous characters like Fatty Arbuckle and mobsters Al Capone and Bugsy Seigel, who played cards in the secret bar downstairs. It had also been the first speakeasy during prohibition in the thirties. Now, it was more of a boutique style hotel with a romantic, bygone era atmosphere and glistening water views.

He climbed off his motorcycle stowing his helmet and riding gloves in the compartment attached, crossed the four lane road, climbed the front steps, and walked through the arched doorway into the lobby. People wandered into the hotel at all hours of the day so no one would give him a second glance. He knew the sorcerer's room number so he bypassed reception and headed for the elevator.

Andre jabbed the call button.

After a couple of minutes the lift door slid open. About to step in, he spotted movement out of his peripheral vision and saw Tom coming up the lobby stairs. The elevator door closed. "What are you doing here?"

"I came to your apartment building and saw you leaving so I followed." Tom walked up to him.

"You know you're not meant to be driving without a licensed driver with you." Andre folded his arms.

"Yeah, I know, but I'm not about to lose you too, Uncle Andre. Why are you here?"

"I came to speak to someone."

Tom tilted his chin. "Who? What about?"

"Nothing you need be concerned about." His eyes moved past the teen, out the front door to the street. "What did you drive here in?"

"One of the vans."

"Ok. Go wait in it until I'm done here. I shouldn't be too long."

Tom shook his head and folded his arms. "Not until you tell me why you're here. Is it dangerous?"

"I'll be fine. Please do what I ask." Andre had given Reece his word he would keep Tom safe if anything were to happen to him.

"He's here to intimidate the sorcerer responsible for resurrecting Jacques and the other Andre." Avalynn's voice echoed into the elevator foyer as she climbed the steps.

The pair swung around.

Tom's frowning gaze moved from her back to his uncle. "Is that true?"

Andre groaned inwardly, giving the witch a stern stare. "Why are you here?"

"I followed the kid." She motioned at Tom with her head. "Someone has to watch out for him."

The teen turned his serious frown to her again. "I can take care of myself. I don't need your help."

"Your uncle will, if he wants to get out of the sorcerer's hotel room alive." Her lilac eyes moved from the boy to the vampire. "You know I can cast a spell to hold him while you get what you came here for. With my help you can get in, get done, and get out without any drama or anyone dying."

"Do you think he won't retaliate if we leave him alive?" Andre asked.

"So you came here with the intention of ending him?"

"Not at first. But do you see any other way?"

Avalynn gave it a moment of thought. "No, I guess not. Let's go up."

"Wait. Neither of you are coming with me."

"Didn't you hear what I said? I can hold him while you…"

"Yes, I heard. I'm not risking anyone else's life tonight."

Avalynn stepped up to the vampire. "I can help you. How do you know if he's alone up there? He could have others with him."

"It's a chance I'm prepared to take."

"Look, I know you're grieving over the loss of your friends but this is crazy. It's suicide. Tom needs you. You're all he has now. So before you go running off to get yourself killed think about the consequences." She wasn't sugar coating it; he needed to hear the truth.

Andre frowned into her lilac eyes for a long time contemplating what she'd said. "All right, but Tom waits in the van."

The teen gave his uncle a severe stare. "Are you kidding me?"

"No, you're waiting in the van. I promised your dad I'd take good care of you if anything happened to him. So go."

Without another word and a disgruntled scowl on his face, Tom turned on his heel and headed back through the lobby to the street.

Avalynn's gaze moved from the back of the teen to Andre. "That went well," she said, sarcasm evident in her tone.

"Yes, well, he'll get over it." He jabbed the call button again. "Let's get this done."

Tom whipped around the corner of the hotel into a driveway on his right. He'd spotted a door leading out of the reception area into the alley on his way out of the building and thought he would use it to get back inside so he could follow his uncle upstairs. Peering around the partition, he raced back up the steps to the elevator foyer. He could hear his uncle and Avalynn in conversation. When the elevator stopped, he double-stepped the stairs up to the fourth floor.

When he reached it he waited. He knew if Andre saw him he would banish him to the van and he wanted to help. He had to make sure nothing happened to his uncle. Peering around the corner of the wall, he watched Avalynn and Andre stop outside a room two doors down on the opposite side of the hall.

His uncle knocked on the door.

After a couple of seconds the door opened and they stepped inside.

Tom eased his tall frame along the passage to the room. Leaning in, he used his Lycan hearing to listen to the conversation. No raised voices, no conflict, as far as he could tell.

As he headed along the hallway to the internal stairs a loud crash emanated from the room.

Tom rushed back to the door. *What should I do?* His breathing quickened and he could feel his wolf trying to emerge. *No. Stay there.* He raised his size 14 sneakered foot and thrust it at the door. It flew back bouncing off the wall. Tom shoved it out of the way as he entered the short hallway, his eyes glowing. He rushed along it to the double curtained glass doors.

Avalynn lay unconscious on the floor. So did the sorcerer.

His gaze roamed the subdued space landing on Andre fighting Andre. The pair of vampires whipped around the room knocking over anything in their path.

Tom's claws elongated through the tips of his fingers, his wolf eager to get into the fight. He held it back. Racing across the room, he made a swipe at the second Andre, his claws connecting with the vampire's back. It wouldn't take long before the toxin took effect. The vampire crumpled into a heap on the floor, bloody tears spilling from his eyes, his mouth contorted in an agonized grimace.

Andre gave him a severe stare as he twisted his double's neck. It wouldn't kill him, the claw marks would. "I told you to wait in the van." Were the first words his uncle said to him.

"I couldn't sit out there wondering if you were coming back. I needed to know you were ok."

Andre walked over to Tom and pulled him into a man hug. "Thank you for saving our lives. By the way, you're grounded."

"Are you serious right now?" Tom whined, huffing out an exasperated breath.

"You bet I am." He realized he sounded like Reece.

Avalynn staggered to her feet holding her head. "What… happened?"

"The other Andre happened. He was behind the bedroom door and hit you over the head with a vase as we walked into the living room."

"I wish I'd seen that coming," she said, raising her hand behind her head to feel the egg on the back of her skull. "Ouch."

Tom's wolf eyes returned to their normal color as his gaze moved to the sorcerer. "Is he…?"

"Yes." Avalynn glanced down at the spell caster. "Better for all of us."

"Now we need to locate what I came here to find," Andre said, walking into the bedroom to check the bathroom cabinet. Nothing. He came back into the room and proceeded to go through the drawers and bedside tables. Nothing there, either. Andre walked into the sitting room and pulled open the doors and drawers on the solid wood, mahogany colored cabinet. *Where could it be?*

Tom got down onto his knees and pulled up the valance on the queen size bed. A metal brief case sat in the center of the carpet underneath. He slid it out and set it down on the white cover. "Maybe in here?"

Andre and Avalynn crossed the room to the bed. "Open it," Andre said.

The case had numbered tumbler locks so Tom used a claw like a can opener to cut through the metal top and peel it back. "Is this what you're looking for, Uncle Andre?"

Andre reached into the padded gray foam lining and tugged a tube free, there were several different glass vials. "Yes, this is it." Andre read each label, horrified to see Dracula's blood in the case. The contents would be disposed of once they were back at the office. He wouldn't take any chances where the bloodthirsty patriarch of all vampires was concerned.

"What do we do about them?" Avalynn asked, glancing over her shoulder at the vampire frothing bloody saliva from his mouth and the stone-like sorcerer.

"I'll call our cleaning service. No one will ever know anything happened in this suite."

"Then we should head back," Tom told them.

Andre turned to Avalynn. "Would you mind repairing the brief case? It would draw suspicion if we carried it out the way it looks now."

"Sure." She twirled her finger and the case looked like new.

"Wow!" Tom said, his eyes wide. "Wish I could do stuff like that."

The three stepped out of the room into the hallway, Avalynn closed the door, and she and Andre followed Tom down the stairs, across the lobby and out to the street.

"You can ride back with me. I'll pick the van up tomorrow," Andre told Tom.

"What?"

"We're not having this discussion right now." Andre gave his nephew a serious stare.

Tom folded his arms. "Fine."

"Good."

Avalynn stepped up beside the pair. "I'll see you there."

"You're coming straight back?"

"Yes. I'll be there when you arrive."

Andre and Tom crossed the busy road to the red Ducati Monster and Andre unlocked the compartment, tossed Tom a helmet and tugged on his own. "Let's go."

CHAPTER SEVENTY TWO

When Andre and Tom walked through the door of Double D Investigations, Ed got up out of Reece's chair and came around the desk. "Where have you two been? Don't you check your phones or what?" The agitation in the ex-Lieutenant's voice was clear. "We were worried about you."

"Sorry, Ed, I had an errand to run." Andre slipped out of his black leather riding jacket and hung it on the coat rack on the wall beside the office door.

"What about you?" Ed pointed to Tom. "Where did you go after we came back here?"

"I – I…" His gaze moved to his uncle.

"I asked him to meet me," Andre told the older man.

Ed folded his arms over his pot belly and scowled. "Oh yeah? Well ya know Tom's not meant to be driving on his own."

"Yes, I do. And it won't happen again. It was a once off." Andre crossed the room and sat in Reece's chair.

"A once off?"

Sarah walked over to Ed and wrapped a comforting arm around his shoulders. "It's ok. They're back now." She knew her husband had been worried about the pair.

Ed cleared his throat, his eyes moving to her. "Yeah, I guess you're right."

Andre's gaze moved to the cot. "Where's Grant?"

"Oh, Anita drove him home. She's going to stay with him overnight to make sure he's ok. By the look of him, I thought he'd feel more comfortable in his own bed," Lozano told him.

"Yes, agreed. Thanks for asking your friend to check him out and stay with him. It's appreciated. I'll do a catch up tomorrow to make sure he's ok."

"Think nothing of it. All in the line of duty." Lozano came over to the group. "I can't believe we lost Reece, Nathaniel, and Todd tonight. I've pinched myself a dozen times to make sure I'm not dreaming." He swiped at a tear sliding from the corner of his left eye. "It's too much to take in."

"I know. I still can't get my head around it," Ed said, giving Lozano a thin sad smile.

Tom plonked himself down on the corner of Reece's desk. "I miss my dad so much. He should still be here. So should Nathaniel and Todd." His heart ached for Reece now he had time to process it. His eyes moved to Sarah. "When can we have the memorial for them?" It would be a triple memorial, not just for his dad.

"Tomorrow, if you like," Sarah told him.

Tom sniffed back the urge to cry and nodded, his voice breaking when he spoke. "Yeah, I would."

"I'll organize it with St. Joseph's in the morning. I'm sure we'll be able to do something in the afternoon." Sarah would call first thing.

"Thank you." Tom swiped at tears sliding down his cheeks. He remembered the dream he'd had about his dad's death. The one he couldn't tell him about. He should've paid attention to it.

"Did Todd have any family?" Ed asked.

"Charlotte told Reece Todd never married and was an only child. Given his age, his parents wouldn't be alive now either." Andre's gaze moved around the office. "Where's Avalynn? Did she come back?"

"Not yet. Why?" Sarah asked.

"She..." Andre realized he'd be implicating himself and Tom in something the others didn't need to know about. "Never mind, I'm sure she'll be here soon."

"Hey, Andre, just so you know... me and Sarah are getting out. For real this time. I can't do it anymore, now Reece is gone. It won't be the same without him. Besides, like I said to him, I'm getting too old for this shit. And what happened tonight is too painful, you know?"

"Yes, I understand why you want to leave. So did Reece. Please stay in touch."

"We will. We're family." Ed swallowed the aching lump in his throat.

"Maybe we should all go home and try to get some rest. It's been a long terrible day," Sarah said. "Why not give Avalynn a call and ask her to meet you here in the morning?"

"I will." Andre's eyes moved to Tom. "Ready to go home?"

Tom nodded. "Yeah."

"Head down to the van while I give Avalynn a call. Won't be long."

Everyone said their goodnights and walked Tom downstairs to the van.

Andre made the call to Avalynn. Her voicemail kicked in. "Hey, Avalynn, it's Andre. We're all heading home. Can you come into the office in the morning at your earliest convenience? Thanks." As he rang off, he wondered where she'd gone.

₱₱

Avalynn entered the hotel lobby and headed straight for the elevator foyer. She climbed the steps, walked up to the lift and jabbed the call button. It was imperative she get back into the sorcerer's suite, hence the reason she hadn't locked the door when she, Andre, and Tom left earlier. The spell caster had stolen an ancient tome more than one hundred years ago from another like him living in the mountains of Nepal, who had been the entrusted guardian of the book, and who he'd murdered to get his hands on it. Witch-hunts were all too common in the region even to this day, and the persecution of individuals believed to practice witchcraft, still persisted in the community. One of the reasons why she was assigned to locate the book and deliver it back to the New Orleans witch council, where it would be placed under lock and key.

The Grimoire, bound in human skin, contained spells, rituals and invocations dangerous to both the witch and human communities across the globe. It was obvious to her now Jacques knew about the book and planned to use it to his own end. She'd arrived at the hotel earlier with this purpose in mind. But when she encountered Andre and Tom she'd invented a plausible reason for being there so they wouldn't become suspicious. There hadn't been enough time to search for the Grimoire while in the room previously, so she returned to do it now.

Avalynn stepped into the elevator, pressed 4, and the door slid shut. She prayed Andre's cleaning crew hadn't arrived yet or otherwise they would have taken the book with them, having no knowledge of what it contained. If so, she would have to confess the other reason for her being in Los Angeles to Andre and ask him to give her the location of the sorcerer's belongings, which she hoped she wouldn't have to do.

Walking along the hallway to the room, Avalynn stopped short when she found the door ajar. She moved up to the opening and listened for any sounds inside. None. She glanced over her shoulder to make sure no one was coming up the stairs or out of the lift, eased the door back, stepped into the hallway and closed the door. She walked into the sitting room, her lilac eyes roaming the space where the bodies still lay. Breathing a relieved sigh, she proceeded to go through every drawer, cabinet, and closet in search of the tome.

Avalynn stood with hands on hips gazing around the suite wondering where the spell caster would hide such a coveted possession. He would not have wanted it to be found by anyone. She walked back into the bedroom, got down on her knees and lifted the valance. It worked for Tom so maybe it would work for her, too, although the teen would have mentioned if a book had been lying on the floor as well. Nothing. "Dammit." She had to find it before the cleaning crew arrived. She stood with hands on hips and did a 360 degree turn, her eyes scrutinizing every nook and cranny. *It must be here somewhere.*

℮)ℛ

Andre and Tom entered the mansion, hung up their jackets and headed to the kitchen, Tom sliding onto a stool while his uncle made them both a mug of coffee. "Here," Andre said, sitting on the stool opposite and pushing the dark blue mug across the counter top.

"Dad doesn't… didn't let me drink coffee," Tom told his uncle. A tear slid from the corner of his right eye and he swiped it away, blinking back more welling in his eyes.

"Well it's better than the alternative." Andre gave him a thin sorrowful smile. The teen was too young to drink anything stronger. Although, under the circumstances, would it have been a bad thing?

"Yeah, I guess." Tom picked up the mug and took a cautious sip. "I…" He stopped himself before he said it.

"I know."

"Dad was your friend long before he knew me. How are you doing?"

"I'm not sure. There hasn't been enough time to process it yet."

"Yeah, I know what you mean." Tom's gaze moved to the open doorway. "I kinda expect him to walk through the door at any minute."

"Yes, me too."

"What are we going to do without him?" More tears were welling in the teen's eyes now.

"We do what he would've wanted. Get on with our lives." Andre sipped his coffee.

"How are we supposed to do that?" Tom swiped at an errant tear sliding down his cheek.

"One day at a time."

"He was a good man, Uncle Andre. He loved me even though I wasn't his biological son… and I loved him. He *was* my dad."

"He was the kind of man who would always do what he could to help people. No matter what it took."

"My mom loved him for that."

"And he loved you both very much."

Tom's chin quivered as he tried to control his emotions. Tears spilled down his cheeks and he let out a huge sob, the ache in his heart too painful.

Andre came around the counter to him and wrapped him in a comforting embrace as they both grieved together.

⁊)(⁊

Avalynn did another sweep of the hotel suite. The Grimoire had to be somewhere. The sorcerer would not have let such a book out of his sight. Her lilac eyes roamed the sitting room. *Where can it be?* Her gaze rested on two wall vents. *Maybe in one of those?* She strutted across the room and looked up at the metal grills. They were slotted into the wall not screwed so they wouldn't be difficult to get open. She pulled a chair across to the first one, climbed onto it and gripped the frame. Giving it a firm tug, the grill wouldn't budge.

She stood on her toes and peered into the dark space before pulling her cell from the pocket of her jacket to shine the flashlight inside. Nothing. She pocketed the phone, climbed off the chair, moved it over to the next vent, stood on the plush beige upholstery and shone the phone inside. *There it is.* About to tug the metal grill free, she heard a noise echo out of the hallway.

Avalynn climbed off the chair, pushed it under the round wood table and darted behind the curtained double glassed doors. Had the bedroom door been closed? She couldn't remember. She waited until the footfalls got closer and whipped into the bedroom out of sight.

The pair of males dressed in blue coveralls carrying plastic tubs stopped at the entrance to the living room. "Ok. Let's get to work," one said. "This place needs to be ship-shape."

Avalynn sidled around the bedroom to the ajar door leading into the short hallway. She eased it back and peered out. The cleaners were busy bagging the bodies. So she could complete her important mission, she would return later to retrieve the Grimoire.

CHAPTER SEVENTY THREE

The next morning, Avalynn hid the Grimoire in the false bottom of her suit case, packed her belongings, and stowed the bag back in the hotel closet. She needed to see Andre to let him know she was leaving. She felt bad for him and Tom – for them all. They had lost good team members in their quest to rid LA of the likes of Jacques and the reptilian creatures, including Nathaniel. She realized, in the time she'd known him, he'd shown her not all vampires were alike. Something she would need to remember. He was an intricate part of Reece's team and had made the ultimate sacrifice to save the life of someone he cared for. They were a family of sorts. The memorial service had been a sad occasion. It had even brought tears to her eyes. Not one to cry often, Tom's beautiful words about his dad touched her heart and she felt so deeply sorry for him because he'd lost both of his parents.

She stepped out into the hallway, about to close the door, when Andre and Tom appeared in the opening elevator doorway. "Hey, how are you?" she asked, not wanting to be her usual brusque self, under the circumstances.

"Doing the best we can right now," Andre told her.

"I understand." Her gaze moved from Tom to him. "Why the early morning visit?"

Avalynn hadn't contacted him after the voicemail message as he'd expected. "I wanted to find out where you went the other night. You didn't come back to the office like you said you would. And you left the memorial service before I could speak to you. Where'd you go?"

Avalynn gave him a sheepish glance. "I had something important to do."

"Like acquire the Grimoire?"

"How did…"

"Not a lot gets past me that I don't know about. Besides, you were spotted at the hotel after we left."

"By your cleaning crew, I assume." She frowned. "How did you know about the book?"

"Sarah."

"Ah, of course.

"She knows someone on your witch council."

"Doesn't surprise me."

Andre folded his arms. "So why didn't you tell Reece the truth about why you were here?"

"The less people that knew the better. There are some who want to destroy the world with it."

Andre's eyes widened. "Like Jacques?"

She nodded. "Him, for one."

"Frig me."

"It's imperative I leave right away to get it into safe hands before someone else comes looking for it."

Andre stared into her lilac eyes. "Ok. I understand. Do what you have to do."

"If you need my help in the future you know how to reach me."

"I do. Be safe." Andre and Tom headed back to the elevator.

"I will. Thanks." Avalynn watched them leave before returning to her room to collect her bag. She had to go… *now*.

ᚸᚩᚳᚱ

Driving back toward Downtown LA, Andre gave Tom a sideward glance. "How're you doing?"

Tom shrugged. "To be honest I don't know."

"I understand. You know you can always talk to me. I'm here for you."

"I know. I think I'd rather not talk about it, right now." He turned to look at his uncle. "Do you mind?"

"Of course not, whatever you need."

Tom gave Andre a sorrowful smile. "Thanks. I wish I knew what I needed."

"You know you don't have to go to school today. Your principal said you could take a couple of weeks off."

"Yeah, I know. I feel like being at school will help take my mind off things. At least I hope it will."

"Don't rush it. Take your time. You need to acknowledge what happened and allow yourself time to grieve."

"Dad wouldn't want me to. He'd want me to continue on... like you said the other night."

"It doesn't mean you can't take time for yourself. It's been a tough couple days without your dad here."

Tom sighed. "Yeah, it has."

"So are you sure you want to go to school?"

"I do. If I feel like I need to come home later I'll tell Mr. Mitchell."

"If you do, give me a call and I'll come pick you up."

Andre pulled the van into the curb outside the high school. "I hope the day goes well."

"Thanks, Uncle Andre." Tom opened the door, tugged his backpack from off the floor and climbed out. "See ya."

"Yeah." Andre gave the teen a thin smile and waited until he'd entered the building before merging back into the traffic. He'd head by Double D Investigations to pick up some case files before driving to the apartment to talk to Lozano about moving back into the mansion with Tom. Would the ex-sheriff want to continue to lease the apartment on his own? And would he stay with Double D now Reece was gone? Something they would need to discuss.

∞C33

Tom walked the length of the school corridor to his locker at the end of the row. As he weaved through the throng of teens making their way to their first class for the day, he realized everyone's eyes were on him. They had obviously heard about his dad's death, at least the news report's censored version of events. The feeling of being under a microscope sat heavy on his shoulders and once at his locker, he opened it, tugged out the books he needed from his bag, and shoved his backpack into his locker. Glancing over his shoulder, he could see all eyes were still on him. "What?" he said, his voice tight.

A guy he hadn't spoken to before came up to him. "We're sorry about your dad, man."

Tom blew out a noisy breath and closed his locker. "Uh, thanks. I appreciate it."

"Let me know if you need anything. I'm Teddy by the way." The kid extended his charcoal fingerless gloved hand.

Tom shook it. "Thanks." He gave the guy a thin smile.

The kid nodded, turned on his heel and disappeared into the crowded corridor.

Tom was about to head off to his first class when he heard another voice behind him.

"Hey, Tom."

Jade.

Why?

Something I don't need right now.

He turned around. "Uh, hi."

A tear slipped down her left cheek and her voice broke when she tried to speak. She cleared her throat. "I – I'm so very sorry… about your dad, Tom. He was a nice man. I can't even imagine what you're going through."

"Um, thanks. Yeah, it's been a tough couple of days."

Her sorrowful eyes met his. "Why are you here? Why aren't you at home taking care of yourself?"

"It's better for me to keep my mind occupied right now."

She touched his arm. "I am so sorry, Tom." Another tear slipped down her cheek and she brushed it away. "Can we talk later? There's something I want to tell you."

He shrugged. "I guess so."

"Ok. In the courtyard? Lunchtime?"

Tom let out a heavy sigh. "Sure."

"Thank you. See you there."

As she turned the corner, Tom wondered what she wanted to talk to him about, and why choose now.

When the lunch bell rang, Tom scooped up his books off the desk and headed to his locker. After stowing them inside, he made his way through the cafeteria out to the courtyard, his eyes roaming the shaded space for Jade. She wasn't there. He wandered over to a vacant table, sat down to wait, hoping she wouldn't be too long. He wasn't hungry and made the decision to go home. He couldn't take anyone else telling him how sorry they were. He knew they were being kind, and he appreciated it, but he'd come to school to get his mind off his dad's death, not be reminded of it every few minutes. His gaze did another sweep of the kids coming outside. Where was Jade?

After waiting fifteen minutes, Tom got to his feet and headed back to the double doors of the cafeteria. Why did Jade stand him up? He couldn't keep doing this with her anymore. He needed to keep away from her, for his own peace of mind, as well as her safety. He realized he still had feelings for her – it didn't matter now – nothing did. Would it ever again?

As he crossed the cafeteria to the busy corridor, he almost collided with her as she came around the doorway. Her cheeks were flushed from hurrying.

"Hey, why are you leaving?" she asked, her voice breathy.

"I've been waiting around for the past fifteen minutes. I thought you weren't showing up." He shoved his hands into the pockets of his charcoal hoodie.

"I'm sorry. I got caught up in class. I couldn't text you because Miss Roberts makes us leave our cell phones in a container on her desk until class is finished."

"Oh, ok. So what did you want to talk about?"

She gripped his arm, walking him out to the courtyard. They sat down.

"Tom," she said, hesitating. She gazed into his beautiful eyes. "I – I want to say I'm sorry for whatever I did to make you mad at me. I want to be here for you." She waited a moment. Should she tell him?

"Look, I'm not mad at you. I don't have time for... Things are different now." He could see tears welling in her eyes and he hated hurting her.

"There's something you need to know."

"What?"

"I remember the night of Tyler's party."

Tom frowned into her eyes. His dad told him Jade might remember over time. Had she?

"Yeah, it was an awesome night."

She rested her hand on his. "No, Tom, I remember what you are."

He gave a humorless chuckle. "Yeah, I'm a sixteen year old goofy kid."

"No." She glanced around to make sure other kids couldn't hear, then frowned at him. "You're a werewolf."

₧₧

Andre sat at the dining room table working on his laptop when Lozano opened the front door. "Hey, Andre. Nice day out there." He took the grocery bag into the kitchen. "Want some coffee?"

Andre got up from the table, walked over to the kitchen doorway and leaned against the jamb. "Yes, thanks."

Lozano dropped a coffee pod into the machine and sat a mug under the nozzle. "Black?"

"Yep."

Lozano busied himself with putting away the groceries while the coffee poured. "Is there something you want to talk about?" The ex-sheriff could see something was on Andre's mind.

"I wondered if you wanted to take over the lease on this place as I'm moving in with Tom."

Lozano handed him the mug of coffee, then popped another pod into the machine for himself.

"I've been thinking about going back to Vegas. I know you need a team for the business, but like Ed said, and no offense, it won't be the same without Reece."

Andre understood. He'd even thought about closing down Double D Investigations, only for a moment. What would the city do without someone to fight the supernatural elements invading Los Angeles on a regular basis? "I know what you mean."

Lozano gave him a painful look. "Of course you do. He was your best friend. I'm sorry to leave without anyone to help you. I'm actually thinking of starting my own PI business back home. We sure could use it there and I know some guys I could get onboard."

"Sounds like a plan. You know you can always call on us if you need help."

"Yeah, I do." He gave Andre a thin smile and took a sip of his coffee.

"Did you have a date in mind?"

"I don't have much here. I came with the bare essentials, so I can leave anytime. But I thought I'd give it till the end of the month."

The end of the month was a couple of weeks away.

"And you'll still work with me until you go?"

"Of course."

"Ok. Great." Andre sat down at the dining table.

Lozano joined him.

CHAPTER SEVENTY FOUR

"The night of the party you called me a monster," Tom reminded. She had hurt his feelings and he'd realized a relationship with anyone was out of the question. Even though his dad said he needed someone in his life, he couldn't do it because he was a monster.

Jade squeezed his hand. "I was in shock. Tyler tried to kill me." A tear slipped down her right cheek and she brushed it away. "I didn't mean it."

"It sure sounded like you did." He slid his hand out from under hers.

"Please. Listen to me. I – I love you."

Tom's heart rate kicked up a couple notches. He realized he couldn't put her life in jeopardy even though he loved her too. "Jade," he said, his voice gentle, "You telling me how you feel doesn't change the fact I'm a danger to you."

She shook her head. "You're not. You could've turned into a wolf the night at the bridge but you controlled it because of me." She squeezed his hand again. "I know you Tom, you're a good person. You wouldn't do anything to hurt me. Look at what happened at Tyler's party. You did everything you could to protect me and the people you love."

That was true. Because of her.

Tom let out a heavy sigh. "I don't know…"

"I do. Please don't push me away."

He stared into her eyes for a long time, his heart in turmoil. How could he let her into the world he lived in? The nightmare world of supernatural creatures and death? "I need time to think about it. You're not going to tell your friends about me, are you?"

Shock crossed her pretty face. How could he believe she would do such a thing? "You know I won't. Not this. You *should* know I could never betray you. Ever." She thought about Nicholas. "How did Nick know about you?"

"I showed him… on the sidewalk."

"How?"

Tom's eyes changed color in front of her the same as they had out at the bridge.

"Oh." She glanced around her again. No one was paying any attention to them. "So he kidnapped us to show me?"

"Yeah, I should never have allowed him to see it. I got angry because he disrespected you. I wanted to wipe the smug look off his face."

"You did that all right." Jade squeezed his hand a little more, smiled at him.

"You said you love me…"

She nodded. "I do."

"I love you, too." He gave her a sad, happy smile. His dad would've been proud.

Jade came around the table, dropped onto his lap, and wrapped her arms around his neck. She leaned in and pressed her lips to his.

ℬℭ

Andre decided to drive over to Double D Investigations to do some work in the quiet of the office. He also needed some time alone. There hadn't been any time to grieve for the people he cared about who were never coming back. Things had been hectic with the memorial and following up on Grant's recovery, and Avalynn, he'd pushed his emotions inside. He opened the door and stepped into the room, his gaze moving to Reece's desk in front of the window. Tears tinted with blood slid down his face as he closed the door. "What am I going to do without you?" He plonked himself down on a chair in front of the desk, brought his hands up to his face and sobbed.

A knock on the door startled him. He'd been consumed by the loss of his friend and hadn't heard the footfalls on the stairs. Andre tugged a handkerchief from the pocket of his jeans, wiped his blood-streaked face, sniffed back the urge to sob some more, got up and walked over to the door. When he opened it Grant Donovan and Evan Osborne were standing at the threshold. "Hey, why aren't you resting?" he said to the detective.

"I'm fine. Well, I will be. Can we come in?"

"Sure." Andre motioned for the pair to enter the office. "What can I do for you?"

"It's what we can do for you," Grant told him.

Andre frowned. "What do you mean?"

Grant pointed across the room. "Let's sit down."

The three crossed the office, Grant and Evan taking a seat in front of Reece's desk. Andre rounding it and sitting in his friend's chair.

"Evan and I want to come work for you."

Andre straightened on his seat. "You what?"

"You lost most of your team this past week. We figured you could use the help," Evan said.

"I could…"

"I'm ready to resign," Grant told him. "I can't do the job I'm supposed to do knowing what's out there. I need to do more."

"I want to stay on the force, so I can work with you on a part-time basis," Evan offered.

Andre knew he could use the help. "When did you want to start?"

"As soon as you need us," Grant said, his gaze moving to Evan.

"Yeah, whenever you're ready." Evan leaned back on the chair, crossed one leg over the other and folded his arms.

"Ok. Leave it with me for a couple of days and I'll get back to you."

"Sure." Grant stood up.

Evan did too.

"We're so sorry for your loss. Take all the time you need. We're not going anywhere." The detective gave him a thin smile, extended his hand.

Andre shook it. "Thanks. I'll be in touch."

After the pair left, Andre sat and gazed out of the window at the perfect blue sky dotted with white clouds. His prayers had been answered. He had part of a team again and would build on it as the opportunity arose.

છ)તૢ

Tom was at the kitchen counter when Andre walked in. "How'd it go at school today?" he asked, climbing onto the stool at the end of the counter and clasping his hands on top of it.

"Tough at first. Everyone kept coming up to me to say how sorry they were. They'd seen the news report on TV, I guess."

Andre reached across and rested a comforting hand on Tom's muscled bicep. "Why didn't you come home?"

"Jade came up to me as well. She said she needed to talk to me about something. So we met up at lunchtime."

"Are you two ok now?"

"She remembers the night of Tyler's party."

Andre's eyes widened. "What?! It's impossible."

"Dad told me it's happened before."

Andre gave it some thought. Reece had been right. "What did she say?"

"She apologized for calling me a monster. She didn't mean it." A thin smile crossed his face. He was so sad at losing his dad – at the same time he wanted to be happy about Jade being in love with him. "She said she loves me, Uncle Andre."

"I'm so happy for you, Tom. It's something I know your dad wanted for you."

"Yeah, he did."

"So you two are good now?"

"More than good. I told her a bit about what we do and she wants to help."

Andre raised defensive hands. "Not a good idea. Do you want to put her life in danger?"

"She won't take no for an answer. I tried to talk her out of it." Tom shrugged.

"Perhaps I could try to remove the memory again."

"No. If she's going to be with me I want her to know the truth."

Andre gave his nephew a serious stare. "You think it's wise, because I don't? What we do is life-threatening. What if something happened to her?"

"You can train her. She wants to help."

"Does she know about other creatures?"

"Like I said before, I explained it a little bit. Maybe you can tell her when you train her." He returned the serious stare. "And there's one more thing. I want to quit school and work with you full time."

"Your dad wanted you to go to college. That hasn't changed."

"Yes, it has. Dad's not here. You are. You need to assemble a new team to fight what's out there. And I'm part of that team."

"Grant and Evan are going to be working with us."

Tom's eyebrows rose. "They are?"

"Yes, they came to see me at the office today. Grant wants to quit the force, work with us full time, and Evan part time."

"That's great. We have part of a new team already."

"Yes, we do." Andre's expression became serious. "You can't throw your future away."

Tom raised his hand. "I won't be throwing away my future. I'll be following in my dad's footsteps helping to protect our city… our home."

Andre understood. "Look, let's stick with what you're doing now and we'll re-evaluate after your birthday. Ok?"

"Ok." Tom let out a frustrated breath. He wasn't happy about it, but he and his uncle *would* negotiate once he turned seventeen. That was a given.

EPILOGUE

Tom passed his driver's test a couple of days after his seventeenth birthday with flying colors. He was now a licensed driver and could drive the van when they went out on raids. His uncle told him he had a surprise for him but wouldn't even hint at what it might be. So curious to find out what the surprise was, Tom's wolf attempted to emerge several times throughout the day due to the adrenalin pumping through his body.

Later in the afternoon, when Andre arrived home, Tom rushed outside to meet him. "So what's the surprise?"

Six months had passed since Reece, Nathaniel, and Todd had been killed and life had taken on a new kind of normal without them. There were moments when deep sadness overtook him and Tom. The thought of not having those they loved with them anymore hurt like hell. Nevertheless, they had to keep moving forward.

Andre climbed out of the van. "Ok, you've waited long enough. Come with me."

He led the teen around to the garage, unlocked the doors and pulled them back. A car sat beneath a cream colored tarpaulin.

Tom's eyes widened. "Is that for me?"

"Yes." Andre walked into the garage, grabbed one corner of the tarp and threw it back over the vehicle.

Tom stood with welling eyes staring at the 1966 Midnight blue Mustang convertible. "Dad's car. How'd you do this?"

"I know someone who is exceptional at repairing written off vehicles. The firies were on scene quickly so the chassis wasn't as badly burned as I thought. It was meant to be a surprise for your dad – because I know how much he loved this car – now she belongs to you."

Tom threw his arms around his uncle, tears spilling down his face. "It's the best present anyone has ever given me. I'll still have a piece of my dad with me every day. I love it, Uncle Andre. Thank you."

Andre handed him the keys. "Want to take her for a spin?"

"You bet I do." Tom walked along the driver's side of the convertible, opened the door and climbed into the seat.

Andre dropped into the passenger seat beside him. "Ok, let's see what she can do."

The teen turned the key and the engine purred to life. His gaze moved to the rear view mirror and he gave a soft gasp. Reece was sitting in the center of the back seat smiling at him. Tom whipped his head around. No one was there. It didn't matter because he knew his dad would always be with him, and he would do his best to live up to his dad's reputation of being a paranormal warrior for their city.

AUTHOR'S NOTE

This is the final book in the Dark Legacy series *for now*. I'll be working on the fourth instalment in the Moon Grove Paranormal Romance Thriller series over the next few months and then the final in that series as well. It doesn't mean there won't be more to this series as I already have ideas for future storylines in a spin off series with Tom as the lead character, taking over where his dad left off. I hope you've enjoyed reading this series and I also hope you'll check out the other books written under my pen name Maggie Anderson. Oh, and by the way, if you enjoyed this book please leave a review wherever you purchased your copy. It would be greatly appreciated.

Happy Reading!

www.ingramcontent.com/pod-product-compliance
Lightning Source LLC
Chambersburg PA
CBHW020333180626
46812CB00001B/187